W9-AVM-287

DISCARD

DEAD RIVER

THE JACKALS

DEAD RIVER

WILLIAM W. JOHNSTONE
AND J. A. JOHNSTONE

THORNDIKE PRESS
A part of Gale, a Cengage Company

DEAD RIVER

DEAD RIVER

PROLOGUE

From Box 31, Folder 7, Perdition County Archives, Crossfire, Texas

Unpublished letters and manuscripts dealing with Purgatory City, other ghost towns, towns that merged with larger metropolises, and uncorporated towns, villages, way stations, and railroad sites.

They called my father a jackal. And that was the most polite word I remember hearing in Purgatory City, Texas. They called him a hard man. They called him lots of things. Well, so did I. There were times when I was a little girl that I thought my pa loved horses — mustangs, mostly — more than he loved me.

Much of my childhood has been forgotten, wiped out by a memory — a nightmare — I will not relate to you or anyone, though it still haunts my dreams. Often, I can't even remember the faces of my late, dearly departed brothers. Or even Mother's face. How beautiful I'd like to think she was.

Yet I just do not know.

But I remember my father.

I also recall vividly a wild Irishman, who loved to take a nip — oh, no, that does not do this man justice. He was a man who drank more liquor than could fill the tank on a fire wagon. He was a man who loved to brawl, no matter that he rarely won a round of fisticuffs, but he loved to fight. He would fight over a drop of a hat or a wink of an eye or just for a bet, even if the wager would win him only a copper cent.

They called him a jackal, too.

Yet I remember him with kindness. Stories around tell he once cared for a little baby in the jail that often served as his second home in Purgatory City. Most people thought this man would eat babies raw and spit out their tiny little bones. Did he? I never saw that. What I remember of this alleged jackal was a man who wore the uniform that freed the Negroes from bondage and prevented the dissolvement of our Union. Yes, I know. Here in Texas most of our great citizens pride those ancestors who wore the gray, who fought under John Bell Hood, Stonewall Jackson, Robert E. Lee, those who "saw the elephant" — as they like to say — in glorious battles at places like Shiloh, Chancellorsville, Seven Pines, Bull Run, Antietam, Kennesaw Mountain, Atlanta, Cold Harbor, and Gettysburg. But even those old soldiers, most of them all gone now, fought for Texas. And well, they also had a strong respect for the men they fought against.

Sean Keegan was one of those men. He also served in the frontier cavalry in Texas, fighting against the Indians that protested white settlers for taking over their country. Sean Keegan might have been branded a jackal, especially after he was court-martialed and drummed out of the service he so dearly loved, but I know this alleged jackal was tried and condemned for doing what any man, woman — anyone — would have done. He did what he had to do to protect the lives of his fellow soldiers. The men who rode with Sergeant Keegan on that day, I have to believe, would never have said anything derogatory about their gallant hero. Most likely, I think now with a great big grin on my face, they kept the man from County Cork filled with Irish whiskey and fine stout Irish beer.

A jackal? I call him a hero. I call him a man.

And I remember someone else, a man whose reputation was lower perhaps than that of my father. Especially after all the dime novels and picture shows and so-called factual accounts printed in newspapers like the one we have here in Crossfire — the county seat. Is it any wonder people frown at the very thought of a bounty hunter — a man who tracks down other men, not for justice, but for the money he might collect?

In this terrible calamity many are calling a Great Depression, I do believe the men sent by banks to foreclose on homes or to kick people off their properties where loved ones might be buried are much more vile than a man who had the courage to bring wanted men — some charged and condemned for the most wicked of crimes — to justice. Jed Breen was such a man, and while nobody recalls his name today, it was bandied around quite often all across this land we call West Texas.

Jed Breen was the third man termed a jackal in the roaring days of the town that is no more than a memory. Purgatory City thrived for a few more years beyond a rip-roaring, Hades-raising decade, till Progress — that awful thing known as Progress — doomed the city. It was nothing more than a few streets of mostly saloons and places of ill repute, when the railroad chose another path.

Fate — and the engineers who picked the path for the Great Texas and California Railway — is why Crossfire has become the seat of Perdition County. Fate is why this letter, this memoir, I write in my feeble hand will be posted to the Crossfire Public Library. And Fate is why Purgatory City is nothing more than a memory to most of us who remember it at all.

Perhaps this letter, these rambling thoughts of an aging Texican, will help people remember where they came from.

I am rambling, of course. I was writing about the third and last jackal, the bounty hunter Jed Breen. They said he had the blackest heart of anyone in the land — a black heart, they said, to contrast with his stark white hair. They said he never brought in anyone alive, but I can deny that as an ugly falsehood. Jed Breen brought in several men alive.

One of them was an Apache renegade named Blood Moon.

It strikes me as strange — no, it is heartbreaking and even numbs my very soul — the Apache Indian who terrorized both sides of the border between our United States and Mexico is the one whose name is remembered. Gridiron teams across the county are called Apaches, Indians, War-

11

riors, Redskins, and I have seen my grand-children shout, "Blood Moon! Blood Moon! Remember Blood Moon!" in pep rallies when their Cowboys, Cavaliers, and "Lions, Tigers and Bears" were going against schools with nicknames that recalled our Red Brothers. That is the only reason anyone remembers Blood Moon except for those weary-eyed historians and old archivists who look through volumes of bound copies of old newspapers, and maybe, in ten or twenty years from now, will be reading this letter . . . if anyone can make out my scratches.

I can barely see well enough to write.

The best historians will be able to tell you Blood Moon was an Apache renegade who waged basically a one-man war against Mexicans and Texans and federal soldiers in the Southwest. He was so vilified and so terrified many settlers the total reward offered for him was a staggering amount today, let alone in the decade after the War Between the States.

Blood Moon was a jackal, too, and perhaps he deserved to be labeled thusly.

Some men have even called another Indian, an Apache, too, who lived most of his life in Mexico, and tried to avoid most white people and most Mexicans, a jackal, as well.

12

Three Dogs, he was named. But if he were a jackal, I never saw him that way. He was like a father to many of his people, and he was like a father to me. For a long, long, terrible while, he was the only father I had . . . or the only one I remembered.

Until one day . . . or weeks . . . and then —

Well, this is no story to be told by an old person whose memory is fading, whose hand has begun to ache, and whose fingers are cramping.

Three men were called jackals in Purgatory City. Matt McCulloch, a former Texas Ranger and a grand mustanger back when wild horses ran free in this part of the state. Sean Keegan, the former cavalry soldier and rumored drunkard. And a bounty hunter called Jed Breen.

These white men were likely despised worse than the Apache butcher we called Blood Moon. And the old warrior whose name was Three Dogs.

One more man from these wild and savage times needs to be remembered, though I cannot attest to his background except from what I've heard. He was a soldier of the Confederacy, too, and his name was Block Frazer.

The way I recall, from my old fading brain, this Block Frazer did not hail from

13

Texas but from some Southern state — Mississippi, Louisiana, one of the Carolinas. I don't think it was as far north as Virginia or Tennessee. After learning the Confederacy was lost, he crossed the border with some of his men at the invitation of the ruler of Mexico. I don't remember that emperor's name, but you likely can find it in some history book. Perhaps even at the library.

I have read and heard stories that other former Confederate soldiers, their egos and will strong, also went to Mexico, refusing to admit defeat to President Lincoln's rule. Some stayed in Mexico, others grew tired or homesick after months or a few years, or they realized their welcome in that fine country was wearing out since Juarez had taken over the country.

Block Frazer, however, remained. I don't know why he stayed and I do not know why he hated Indians so much, but Block Frazer became — the way I remember things — a true jackal. He was an evil, evil, evil man, and he had his men do evil, evil, evil things.

Block Frazer was a jackal, though as far as I can tell, no one in either Mexico or Texas called him such.

I did not know Block Frazer. He came into my life just once. I did not even know his name until months after I saw him try

14

to kill my father.

Here, my dear readers, is what I know, and what I remember, and what in my aching heart is true.

Matthew McCulloch, Sergeant Sean Keegan, and Jed Breen are whom Purgatory City, Perdition County, Texas, branded jackals. But if it were not for those three men — and, I can say with a weak smile, one of them, in particular — I would not be here to write this piece of minor trivia, minor history.

Believe me or call me a fraud. That is your right.

McCulloch, Keegan and Breen were jackals to many, but they will always be heroes to me. And in their own way, Blood Moon and Three Dogs, were heroes, too. Block Frazer, well, he was a scoundrel and the vilest of men and though I should not think such thoughts, I hope he has been burning in Hell for many, many years. And that he will continue to rot in misery for he was a true jackal.

Note from J.S.T. Cohen, Archivist, Crossfire Public Library, November 13, 1936. This letter arrived on October 1, postmarked Crossfire, but with no return address and was not signed. While we are unable to verify the

15

veracity of this — woman's from the look of the handwriting — account, research in our own archives has turned up some supporting evidence that warrant its claims.

An editorial from the *Herald Leader* of Purgatory City — no longer, as the letter writer observed, existing — indeed ran a page 1 article in the [illegible] under this headline.

THE TIME HAS COME FOR OUR CITIZENS TO STAND UP TO THE JACKALS OF WEST TEXAS AND MAKE A STATEMENT FOR LAW

The rest of the headline has been torn.

The editorial does, however, cite a Texas Ranger named Matthew McCulloch, a federal Army sergeant named Sean Keegan, and a bounty hunter called Jed Breen as the so-called jackals.

If what the editorialist, one Alvin J. Griffin IV, wrote is even half-true, then it is my opinion that these men were indeed jackals, and that is an understatement.

Other articles found in various Perdition County newspapers from 1871–1883 (the last year was when the railroad bypassed Purgatory City that led to the town's collapse) have scant mention of McCulloch, Keegan, and

Breen, but their names do pop up and some-times they were still called jackals.

Letters to state archivists in the states mentioned by the anonymous letter writer regarding Block Frazer were returned with regrets that no one under that name for the period cited were found in city directories or newspaper searches or just not returned at all.

There are a few spotty mentions of one Blood Moon in Perdition County newspapers, but the National Archives and Records Admin-istration said several pages of official military correspondence mention the name of the Apache Indian from as far east as San Antonio to as far west as Fort Inferno on the Arizona–Colorado border.

The Apache Indian named as Three Dogs has not been found in history books on this library's shelves, and the archivist at the National Archives and Records Administration said no name popped up in a casual search.

We are waiting to hear back from the ar-chives in Mexico City. [No record of any reply has been found as of this date, 7-11-1953, BKJ.]

Therefore, it appears three men in this county were known as the jackals, and they might rank up there with Jesse James and

William Quantrill in their bloodlust and butchery.

It is, however, with deep regret that the person who wrote this account did not sign her (or his) name, but provided enough material and enough names and items that have been verified to make the staff and I believe this letter is worthy of being filed here.

But the county officials and the state archivists in Austin all stress that in no way are we endorsing this letter.

That is something we must leave to the individual readers.

CHAPTER ONE

Ugly Juan Maldado had put up quite the resistance in an arroyo near Devil Ridge, east of Fort Hancock, till a round from Jed Breen's Sharps rifle busted the murdering rustler's left shoulder. Although Breen cauterized the wound, he half expected Maldado to die before the reward could be claimed — especially when the soldier boys at Fort Hancock refused to take Maldado since he had never stolen government horses or mules. The post surgeon declined to operate on the badly wounded Mexican because he had not been wounded by a bluebelly or had ever worked as a civilian contractor for the United States Army.

The army boys decided to be uncooperative, Breen figured, because they wouldn't be claiming the reward on Ugly Juan Maldado, but that wasn't Breen's fault. Breen had earned this one, wearing out two good horses, spending six weeks sleeping — when

he could risk sleep — in the scorching fur-
nacelike heat, getting his fine new Stetson
punched through the crown with a .45 slug
that, two inches lower, would have blown
off the top of his head.

He thanked the boys in blue for their
trouble — at least they hadn't denied him
water or a sip of the surgeon's brandy —
and pushed on.

Two and a half more days of traveling
along the road that paralleled the Río
Grande he finally reached El Paso.

Sheriff Burt Curtis shook his head when
he examined Ugly Juan Maldado. "I'll be a
suck-egg mule," he exclaimed. "This ol'
greaser ain't dead."

"That's right," Breen said with relief.
"Now if you'll just sign the affidavit that
says he was delivered to you alive and well."

Curtis looked up, narrowing his eyes. "He
ain't exactly alive, though. And sure ain't
well."

"Not many men would be called *well* after
having a Sharps blow out most of his
shoulder blade." Breen extended the white
piece of paper and pencil.

The sheriff looked at the paper without
moving. "Why didn't you amputate?"

"My pocketknife was dull."

"You coulda took him to Fort Hancock."

"I did." Breen waved the paper. He wondered if Curtis was hoping the outlaw would die so he wouldn't have to sign the paper. Or maybe Burt Curtis couldn't read or write. "The good boys in blue declined to be of service." That proved to be the right thing for Jed Breen to say.

Burt Curtis, who had fought under John Bell Hood in the late War Between the States, began spitting out all sorts of profane thoughts about bluecoats and Yankees in general. When he finished, Breen still held that paper tightly so the wind wouldn't snatch it away and blow it to Mexico.

"Maldado's not dead," Breen said. "And that means five hundred extra dollars." He held out the paper and pencil again. "If you'd do me the honor, Sheriff Curtis."

The county lawman rolled his eyes, spit onto one of Ugly Juan Maldado's brogans, and took paper and pencil. "Maybe the murderin' piece of scum'll live long enough to hang. That way the county gets paid for the gallows buildin', the printin' of the invites to the hangin', and the buryin' and such."

"You mean you get paid for all that." Breen smiled as the sheriff returned the signed document.

"But it ain't nowhere near as much as the

extra five hunnerd you be gettin'."

Indeed. The Joint Citizens Committee of El Paso, Brown City, and Sierra Maloliente had specified that fifteen hundred dollars would be paid upon positive identification of Ugly Juan Maldado if the outlaw was dead. Another five hundred dollars if he was brought in alive. Breen wasn't exactly sure why. Bringing in a corpse would save expenses, so to a professional manhunter like Jed Breen it seemed more logical to pay more for a dead man than a fellow you'd have to feed and house and, as in the case of Ugly Juan Maldado, splurge on a doctor to keep the man alive long enough to be executed. Breen figured the citizens of El Paso, Brown City, and Sierra Maloliente wanted the honor of dragging the scoundrel through prickly pear and rocks before stringing him up. Maybe that was worth paying five hundred bucks.

"If he dies, you could still hang him," Breen said.

The sheriff looked up, eyes registering the truth of Breen's statement. "Reckon I could at that."

"But," Breen said, "maybe you ought to fetch a doctor to look at Maldado. See if he can't do a better job of keeping him alive to drop through that trapdoor." Feeling generous, he reached into his dust-covered vest, pulled out a half eagle, and tossed it to Burt Curtis. "Keep the change from whatever the sawbones charges you . . . I mean . . . the county."

Burt Curtis bit into the coin to make sure Breen wasn't cheating him.

"And join me at the Exchange Saloon when your prisoner is comfy in your best cell. I'll buy you supper and a bottle of rye to wash it down."

It paid, Breen had learned in his years plying his trade, to keep the law dogs happy.

Two weeks later, Jed Breen could hardly remember the last time he had felt this fine. He was riding back toward Purgatory City from El Paso on a fine strawberry roan won at a card table — aces full over jacks beating kings full over deuces — and had two thousand dollars in his saddlebags for turning in Ugly Juan Maldado to the county sheriff, alive and likely to live long enough to be lynched or tried and hanged legally. Breen's stomach was full from the fine cuisine one could find in a city like El Paso, even if that chow didn't taste anything like a man of means could enjoy in some real town with real class and real food — New Orleans or Kansas City or Memphis or St.

Louis or Galveston — but it sure beat what passed for grub in Purgatory City.

Suddenly, Breen started thinking about taking a vacation or a leave of absence. Bounty hunting proved to be hard work, and often work that never paid much money. Plus, it was tough on one's backside riding hell-bent for leather across the dusty inferno called West Texas. Unless you were going after pickpockets or runaways, the job could be downright dangerous, bringing in owlhoots who did not want to spend twenty years in Huntsville or get their necks stretched on the gallows or nearest hanging trees.

San Francisco perhaps. Hell, right now Fort Griffin or Fort Stockton would feel like Paris or Rome.

He stopped daydreaming and decided on something more reasonable. When he got back to Purgatory City, he would treat his friends, or the closest men that came to being his friends — Matt McCulloch and Sean Keegan — to supper and whiskey at the finest establishment in that hellhole. That would likely set Breen back ten bucks. If that. Depending on how drunk Keegan got or how many fights he started. A grin stretched across Breen's stubbled face as he pictured the look on Keegan's face when he showed him the reward money.

An instant later, the grin died.

Jed Breen saw black smoke coming over the top of the ridge. He reined in the strawberry roan, while reaching down first for the Sharps, then stopping and dropping the right hand to the butt of the double-action Colt Lightning holstered on his right hip.

The roan snorted. Breen wet his lips with his tongue. The wind blew hot, sending the smoke toward the east. He tried to get his bearings, figure out how far he was from Purgatory City, whose house or stagecoach station that might be. But Jed Breen had never been known as neighborly and even the most God-fearing and generous Christian in that part of the Western frontier likely wouldn't feel neighborly toward a bounty hunter, especially one known as one of the three jackals.

Matt McCulloch and Sean Keegan were the other two.

It wasn't a grass fire. Not smoke that thick and dark, and it wasn't like there was much grass this time of the year — or any time, really — to burn.

He listened, but heard only the wind. Then he clucked his tongue and gently spurred the roan. The hooves clopped and

25

Breen drew the Lightning from the holster, keeping the barrel pointed at the ground and away from the roan's belly.

At the ridgetop, Breen reined up and saw the homestead about a quarter mile off to the east at the bottom of the hill. It was a dirt-and-adobe structure, so only the roof and door were burning, along with the privy over toward the corral. He saw a patch of white and blue between the burning home and the empty corral. Breen didn't know who had tried to homestead there, but he damn well knew what that patch of white and blue meant.

He thought about grabbing the binoculars out of his saddlebag or using the telescopic sight on the Sharps, but the sun was at ten o'clock or thereabouts, and he didn't want to risk the rays reflecting off the lenses . . . if any of the butchers remained nearby.

For fifteen minutes, Breen studied the homestead and every inch of ground within a rifle shot. Finally, he kicked the horse into a walk, and tried not to hear the hoofbeats or the wind, but something else — the click of a weapon's hammer, the call of a hawk or raven, a coyote's yip.

A war whoop.

When he reached low ground, the roan turned skittish.

"Hell," Breen whispered. "I smell it, too, boy." His throat turned to sand.

Fifty yards from the flames, he pulled on the reins. The roan had been fighting the bit for about twenty-five feet, and Breen wasn't the kind of scoundrel to force a horse or anyone into the scene. Without holstering the Colt, he dismounted. Only after turning the horse sideways, keeping the ridge and road he had just descended to his back, did he holster the Colt and open the saddlebags — just not the one that held the reward money.

He found the hobbles and quickly secured the roan's forefeet. Rubbing his hands on the gelding's neck, Breen rose and looked over the saddle, staring at the surrounding countryside and the inferno beginning to burn itself out. He grabbed the canteen, uncorked it, took a mouthful to rinse out the gall and sand, and spit it onto the dirt. The next mouthful he swallowed.

The roan let Breen know he was thirsty, too.

"I know," Breen whispered, corking the canteen and wrapping it on the saddle horn. "But you'll have to wait."

He slid the Sharps from the scabbard and patted his trousers pocket. Three shells. Five already in the Colt, plus a shell belt filled with .38-caliber bullets. He tugged on his Stetson's brim to pull the hat snug before he moved off the road on the right, nearest the burning homestead, and crouching, he sprinted twenty yards, stopped, and dropped to one knee. Again, he studied the terrain.

If the fire was burning out, he told himself, whoever set it had to be long gone. That was common sense. Again, he wet his lips. Again, he remembered that common sense had gotten many a man killed in that savage, lawless country.

Men who took their time lived longer than men who acted recklessly.

For ten minutes, he moved little more than his eyes, although the wind blew his prematurely white hair, and he now wished he had told the El Paso tonsorial artist to take more off the length. He was paranoid enough from the smoke and stench of death that he thought his hair, especially white as it was, might be enough for some murdering prairie rat to draw a bead on. His stomach and nose began to protest the wretched stink. Looking at the roan, he wondered how long the horse would just stand there before trying to break free from the hobbles and gallop back to the gentleness and comforts of El Paso.

Another five minutes stretched past in

agonizing silence.

Finally, Breen raced to the well on the western side of the burning house. The stench gagged him, and he pulled the bandanna up and over his nose. Wood and grass weren't the only things the fire was consuming inside, and what Breen smelled, he understood, was not a side of beef. Again, he looked at the patch of blue and white, clearer now, with a definite shape and form.

He held his breath and ran to the woman.

Choking down the bile, Breen made himself close her green eyes. Two arrows, shafts broken when she fell, remained imbedded in her back. She must have been running from the house for the corral when the Indian — Apache by the arrows — killed her.

The corral was empty.

A noise made him point the Lightning toward the line of scrub beyond the burning outhouse, and he almost put a bullet into the head of a mule. Breen's gun hand dropped like an anchor, and he struggled to catch his breath. He looked for tracks, but saw none, though the wind likely had wiped most of them out. He tried to think. Apaches or an Apache had killed the couple homesteading here. Why leave the mule?

At that moment, another noise tore through Breen's composure. He whirled around, and saw a juniper about thirty yards toward the east.

The crying sounded louder.

"My God," he whispered. Shoving the .38 into the holster, he grabbed his Sharps and ran to the stump of a tree, sliding, turning, and looking behind him before he glanced down at the swaddled infant. The green-eyed baby wailed as the mule stopped near the edge of the corral and brayed.

Breen glanced at the dead woman. Would she have run so far from the corral, left her little baby under the tree, then sprinted for the mule or horses? From where the body lay, it sure as hell looked like she ran from the house and was making a beeline for the corral or the scrub brush and arroyo beyond it when two Apache arrows had ended her life.

Breen tried to comprehend what all had happened, but before he could put together even one thought that made a lick of sense, he heard another noise.

One that practically stopped his heart.

Hoofbeats pounded the hard-packed road. The smoke stung his eyes as it wafted above and all around him, and he squinted, cursed, and saw the strawberry roan galloping up the road. On the back of Breen's horse sat a black-haired Apache. The very same red devil who'd killed the man — likely burning in the remnants of the home — and the woman. The miserable son of a cur had left the baby to die a slow death. Somehow, the Indian had managed to release the hobbles on the roan and keep the horse quiet. The Apache must have been a ghost, but a ghost Breen could see. The bloody thief was leaving Breen afoot.

And galloping away with his horse and his hard-earned two thousand bucks.

CHAPTER TWO

It was a hell of a lot cooler in the Davis Mountains than it was in the rest of the Hell that was West Texas, but still Matt McCulloch wiped his damp palms on his leather chaps. Squatting, he felt the sharpness and coolness of the moss-covered boulder of lava as he leaned back and bit his bottom lip. Waiting was the hardest part of his job.

Well, maybe the hardest part came at various times of the day. Sometimes morning, often at night, especially through the long days when he just sat and waited after he had constructed makeshift corrals around a watering hole and had nothing left to do but capture a herd of West Texas mustangs. That's when memories would break free and flood his heart and soul.

The Indian raid all those years ago had left him burying his wife and all but one of his children. Though less frequent the past few years, the nightmares that never ended were of his daughter — the one the Indians had not butchered at McCulloch's horse ranch. The one they had taken with them across the border into Mexico. The one McCulloch had kept searching for until he'd had to give her up for dead.

He had joined the Texas Rangers partly to fill his time and to get him away from the ranch and its memories, but a few years back, the Texas Rangers had kicked him out. They figured he wasn't a man anymore, just a shell of what he had been. They said he had turned into nothing more than a jackal — at least, that's what some no-account muckraking editor had labeled him, and the word had stuck.

He had become one of the three blights upon Purgatory City's good name — as if anything good ever came out of that cesspool of a town. *Matt McCulloch,* the Ranger gone bad. *Sean Keegan,* the cavalry sergeant who shot his own commanding officer (overlooking the fact that the coward had been deserting his own command, taking water and ammunition with him, and leaving Keegan no choice but to put a bullet in the back of the yellow dog or risk everyone else being killed). And *Jed Breen,* the bounty hunter who brought all of his men in dead, which was a lie. Breen knew just how much easier it was to bring in a man alive, and he had collected more rewards on living hombres than those slung over a saddle and draped with a blanket.

Maybe Matt McCulloch was the only true jackal of the trio.

He made himself block those thoughts from his mind. Forget about his past, if just for a few tense minutes. Forget about the dead and the memories. For the past few years, despite a few interruptions that had required saving his own hide and the lives of others, he had been doing what he'd always dreamed of doing. Doing what he had been doing before his family had been massacred. He was a horseman. A mustanger. He was regaining the respect he had earned before the horrible tragedy.

And he had a chance, a once-in-a-lifetime opportunity, to make that respect stick.

If only . . . if only this time . . . that gray horse would cooperate. Well, that would be the first step, but far from the last one. Catching a mustang, especially a strong, savvy one, would just start the ball.

The shining mustang sniffed the air, then let out a whicker. McCulloch tensed. He had muzzled his roan, and being a McCulloch-trained horse, the gelding did not even stamp his feet. The gray stallion below had Arab blood in him — by the way the shoulders sloped and the high arched tail. The head was small, too. It made sense to the seasoned mustanger. Even West Texas had seen people moving in since the end of the War Between the States, and that meant more horses. Horses of all breeds. Mostly quarter horses for the cowboys or draft animals to pull heavy wagons, but some thoroughbreds and Morgans, even a Tennessee Walking Horse. And Arabs.

Bloodlines were mixed as they mated and reproduced, giving some special horses the best of various breeds. Horses had minds of their own. So did Comanches, the best horse stealers in the business. Horses escaped from barns and corrals and found a haven in these mountains that offered an oasis in the Chihuahuan Desert. And lucky, or just smart, stallions sometimes even escaped from the Comanches.

The gray stallion might be the best mustang-mix Matt McCulloch had ever seen.

For four evenings, he had been waiting, watching, feeling his stomach twist itself into knots while he hoped and grimaced. The stallion knew water waited for him and his herd of mares and a few young colts just beyond the rocky entrance, just narrow enough for a mustang to slip through, one at a time. Four times, though, the smart gray had whirled around after pawing the earth and sniffing the air, and with a scream had taken off at a high lope. His mares and young sons had followed, raising dust in the twilight, vanishing over the next ridge.

Leaving behind the cool, fresh water in the deep spring.

Leaving behind Matt McCulloch, shaking his head in deep appreciation for the gray's instincts and a growing dread for another camp on hard ground.

He expected the same result this evening. The mustang would gallop off and his herd would follow, and McCulloch would grain his roan, eat more jerky and hardtack, wash it down with water from that wonderful spring, roll out his bedroll, and wait for another chance tomorrow.

Coffee would have been wonderful, as would a hot meal, even just heated up jerky in a skillet. But he didn't want to spook the gray with the smell of ashes even twelve hours old. He wanted the spring he'd discovered by accident to seem just the way it had been for as long as the gray had been watering there.

The stallion must have caught the scent of McCulloch. He didn't think the roan would have made the horse suspicious. Enough tracks told McCulloch other horses watered there, along with black bears, deers, pronghorn. He had even seen a good-sized ocelot drinking water, ignoring the presence of the Texan and a Texas mustang, just that morning.

The gray could smell him.

McCulloch smiled at the thought. That would be a shock to Jed Breen and Sean Keegan when McCulloch told that story. They had always claimed horse blood, not human blood, flowed through his veins — that McCulloch was more mustang than man.

His attention was drawn by movement near the entrance. Sure enough, the mustang moved closer, sniffing the boulders on both sides, then the dirt. It raised its head, beat the ground with its forefeet, backed up, looked north and east, shook its head, took one step toward the passageway, and then wheeled around and galloped off toward the waiting horses on the hillside just below the ridge.

McCulloch did not react. A Vermilion Flycatcher flew off a branch of a piñon, and McCulloch watched the bright body of the bird for several seconds, trying to appreciate the beauty of the brilliantly covered bird, but mostly to take his mind off another lost chance. And like most Texans, he was the kind of man who never paid attention to any bird, unless it was a turkey buzzard circling or a flock of some winged critters spooked by something that might be out to kill a white man.

The pounding of hooves stopped, and McCulloch looked up the slope leading to the boulder-strewn canyon he had been calling home for several bone-aching days and nights. The gray had stopped halfway between McCulloch's perch and the stallion's family.

McCulloch's lips tightened, but he did not make a sound, didn't even wet his lips. He narrowed his eyes to keep from blinking and breathed steadily. His heart raced wildly. The mustang with Arab blood reared, front feet doing a dance in the air, and he screamed at the mares and colts. A moment later, he turned and thundered back toward the entrance.

McCulloch stopped breathing. He smelled his own stink after spending days in the mountains.

The gray stopped again at the narrow path left by an ancient volcano and led to the spring. The horse spun back, shook its head with intensity, and gave a loud whinny, ran back just a few yards toward the herd, whickered again, and then turned around. Again, hooves scraped the sand, stones, and weeds before the mustang moved to the entrance and moved in quickly.

McCulloch jerked his head toward the herd. But the mares and colts did not follow. He started to think what a great leader the gray stallion had to be. It must have warned the horses not to follow. The gray was investigating, and if he deemed the water hole safe, he would return. Suddenly, McCulloch realized maybe the herd had not had much water over the past four days. Yet the gray would not risk his family.

He didn't often have the chance to catch a mustang like that one. McCulloch pushed himself up with his arms on the giant piece of ancient lava behind him, threw his left leg over the boulder in front of him, followed with his right, and slid down the rocks to where the mustang had stood just a few moments earlier.

The usual plan for a mustanger with Matt McCulloch's savvy was to catch the whole damned herd. Sort out the best, geld most of the young studs, turn loose the old and weak ones, keep some mares for breeding, and either keep the leader, or sell him for a fortune. But McCulloch figured he had no chance at the herd, and he wasn't going to lose what might be his only opportunity to catch the mustang stallion of a lifetime.

Hooves thundered from the other side of the entrance, leaving McCulloch no time to spare. The gray blocked out the openness behind him as it moved with intense purpose through the short path. Rainwater over thousands of years had carved a hole in both sides of the opening, just big enough to hold two cedar limbs. McCulloch found the first, a hard cedar pole he had hidden in the rocks, and rifled it across the entryway. He had just enough time to slide the second limb atop the first. The volcano-forged rocks would hold the limbs tightly, leaving no way for the horse to go under the makeshift gate, or leap over it, especially considering just how tight the path was.

It didn't stop the mustang from slamming into the poles, just as McCulloch pulled his hands way from the top cedar limb. The wood creaked and dust flew from the boulders. The blow and all its fury took McCulloch by surprise and he fell backward, landing hard, but coming up quickly. The gray slammed again, and McCulloch shuddered harder than the two cedar limbs did. Again the horse rammed the gate, and dust and gravel flew from both sides of the entrance.

McCulloch rose quickly. The gray backed up and charged again, but he could not get up much speed in those tight confines. The cedar gate held again. An agonizing scream came from the Arab mix, and the mustang tried to rear, to pound the blocking instruments with its forefeet, but the passageway proved too tight to get more than eight inches off the floor.

Hooves thundered again, but from the ridge, echoed by whinnies and screams. McCulloch spun around, and saw the herd raising dust on the slope.

They would have earned McCulloch a pretty good chunk of silver, but that didn't bother him. Mustangs were something to watch in the wild, and he soaked it all in, watching the young studs lead the mares and a few colts and fillies to the ridgetop, then disappear on the far side, leaving nothing behind but raising dust and the sound of hooves galloping away.

Behind him, McCulloch heard the agonizing scream of the gray stallion. It sounded like the mustang's heart was breaking, and he knew why.

The gray had lost his herd. Those young studs would fight it out for supremacy in the days to come, and one would become the new king. As kings went, he figured the new stallion of royalty would be something along the lines of King George. At least, McCulloch thought that was the Brit in charge of the colonies back when the Revolution started and America won her independence.

Let that herd stay free for a while. Matt McCulloch had Louis the Fourteenth trapped in a box canyon. He had the king of all mustangs.

The gray rammed the cedars once more, then snorted. It urinated on the dusty ground, probably telling McCulloch what he thought of him. A moment later, the horse tried to turn in the canyon, but quickly realized he had only one choice — to back up into the clearing. His flaming eyes showed he did not like the idea of retreating.

Those eyes also told McCulloch something else.

As did all the busted bones in McCulloch's body, especially the most recent bad break in his left leg, which began reminding the former Texas Ranger just what he was in for.

"Well, you damned ol' knucklehead," McCulloch drawled with a weariness he hadn't felt in some time. "You got what you wanted. Now all you got to do is not get

42

your brains bashed in trying to break this cocksure little man-killer."

At least he didn't have to worry about the smell of burned wood or ashes spooking off a prime mustang anymore. Tomorrow morning, he could have a hot breakfast and coffee to wash it down.

Hell, McCulloch thought, a man deserves hot chow and strong coffee for what might be his last meal.

CHAPTER THREE

When he bellied up to the bar at The Palace of Purgatory City, Sean Keegan was in fine spirits — having shared a bottle of real Irish whiskey, not rank forty-rod rotgut funneled into a bottle with an Irish whiskey label, with Corporal Dickie McGee in a livery stable.

The Palace was a new saloon enjoying its grand opening on that lovely evening, lovely on account Sean Keegan was in his cups and Dickie McGee had dared him to go into the fancy drinking place. Dared him by offering him two dollars and sixty-one cents. So while the corporal waited on the board-walk across Purgatory City's Railroad Avenue — even though the railroad hadn't seen fit to come to Purgatory City — Keegan slipped through an opening at the bar before a man in a black broadcloth suit and bowler hat could get there.

The Palace of Purgatory City advertised

itself as having an Elegant Decorum.

**Serving the Best Cold Beer, Gin
The Best Wines from California,
Missouri, and Europe
Genuine Kentucky Bourbon
True Tennessee Sour Mash and
London Distilled Gin**

Games of chance of faro, poker, hazard, chuck-a-luck and blackjack could be found on the second floor. Above the back bar, a sign read:

☞ **PROCURE YOUR PLACE IN THE
GRANDEST DRINKING HOUSE** ☜
BETWEEN ST. LOUIS AND SAN FRANCISCO

Keegan smiled. He had indeed procured his place there.

And that, Keegan understood as his grin widened, explained why Milt the bartender was frowning underneath his waxed and twirled mustache. Slapping a nickel on the bar, the Irishman said, "Milt, let me see how cold your best beer is on a hot evening like this one, laddie."

Milt busied himself cleaning a mug with a towel.

"Milty, me lad, I'm hot and I'm thirsty,"

45

Keegan said.

"I don't want no trouble, Sean." The barkeep wasn't tan — men who slept all day and worked all night in a smoky saloon rarely got past the pasty look — but he looked paler than the West Texas sun.

"Bring me a mug of beer, more beer than suds, and we shan't have any trouble, me good man."

The cowboy on Keegan's left and the muleskinner on Keegan's right pushed themselves a little farther away, giving the former cavalry sergeant a little more elbow room, but not very much, crowded as The Palace of Purgatory City was that fine, sultry evening.

"Dankworth!" a voice called from behind Keegan and to his left. "If you serve that dastardly jackal, I'll see that you never pour another drink in this part of this godforsaken hellhole."

In the suddenlty quiet saloon, Keegan thought, *Dankworth. Now I know why he calls himself Milt.*

Milt Dankworth's Adam's apple bobbed as he stopped messing with the clean beer mug and seemed to turn even whiter, a stark contrast to his black mustache.

Slowly, Sean Keegan turned around, resting his arms on the bar and putting a worn

46

cavalry boot on the brass footrail. The man who had spoken stood in front of a table about twenty feet away. He wore a spit-and-polish uniform of a soldier of the United States Cavalry and a sharp-looking kepi. A second lieutenant, he had to be new to Fort Spalding, the Army post a few miles from town, and looked as if he had just gotten his commission from the United States Military Academy at West Point.

Officers seasoned by a month or two of summers in West Texas quickly learned that a kepi wasn't worth a damn for anything other than a dress parade. The green officer's face already showed signs of sunburn, and Keegan figured his neck would be blistering.

A redheaded saloon girl stopped a couple of feet from the blond, fair-skinned Army officer. He sort of reminded Keegan of that idiot and yellow-livered officer he had been forced to kill to save the rest of the command a few years back.

"And who do I have the pleasure of addressing, sir?" Keegan said as he began drumming the fingers on his right hand on the fine, cool mahogany bar.

"Lieutenant Charles Tibbetts. And I have heard of you." He tried to spit — saliva, not tobacco juice — at the closest spittoon but came about two feet short. Some dribbled down his chin.

"Aye," Keegan said. "I've never heard of you. Probably never will."

A slight murmur rose within the saloon.

Keegan smiled again. It felt good when he could make men laugh.

Lieutenant Charles Tibbetts wasn't laughing, of course.

"The Palace of Purgatory City is for gentlemen," Tibbetts managed to say after a long while.

Keegan glanced at the cowboy, then at the muleskinner, and finally looked back at that uppity snot-nosed West Pointer, Second Lieutenant Charles Tibbetts. "Then how in blazes did you get past the bouncer?"

Finally, color, albeit red, covered the green punk's face.

As Lieutenant Tibbetts was struggling to find a proper response, the cute little redhead with the tray of drinks slipped closer to the table and the officer. Her voice carrying in the once-again quiet, new and fancy saloon, she said, "Soldier boy, honey, don't pay that Irishman no never mind. He ain't worth the trouble, and he's always causin' a ruckus, I hear. So here, honey, you take this rye and —"

Tibbetts slapped her savagely, sending the

48

rye she was trying to pass off to him flying onto a table filled with stinking buffalo hunters. The tray with the other drinks crashed onto the floor, and the cute little redhead fell hard onto the sawdust and the green lieutenant's spittle. Her head hit the spittoon, knocking it over, and she lay there, staring up at this monster in blue. Her eyes filled with tears. Blood streamed from her busted lip.

No one spoke in The Palace of Purgatory City.

And Sean Keegan began walking away from the bar, Milt Dankworth, the cowboy, and the muleskinner.

His neck was turning hot and the blood kept rushing to his head, back to his heart, back to his head, pumping at the speed of a steam engine taking the mail to Fort Worth.

Somehow, Keegan found his voice. "Like I said . . . this place can't be for gentlemen."

The lieutenant took a defensive step back into the table. The men sitting with him looked at Keegan, who stopped, knelt, and found what passed for a clean handkerchief in his trousers pocket. He held it out to the redhead, and she took it with a trembling hand.

"Ye'll be all right, honey," Keegan said softly. "And don't worry about this young

49

whippersnapper. He won't never pester ye again." He kicked the spittoon toward a table where merchants sat, and gently raised the saloon girl to her feet. *Gosh darn, she sure smells pretty. At least different from the stink of whiskey, plug tobacco, and cigarettes.*

When she seemed steady enough, he let go of her arms and smiled his best County Cork smile. "Better?"

She kept the handkerchief against her lips and nodded. The tears kept leaking, but Keegan figured she'd be all right.

"Go on back behind the bar, lassie," he told her. "Tell Milt Dankworth to give ye a bracer and put it on me bill." He watched her walk away, and did not turn around until she was behind the bar.

She'd be safe there. Milt had worked in quite a few buckets of blood before landing the swank job at this polished hellhole. He was savvy enough to know to pull her behind the expensive, solid mahogany if lead started flying.

Then Sean Keegan turned back to stare into Second Lieutenant Charles Tibbetts's reddening face. "Laddie, I thought I was making a wee little joke when I suggested that ye were not a gentleman. But as we have all seen this lovely night, I misspoke. Not a gent? Nah, laddie, ye happen to be lower than a rattlesnake or a squire from London. Where I come from, and where I live now — yes, Purgatory City — men don't strike women. Never."

"She's no woman. She's a —"

Keegan's backhand sent the blond idiot falling back onto his table, knocking a commissary agent from Fort Spalding to the floor. Keegan took in the others sitting with Lieutenant Tibbetts, wondering how many he'd have to take on, but realized he was in luck. The soldiers sitting with the damned fool and ungentlemanly sidewinder were penny-pinching officers from the hospital and headquarters — not commanders of cavalry troops. They might have been good at keeping the soldiers clean and fed, and paid whenever payrolls actually came through, but fighting was out of their element. Those types didn't even care to watch a soldier's fight or a boxing exhibition in the stables of Fort Spalding.

His face redder than a radish, Tibbetts turned to push himself off the table. His right hand began fumbling with the flap that protected his Army-issued revolver.

"Nay," Keegan said. "This is not a gunfight, laddie. It's a saloon fight." He kicked Tibbetts in the groin.

The look of the radish vanished, and Tibbetts's face went back to the pale, sickening, ugly look. As he doubled over, his nose and forehead met Keegan's knee, and he fell hard to the floor.

With his left hand, Keegan bent and jerked the officer to his feet. His right hand reached over, found the butt of the silver-plated service revolver, pulled it from the holster, and tossed it onto the table where the lieutenant's companions stared at it as if it were a pack rat.

Keegan slapped the soldier's face four times, punched him in the gut, and stepped back to let the officer puke out his guts without getting any of that mess on Keegan's boots and pants. A few men gagged.

That struck Keegan as funny. Men out here could look at a disemboweled gent who wound up on the wrong side of an Arkansas toothpick, or a family butchered by Comanches or Apaches, and not give it much thought, tears, or gags. But a little vomit from a dumb little shavetail . . .

Keegan slammed a haymaker that sent Tibbetts spinning, and then the fine-spirited Irishman leaped across the puddle the lieutenant had created, and snatched a hold of his blouse before he fell onto another table. Keegan slapped him twice more, put a left into the boy's sternum, then grabbed him by the collar of the army tunic and threw him across the room.

Dickie McGee was going to be sorry he had wagered on the dare. Sean Keegan was going to walk out of The Palace of Purgatory City on his own two feet.

But Keegan realized a moment later the error of his ways. He should have looked before he had thrown the army greenhorn. That damned little snotnosed officer had crashed himself right onto the table of buffalo hunters, busting the bottles of rotgut, knocking over the glasses, and sending two of those burly men onto their hindquarters, one of whose rear end fell right into the river of tobacco juice and spit that had flowed from the overturned spittoon.

"Aye," Keegan whispered. "Ay-yi-yi."

Well, he couldn't let a bunch of Texas hide men see him run or try to get out of a mauling, so Keegan strode toward the table, helped one of the hide hunters up, and dusted off his collar. "I'll set ye boys up when I'm through with this worthless damn Yankee."

He hoped *damn Yankee* would appease the stinking buffalo men, even though Keegan had been wearing the blue since the War Between the States. He hoped, but pretty much figured he was right, that these stinking, burly brutes were Texans or at least Southerners. He also hoped he could kick Lieutenant Tibbetts all the way out of The Palace of Purgatory City, and disappear himself — on his own two feet, of course.

He pushed Tibbetts farther, lifted him off the floor, slammed a left uppercut to the jaw, dropping him again like a sack of something. He grabbed him by the collar, pulled him up and yelled, "And don't come back here till ye learn how to behave."

The lieutenant's head and shoulders pushed open the batwing doors, a couple of horses tethered to the hitching rail snorted, and he heard the *whoomp* as Tibbetts hit the sand of Railroad Avenue.

"I'll be back after I clean that litter off the street," Keegan said. He had his right hand on one of the batwing doors, when he felt himself being jerked back. "Hell." He spun around to feel a smelly, hairy-knuckled fist loosen some molars and send him crashing into a drummer's legs at the bar.

The drummer cried out as he fell over Keegan's body. Two of the buffalo hunters jerked the little man up and tossed him over the bar. Keegan came up and felt the wind rush out of his lungs, and he doubled over and dropped to his knees. For a moment, he felt as if he would vomit, but rough

54

hands pulled him up, sending that bile in his throat back into his gut, and then the pounding felt like the herd of shaggies those ol' boys had just left rotting, except for the hides, on the plains north. Fists and boots popped him just about everywhere, and Keegan began to think those boys wouldn't stop until he was a puddle of Irish sogginess.

A gunshot rang out and The Palace of Purgatory City fell silent after the ringing subsided and the plaster stopped raining down from the ceiling.

"That's enough," a Texan drawled. "Who started this?"

"He did," one of the buffalo men said in a whiny voice.

"He whupped that damn Yankee, too," said a buffalo man who sounded like a hide hunter should.

"Is that true, Milt?"

"Reckon so." The bartender's voice sounded ten miles away.

"Figures."

Keegan heard iron scraping leather, and figured the deputy was holstering his pistol. Rough hands grabbed Keegan's boots, and he felt himself being pulled across the floor and through the batwing doors. He heard them banging behind him, then his back

55

and head smacked the sand of Railroad Avenue as he was dragged toward a place he knew quite well — the jail at Purgatory City. It was a new jail, about eight months old.

"Wait," Keegan called out. "There's a nickel of mine on the bar. I never got my beer!"

CHAPTER FOUR

For three years, Major Block Frazer had been in command of the Río Sangrieto *Rurales* out of the village known as El Pueblo de Cebollas Verdes. For just shy of ten years before that, Major Block Frazer had served under Ferdinand Maximilian, the Archduke from Austria who had ruled Mexico until the Mexicans decided he wasn't worth spit, and Benito Juárez's boys had lined the sorry excuse of a leader against a wall and filled him full of bullet holes. Then Block Frazier had tried being a gentleman farmer, as he had been in Alabama before the damned Yankees put their Northern noses in Southern affairs. He had grown peaches and onions, but after Maximilian, most of his gringo neighbors had given up, left their plowshares and Mexican donkeys, and headed back for what had been home in the United — not the Confederate — States.

Hell would be colder than a winter in the

heart of the Sierra Madres before Block Frazer ever went sniveling back to the Tombigbee River. He had never been much of a farmer. Never could have gotten cotton to grow if he hadn't had all those slaves working the fields in the worst hell of summers and the muddiest of springs. Soldiering, though, that was one thing Block Frazer was good at. Just ask General Nathan Bedford Forrest, and he would affirm that quick as a polecat.

Three years back, Señor Miguel Blanco, alcalde of El Pueblo de Cebollas Verdes, and a capitán from Ciudad de México, sent by Sebastián Lerdo de Tejada, the Mexican who had replaced Juárez, had come to Frazer with a proposition. If he could get the ten men who remained with him since serving in Frazer's Legion during the War for Southern Independence to protect the village and the surrounding community, they would make him lieutenant of the Rurales del Río Sangrieto. Lerdo's government would pay them a fine salary, and the good alcalde would pay a bounty for every Apache or Comanche scalp they brought in. One hundred pesos for a man's topknot. Fifty for a woman. Twenty for a kid.

"I ain't no snot-nosed lieutenant," Block Frazer had told them. "I was a major under

Forrest, and I'll be damned if I'll get busted down for you brown-skins."

The Lerdo man and Señor Blanco agreed.

Lerdo was gone now, replaced by some other rotten Mex named José de la Cruz Porfirio Díaz Mori. Everyone had more names than some counties back in Alabama; Frazer never could get used to that. But the money was the same. After thirteen years in Mexico, Major Block Frazer was finally enjoying life south of the border. At last, he had found something he was good at.

"What do ya think, Major?" Oaxaca Joe said. His real name, back along the Tombigbee had been Joseph William Henderson III, and he had been one of the best horsemen in Forrest's cavalry, but, two years back, he had taken the nickname Oaxaca Joe after deciding that Oaxaca José just didn't fit, what with his blond hair, fair skin and blue eyes.

"It'll be easier than the time in '62 when we sent them bluecoats swimmin' through cottonmouths and gators at Bayou Pierre in Mississippi," said Billy Ray Ferguson.

"Are you answering for me now, Billy Ray?" Frazer said without removing his binoculars as he studied the camp below the hill. He could hear Billy Ray Ferguson swallow hard.

59

"No, Major, suh. I was speakin' my own mind."

"Did Joseph ask what you thought?" Frazer refused to use any Mexican nickname on a God-fearing boy from the great Southern state of Alabama.

"No, suh."

Frazer raised the binoculars higher, scanning the country to the south, then the east, finally the west. Seeing no signs of life in the miserable patch of desert, he lowered the binoculars. Without looking toward Ferguson to his left or Henderson to his right, he said, "Bring the scout up here, Joseph."

Instantly and eagerly, Joseph William Henderson III wheeled his dun around and loped off to the back of the column. While the dust was settling, Frazer pulled a Mexican cigarillo — one of the few pleasures he had discovered in Mexico — from the inside pocket of his well-worn Confederate shell jacket, stuck the slim cigar into his mouth, and turned toward Ferguson, who was already striking a match on his saddle horn.

Frazer waited for the Southern soldier to light the smoke then said, "Check the caps on your revolver, son. Make sure you have six good shots." He spoke without removing the potent tobacco as the smoke comforted his throat.

"Don't need caps no more, Major," Ferguson said. "You oughta get yerself a Colt that fires brass cartridges instead of havin' to mess with 'em percussion caps and paper ca'tridges."

Frazer pulled the slender six-shooter from the holster on his right hip. Draping the reins over his gelding's neck, he removed the Mexican smoke to speak. "This is no Colt, son. It's a Leech and Rigdon, built at the fine city of Greensboro in the great state of Georgia, and it has served me well since '63, and it will serve me well for years to come."

Hooves clomped on the ground to the north, and Frazer called out, "Be ready, Alabamans. Ready to ride — and kill — you Rurales." He laughed at the word. *Rurales.* There wasn't a Mexican in the bunch. The cigarillo returned to his mouth, and he lifted the reins with his left hand, and turned as Joseph William Henderson III and the Mexican scout reined their horses to a sliding stop.

Major Block Frazer let the wind carry away the dust before he turned his head and looked at Henderson and the dark-skinned scout.

"Ask him why we haven't found signs of those Comanches he told us about," Frazer

61

ordered.

Joseph William Henderson III spoke in rapid, fluent Spanish. The kid had a gift for gab in any lingo. Frazer knew but a few phrases in Spanish, but this old boy had been speaking the tongue like he was a bean-eater almost as soon as they had settled there under Maximilian's protection and invitation.

The scout, a slender Mexican with a stringy mustache, and lustrous black hair almost to his shoulders, answered quickly. Some people called the Mexican language beautiful, but it just made Frazer's head scream in agony.

"Juanito says the Indians pulled out from the column one at a time, going east or west or continuing south, but he thinks they will likely regroup in a few miles. Leaving the party was a diversion to split us up as he told you when we last rested our horses. They will probably attack one of the smaller farms four or five miles south, steal horses, and make for the Río Grande and back into the United States."

Frazer closed his eyes. "Joseph, how many times have I asked you never to use the words *United States*?"

"I did not use them, Major," the young

man answered. "Juanito did. *Estados Unidos.*"

The major's eyes opened, and he sighed before tilting his head off toward the northeast. "Might that column of smoke rising over the hills be the handiwork of the Comanches we have been allegedly trailing?"

He watched as every man in the column found the smoke. They were still young, still eager, but they lacked the sense God gave survivors. *Hell,* Frazer sometimes thought, *with men like this under my command, is it any wonder we lost that damned war?*

The Mexican scout whirled his horse around. *"Dios mío,"* he whispered, then spurted out a string of nonsense that made Frazer squeeze his eyelids tightly for a few moments to dull the pain in both temples.

"Juanito," Henderson began translating, "says they must have hit the Delgado place instead. He says if they have already set the rancho of Señor Delgado afire, the red devils are running north. And there's no way anyone can catch a Comanche buck when he's riding for his home."

"Indeed," was all Frazer said.

On the other side, Ferguson swore. "Well, I swan, we ain't got no Comanche scalps to buy us tequila tonight. And after all this

63

hard ridin' we done."

"Don't jump the gun, soldier," Frazer said and turned to look at young Billy Ray Ferguson. "How long is Juanito's hair, boy?"

Ferguson's eyes turned briefly to the scout. When he looked back he said with a snigger, " 'bout as long as my sister's."

"Or some Indian buck's?" Frazier asked.

The light finally shined in Billy Ray Ferguson's eyes.

Major Block Frazer turned to the scout, raised his Leech & Rigdon and put a .36-caliber ball through Juanito's heart, sending him somersaulting over the back of his horse, which screamed, and took off, loping for parts unknown.

Spitting out the cigarillo, Major Frazer raised the revolver over his head and yelled, "Charge. Take no prisoners. Put them all to the sword."

His spurs raked the gelding, and he felt the glory of wind, smelled the taste of battle, and his eyes shown with delight when those who rode behind him, those brave Alabamans of the Río Sangrieto Rurales cut loose, to a man, with rebel yells.

Frazer shot the white-bearded hombre between the eyes, and watched the man fall face-first into the fire. It was no loss to Frazer, for the dead Mexican's white hair would never have passed for a Comanche or an Apache scalp back at Alcalde Miguel Blanco's office in El Pueblo de Cebollas Verdes.

Gunfire erupted all around him and for a moment, just a brief reliving of glory, Frazer remembered the joy of battle, the grandness of fear, and the trembling of emotions while watching the bluecoats scatter and run. Had Block Frazer been allowed command, Robert E. Lee never would have surrendered. The North would lie in ruins, the South would be the most powerful nation in the world, cotton would be king, and Block Frazer would be back on the veranda of his mansion, sipping lemonade and, maybe, just maybe, enjoying an even better cigarillo than could be found so far from Veracruz or Mexico City.

He killed another Mexican, saw him slam against a wagon wheel, spin around, and drop in a heap.

Low in the valley, the Mexicans had been making an early supper, and likely had not seen the black smoke from that rancho. Otherwise they would have been prepared. Obviously, they had seen Frazer and his men, but with the flags of Mexico and the Rurales being carried by Homer Witherspoon the peaceful men had not worried about being shot to pieces.

Frazer reined in his horse beside a covered wagon, the largest in the wagon train, and watched a Mexican running up the hills. His pistol was empty — Frazer had learned to count his shots. He shoved it in the holster and reached down to draw the Mississippi rifle he had been carrying with him since his first trip south of the border, during the war that started in 1846, the war in which he had helped bring more land to what could have been, what should have been, the Confederate States of America.

With the stock braced against his shoulder, Frazer eared back the hammer, adjusted his aim for range and shooting uphill, and touched the trigger. His horse did not flinch at the cannonlike noise, and Frazer grinned when the fleeing bean-eater slammed into the earth and slowly began rolling back down the hill.

One of the boys galloped off toward the dead man, yelling out, "Hurrah! Hurrah for Major Frazer! Hurrah!"

A moment later, the ringing left Frazer's ears, and he breathed in deeply, hoping to hold the smells of gunsmoke, of blood, of burning flesh for as long as possible. But he knew better.

A soldier ran up to him, and Frazer tossed

66

the kid the Mississippi rifle and then handed him the empty .36-caliber pistol. "Reload both, Tim. Six beans in wheel in the .36. Make sure the caps are secure." Twisting in the saddle, he barked, "Take scalps of those whose hair will pass for a red buck devil's! Billy John, grab anything of value from the wagons, and set this one — the big one — on fire. Butcher the bodies the way a Comanche would then throw the bodies in the burning wagon. Harry, you and Bubba make sure our horses don't run. Hobble them. Ferguson, you get your arse back up on the road, and keep a lookout for Apaches and Mexican troops. Logan, grab some arrows out of your saddlebags and put them in some of the wagons. I want this outfit to look like it was attacked by every damned buck in the entire Comanche nation! Now hurry up with this butchery, and let's lope back for home." He caught his breath, swung out of the saddle, and swapped the reins of his gelding for the Mississippi rifle and the revolver, sliding the latter into the holster.

Turning back to most of his command, he continued issuing orders. "Fill some bodies with arrows, too. When we get back to the pueblo, remember this. We did not see this massacre. We know nothing about it. We

67

caught a bunch of bucks when they were loping north, at Dragoon Springs, which we all know is dry right now. We killed these Indians — Henderson will give us the tally when we're all done here. Any questions?"

Logan stood. "What about the horse tracks? We're ridin' shod mounts, Major. That might cause suspicion."

"Comanches steal shod ponies, soldier. And when we're back on the road, we will cover our horse's hooves with rawhide. By the time Rurales get here, the wind will have blown most signs away. Remember that. And remember what a redskin's scalp — or a greaser's for that matter — will bring us when we get back to the pueblo."

Frazer sucked in a deep breath. "Any more questions?"

Silence.

"Then get busy and let's get out of this stink hole."

A figure leaped from the covered wagon.

Whirling, Major Block Frazer brought the Mississippi rifle to his shoulder, but quickly lowered it as the figure of an attractive Mexican woman wearing a brightly colored dress ran toward him. Tears streamed down her face as she clasped her hands and fell to her knees. She looked up at him, crying and praying and pleading and clasping her hands in prayer.

Frazer did not need to know any Mexican lingo. The pretty gal could have been speaking Paiute or Russian or some Oriental tongue and he still would have known exactly what she was saying.

Begging for her life.

He licked his lips. She probably would offer him anything to spare her life. *Anything at all.*

As good as she looked, it damned well might have been worth it.

Her hands released their prayer-hold and she fell to the ground. Her arms held her up, but her head dropped down as she sobbed and choked out a few more words.

Damn, but she was one pretty girl . . . for a Mex.

He lowered the hammer on the Mississippi rifle and shook his head. He used both hands to raise the rifle over his head. Yes, she was lovely. But an Indian scalp on a woman was still worth fifty pesos back at El Pueblo de Cebollas Verdes.

The stock of the .54-caliber long gun came down and crushed the woman's skull.

The scalp would be a bit messier, but it would still pass for a Comanche's at the office of the alcalde.

69

Chapter Five

Jed Breen ran as he holstered the Colt Lightning, ran as though he had to catch the strawberry roan. Fat chance of that, but he knew exactly what he had to do. While he ran toward the road and the dust, he envied the Apache stealing his horse. Breen had always known that Indians, and especially Apaches, had patience and nerve, but this horse thief and murdering devil must have gotten triple doses of both . . . and plenty of gall for a chaser.

Breen reached the corner of the corral and braced the Sharps on the top rail while he adjusted the brass telescope's sight for range. He focused on the top of the hill above the road, well ahead of the dust. Though he knew it was useless, he tried to control his breathing and then braced the stock against his right shoulder and leaned forward, positioning his feet so he would be as steady and still as humanly possible.

Another disadvantage, he thought. *Human.*

A jackal, certainly, but he was a human being. The Apache on the roan . . . well, that monster was something entirely different. Breen blinked, drew in a breath, opened his eyes, and slowly let out the breath.

His finger touched the set trigger and heard the click. He waited, both eyes open, one watching the road, the other staring at the crosshairs on the sight.

Now, he thought, still holding his breath, and before the target appeared in the sights, he touched the second trigger. The stock slammed against his shoulder, the roar of the cannon he held rocked his ears, and his nose and mouth breathed in the acrid smell of gunpowder. Already running, he found the road and raced up the hill, fumbling to eject the brass casing and replace it with a fresh load.

The strawberry roan was down, struggling but unable to rise. Breen refused to feel anything. Even Matt McCulloch, who loved horses more than he loved people, would understand. A man did whatever it took to survive. A man did whatever he needed to when it came to avenging the murder of an innocent young mother and her husband. A man did whatever he had to when it came to making a butcher like the Apache pay for

71

leaving a little, bitty baby to bake and die underneath the brutal West Texas sun and wind.

He shifted the Sharps to his left hand and drew the .38 with his right.

Reaching the hill, he saw the signs. The Indian had been thrown forward when the horse somersaulted. He had dragged himself into the brush. Breen's instincts took over and he dropped beside the strawberry roan just an instant before a pistol shot whistled past his ear.

The Apache was on the downslope. He hadn't been able to see Breen until he reached the top where the dying horse snorted and bled. Three legs were broken, and the lead bullet had torn through the roan's lungs.

A kind man, Breen figured, would put a bullet from the Colt into the animal's brain, end its suffering, but he wasn't a kind man. And with an Apache lying in the brush with a revolver of some kind, Breen knew he might have need of every bullet he had.

The wind blew hard down the hill, bringing dust and the smell of dry air with it. That gave Breen an idea. Easing the Colt and the Sharps onto the ground near the horse's belly, he crawled around the dying animal and through the manure and urine the roan could not control. He moved as close as he could to the brush then fingered the poster he had taken off the post office wall in El Paso. Wanted for murdering a dance-hall girl in Arnold's Town, R.G. Cordell might have to wait a while.

Ignoring the loss of the $250 bounty, Breen fished a match out of his vest pocket, struck it against his thumb, and held the flame at a corner of the wanted poster out of the wind, watching it catch easily. Then he stretched out his arm and dropped the burning poster on dead grass and dead brush.

Texas is a funny place, he thought as the flame grew. Down where the homesteaders had claimed their acres, a body could hardly find anything other than cactus that would grow. But on the ridgetop and the other side of the hill, grass and brush grew then died from the lack of water. *I wonder why those folks decided to claim land on that side of the hill, instead of the other. Not that it matters now.*

The Apache would have killed them no matter where they had decided to put down their roots, unless they had filed a claim on land in, say, Montana Territory. Even there, they would probably have been killed by Cheyennes or Sioux.

73

Fueled by the strong, hot wind, the flames found fuel, grew intensely hot and large. The crackling became louder, the smoke thicker, and Breen moved back, still using the horse's trembling body for a redoubt, and found the Sharps and the Colt. He crawled through a river of blood to the horse's head, heard a snort and what sounded like a human groan. With the wind and the roaring of flames to his left, he couldn't be certain.

Then he knew.

Lifting his head, he saw the horse's eye. The strawberry roan was dead.

"Damn." He felt anger rush to his head. "Damn. Murdering Apache devil."

That strawberry roan had been a real fine horse. It should have been. It was one of Matt McCulloch's horses, and the Indian had forced Breen to shoot it down. Only six years old, it could carry a bounty hunter miles and miles, and should have lived to a ripe old age.

Breen pulled both weapons in front of his head, looked at the ground where the Apache had hit the dirt hard, and read enough signs to tell him the Indian had dragged himself into the bush. The flames were about twenty feet uphill of that spot.

Breen looked east, and saw the ditch

formed by rainwater running downhill, away from the burning homestead below. "Greenhorns," he said aloud, just so he could hear his voice, hear what he was thinking as the roaring furnace to the west became deafening. Another reason they should have claimed the land on the northeast side of the hill.

Holding the Sharps in his left hand and the Colt in his right, Breen moved away from the heat and rolled into the ditch. Moving faster going downhill, he measured himself as he crawled like a snake. Fifty feet later, he stopped and chanced a look. The wind was blowing to the northwest, carrying flames and smoke toward the high desert mountains, leaving Breen with a clear view. It moved faster than he had expected, but it would run out of fuel in four hundred yards and die out.

Fire could be wondrous, Breen marveled as he remembered watching a house of ill repute burn down in Gibsonburg toward the Río Grande. No man, especially a man who had been thrown from a galloping horse headfirst onto hard West Texas turf could outrun a fire. Especially not flames powered by a hot, dry summer and a brutal West Texas wind.

He saw the Apache standing about thirty

yards downhill, off on the other side of the road, naturally. And just about where Breen expected to find him.

The man was brave and cunning. Breen had to give him that. And he was far from a fool. The dirty dog ran. Ran as hard as he could, despite the limp in his left leg and carrying a Winchester repeater in his right hand. He reached the road, clear of the flames.

By then Breen had dragged the Sharps to his shoulder. He eared back the hammer, tightened the stock against his shoulder, and touched the set trigger. Then the second trigger.

The cannon roared again. Breen let the Sharps fall into the ditch while he stood, palming the Lightning in his right hand. The bullet had splintered the stock of the Winchester, sending the rifle flying back toward the rushing flames, and dropping the buck to the ground.

He rose to his feet and reached for a sheathed knife, only to stop suddenly. Breen held his .38 by both hands, six feet away. His arms were not shaking.

"Drop it." Breen repeated the phrase in Spanish. He didn't speak Apache, and he doubted if this warrior savvied English, but most men in that part of the country could understand some Spanish.

The Apache froze, his black eyes stared harder at Breen. *"Mátame,"* the warrior said. *"Ahora."*

Kill me. *Now.*

Breen shook his head. *"Nada."* He motioned with his head. The Lightning did not move half an inch.

The warrior understood. His right hand found the deer-horn handle and easily drew the knife from the beaded sheath, but his black eyes never looked away from Breen. The knife flew into the dirt.

Far too experienced to look at anything but the Apache, Breen motioned with the Lightning's barrel, and the Apache pushed himself to his feet.

Breen backed up far enough to pick up the Sharps and tilted his head up the slope. "You first," he said in English. "Back to the homestead." He started his best approximation of the order in Spanish but stopped when he saw the Indian's left hand.

It was more than red, more than the copper-colored skin of an Apache. It was wretched, shriveled, and pinkish.

Jed Breen knew exactly who he had caught. "Blood Moon," he whispered.

"Lucky *norteamericano* pig," Blood Moon said, and then he smiled.

Breen steadied his breathing and his heart. "You speak English."

The Apache's face turned into stone.

"Move." Again Breen waved the Colt. He stepped back, keeping a good, safe distance from the Apache butcher, and let the man pass.

Twenty yards past the dead roan, Breen made him stop . . . just long enough to grab the canteen and saddlebags off the horse.

"Andar," Breen commanded, and he followed Blood Moon, the most notorious of all Apaches on both sides of the border, down the hill, still favoring one leg.

Flames burned down the far side of the rise. The fire was burning out at the homestead below.

Reaching the homestead, Breen made the Indian stop again. He pulled out the manacles from his saddlebags, tossed the irons toward Blood Moon, and watched him clamp on the cuffs. Breen ordered, "Lie down."

The Apache obeyed. Breen put the leg manacles on the Indian himself, then checked the wrist bracelets, and searched the Indian for any other weapons. He found another knife and a pocket derringer. He took a sip of water from the canteen.

"Agua," Blood Moon said.

78

Breen capped the canteen. "No. No water for you. You'd probably just pour it out."

That brought a smile to the Apache's face and warmth into his eyes.

Breen laid the canteen away, grabbed the length of chain connecting the ankle manacles, and dragged the Apache close to the dead mother's body.

It was the only time Blood Moon showed fear.

"If you move an inch," Breen whispered, "I'll kill you."

Blood Moon frowned.

"Stay here."

As expected, Breen had found Blood Moon's weakness. Apaches feared no man, no weapon, no god, but they were scared of the dead.

Breen spoke some gibberish, hoping the Indian might think he could speak to the dead, and then he hurried off to find the baby, no longer crying, but asleep. *Alive, at least,* Breen thought as he carried the little kid back to his prisoner and a corpse.

"All right. Move."

Blood Moon rose and scurried away from the dead body. The baby still slept.

Breen pointed at the garden.

"There's a hoe. Dig a grave."

The warrior frowned.

"As deep as you can. In the garden. We've got a mule."

"Good," Blood Moon said. "I am hungry."

Breen's head shook. "The mule will carry the baby. And most likely me. You'll walk. With luck, we'll be in Purgatory City in three or four days."

CHAPTER SIX

The last time Matt McCulloch went mustanging in these pretty mountains — well, pretty to him, who had only seen the Southern Rockies; and pretty, considering it was Texas — he had run into white scalphunters. The lowest form of humans, if you could call them human, were men killing Indians for scalps to peddle to the government in Mexico. He had also run into a Comanche boy.

So as the middle-aged horseman enjoyed his morning coffee, he made damned sure he kept the fire small and that the wood didn't give off much smoke. Coffee only. No hot food, not even warming up jerky in a skillet.

Besides, breaking a horse like the snorting gray stallion in the pen McCulloch had built was not something anyone with a lick of sense wanted to do on a full stomach. He sipped his coffee with relish, letting it last but not get cold, while watching the magnificent piece of horseflesh trot around the fence, testing the cedar posts and rails, snorting, sniffing the ground, pawing up some dust, trying to find a weakness, a chance of escape. The tail remained arched, for this horse might lose its freedom, but never would lose its pride.

He brought the tin cup to his mouth and frowned. The cup was empty. Lowering the old piece of battered tin, Matt glanced at the blackened pot on a stone by the fire. He could use another drink. Another cup of coffee, another ten minutes of pleasure. That wouldn't be a bad thing.

A sigh and a grunt followed as he rose off the boulder on which he sat. His left boot kicked sand over the flames and hot coals, and he put the cup on his makeshift chair of ancient lava rock.

His chaps flapped as he ambled toward the corral, unbuckling his gun rig, wrapping the belt over the holster, and laying that on a flat piece of granite on the eastern side of the pen. The stallion snorted, flashed angry eyes, and loped to the far side. Which was fine with McCulloch. The farther those unshod hooves were from stoving in his head, the better. Grabbing his rain slicker — though the sky remained a pristine blue with not a cloud within miles — off the flat rock, he slipped between the lower and middle rails and entered the corral.

The stallion gave an angry snort as the former Texas Ranger fished the deerskin gloves from the back pocket of his woolen britches and tugged them on slowly, keeping both eyes trained on the wild mustang. The gray's head dipped, then came up, and the animal let out a snort, probably profanity in mustang language. Issuing his challenge. Daring the man to take one step closer. The horseman didn't. Not yet. Breaking a horse was something a man did with patience.

McCulloch fetched the coiled lariat hanging over the top of one of the posts, and let the yellow slicker drape over the top rail.

He shook out a loop. It came as natural as drawing a Colt. He moved easily, whispering like he was coaxing a newborn to go to sleep. The stallion bolted, and McCulloch turned slowly, still moving toward the horse. When the gray went to another part of the corral, McCulloch never stopped his methodical stride.

The horse turned; McCulloch turned. The horse backed up; McCulloch went forward. The loop widened as the horseman began closing in, the hemp reata whistling through the air over his head. When the horse bolted, McCulloch let the lariat sail. A perfect throw landed the loop over the gray's small head, then slid down the neck. The horse kept running, and McCulloch deftly braced the rope behind his back, holding tight with gloved hands on both ends of the rope.

The fun began. The rope burned through McCulloch's corduroy vest, the winter shirt he wore despite the heat, the cotton underwear, and through maybe a layer of skin across the mustanger's lower back. The gray reared, crying out a savage roar, and McCulloch ground his teeth, thinking if not saying every swear word he had ever heard. He was sweating like his body had opened up all the spigots, and he made his way back, the horse fighting him at every turn.

Breathing became a chore, almost impossible.

McCulloch felt the snubbing post next to him. He used every muscle he had and summoned up enough grim determination to put the lariat on the other side of the thick post. Quickly he made a single dally, wrapping more of the lariat against the snubbing post. The horse bolted. Smoke rose from the friction as the hemp tightened and pulled hard against the cedar.

His hands ached, burned by the rope despite the gloves, but McCulloch kept up his job. He ducked underneath the rope as the horse began circling. Throwing another dally around the post.

He felt lucky. Some horses would keep the fight up for hours, but the gray seemed to know fighting was fruitless. The horse stopped, turned to face McCulloch, and flared its nostrils, stamped its forefeet, and snorted twice. Then it backed up just enough to add tension to the rope that held him securely to the snubbing post. And urinated.

As if telling McCulloch exactly what the proud king with blood from Arabia thought of a puny white man in dust-covered clothes.

McCulloch tried to swallow and felt dust carve the back of his throat. His left leg ached something fierce — the reminder of a bad break he had taken about a year or so back.

Quitting — even for a moment to slake his thirst with water from a canteen — seemed inviting, but McCulloch wasn't always patient. He limped back to fetch his rain slicker and slowly moved back to the horse. The gray snorted, twisted, grunted, and backed away as far as it could before the lariat tightened.

"Easy, boy," McCulloch said.

"Easy . . . easy . . . easy . . . why . . . don't you . . . go to . . . sleep."

He was lucky. As he spoke, the horse focused on his face.

McCulloch flung the slicker perfectly over the gray's eyes. The horse straightened, turned once to the left, and then froze. Blinded by the slicker, not knowing what to do, the horse became a statue. Its body, shining with sweat, trembled.

Pulling a small strip of calico from the mule-ear pockets on his pants, he used it to tie the slicker on.

"Easy, boy. Easy." Slowly he backed away several feet before turning and moving with a purpose to find a canteen and the other items he would need for the real work.

He worked the saddle blanket only. Putting it on the horse's back. Letting the horse smell it, feel it. Taking the blanket off. All of this McCulloch did with the slicker still serving as a blindfold on the mustang. Before the sun moved directly overhead, he was letting the horse get used to the saddle. Smell it. Feel it. Figure out the weight. He wouldn't start cinching it until later.

After that, he removed the slicker and draped it over the snubbing post. He dragged a bucket of water to the stallion, let it drink, and found some grain, which he dropped beside the bucket. It was chow time for the horse while McCulloch dragged his aching body through the corral, found the tin cup and old pot, and had his noon meal of cold coffee and nothing else.

The afternoon passed as methodically as the morning. Blindfolding the stallion with the slicker. Blanket. Saddle. Blanket. Saddle. And then cinching the saddle, which took considerably longer. Before dusk, he climbed into the saddle and sat there. Even though the temperature cooled, his body flooded with sweat. He could feel the tension in the gray, but the horse did not buck. He dismounted, slowly, letting the horse get used to him then grabbed the horn, stepped into the stirrup, and swung into the saddle again. And again. And again. After removing the slicker, McCulloch rewarded the gray with a carrot, though he did it more to let the stallion smell his hand.

Don't bite the hand that feeds you, he thought with a smile. *And tomorrow, don't buck the crazy fool off.*

It didn't work.

The next morning, after another breakfast of coffee and cold jerky, McCulloch repeated the process with the stallion blind-folded by the slicker. Then he took the slicker off, and, after the noon feeding and watering, he kept it off.

The saddle blanket he held under the gray's nose, letting the horse catch the scent, and slowly put the blanket over the back. The horse turned to look, but since it was still secured by the lariat to the snub-bing post, it did not buck or jump or kick out with its hind legs.

The saddle came next. The horse nosed the seat, the cantle, the horn, latigo, cinch, and both stirrups. McCulloch moved the saddle around in the air, so the creaking of the leather and the bouncing around of the stirrups wouldn't spook the gray — well, maybe not too much. Again the horse turned to watch, always suspicious, as Mc-Culloch hefted the saddle, and tried his best to ease the heavy mixture of wood, leather, and brass atop the thick blanket.

"Easy," he said as the horse danced and twisted. "Easy." He wished he had a voice that animals found soothing, but he knew he would never win any ribbons in a singing contest. Hell, he could barely hum.

After a long while, the gray stopped trembling and twisting as the weight became familiar. McCulloch bit his bottom lip as he knelt, reached under the gray's belly and found the cinch.

Exhaling after not getting kicked or stomped or urinated on, he tightened the cinch, and stepped back.

Now came the hard part. McCulloch walked back to the corral post where he had set his cup of coffee. He drank what was left, wiped his mouth with the dusty shirt sleeve, and returned to the horse. The slicker was again thrown over the gray's head, and once it had stopped moving, McCulloch began whispering nonsensical words as he eased the lariat over the gray's neck and head. The rope dropped into the dust, and McCulloch found the hackamore he had brought into the corral earlier.

The hackamore, he had told himself, would be easier on the wild animal than a bridle and bit. He slipped it over the horse's nose, threw the rope over the neck, and grabbed hold of the horn. Still blinded by the slicker, the horse tensed, but remembered the noise of creaking leather and the weight of McCulloch as he moved his right leg over the saddle, and let his boot find the far stirrup.

It seemed as if the wind had stopped blowing, that the birds had stopped singing, and the clouds — a change from the previous day — had decided to stay put.

Probably, McCulloch thought, just to watch the show.

Gripping the hackamore with his gloved right hand, McCulloch leaned forward, held his breath, exhaled slowly, and left his left hand slide the slicker off the gray's head.

He waited an instant, if that.

Suddenly he felt the hell about to be unleashed, and at that moment McCulloch dropped the rain slicker. Anticipating the horse's first jump, he raised his left hand over his head and felt his buttocks pulled upward by the thrust. The tops of his boots caught the uppers of his stirrups, and as the gray came down, McCulloch's back ached at the impact of his bottom with the saddle.

Again. And again. Twisting, the horse kicked and thrushed, spun like a twister. Six jumps later, McCulloch understood what a bird felt when it was flying. A second later he understood what a chicken egg felt like when he dropped one onto the floor of his kitchen.

That's pretty much how the rest of Matt McCulloch's second day with the gray mustang in the Davis Mountains went.

He dabbed the scratches and cuts with a wadded up bandanna he had dunked in the stream. The muscles and some of the ugliest bruises he touched up with a concoction a broken-down horse trader had taught him how to make. Mix molasses and vinegar with gunpowder, chili powder, and horse liniment. Boil water with chewing tobacco and a peppermint stick, and mix the two parts together. Chewing jerky hurt his mouth and most of his teeth felt as though they had been loosened considerably from all the jarring in the saddle and hard lands on the earth. Even swallowing coffee came hard.

But McCulloch made his way back to the corral and spent the rest of the next morning trying to ride the rank off the beast. It would take time, of course. He knew he couldn't gentle the gray and doubted if a horse like that would ever be considered completely broken. He planned to ride it enough to pull it behind his gelding to the ranch outside of Purgatory City. Then at least he could sleep under his own roof and in his own bed and not on the hard, cold ground of the Davis Mountains.

Besides, the way he had things figured, the temperature didn't top eighty-five degrees at that elevation, while down below on the West Texas plains near Purgatory

City, it would be ninety-six degrees in the shade.

And shade was mighty damned scarce in Purgatory City.

That was the plan. That had always been the plan. But after he had been tossed three more times that afternoon, McCulloch changed his mind.

He shook out the stiffness in his left shoulder, which had broken his last fall, and thought a little harder landing would have broken his collarbone for the umpteenth time. Wandering back to the corral fence and more important, the canteen, he considered how wise was it for a man of his years to be breaking wild horses alone in the mountains. It wasn't that he was old or that his hair was gray. It was certainly a whole lot darker than that bleached white that covered Jed Breen's head, but West Texas aged men more than even an Austin courthouse.

He sipped water, wiped his lips, ran his tongue over his teeth to make sure he hadn't lost any in his last wreck. Then he looked up.

And froze.

Only for a moment, only to recognize what he saw and understand what it meant.

Smoke. But not from some greenhorn

who hadn't seen what Comanches, Kiowas, Apaches, or white renegades could do to a damned fool. Not from a wildfire. And not from a burning building. It was signal smoke. Indian? Maybe, probably even likely, but it could be from scalphunters or other renegades.

CHAPTER SEVEN

The squeaking of the cell door being opened made Sean Keegan's head hurt. He would have rolled over or at least covered his ears with his arms, but that would have required moving. Keegan didn't think he could move even a finger, just yet. Squinting his eyes sent bolts of lightning through his skull, and got his stomach to rocking.

Something grunted. Boots dragged across the floor. The door squeaked again, slammed, and while Keegan cursed, he heard the keys grating in the lock — something he had not heard when Purgatory City's jailer must have unlocked the cell.

The grunt came again.

Keegan got a whiff of something incredibly foul, and being experienced with hangovers and drunken benders, he understood the odor did not come from him. Nor did the grunt, which sounded partly human.

"Move."

His eyes opened, and Keegan turned his head slightly.

A high-crowned black hat covered with dust and grime and filled with holes, covered the man's thick black hair. The forehead, cheeks, and nose had been burned to some color between brown and a bottomless pit, but most of the face was a filthy black beard streaked with gray . . . or maybe that was drool.

Keegan's eyes had a hard time focusing.

The voice, guttural but commanding, spoke again. "Move, damn you."

A laugh echoed, and that came from the other side of the iron bars in the relatively new Purgatory City jail cell.

Keegan made out the wretched buckskin shirt on this . . . this . . . this . . . *man* the size of a mule. A belt with a big buckle strapped across the massive belly, and more buckskins, even more foul than the shirt, stretched down until dingy, stinking, ancient brown boots scuffed closer to the bunk Keegan occupied.

"I count three," said the man. Or was it a monster?

Keegan thought he might be dreaming, but he never had nightmares. He made himself move until he sat on the bunk, and when his eyes focused, he realized he had a cellmate, one of the hide men from The Palace of Purgatory City the evening before.

Heeheeheeheehee came the nasal laugh, but not from the six-foot-five beast now drooling next to the toes of Keegan's cavalry boots.

Looking away from his new bunky, Keegan found the jailer.

"Slim" — he was surprised he could speak without throwing up — "what the hell are you doing to me?"

"Heeheeheehee," the old jailer laughed again.

"Move or you eat tooths for breakfast," the hide man said.

"Hold ye horses, ye bloody rube, and let me see what's going on here." Keegan slid down the bunk to the brute of a man — no, Keegan didn't consider buffalo skinners men — so he could look at Slim Van Horn, taking in a quick scout of the cell to Keegan's left. "That cell's empty, Slim, what's this —"

Massive hands gripped Keegan's shirt-front, and a moment layer Keegan felt himself sailing faster than a catamount could jump. His right shoulder slammed into one iron bar, and that lessened the impact when his head met the next bar, splitting his forehead about two inches instead of spilling his brains onto the floor. He twisted, felt bruises forming on his back when that part of his body met iron, and the next thing he knew, his legs were stretched out northeast and northwest on the floor, all sorts of brilliant colors flashing across the cell before the blood blinded his right eye.

The way the light shined through the barred windows, Keegan knew it was late afternoon. Too late to be bringing in a drunk from last night, and far, far too early to be jailing a drunk on that fine day for a hangover.

Keegan sat for what felt like ten days, but only a few seconds could have passed. Moving seemed dangerous since his spine might have been dug into the cell's stone floor like a fencepost at the nearest livery stable's corral. Pain shot from his pelvis to the back of his skull. He slowly wiped blood out of his eye and off his face, and turned just a wee bit to see Slim Van Horn making his way toward the door.

Keegan's mouth moved, and he knew he had spoken, though he couldn't quite figure out what he had said. Most likely it had been directed at Slim Van Horn. The jailer was grabbing a hat off a big deer horn next to the potbellied stove. The keys to the cells were flipped to the town marshal's desk.

"Slim!" Keegan heard his own voice.

"You boys figure out who gets the bunk," Van Horn said as he opened the door. "And try not to kill one another."

The door closed.

Keegan pressed a palm — though he couldn't have told a priest if it had been his left or right one — against the cut in his forehead and looked up with his good eye at the monster that had become his cellmate.

Six cells were in the new jail. And when Keegan had been dragged in the night before, every damned one of them had been empty. Since the only things Keegan could hear were his pounding heart, his literally and figuratively splitting skull, and the shuffling of old boot soles against a cold, stone floor, the Irish former cavalryman knew only two men were in jail. In one cell. It wasn't Friday or Saturday night, and it was the middle of the month so nobody who had a job had gotten paid. No one in the town's law enforcement thought there would be a lot of drunks and brawlers to arrest.

Which meant only one thing.

"I rip off arms first," said the beastly fiend towering above Keegan. "Right or left?"

Keegan didn't answer, and since he was holding his left hand against the cut in his forehead, the buffalo skinner jerked Keegan's right arm, came a fraction from pulling the shoulder out of the socket, and sent Keegan flying against the stone wall, knocking the breath out of him and into next month.

Keegan fell hard onto the bunk, breaking it in half.

In the old days, back when he was a wee bit younger, he would have enjoyed the fact that he faced another fight. The queasiness in Keegan's stomach had vanished. His head hurt, but no longer because of a hangover, replaced by the pain from those handful of dents and cuts walls and jail bars had left on various parts of his noggin.

The big, stinking, savage man had stopped shuffling his feet and was kneeling, still grinning, and pulling up the buckskin britches over his right boot. The filthy hand reached inside and drew a knife, the silver of the steel shining like the eyes of a diamondback rattlesnake before it struck. The skinner straightened and said, "Cut off arm now. Then gut you."

Keegan raised his left hand and wagged a finger at the slow-moving scoundrel. "You . . ." he said, his memory clearing.

"You weren't with those hide men I whupped at The Palace." He knew he was right. Keegan's memory wasn't what it had been back during the War of the Rebellion — for that was many bottles and kegs of whiskey ago — but he knew he never forgot a face. And a face like the bearded one above him was something no one would ever forget.

"Cut off finger," the brute said, "if you no stop waggin'."

The man dragged his feet a bit faster, and Keegan kept wagging his finger. He waited, then flung the filthy waste bucket his right hand had found, sending urine and excrement and probably vomit from prisoners two days ago at the man.

"Arrgghhhhh!" the big hunter cried as he spun around, spitting, coughing, gagging. The effect surprised Keegan as he scrambled to his knees, grabbed a broken leg of the bed, and made himself stand and stagger to the far corner of the cell.

"What's the matter?" Keegan taunted. "The smell of piss and dung and whiskey vomit drowning out that perfume ye been breathing from your own body?"

The man roared, the knife flashed, and the behemoth who moved like a slug, tripped over the slop bucket, and fell face-first onto the floor.

Keegan stepped toward the skinner, intent on kicking his teeth down his throat, but for a man whose legs did not work worth a tinker's damn, the man was fast with his arms and hands. The knife slashed forward, causing Keegan to gasp, twist his calf from the razor-sharp blade, and leap back. The man reeking of buffalo guts and human waste put both hands on the floor, the right one still clenching the knife's rosewood handle, and began pushing himself to his feet.

Taking advantage, Keegan made two quick steps, brought up his left leg. The toe of his boot connected under the big man's jaw and sent him crashing back.

Moving in again, Keegan had to leap out of the slashing blade's arc. He backed up to catch his breath, knowing the hangover and the beating he had earned last night kept taking its toll on him. Again, he wiped the blood out of his eye.

The big man reached up with his left hand, gripped one of the crossbars on the cell, and started to pull himself back to his feet. Keegan charged, deflected the slashing blade of the knife with the busted wood that had been the bunk's leg, then dropping the chunk. Both hands reached up and snagged hold of the top of the bars.

The builders had been sloppy. The bars didn't go all the way to the ceiling, not that anyone cared; it wasn't like some drunk or murderer or bank robber could escape through a six-inch hole, but that gave Keegan the leverage he needed. Both feet smashed into the man's left arm. The snapping of both bones in the skinner's forearm seemed louder than a gunshot.

The big man screamed in agonizing pain, sounding more like a woman than the massive fellow he was. The knife fell to the floor as the man spun to grip his mangled arm. Keegan took advantage again, pressed his boots against the bar, and kicked himself back. Landing mostly on the liquid and stinking waste, he slipped, fell hard onto his left shoulder, grunted, rolled, and kept moving until the bars on the far side of the cell stopped him.

He tried to catch his breath in a second, while realizing any decent laundress would charge him triple, maybe even more, to wash his clothes. The skinner grunted in pain and spat out choking, garbled words. Seeing the knife on the floor, Keegan made himself stand. But the buffalo man had seen the look in Keegan's eyes, and he stopped gripping the busted arm and found the

102

knife's handle.

The man moved faster, but still could barely beat a sloth in a race. The blade ripped through Keegan's trouser leg just above the top of his right boot. Keegan watched the big man try to stand and saw another opportunity. He moved to the busted bed, grabbed the smaller part of the bunk, letting the sawdust-filled mattress and wretched blanket of more holes than wool drop to the floor. He raised the splintered wood over his head and brought it down on the man's head. The momentum carried Keegan past him, and the brute's right arm managed to punch Keegan's left ankle, tripping him and sending him into the bars.

Keegan stopped himself with his hands, spit out blood and saliva, and whirled around. Through sweat and blood and instinct, Keegan saw the hider still on his knees, searching for the knife. Keegan spotted it first. He charged, not for the knife, but for the skinner. His right boot came up, caught the man's bearded face and smashed him backward. Keegan hit the floor, too, rolled over through the stinking wretchedness, and grabbed the knife's handle. He scurried back and flung the blade through the bars.

The brute's eyes turned dull.

Keegan pushed himself up and braced his back against the cell door. Breathing hard, he managed a smile.

"Knives make things messy," he said between gasps. "Let's try those bloody old Marquis of Queensbury rules."

The leviathan grunted, spit, slipped once, and came back to his knees. Keegan, spitting out froth and wondering if any part of his body wouldn't be blacker than the brute's beard and soul, found his feet again, and kicked the hide man in the chest, sending him spread-eagled on the floor.

"I . . . hate . . . Queens . . . bury . . . rules." Taking advantage of the position of the man's legs, Keegan's right boot found the hider's groin.

The man gasped, grunted, and his sunburned face turned countless shades paler. Keegan sat on the man's stomach, his right hand found the slop bucket, and he slammed it onto the man's face. He raised the bucket again and brought it down harder. And again, this time on the big man's forehead. The well-seasoned bucket busted, and the man let out a long sigh.

Keegan fell off the man, trying to find some fresh air to fill his lungs. He didn't. He reached forward, hoping to reach the bars and pull himself up, but the walls and doors of the cell felt fifteen miles away.

So he crawled. Crawled across the floor of a cell that was twelve feet by ten feet, through urine and unimaginable filth, which he quickly added to by vomiting twice. He dared not wipe his mouth with his shirt sleeve, as filthy as it was. Finally he felt the coldness of the iron and his fingers tightened against the bars. He pulled himself forward, pulled again till his aching head touched the iron.

Rolling onto his back, Keegan stared at the ceiling, told himself to keep breathing, told himself that Slim Van Horn would pay bloody hell for such a shameful act.

A minute passed. Two. Five. Ten. Maybe more. Keegan wasn't sure, but at some point his right and left arms obeyed his commands and rose above to find a crossbar. What felt like weeks later, Sean Keegan managed to pull himself to a seated position.

He focused on the giant, saw blood streaming from the man's head, nose, and mouth, running down the cracks in the stone floor, mingling with other nasty liquids. Keegan hurt so much he couldn't smell, and that was more than a small blessing.

He couldn't see out of one eye. He didn't

think he was blind, but ruled that the blood was starting to congeal from the cut in his forehead. The other eye focused on the man who had tried to rip off his arms, stab him to death, crush him till he was a drooling dummy. He stared, watching the buckskin shirt, watching it rise and fall, rise and fall, rise and fall.

All right, he told himself. *They can't hang me for murder. And maybe if this son of a dog ever wakes up, he'll tell me what this little set-to was all about.*

Ten minutes later, the door to the jail opened.

Keegan grinned at the gasp.

Though he didn't figure his voice would carry as far away as the front door, he said, "Slim Van Dorn, next time you put a man in this jail to kill me, you bloody well better make sure the gopher's knees can bend."

CHAPTER EIGHT

The woman named Litsog came out of the Apache wickiup in the Sierra Madre range, but this time, the old hag with only three teeth — two uppers and a molar in the back — did not whip Litsog's back with the cane switch that sometimes reminded her of that other life she once lived.

Hates Everyone, the shrivel-faced, practically toothless, gray-headed woman, had stepped aside, and was silent, not hurling insults, not singing a song while she beat Litsog with the cane. She even bowed her head.

Litsog's green eyes lifted, and she saw two men standing before her. One was Three Dogs, the leader of this group of Chiricahua Apaches. Three Dogs had much power, and even Litsog had to agree, had treated her kinder than most of the Apaches had. He had even kicked Blood Moon out of the village, driven him back into the country of the bluecoats and — she tried to block away those memories, for after all these years, she knew better than to think of her past life. What was here, was now, what would be, and would always remain, forever.

She was Apache. Now. Despite the color of her eyes and the shade of her hair. Litsog had been her name for many, many moons. The earth had turned so many times she had trouble recalling the language she once spoke. But she could still remember some things — when she had to — but not during the day. Never during the day.

Something was wrong, Litsog knew. She held her breath, wondering, looking around. It seemed as if all the village had come out.

Maybe, she thought, this was the day that she once prayed for every night, and sometimes, every waking moment. This was the day that the Chiricahua Apaches would do what they usually did to white captives. This was the day when they would kill her.

She prayed God to forgive her for wishing that they would. Finally. End the misery. End her life that had really ended so many years ago.

The holy man, Yo-íí, raised his short, stocky arms over the buffalo headdress he had traded with a Comanche before Litsog was ever born, and began singing. She could not make out most of the words, but when the other women began singing, and crying and sobbing, and when the mother of Litsog's husband fell to her knees and wailed like a dozen banshees, she knew. Even before Three Dogs spoke, Litsog knew.

"Killer of Cougars is dead," Three Dogs said. "Hear me again. Killer of Cougars is dead. He was killed fighting — as he would want. He was killed fighting for his people. He was killed with honor. Sing songs for him tonight, then never, never, speak his name again."

Looking back at Litsog, Three Dogs drew a large knife from a fringed and beaded sheath on his left hip. He hefted the blade, nodded at Yo-íí, who sprinkled some dust over the forged steel, and covered the paces that separated the Apache chieftain from Litsog. Like the expert he was, he flipped the knife up and caught it with his hand, gripping the blunt side of the blade with his fingers, then lowering it toward Litsog.

She took it. She knew what was expected of her. Four years ago, five, or even last year, she would have taken the knife and screamed at Three Dogs, at Yo-íí, at Hates Everyone and shoved the knife to the hilt between her breasts. But now, she fell to her knees, hung her head and began singing in Apache the best she could. Her voice quavered. She felt tears in her eyes.

Tears. Over Killer of Cougars? Over her husband? No, that couldn't be.

Three Dogs grunted something in Apache that Litsog could not understand, but she heard him walk away, even above the singing of mourning songs by village women, even over the shouts of the warriors who had abandoned Killer of Cougars to his fate.

His body was not here. They did not bring Killer of Cougars home to the Sierra Madre range. They did not bring him to the Dead River.

Yo-íí knelt beside her, and said some Apache prayer.

A wild thought flashed through her mind. *Apache prayers are so much shorter than the Reverend Thurmond Benson Kelsey's were back . . .*

It was something she recalled her father saying. Her white father. So many lifetimes ago. He would say it often, and Litsog's mother would scold him, shame him, with a blistering attack on what is proper and what is sacrilegious. Litsog stopped herself. *No. Do not think that. Do not torture yourself with memories. Not now. Now while the sun shines.*

"Where is my husband?" she asked.

Yo-íí grunted.

110

She tried again. "Why did not they return him to his people?"

The holy man tried to explain, but Litsog only caught half of what he said as she stared at the shining blade of the knife of Three Dogs. She saw her distorted reflection in the Damascus steel.

Damascus. Da-mas-cus. What a strange word, she thought. *Where does it come from? What does it mean? Shiny? Picture? Reflection? Deadly? Sharp?*

At length, Yo-íí stopped talking like a man of faith, a man of wisdom. When Litsog lifted her head and looked into his black eyes, she saw the sadness, the weariness, and the old man wet his dried, ugly lips, and he spoke softly. "The Mexicans caught him. He stayed behind so others might live. He was brave in death as he was brave in life. But . . . the Mexicans — no, not Mexicans, but the pale eyes who left their country with the bluecoats and the Tejanos — those evil men. They are who caught your husband. And they are the ones who took his scalp."

She stiffened, understanding, and felt a terrible sadness for her Apache husband. Not that she ever loved him, not that she ever could love any Apache man. Love Killer of Cougars? How did he get such a

111

name? She had never seen the hide of a mountain lion, and he had never mentioned mountain lions, catamounts, panthers, or any such name. He had beaten her three nights a week, usually for no reason, except because he could. He had raped her. He had dragged her by her hair, threatened to cut her throat, or carve out her eyes. He had been a monster, one even more cruel than Hates Everyone.

But there was something decent in Litsog. There was something human. As wretched a husband, as cruel a human being was Killer of Cougars, even Litsog did not wish for him to have been scalped. She knew what Apaches believed and their own religion. An Apache mutilated would never be a whole man in the hereafter.

Killer of Cougars was doomed to Apache purgatory or Chiricahua hell.

Around her, Apache women wailed and some sang songs of mourning. When she looked up, the blacker than midnight eyes of Yo-íí bore through her, and she knew he was waiting. Waiting for her to do what was expected of an Apache widow. She found the handle of Three Dogs' knife, and brought it up. In the eternity of hell she had spent since being taken from her home, she had seen how these people mourned their dead. Doe With Horns had cut off the pinky on her left hand and the tips of both ears. Others had maimed themselves in other ways.

Closing her eyes and biting her lip, Litsog began singing her own mourning song.

Killer of Cougars
I will never say your name
After tonight
But you will always remain in my heart
Forever
Forever
Forever
Killer of Cougars
You will always be my husband
Your spirit will live on
Your bravery, too
You saved many of our young warriors
Our people will remember you
Forever
Forever
Forever

She sliced her right forearm with the blade of the heavy knife. Felt the blood running down her arm, spreading down her hand, dripping off her fingertips. She changed hands, the blood sticky on the handle of the great Apache chieftain's knife. The blade

113

carved a slash down her left forearm and blood spilled freely.

Her eyes opened. Yo-íí's face remained ugly and stern. Two cuts down both arms must have seemed like a pittance when it came to Apache mourning. The great holy man wanted more. So Litsog lifted the heavy knife with her right hand and brought it to her head.

And when she started cutting, all singing stopped. A few women gasped in horror. The silence proved deafening, but Litsog cut and cut and cut, and began to sing. Tears blinded her, but not before she saw the stunned expression on the grizzled old holy man's face. Even Yo-íí had not expected this much grieving from a woman who was not even truly an Apache.

A young brave began his own song.

Look what she does
Look what she does
Litsog loved her husband
Litsog loved her husband
See what she does
See what she does
Litsog loved her husband

She moved the knife to the other side of her head, and continued the butchery. Her arms hurt, and the blood still flowed like small creeks in the rugged mountains of Mexico.

At length, the knife of Three Dogs went to the top of Litsog's head.

When she started carving, Three Dogs had returned. "Enough!" the leader shouted.

Litsog pulled the knife away from her head, and let it fall to the ground.

She realized she was on her knees, swaying from shock, or heat, or the loss of blood. At first, she looked at Three Dogs and at Yo-íí. Finally she turned to the villagers, the warriors whose lives might have been saved by her wretched Apache husband's bravery and sacrifice, and then at the chopped long locks of her blonde hair that scattered the ground as the wind blew her mourning away.

For the Apaches, Litsog's yellow hair had been something they envied, something strange and wonderful. Killer of Cougars had said it was like rays of sunshine, even warm to the touch. *He could be poetic, sometimes,* she thought, *for such a cruel man.*

Black-haired Indians marveled at her hair, which stretched to her waist. Or had, after so many lifetimes in captivity. But now her hair was short, and would have been even shorter had not Three Dogs ended the butchery.

She stared at the hair for just a moment, because Yo-íí and even Three Dogs himself knelt beside her, binding the cuts in her arms. The chieftain lifted her to her feet, and helped her to the wickiup she had once been forced to share with Killer of Cougars.

The young warrior began singing again.

See what she has done
See what she has done
Litsog loved her husband so much
Litsog loved her husband so much
See what she has done
See what she has done
Litsog loved her husband so much
We should all be blessed
To have someone love us that much
See what she has done
See what she has done

Inside the wickiup, Three Dogs eased Litsog onto a blanket of various colors the Indians had traded for. He brought a ladle to her mouth, and she tasted water from a pot. The water revived her. Something close to sanity returned. And maybe vanity, too.

"Am I no longer beautiful?" she asked, suddenly fearing what might happen to a widow with butchered, chopped-up yellow hair.

"You are more beautiful than ever," Three Dogs said and let her drink more water.

"More?"

Her head shook.

He nodded. "Rest," he ordered. "Sleep." He rose. "We will speak tomorrow."

She asked again, still fearing for some crazy reason that she would be tortured and killed in the morning. "Am I no longer beautiful?"

"You are more beautiful than ever," he said again. "If I did not have three wives already, and all of them jealous, I would begin a courtship of you." His eyes twinkled, and then he was gone.

Both arms started to hurt, but she blocked out the pain and lifted her right hand to her head. *What have I done?*

She realized she was alone, and when the sun went down, and the songs of mourning faded as well as the song the young warrior had sung to honor her, and there was nothing to hear except horses grazing, wood crackling in fires, and maybe a dog snoring on the far side of camp, Litsog began the ritual she had started when she first arrived at a camp of the Apaches.

She spoke words in a tongue that sounded

117

strange to her, and on this night proved even more difficult to remember.

"I am from . . . T-T-Tex-as. I am from . . . T-Texas. Texas.

"My name is Lit— No! My name is M-M-M-M . . ."

She frowned, bit her lip, and tried again.

"My name is See . . . See . . . Sin . . . Sin-theee-aa. Cynthia."

She breathed in deeply, held it long in her lungs, and exhaled. "My name . . . is . . . is . . . My-me-M-M-M . . ."

Finally it escaped like a curse.

"McCulloch."

CHAPTER NINE

Whenever the baby cried, Jed Breen cursed. It never stopped the infant's bawling, which pricked the bounty hunter's nerves more than the malevolent stare Blood Moon always had on his ugly and cruel face. Breen usually rode the mule, holding the kid in his left hand and the double-action .38 in his right. The Apache walked ahead, silent, shackled, moving without complaint, but something about the way he moved, how tall he stood, told Breen there was not an ounce of fear in the cold-blooded killer. And the Indian likely was not concerned in the least that he was being taken to a people who would kill him as quickly as they could.

Breen didn't need the reins. The mule had the slowest walk of any four-legged critter he had ever seen. He could walk faster than the mule, but that would mean carrying the baby and keeping an eye on Blood Moon. So Breen sat on the mule's back, tried rocking the squalling brat, even tried singing to it. "Dinah, Dinah, Show Us Your Leg" apparently upset the child more than the sun in the kid's eyes.

Sometimes the kid would cry itself out, but a mile later, Breen knew he wouldn't last another mile. His ears ached and his head was splitting. Still holding the Lightning, he picked up the reins draped over the mule's neck and pulled hard. The mule snorted and slowed and finally came still.

Blood Moon kept walking until Breen ordered him to stop. The Apache obeyed, but did not turn around. Just stared ahead seeing only the long road to oblivion.

Breen swung his right leg over his saddle, which did not fit the mule's back worth a damn. Still holding the kid, he dropped to the ground and cursed as he stumbled toward the edge of the road. His legs went out from under him, and he landed hard, jarring his spine but keeping a firm hold on his revolver and the crying kid. He closed his eyes tightly for just a moment, but jerked up and leveled the revolver at the figure of Blood Moon.

The Apache still stood in the road, looking northeast, unconcerned.

"Lousy Apache must be deaf," Breen said.

The baby screamed. The mule urinated.

Breen grimaced as he came to his feet, still holding the crying baby and walked around the mule, pleading with the kid to just be quiet, if only a few minutes so he could think. Being a midwife wasn't the job for a bounty hunter . . . if midwives actually took care of crying babies after the moms had given birth. He looked upward at the sun, and began to think maybe the kid was hot. West Texas wasn't cool that time of year. Breen twisted, glanced over his shoulder at the still unmoving Apache, and then hurried off the road. He found a dip off the road, saw the shadows, and placed the kid in the shade. It still screamed its little head off, eyes closed tightly, wailing like ten million coyotes. Breen thought and thought, or tried to, but who could think clearly with the kid's nerve-splintering wails.

He hurried back to the mule, opened the saddlebags, found a sack and tugged at the drawstring. A moment later, he pulled out a piece of beef jerky. Maybe the kid was hungry. Hell, Breen was, so he put one end of the dried beef in his mouth, tore off a mouthful and chewed.

He'd never get to Purgatory City if he had to stop every couple of miles because the little baby wouldn't stop crying. He'd never collect that beautiful bounty for bringing in

121

the most wanted Indian since . . . hell, Te-
cumseh?

The jerky was supposed to taste wonderful, but Breen couldn't taste a thing. Not
with all this — silence.

Breen looked over the saddlebags. His face
turned white, and the Colt came up in his
hand, as he moved away from the mule and
hurried back to the dip on the other side of
the road. "Get away from that baby!" he
bellowed.

Blood Moon held the kid in both arms.
The Apache looked up, black eyes unread-
able and unblinking, and said nothing.
Breen had been in the country long enough
to know what Indians would do to squalling
kids. He'd seen — well, not exactly *seen,*
but *heard* Texans in saloons and read newspaper accounts about murderous raids and
kidnappings and some posse finding a baby
with its brains bashed against a rock, tree,
or cactus.

"Put him down!" Breen ordered, leveling
the revolver.

As the Apache rocked it in his arns, the
baby had stopped crying. Then the kid
began sniffling, and suddenly it was crying
again.

"I said —"

"Hand me your scarf," Blood Moon said.

The words were in English, guttural, but easy enough to understand.

"Scarf? What?"

"And bring me a canteen."

Breen weighed his options. He could put a bullet between Blood Moon's eyes, but if the Apache fell on the kid or dropped it onto the rocky ground, the baby might be seriously injured, or even killed.

"Muy pronto." The Apache spoke in Spanish, and the baby's sobbing turned louder.

Breen moved back to the mule, found the canteen. He started to holster the Colt, reconsidered, then swore and shoved the hot iron into the leather. While he carried the canteen back across the road, he began tugging at the knot on the piece of blue and white silk that hung over his neck.

The Apache was kneeling, placing the baby on the dirt. When Blood Moon looked up at Breen, he reached out with his left hand. Breen held out the bandanna, but the fierce Indian's head shook, so he tossed the canteen then stared in utter silence.

The Apache raised the tiny little nightshirt over the baby's fat little legs, pulled off stained white unmentionables, and tossed the diaper aside. Breen caught a whiff and frowned, then sniffed. Well, no wonder he hadn't smelled the excrement. He stunk to high heaven. Riding through the heat, setting grass afire, and coming through a fight with a murdering Apache renegade would do that to just about anybody.

The Indian turned the baby over and poured water over the kid's hindquarters. Breen swallowed.

"What are you doing to him?" Breen asked.

The Apache held out his left hand, and Breen tried to comprehend, but the Indian crooked the pointer finger and Breen remembered the silk bandanna he held. He moved closer, held one end of the sweaty piece of fabric in his left hand, and kept the Colt Lightning steady in his right.

A second later, the Apache held Breen's bandanna and began wiping the baby's pink little butt.

Breen frowned. "That cost me seventy-five cents in El Paso."

The Apache finished cleaning, and held the sopping, stringy, stained bandanna out toward Breen.

The head on his shoulders shook, though Breen had no memory of shaking his head, and the stinking bandanna dropped onto the dirt. Slowly, the Apache pulled the red silk headband off his head and began unfolding it. Fascinated, Breen watched as the

124

bandanna was transformed miraculously into another unmentionable, and suddenly the little squirt wasn't crying.

"Is he all right?" Breen whispered.

"She."

Breen stared. His lips moved, but it took several seconds before he spoke again. "Huh?"

"She," Blood Moon said. "Little girl. Not boy. Damn fool."

Damn fool, Breen determined, was aimed at him.

The Apache looked up, eyes trained on the jerky, and he held out his hand again.

Breen understood and handed the Indian the dried beef and he took it in the mangled, ugly, red hand.

"Is he hungry?" Breen asked, then remembered. "She. Is she hungry?"

"No teeth," Blood Moon said. "But can suck." He stepped out of the dip, and nodded at Breen's seventy-five-cent, manure-and-urine-stained silk bandanna from the Southwestern Gentlemen's Emporium in El Paso, Texas.

"I'm not wearing that around my neck," Breen barked. "To hell with getting the back of my neck burned by the sun."

"Bring, damn fool," Blood Moon said.

Breen didn't know why he did it, but he

125

picked the filthy fabric off the dirt and shoved it into his back pocket. The Indian sat on a rock on the other side of the road, pulled a small deerskin pouch that hung over his neck, and emptied the contents, letting a slight breeze carry whatever dust or herbs or powder down the trail. Then the Apache poured precious water from the canteen onto the small piece of faded deerskin.

"Damn it," Breen said. "Don't waste water. There's no water —"

He stopped speaking as Blood Moon removed the jerky from the kid's mouth, and let the baby suck on the deerskin.

"Need milk," Blood Moon said as the baby sucked.

Breen studied the Apache's dark eyes. Then shook his head. "Fat chance of finding mother's milk, or even a damned cow in this hellhole."

The Apache took the pouch and soaked it again with water, then returned it to the baby.

"Easy with that water, boy," Breen snapped again. "The nearest water hole is twenty miles from here."

Blood Moon did the damnedest thing. He looked up at Breen and smiled. "Much closer." He added, "Damn fool."

That evening, Breen stretched out underneath a juniper and sucked on the bone of a plump rabbit Blood Moon had caught with a snare, while soaking his feet in the cool spring the Apache had led the mule, the baby, and the bounty hunter to. A smokeless fire heated the coffeepot and Breen took a sip from his cup, then thought about his greed, his stupidity, and his ungentlemanly ways and offered the cup to the Apache.

"Too hot for girl to drink," Blood Moon said dismissively.

"Not for the baby, damn you. I ain't that ignorant. For you."

"White man coffee?" Blood Moon spat.

"Well, we ain't got no tiswin here," Breen barked back. Tiswin was the weak beer Apaches drank.

Soon, the baby slept. The Apache asked for Breen's stinking bandanna, which he then turned some cactus pad into some kind of soap, and used water from the spring to soak and clean the seventy-five-cent silk. He also used the skin of the rabbit flesh side out as a bonnet for the baby's head.

The baby looked damned ridiculous, but it wasn't bawling its tiny little head off.

At least for the time being.

Breen finished the coffee, hoping it would keep him awake. Blood Moon might be chained, but he was still the most dangerous man in the Southwest, and Breen wasn't about to get too comfortable. So when Blood Moon backed up, Breen rose, dropping the tin cup, and palming the .38-caliber revolver.

"We go," Blood Moon said. "Now."

"Now." Breen shook his head. "It's a new moon. And it's pitch dark."

"Sun too hot for baby," Blood Moon said. "We travel at night. Day for rest. Better for baby sister."

"Baby sister my ass," Breen barked. "You butchered the kid's mother, burned the dad alive, and left this kid in the bushes as coyote bait. You don't give a damn about this kid. And if you think I'm riding in the dark with the likes of you so you can slip away and vanish —"

"We go now," Blood Moon interrupted.

Breen leveled the .38.

"Damn Fool," the Indian said.

Breen realized that had become his Apache name.

The savage killer smiled. "You will live to see White Eye town." He struggled with the name. "Pur-ga-tor-e Cit-teeeee."

Breen frowned. "You killed his . . . her . . . parents."

"Needed horse."

"You could have taken the mule," Breen pointed out, nodding at the tired animal still lapping up water from the spring like a dog.

"Mule good to eat," Blood Moon said. "Not ride."

"I thought Apaches would rather walk than ride."

"We go now," Blood Moon said again. "Move in darkness. Rest when sun burns."

Breen wet his lips.

"You will live to see White Eyes town," Blood Moon repeated, and turned away. He moved to the other side of the spring, and grabbed the reins on Breen's bridle and led the mule away from the water.

"Hold it!" Breen barked. His Sharps was still in the scabbard.

Blood Moon turned and grinned. "If dead I want you, dead you be." The Apache pointed a shriveled finger at the sleeping baby. "Carry sister. We walk."

"Why not ride?"

"Mule bloated with water now. And riding wake up baby." The Indian's teeth shown in a wide smile, reflecting the flames from Breen's nice fire.

"Just stand still." Breen walked to the mule, keeping his distance from the Apache who still held the reins, and moved to the other side of the horse. He put his free hand on the stock of the Sharps. "I'll carry this, too."

"Damn Fool," the Apache said. "How you carry baby sister and loud gun at same time?"

Breen had the rifle halfway out before he cursed and shoved the Sharps back inside. Then he thought again, pulled the heavy rifle out, and ejected the cartridge. When the rifle slid back into the leather, he stepped aside and picked up the heavy brass cartridge. "There. It's empty. Won't do you a damned bit of good, will it?"

The Apache nodded, and as Breen walked back to the coffeepot, he heard the Indian say, "Unless I break head open with loud gun while Damn Fool sleep."

Breen stared. The baby girl cooed.

"You will live," Blood Moon said one more time. "Unless rattlesnake bite you. Or lightning strike you."

Breen felt unsteady, uncertain, and anyone who had ever had much to do with him knew the bounty hunter never felt unsteady — even when he was drunk — or uncertain, even when he found himself in a deadly pickle.

He found the coffeepot, lifted it over the fire, and emptied the remaining blessedly hot liquid over the flames, the coals sizzling but providing enough light as he tossed the pot and the cup toward the Apache's moccasins.

"Put those in the saddlebags," he ordered. Finally, he holstered the Colt and moved to the kid, picking up the baby, and praying to every god he could think of that the little boy — *girl,* damn it — wouldn't wake up.

They walked back toward the road, and Breen realized he'd never be able to find the hidden spring again if he searched for ten years. Moving slowly, they reached the road, and the Apache let the mule lead the way. They followed in the darkness by the sound of the hooves. When the mule stopped, Blood Moon would let it rest a moment, then pat its rump, and the mule would continue the slow walk, up and down the hills, until the country flattened.

When the skies turned gray and eventually dawn began breaking, the Apache moved ahead of the mule, took the reins, and led the beast, Breen, and the baby off the trail about four hundred yards to an arroyo deep enough to protect them from the wind and the sun, and keep them out of sight.

Blood Moon changed the baby's diaper, and let it suck on the water-soaked pouch and gnaw on the jerky. Breen stretched out his weary legs, and got a fire going, just long enough to heat up coffee. He offered his cup to the Indian, but the head just shook.

When Breen was sipping the hot brew, the Apache took the baby in his arms, squatted with his back against the arroyo wall, and began singing a soft guttural song to the quiet baby.

"Apache girl," Blood Moon said. "No cry no more."

After kicking out the fire, Breen let the coffee warm his throat and fill his stomach. The Colt lay on his thigh; the Sharps, still unloaded, leaned against the far side of the arroyo wall. He cleared his throat and asked, "Why in hell do you want to get to Purgatory City?"

The Apache did not answer until he had finished singing to the baby, and the baby girl was asleep. Then he stared across the harsh twenty yards at Breen. "I find Mac-Cul-Lock."

CHAPTER TEN

Matt McCulloch left the gray mustang stallion in the corral, buckled on his belt, and drew the Colt from the holster. After opening the cylinder gate, he pulled the hammer to half cock, then rotated the cylinder. His left hand dropped to his waist, pushed out a cartridge from the shell belt, and dropped the bullet into the empty chamber. There were times when five bullets in a six-shooter seemed reasonable, and safe, and there were times like now.

After easing the Colt back into the leather, McCulloch moved to the kicked-out fire and quickly packed his meager belongings. He saddled his roan gelding quickly, expertly, checked to make sure there was a round in his Winchester, and returned to the pen he had built. He wrapped the reins around one rail, grabbed the lariat, and ducked back into the pen.

The gray started trotting around, and Mc-

Culloch let the loop sail over the horse's head again. The fighting wasn't as hard as it had been, and he lessened the stallion's resistance more when he put the slicker over the contrarian's head. He tightened the saddle cinch on the roan, and led it to the corral, kicking down the lower rail, and using his free hand to remove the other two. The clanging of wood on dirt and stone made the horse pull back a bit, but not enough.

McCulloch looked up at smoke, spit, and gave the lariat three dallies over the horn, tied it off, and swung into the saddle on the roan. Spurring the horse, he felt the gelding spring into a lope, and the gray mustang was forced to follow.

Having mustanged for years in those mountains, he knew to let the roan pick its own path. A horse's eyes, he had learned many, many years earlier, were better than any man's vision, and a wrong step could leave a horse with a bullet in its head or the throat cut after breaking a leg and thus a man afoot. Nobody ever wanted to be left afoot in country like West Texas, but the smoke McCulloch had seen doubled or even tripled the dangers.

Eventually, he found the creek bed, though the water flow had slowed to mostly a trickle, and he rode along its banks, the horses' hooves pounding on the rocks. Traveling above the creek might have been easier, but it was also dustier. Until he was out of the mountains, McCulloch did not want anyone to see the dust two horses would raise. Once on the flatlands, dust would become inevitable, but he could ride his horse like hell by then. Another reason to stay in the creek's twisting path was that it would be harder for anyone to see him.

The smoke, of course, could have been anything. Some trapper or even another horse hunter too careless with the size of his cook fire or the wood he had chosen to burn. Homesteaders — plenty were trying to claim their one hundred and sixty acres these years, even though a man couldn't do much with that little bit of land in West Texas country.

It paid to play things safe, be careful and cautious, so McCulloch rode.

After a while, he reined in the roan. The gray tried to turn and run, but the lariat held firm, and the roan was smart enough to set its legs firm, lower its head, and hold its ground.

"Good boy." McCulloch praised the horse and rewarded it with a few gentle pats on the neck. He let both horses drink from a shallow pool where the river bent with the hills and hard boulders, but not too much. Then he let the horses walk for ten minutes, and afterward put the spurs back against the roan's belly, and they loped another couple of miles.

He could feel the change in elevation. West Texas turned warmer and before the sun had risen straight over his head, he was out of the mountains. As he rode, he wiped his forehead with his shirtsleeve.

The nearest town was Fort Davis, filled with gamblers and whiskey drinkers and blue-coated Yankee soldiers. It wasn't a big town, considering that the U.S. Army post was pretty damned big, but it did have the law. It also was known to be a popular place for horse thieves and murdering scum.

Home lay north, the way he pointed the roan. The gray stallion had stopped resisting and ran when McCulloch wanted to gallop, ran as though he enjoyed running, as though he did not mind the rope around its head. McCulloch figured the gray ran to lull the mustanger into a sort of complacency, so he could jerk the damned saddle off the little gelding and ride like hell till the rope broke, the saddle tore free, and the gray was free to go back and reclaim his herd of mares.

McCulloch slowed the game roan gelding to a trot, then a walk, and frowned as he saw three riders ease out of an arroyo and wait for him in the center of the road. He did not stop riding toward them. He did not turn around and ride back toward Fort Davis. He couldn't. He heard the clopping of hooves behind him and knew there were four men. The three ahead of him and one behind.

The one behind, he figured, had lighted the smoky fire.

"Smart," he whispered.

He remembered seeing the prints left by shod horses when he had first arrived on the mustanging expedition. He remembered reading the tracks enough to know one of the horses had leather socks over the hooves, a ploy used by men on the owlhoot trail to make the tracks harder to follow. Hell, not only outlaws used that trick; McCulloch had been known to do it himself, whenever situations called for such tactics. He had been in West Texas long enough to tell when a horse riding behind him was wearing leather socks to hide its tracks.

McCulloch kept the horses moving and finally reined in about twenty yards from the three men still on horseback blocking the road. He let the reins drop over the roan's neck, and pushed up the brim of his battered hat.

"McCulloch," said the red-bearded man with the twin bandoliers crossing the dusty plaid shirt.

"Red." McCulloch nodded at Red Nixon. "I thought they hanged you in Laredo."

The outlaw's dark eyes brightened.

"They did. Rope broke."

The men on either side of him laughed. One was a Mexican, wearing a beaded sugarloaf sombrero, who twisted his thin but long mustache. The fat man on the pinto horse braced the shotgun on his left thigh, and let the thumb pull back the twin hammers.

"Did it, now?" McCulloch said casually, grinning as though he had not heard that dreadful sound of a sawed-off Greener ten-gauge being cocked.

"Well," Red said, shrugging. "The knife in Pedro's hand probably had somethin' to do with it."

Pedro stopped twisting his mustache, reached down toward his left boot, and withdrew a slim dagger with a blade that reflected the sun's rays.

"That must be Devil Stillman behind me then," McCulloch said.

"That's me, Matt," Stillman said in a nasal drawl.

"Nice-lookin' stallion you got there, Matt," Red said mildly.

"Since when did you turn to stealing horses, Red?"

"Oh, now, Matt." The killer grinned as he leaned back in the saddle, removed his hat with his left hand, and wiped the sweat off his forehead with his shirtsleeve. "I ain't never stole no hoss, Matt. You know me better 'n that. But you ain't gonna have no use for that gray stud or that roan you be sittin' on once yer dead."

Fatso with the cocked Greener chuckled.

"Red," McCulloch said. "I'm no longer a Texas Ranger. They kicked me out some while back."

"So I hear tell." Red still held the hat.

"I hear tell he's a jackal," said the fat man with the shotgun.

"Shut up," Red Nixon told his companion.

McCulloch waited a few seconds, seconds that felt like days, wet his lips, and tried again.

"I don't have a warrant for you." The former Ranger raised his voice. "Or even you, Stillman."

Stillman chuckled like a hyena. A rabid hyena.

"I don't even know these two other gents. So there's no quarrel between us, now, is there?"

"Isn't there?"

McCulloch tilted his head. He had chased after Red Nixon for a number of years back when he was Rangering, but had only seen him a couple of times, and those had been brief meetings — during a bank robbery in Peaceful Valley, which hadn't had a moment's peace in fifteen years being that close to the Río Grande; and when Nixon's gang ambushed a Ranger patrol not far from that very spot when McCulloch had first joined the Rangers.

He waited.

Red Nixon would explain, and it was too damned hot to ask pointless questions.

"You kilt my brother, Matt."

McCulloch turned his head slightly, shook it, and looked back at Devil Stillman, who sat with his arms crossed. The tall, glassy-eyed man in a tall silk hat held on his head by a piggin' string was not holding the reins, and his rifle was still in the scabbard under his leg. "You know what he's talking about, Stillman?"

The outlaw just laughed.

McCulloch looked back at the three men in front of him. "I don't recall ever meeting

140

your brother, Red. Don't recall even knowing you had a brother."

"I did. Ten years my junior. You killed him."

"You'll have to tell me —"

"He rode with Don Marion Wilkes."

"Oh." McCulloch had never even heard of Don Marion Wilkes until a fracas in Arizona Territory in which Wilkes, a cutthroat, had tried to start a war against the Navajos, tried to butcher a number of pilgrims, and had paid for his crimes with his life.

McCulloch very well could have killed Red Nixon's brother. Or Sean Keegan or Jed Breen might have gunned down the boy. Or one of the pilgrims, who were hardy Arkansas boys who knew how to fight. Or the brother could have died by Navajos or even Comanche Indians. It had been a wild fight on the Dead River.

McCulloch's head shook. "Your kid brother should have picked a better outlaw to ride for." He smiled then. "He should have ridden with you."

Red Nixon grinned. "Well, Matt, I thank you for that. Kind sentiments. I truly hate to kill you, but, well, you know the sayin'. Blood's thicker than . . . well . . . somethin'."

McCulloch nodded as if he understood. "Red, you were one of the best for a long time, but you shouldn't ever have gotten so damned cocky."

The Colt was in the former Texas Ranger's hand in an instant, cocked and roaring as his left hand gripped the reins tightly. The bullet caught Fatso in the sternum, killing him instantly and causing his fingers to touch off both barrels of the Greener. A ten-gauge roared loud enough when just one barrel went off, but when two roared and Fatso flew off the back of his pinto, Red Nixon and Pedro's horses reacted.

Pedro's horse twisted, slamming into Nixon's mount and sending the horse bucking. Nixon was unprepared, for he still held his hat in his hand, and his other hand had a loose hold on the reins.

The Mexican tried to recover and draw his pistol, but the momentum of the horse loosened him from the saddle and he hit the ground with a thud. His right foot caught in the stirrup and he screamed briefly as the horse bolted toward Fort Davis, dragging him like a rag doll.

McCulloch hardly noticed. The roan was running straight ahead, pulling the roped gray behind him. He turned back toward Devil Stillman after his first shot. Although a pro and his horse well-trained, Stillman was too slow. McCulloch put a bullet in the skinny killer's gut, sending him into the ditch.

McCulloch had not wanted to kill the man slowly, but the roan was running and he had missed his aim. Devil Stillman would die, of course, but it would take him a couple of days.

The roan thundered, and McCulloch leaned forward, trying to find Red Nixon in the sights of his long-barreled revolver. He just caught a glimpse of the wild-eyed killer as he came to his knees and palmed his big Schofield .45. McCulloch couldn't get a shot off, but he didn't have to. The roan pummeled Red Nixon to the ground, and the galloping gray stallion's hooves finished the job.

McCulloch leaned forward in the saddle and thought about turning around, but it did not matter. Four outlaws were on the ground, one being dragged to Fort Davis. When the law came to discover the mess, they would celebrate that somehow, Red Nixon was dead, Devil Stillman would soon be joining him in Hades, and some fat, dumb unknown outlaw was dead with them.

Not one man or woman in West Texas would care who'd killed those men, what

143

had caused it, or why it had happened. It would be a hot time in Fort Davis and telegraphs would be burning the wires with news of Red Nixon's long overdue demise to be printed in newspapers in Dallas, Fort Worth, and probably all the way to New York City.

By then, Matt McCulloch would be back in his hard-scrabble ranch outside of Purgatory City, sleeping in his own bed. He would be gentling the masterful gray stallion in his own round pens, and stabling him in his own barn.

The day had turned out to be not so bad after all.

Fifteen minutes later, he reined in the roan, walked him for fifteen minutes, then put both horses into a trot.

CHAPTER ELEVEN

"Harry," Sean Keegan began, but the judge cut him off.

"It's 'Your Honor,' " Judge Harry Fellow said.

"Well, Your Honor, I —"

"Do you have counsel?"

Keegan sighed. The law in Purgatory City was getting more and more ridiculous. Harry Fellow had been serving as the district judge for what had to be going on a year now, and Fellow had tried and sentenced Sean Keegan enough to know that Keegan never had a lawyer. He just pleaded his case, took his jail time, and didn't have to worry about food and grub for usually thirty days or thereabouts. It was sort of like what some folks — or at least Jed Breen — called a sabbatical. 'Course, those month-long sabbaticals had been a lot more pleasant before Slim Van Dorn became the jailer. West Texas sure was going to bloody hell in a hurry.

"Well?" Judge Fellow removed his spectacles and when he did that, he looked meaner.

" 'Course not, Harry — yer honor."

"Let the record show that the defendant waived representation and will serve as his own counsel." Someone scribbled down what Harry Fellow said.

Keegan tried something new, smiling at his brilliance. There was one good thing about spending three months in jail during a year. He got to read newspapers, books, and illustrated magazines to while away his time — when he wasn't digging privies or sweeping out the cells, or busting rocks, or mucking stalls or whatever the leading citizens of Purgatory City needed done. "Your Honor," Keegan said, "I object to this entire farce that you call justice. This is not a courtroom. Therefore —"

"Do you need the court to remind you, Sean Keegan, that this trial is being held in the Purgatory City Jail because you burned down our courthouse?"

"That was never proved," Keegan objected.

"It's getting near suppertime," Judge Fellow said, "and this being the last case, I'd like to get it over with. Stand up, Sergeant

— *Mister* Keegan."

Keegan pushed himself off the cot in his cell. A hell of a thing, he thought, being tried while he was sitting in a stinking cell. That was sure to make the jury think less of him. Keegan looked around, blinked, and shouted, "Where's the jury?"

"There's no jury. I'm trying you." The silver-haired jurist looked over the papers in Slim Van Dorn's desk. "The state calls Lieutenant Charles Tibbetts."

The slimy little shavetail rose from a bench near the potbellied stove and raised his right hand.

"You're an officer of the United States Army," Judge Fellow said. "There's no need to take the oath."

Keegan cut loose with a stream of profanity.

"That'll be five dollars, Sean," the judge said without pounding the Remington .44 he used as a gavel or even looking away from the snotnosed little scumbag of an Army officer. "Contempt of court." The jurist nodded at the punk. "What happened to Tiny Olderman, Lieutenant?"

"Who the hell is Tiny Olderman?" Keegan railed.

This time the butt of the hammer struck the cheap pinewood desk. "Ten dollars."

147

Keegan shook his head and spit on the floor of his cell.

"Tiny Olderman is a former buffalo skinner who was serving a one-day sentence in jail for forgetting to tip his hat to a lady and this man — the defendant — attacked him viciously, almost killed him, in that very cell where he stands now."

"Tiny?" Keegan shook his head.

"You'll get your chance to cross-examine the witness in a minute, Sean. Till then, unless you want to pay fifteen dollars or add fifteen days to your sentence, just stand there and look innocent."

Keegan mumbled what he hoped Judge Fellow would take as an apology, and he gripped the bars on the cell till his knuckles whitened as Tibbetts began a string of lies that would make a great liar like Sean Keegan admire, were he not in jail, and had he any respect for the weasel wearing the blue of the greatest cavalry in the world.

The way Charles Tibbetts told the story, Sean Keegan had instigated the attack on that big old hide hunter who had damned near broken every bone in Keegan's body. The way the lying Army officer testified, Tiny Olderman was about as close to one of the twelve disciples as a body could find in a hellhole like Purgatory City. Officers

148

were not supposed to lie, especially under oath, but the only honest words Tibbetts said was when he stated his name and rank and posting at Fort Spalding.

"Your witness," the judge instructed Keegan after Tibbetts had finished his six minutes of lies.

After releasing the iron bars from his death grip, Keegan wiped his mouth and tried to remember how prosecutors had talked during the dozens of trials that had left Keegan in jail.

"Why was this Tiny — what a joke of a name for a man the size of a bull moose — put in my cell when all the other cells were empty?"

"I have no idea," Tibbetts said with a grin. "I am not the jailer."

"Where is Slim Van Dorn?"

"Who?"

"Van Dorn. Who put Tiny in this cell? The damned jailer!"

Judge Fellow yawned. "Profanity does not look good in transcripts of a trial, Sean. Watch your language." He hefted the Remington. "I don't want to put too many dents in property of the city constable's office any more than you want five more dollars or five more days added to your sentence after you're convicted."

Keegan sighed, thought about changing his plea to guilty and throwing himself on the mercy of the court, but began another attack. "Were not you in The Palace of Purgatory City Saloon a few nights ago?"

"I believe I was there on the night you practically tore the fine establishment off its foundation and caused, according to this morning's newspaper, three hundred and fifteen dollars' worth of damages," the officer answered.

"How much damage would you say I done to you?"

Tibbetts rubbed his jaw. His lip remained swollen. "Sticks and stones may break my bones, but an Irishman can never hurt me."

Keegan's hand returned to squeeze the life out of the hot iron bars.

"Did not you bribe Slim Van Dorn to put that scoundrel and brutal, stinking buffalo skinner in this cell as an act of revenge, to beat me to a bloody pulp, to kill me, just to exact your revenge for humiliating you in The Palace of Purgatory City Saloon that night?"

There. He saw in Judge Fellow's eyes that the honorable jurist knew Keegan was telling the truth, and he saw the hatred in the punk shavetail's face.

"Mr. Olderman is no longer a skinner of

150

hides," Tibbetts answered, "but a loyal scout for the federal soldiers posted at Fort Spalding."

Keegan sighed, turned around, and sat on his bunk — the new bunk, well, at least the one Van Horn had dragged from the third cell over after Keegan had done his damnedest to keep Tiny Olderman from killing him.

"Are you done with this witness?" Judge Fellow asked.

"Not hardly. I ain't done with this lying skunk, Your Honor. He'll see me after I've done my time, and he'll regret he ever mistreated Sean Keegan, and doubly regret besmirching the Irish."

"Does the state have any other witnesses?" The judge did not wait for an answer, since he already knew it. "The state rests," he told himself, "and now the defense can take over. Any witnesses, Sean?"

Keegan shook his head. "It don't matter what I say. I know the truth. So does this lying sack of donkey dung."

"Well then . . ." The judge rose, nodded for Charles Tibbetts to sit down, and said, "it's time for the verdict and the verdict is —"

The door swung open, letting in daylight, the blast of hot wind, and the wails of a screaming baby. An instant later, a menacing figure filled the doorway, and Lieutenant Charles Tibbetts let out a gasp as he staggered back, tripped over a stool, and crashed to the floor while he was fumbling to unfasten the covering and get to his service revolver. Judge Fellow, of course, had no problem with his Remington. He reversed the grip like a professional gunman — which he had been during the late War of the Rebellion when he had ridden with Quantrill's boys in Missouri and Kansas — and had the revolver cocked and aimed at the towering Apache that slowly moved into the jail. He was manacled, and the keen-eyed judge saw that, too, and the figure behind the Indian.

Jed Breen slipped through the crack of the doorway, looking like he had been dragged from the Texas Piney Woods near the Louisiana border, up and down the Hill Country, then along the Río Grande and through the Big Bend and all the way north through the Chihuahuan Desert to the end of the line that was Purgatory City.

The racket that split Keegan's ears came from this little bundle that Breen held against his left shoulder with his left arm. His right hand held the Colt .38 that was aimed at the big Apache brave.

Lieutenant Tibbetts managed to back his

way across the floor to a nearby empty cell, and finally pulled the hogleg from his holster.

"Don't shoot!" the judge roared, and added, "you damn fool."

He had to yell. The package the sunburned Breen clutched raised more noise than Comanches on a murder raid.

"Give me," the Apache said, though Keegan wasn't sure he heard correctly, considering the whimpering coming from Lieutenant Tibbetts, the blasting howl of the wind, and that infernal screaming from what had to be a baby coyote or a damned kid in Breen's left arm.

Yes, Keegan realized, he had heard right, because the bounty hunter dropped the revolver into his holster and handed the bundle to the manacled Indian.

"No, you damned fool!" Judge Fellow bellowed at Breen, but the bounty hunter gave the swaddled baby — not a coyote, Keegan could see now — to the giant Apache.

Instantly, the noise ceased.

Breen kicked the door shut, looked around and recognized Keegan.

"Where's the marshal?" Breen asked.

"Delivering a prisoner to Freemanville."

"Sheriff?"

"Serving as the marshal's deputy."

Breen saw the coffeepot and made a beeline to it. He poured a cup, and guzzled it down, poured a second cup for himself, and a third, which he brought to the Apache.

The Indian stared at Breen, then at the cup, and said, "How do I drink and keep Baby Sister quiet?" The warrior rattled his chained wrists.

"What the hell is going on here, Breen?" Judge Fellow demanded.

Breen brought the coffee cup instead to Keegan, then turned to the judge.

"I found him — or he found me," Breen began, and leaned against the iron bars of Keegan's cell. "On the El Paso pike. Homesteading couple had been murdered, this baby girl left in the shade." He raised his coffee cup at the Apache. "This is the one who did it. This, gents, is Blood Moon."

"My God!" Lieutenant Tibbetts brought his gun up again, but couldn't keep it from shaking.

"That's twenty thousand dollars coming to me," Breen said, and let Keegan's mug toast his. "Payable in U.S. script upon delivery."

Charles Tibbetts managed to pull himself to his feet, and holster his revolver. "I should report this immediately to the colonel," he said. "With your permission, Your Honor . . ."

He did not wait for Judge Fellow's approval, and gave the baby-rocking Apache a wide berth as he cracked the door open, slipped through it, and slammed it shut.

"My God," Judge Fellow repeated.

Keegan sipped his coffee while Breen went into action, explaining the massacre, the trap Blood Moon had set, the long journey from the burning homestead to Purgatory City. He found the keys to the cell next to the judge, opened the shadiest, coolest, and largest cell, and held the door open as the Apache made his way into the cell, still holding the baby. Once the door was closed and locked, Breen unfastened the manacles and took them through the bars. The Apache still held the baby, and now he moved to the bunk in the coolest part of the cell and sat, still rocking the baby in his arms.

"You can't leave an infant in there with that murdering savage," Judge Fellow said.

"He's the only one who can keep the kid quiet." Breen finished his coffee and went back to the stove for his third cup. "We'll need . . . um . . . diapers, and soap, and a new silk bandanna for me. A little tub to wash the girl."

"What's her name?" Keegan asked.

"I don't know." Keegan picked up the chair Tibbetts had knocked over and slowly sat down, stretching out his legs and moving his dusty boots one way, then the other.

"We can't leave a white child in that jail with that murdering fiend," the judge said. "We must find a decent white woman to take in the baby."

"Good luck finding a decent woman within fifty miles of Purgatory City," Keegan said. The coffee tasted pretty good, and he felt refreshed. Even the bruises and cuts Tiny Olderman had given him no longer hurt.

"Milk," Blood Moon said from his cell.

Breen snapped his fingers. "Yeah. Milk. Canned milk or goats milk. Milk. The baby has been living off water and beef jerky."

"Beef jerky," the judge said. "My God."

"There are decent women here," Breen said. "The gunsmith's daughter and . . ."

"She can't give no kid mother's milk," Keegan pointed out.

"Well, damn it, we can worry about who's gonna mama this child later. Right now it — she — needs to be given some warm milk and given a bath and given something decent to wear."

The judge had lowered the hammer on

his Remington, and now he banged the butt on the desk. "All right. Keegan, you're sentenced to thirty days in jail for destroying The Palace of Purgatory City and for assaulting the prisoner Slim Van Dorn."

"Tiny Olderman," Keegan corrected, "but I'll gladly thrash the no-account, scheming and conniving bucket of manure that is Slim Van Dorn. Slim and Tiny. There's a couple of little gophermutts that deserve a big whipping."

"Thirty days," Judge Fellow said. "We'll credit you with the time served in jail." He rose, holstered the big hogleg, and found his hat. "Breen, you stay here, guard the prisoners. I'll gather up some Christian ladies and put them in charge of the baby. I'm certain that moron of a lieutenant will alert the damned Yanks at Fort Spalding. We'll get supplies for the kid, and I'll have a telegraph sent to Austin so that the state knows that Blood Moon's bloody reign of terror has ended." He put his hand on the knob, but looked back at the bounty hunter before opening the door.

"Is there anything else you need, Breen?"

"Food," the bounty hunter answered, and nodded at Blood Moon. "For the both of us. Rye for me. Maybe a woman."

"I know. For the baby."

"No," Breen said. "For me. One of Miss Holly's . . ."

The door opened, and slammed shut. Breen moved to the desk the judge had vacated, and settled into the chair, and slowly, with audible groans, lifted his legs and put them on the top of the battered desk.

"Twenty thousand dollars," Breen said, and smiled.

"Ye'll buy your ol' pard Sean Keegan some Irish once you get it, won't ye, my fine friend?"

"You bet."

The baby remained quiet.

Keegan felt pretty good for a man facing a long hot month in a dismal Purgatory City cell.

Silence — even the baby in the Apache's arms remained quiet, perhaps had fallen asleep — filled the room.

Then, Blood Moon spoke to the bounty hunter.

"Bring me Mac-Cul-Lock."

CHAPTER TWELVE

Joseph William Henderson III, alias Oaxaca Joe, had taken the rest of the Río Sangrieto Rurales to La Cantina de Setenta y Tres Borrachos while Major Block Frazer rode his horse to the office of Miguel Blanco, alcalde of El Pueblo de Cebollas Verdes. The village priest, Padre Eugenio José Francisco de la Santúsuna y Gutiérrez, opened the door, bowed slightly, and led Frazer through the narrow, dirt-floored hallway and through a series of small rooms to the shady part of the adobe home where Blanco sat fanning himself with a newspaper from Mexico City.

The priest then led the prayer, which, Frazer thanked his lucky stars, was shorter than the holy man's name. Before leaving the defeated Confederacy for Mexico, Major Block Frazer had always wondered why so many Alabama families thought they had to give their sons and daughters the longest names known to mankind. But after living in Mexico all these years, he had come to appreciate the terseness of a Billy Ray Ferguson or a Joseph William Henderson III.

After the amen and genuflecting, Frazer helped himself to the bottle of Napoleon brandy and filled a snifter with the dark liquor. He held it up in a toast, and waited for the speechfest to begin.

As Alcalde Miguel Blanco cleared his throat and Frazer sipped the sweet booze, the Alabaman thought, *Surely, Miguel Blanco can't be this greaser's entire name.* And he wondered why he had never thought about this before, but before he could ponder on such heavy summer pontificating, the old priest kissed his cross and said something that made Frazer gulp down the gentlemen's sippin' likker.

"How would you like to take the scalp of the Apache killer named Blood Moon?"

Though the priest could not — or refused to — speak English, Frazer had been south of the border long enough to savvy a few Spanish words, especially *Mano Ensangrentada* — Blood Moon — and *asesino* — killer — and Apache was the same in any tongue. Frazer waved off the alcalde's translation into English before he could get halfway.

160

"You found that black-hearted devil?" Frazer demanded.

He had to wait while Miguel Blanco translated the question, which was direct and to the point, in some long-winded gibberish to the padre. But he had to give the priest credit for his answer. It was just a slight nod.

The alcalde refilled Frazer's glass, then poured healthy portions for Father Eugenio and himself.

"Your competition did," Blanco said after taking a small sip of his brandy.

Frazer found a Mexican cigarillo, bit off an end, and dipped it in the brady before fishing for a match. "There are many scalphunters in Mexico," he said after he struck the match on his thumbnail. "Just none as good as me and my boys." He brought the match up to the tobacco, and once he was drawing good smoke, he shook out the match and pitched it into the brass ashtray on the alcalde's desk. "But by my figgerin', only El Hombre del Pelo would have enough gumption to make the claim that he can find Blood Moon."

El Hombre del Pelo was the moniker these stinking greasers gave Santiago Vasquez. That was another bit of Spanish Frazer knew all too damned well. *El Hombre del*

Pelo. The Hair Man. He was good at his job, and he didn't even have to kill peaceful Mexicans and pass off their scalps as that of Apaches, Yaquis or Comanches.

"*Sí,*" the priest said, and stared at his brandy.

Frazer filled the silence by smoking the little Mexican tobacco and sipping the expensive brandy. His hosts remained respectfully silent, and would have waited till Judgment Day before they started talking, so Frazer spoke.

"Let me guess," he said, and again dipped the slim cigar-cigarette half-breed smoke in the snifter of brandy. "Santiago Vasquez ain't got the *huevos* to take his boys into an Apache camp, well, not this Apache camp. Since everyone between the Isthmus of Panama and the territory of Colorado in Yankee America knows that Blood Moon is one of the braves led by Three Dogs. And Three Dogs is bigger than Mangas Coloradas, Cochise, Geronimo and fifteen other Apache butchers combined. So Vazquez figures he needs some able-bodied men to ride with him."

Frazer smiled.

The alcalde glanced at the priest, who was glancing at Blanco, and then both Mexicans turned to the Southerner.

"Sí," both said.

After a short grunt, Frazer killed his brandy and set the empty glass on Blanco's desk. When the alcalde reached to refill, Frazer shook his head. "No, no more for me." He flicked ash onto the floor. "Where's the Apache camp?"

Once again, the priest and the alcalde ignored Frazer long enough to study each other. The padre spoke lengthy in a whisper, as though he wanted to make sure the commander of the Río Sangrieto Rurales did not understand, even though Major Block Frazer could care less. He finished his little Mexican smoke, and reached over and snubbed it out in the brass ashtray while Alcalde Blanco responded to whatever the hell the padre had said. Then Frazer leaned back and listened as the alcalde explained.

"Señor Vasquez came across a war party of the red devils three hundred kilometers west and south of here." The alcalde spoke slowly, clearly, trying to eliminate most of the Spanish accent — as though after all these years in this arid wasteland, a brilliant mind like that of Major Block Frazer couldn't savvy what he was hearing. Frazer listened as Miguel Blanco continued.

"One of the demons was captured, terribly wounded. He told of the general location of the camp." The alcalde grinned. "Before he was killed."

That was a damned lie. An Apache never talked. If Vasquez knew where that Apache camp was, he had learned it some other way. And even if he had . . . Frazer snorted. "The Apaches will move camp. Three Dogs is smart. Too smart to risk getting his entire village wiped out."

The grin that stretched across Miguel Blanco's face surprised Frazer. "Perhaps," the alcalde said, shaking his head. "But this is the best chance we have at ridding Mexico of this fiend from Hell."

Frazer wiped his mouth. "You didn't answer my question. Where's the camp of Three Dogs and his redskin butchers?"

Miguel Blanco smiled. "Señor Vasquez says for you to meet him at Río Muerto — the Dead River — and you and he will make arrangements. Then he will lead you to the camp of those evil murderers. It has been agreed that we will double the bounties for any scalps you bring from the camp of Three Dogs. And we will pay even more, a king's ransom, if you bring us the heads of Three Dogs and Blood Moon."

Silence returned to the room, so still and quiet, that Major Block Frazer would have sworn that he could hear the beads of sweat rolling down his cheeks.

"What is your answer?"

But for a brief moment, Major Block Frazer was no longer in El Pueblo de Cebollas Verdes. He was at his hacienda, twenty miles west of the Mexican village, and eight years earlier.

"God have mercy. God have mercy. God have mercy."

Ol' Cookie Roberts, who had been feeding the boys since Paint Rock Ridge in '62, kept whispering, as his son, Tim Roberts, who'd been a drummer boy for Frazer's command, tried to keep his pa's guts from spilling into the dirt. Frazer had lost track of all the times his soldiers, in the Confederate South and down here in Mexico, had joked that if Ol' Cookie tried eating the grub he cooked for his men, his guts would rot out.

"Billy John," Frazer said to the wide-eyed trooper trying to untie the rawhide that held Cookie's arms to the corral posts. "Take Tim away."

Tim looked up. "No," he said, swallowed. "No, no . . ." But he offered no resistance when Billy John Carter moved away from the corral at Frazer's hacienda and eased the boy toward what had once been the

165

main house.

Then Frazer drew the Leech and Rigdon and sent a ball into Ol' Cookie's brain, ending the suffering. The echo of the revolver's report was lost to Tim Roberts's wail of pain, remorse and thanks.

Men coughed from the smoke. Those who didn't gagged at the remains of their friends, their families, their dogs, their homes. Blood stained the ground, and bodies littered the field. Bodies? That was hardly the word to describe what Major Block Frazer saw, not after the handiwork of the Apaches.

Joe Henderson was walking over holding an arrow in his hand. He would get here soon enough, Frazer figured.

Smoke filled the air, but the smoke did not smell just of burning cottonwood, hay, thatch, or the cherrywood furniture Frazer's wife had always loved. Frazer remembered the smell of burning flesh from the war, and he recalled that fight on Bluewater Creek, when Yankee canister had set the woods afire, and men wearing blue and butternut had been caught by the wind-driven flames. You didn't forget those things. That's what soldiers said.

But Block Frazer knew he would never again remember the atrocities, the horrors, even the triumphs he had experienced while fighting to preserve the Southern way of life. He would remember nothing from this day forward but . . . this.

Joe Henderson held out the arrow.

"Apache," Frazer said after just a quick glance at the arrow. Half of the shaft and the flint arrowhead were stained with dried blood.

"Not just any Apache, suh," Joe Henderson drawled. "This is the mark of only one of those killin' scum of the earth." He pointed to the thumbprint of blood just below the turkey feathers at the end of the arrow. "It's Blood Moon's own mark. Blood Moon himself led this raid."

Frazer turned his head and spit, or would have, had he any saliva left in his mouth.

He wiped his mouth anyway with his sleeve, drew in a short breath, and looked around at the smoke and death and destruction, before he had enough resolve to face Captain Joseph William Henderson III, one of the best soldiers ever to come down from Cheaha Mountain and put on the gray.

"Have you found my wife?" Frazer asked.

Henderson held his breath.

Frazer thought now that he could smell his wife's favorite perfume in the smoke. He knew that couldn't be the case, but it would have been a blessing. Burning to death, or burning after death, anything would be better to learn that the love of his life, the mother of his children — now all dead to typhoid and cholera and a heart condition — had not been taken alive by the Apaches — for that was worse than death for any Alabama belle. Or any white woman. Any woman at all.

It took a minute or more before Captain Henderson could formulate a proper answer. When he held out the arrow, and when Frazer's eyes looked down at the feathered little stick, Henderson spoke:

"I pulled this out of her body, Major." He must have gestured toward the gazebo that she had begged Frazer to build. That's where she had been, and if she had to pick a place to die, that would have been it — since she knew she would never die at home in Mobile by the bay.

Frazer took the arrow and stared at it.

"From the little blood, and seeing that the arrow must have hit her heart," Henderson said, "it was quick. Instant. She did not suffer. And she was not molested in any way. A blessing, Major. I mean . . . not a blessing but . . . well . . ."

"I know what you mean, Capt . . . I know what you mean, Joe." Frazer tried to smile, but that was impossible. He held out the arrow, and let Henderson take it.

"I'm sorry, suh," Captain Henderson said.

Frazer nodded and tried to think of what he should do. He was the commander of these Southern men. And he knew what he had to do.

"Blood Moon will pay," Frazer said.

"Yes, suh," Henderson said.

"Every damned Apache will pay for their savagery."

"We'll follow you all the way to Hell, Major!" called someone whose voice Frazer did not recognize.

He looked up at Captain Henderson. "Tell me, Joe, you can be honest, just tell me, did they . . . did they . . . ?"

"I told you the truth, Major," the young Alabama mountain boy said. "One arrow struck her on the gazebo in the heart. I'm not sure the Apaches even checked on her afterward. There were no signs, no moccasin prints, no horse tracks there. They likely had their hands full. She was not . . . not . . . they did not even take her scalp, Major."

"Apaches do not take scalps, Captain," Frazer told him.

"Yes, suh. You're right, of course, suh."

"Capt'n Henderson!" a Southerner yelled out from the burning smokehouse. "We've found . . . yer wife . . . her . . . body . . . suh."

The flames licked, the smoke rose, some men cried, most of them cursed, and Captain Henderson's voice trembled as he said, "If . . . you will . . . pardon me . . ." Then it broke entirely. "Major . . . suh . . . Oh, my God!" And Frazer heard Henderson's boots on the dirt as he ran toward the smokehouse.

Block Frazer just stood there, alone, mind rushing, pain fading, all feeling leaving him at that instant.

He looked up, staring, memorizing every detail of the carnage that had once been his home in exile.

"Apaches do not take scalps," he heard himself say. "But, by thunder, I will."

And just like that Major Block Frazer was transported eight years and twenty-five miles back to the office of Alcalde Miguel Blanco in El Pueblo de Cebollas Verdes. He stared hard at the alcalde, then shot the priest a quick glance, and again looked at Blanco. The alcalde wet his lips and started to repeat his question — *What is your answer?* — the Mexican imbecile.

"You know my answer," Frazer hissed.

CHAPTER THIRTEEN

"What the bloody hell did that murdering buck just say?" Sean Keegan stood, his fists clenching, his hard eyes blazing, not at Jed Breen, but the Apache in the jail cell.

"You heard him," Breen said. He felt as though he had been awake for fourteen straight days, and had walked from El Paso to Purgatory City. He could use about a monthlong rest, just him in a nice bed of down and a dozen pillows. Not even a woman. Not even whiskey. He'd just sleep till he was done.

Hell of a chance of that happening, though.

"He wants to talk to Matt," Breen said.

"What the bloody hell for?" Keegan strode to the cell. "What business do ye have with a Texas Ranger?"

"Former Texas Ranger," Breen said after stifling a yawn, but Keegan didn't hear.

"Tell me!" Keegan shouted.

171

"Shut up, Sean," Breen said. "You'll wake up the baby."

The Irishman turned, and Breen went to the wash basin to scrub off some of the dirt. "Let me see what I can do to find a part-time mama for that baby. Then I'll rent a horse from the livery and ride out to Matt's place." He stopped. "You don't know if Matt's there, do you?"

Keegan's head shook. "Haven't seen him in town in a month of Sundays, but you know Matt. If he's not there, he's out hunting horses, or maybe driving some over to Fort Spalding or some other outfit to make enough money to get that spread of his back into something more . . . fit for a human being."

Breen toweled off his face, then looked at the towel and frowned with disgust. Maybe after he had fetched Matt McCulloch, he could get a real bath in a real hotel and find a decent bed, though he knew there would be no down and little comfort to be had even in Purgatory City's best hotel — where even the brothels weren't close to top of the line.

"I'll try to find some milk for the baby, too," Breen said. He grabbed his hat, nodded at Keegan, and walked outside.

The judge was across the street talking to

172

a banker and several other men. Most of the men listening to the judge were staring at the jail. That lieutenant had not gotten far, not even to the telegraph office to wire the fort. He was talking to a few men in front of a saloon with one of the windows boarded up — The Palace of Purgatory City, read a crooked sign, leaning more toward the busted boardwalk. That, Breen figured, explained Sean Keegan's presence in the jail. A rider, some cowpoke from one of the spreads nearby, reined up his Appaloosa and leaned from the saddle, shook one of the town merchant's hands, said something to the judge, and then stared at Breen and the jail.

"Hell," Breen said. "It figures."

He walked to the mule, pulled his big Sharps from the scabbard, and returned to the jail, opening the door, stepping inside, shutting the door.

"Sean." He found the keys and unlocked Keegan's cell, then handed the former cavalry trooper the heavy rifle.

"Better take this," said the bounty hunter, tilting his head to the window.

Keegan took the rifle and followed Breen to the front of the jail. Both men peered through the dirty glass. "Aye," Keegan said. "Just like those rogues. I'll load me a pair of scatterguns, too."

"Thanks," Breen said.

"If there's one thing I despise," Keegan said. "It's a lynching. Even lynching a low-down, man-killing, woman-raping, baby-abusing fiend from hell like that black-hearted, red-skinned devil."

"They're probably nothing but talk," Breen said. "But don't let them take Blood Moon out of this jail — at least, not before I collect that reward."

There was one shining treasure in the rawhide town of Purgatory City, maybe the reason Breen had made this miserable speck of earth his base of operations, and Breen smiled as he opened the door, hearing the bells chime above it, and stepped inside Bonderoff's Gun Shop.

Pretty Ramona looked up from the ledger book, then laid a .36-caliber Navy Colt, ivory grips and silver plated, on the counter. "Why, Jed Breen, well bless my soul, every time I see you you look like something the cat drug in." She smiled. "But you're still mighty handsome."

Damned if Breen didn't think his face was flushing, but he managed to choke out a question: "Is your pa around?"

She shook her head so hard her locks

bounced this way and that. Ramona Bonderoff had some lovely hair.

"He's delivering an Allen and Wheelock .44 to One-Eyed Jack Coe at Thompson and Bicknell's Gambling Emporium," she said.

Coe was the cheat who ran the faro layouts at that den of inequity.

"Don't see many of those revolvers around these days," Breen said, just to say something.

"Jack wanted it converted from percussion to take modern cartridges."

"Makes sense."

"How's your Sharps shooting?"

"Fine. Tell Bondy he did a good job of sighting it last time I brought it here."

She smiled, then laughed. "Pa'll appreciate such fine praise from you."

Breen turned to stare through the storefront window, remembering at last to take off his dusty hat, and he hoped he would see Ramona's father coming back from Thompson and Bicknell's. What he saw, unfortunately, were more men heading toward the saloon where Lieutenant Charles Tibbetts was working up some overheated zealots into a fury, and more of the town's more reputable vermin listening to the judge talk.

"Does your Colt Lightning need something, Jed?" Ramona asked.

Breen blinked, looked away from the window, and then glanced at his .38. "No," he said after a long while. "Probably needs a good cleaning."

"I'll be happy to look at it for you, Jed."

Breen drew the revolver, sighed, and started pushing out the cartridges as he walked over to the counter, catching the scent of Ramona's shampoo and whatever perfume she might be wearing. She took the revolver with her small, white hands, laid it on a towel next to the ledger, which she closed, and then shook her head and let out some soft *Tks, Tsk, Tksssss.*

"Jed Breen, a man like you — especially a man like you — ought to take better care of your firearms." Ramona reached under the counter and came up with oil, a rag, and a cleaning brush and went to work. Breen turned around and stared as more and more men gathered on both sides of the intersection, businessmen and even a couple of ladies listening to the judge, and saddle tramps and the scum of the earth listening to the shavetail Army officer.

Breen ran his right hand through his white hair, which he realized needed a good scrubbing, too.

Ramona was finished in a few minutes,

and Breen took the .38, and began reloading the bullets. Feeling that bit of intuition, he pushed a sixth shell out of his shell belt, and fed it into the last empty cylinder, then lowered the hammer, and let the Colt slide easily into the holster.

"How much do I owe you?" he asked, though he kept staring out the window, only this time he was hoping to see Bondy coming back to his business.

"Oh, shucks, Jed, don't be so silly," Ramona said. "There ain't no charge for cleaning a tiny little .38. Especially when it belongs to a great customer like you."

Breen made himself smile, and turned around and looked at the pretty girl . . . Girl? . . . Hell, Ramona Bonderoff was a full-blooded woman, and Breen had known that for a year or two.

He looked for his hat, realized he had dropped it by the front door, understood that he was going around the bend, and then he stared into Ramona's pretty eyes. He couldn't wait for Bondy to show up. He needed to get to a livery and light a shuck for Matt McCulloch's horse ranch.

"Ramona," he said. "What do you know about babies?"

To Breen's amazement, she didn't slap his

dirty face or curse his dirty mind.

Her eyes brightened, and she laughed.

Ramona wasn't laughing after Breen explained what he needed from her, and gave her a quick and condensed version of what brought him into Bonderoff's Gun Shop.

She grabbed her bonnet and purse, and Breen wound up following her out the door — the bells ringing ominously this time — and up the street and away from the jail before she stopped at Simms's General Store. Ramona told Leon Simms to charge everything to Bondy's account, and Breen followed her out the door, carrying two wrapped packages under his left arm and wielding a wash tub — twenty-one inches in diameter, twelve inches deep, the only size Simms had in stock — in his right.

Down the boardwalk they went, Breen struggling to keep his balance and not drop anything, while people cleared a path for the fast-walking Ramona. Breen wanted, dared even prayed, for Tibbetts and his crowd and the judge and his listeners to see what was happening, but he dared not move his eyes from where he was walking because Purgatory City's boardwalks had been known to break a few ankles and legs of careless pedestrians.

They reached the jail, and Ramona jerked open the door, and stormed inside.

"Give me that baby, you stupid men!" she snapped.

Breen tried to catch his breath, but before he backed inside the Purgatory City jail, he looked across the street, and felt a great relief. The Tibbetts boys and the judge's men were staring, gawking, stunned at this turn of events. Breen backed into the jail, and used the wash tub to slam shut the door.

Once he had deposited the items, and once Ramona had the little baby and was ordering Keegan to heat up some water and find some clean blankets that could be used for a bed, Breen announced, "I'll be back with Matt as soon as I can." He wanted to smile at Ramona, to thank her, but she busied herself with the baby and Keegan locked the cell door again and tossed the keys onto the desk.

Blood Moon rattled his way to the bunk, and sat down, but he nodded in what Breen figured was appreciation as Ramona Bonderoff took charge of the baby girl.

At the door, once Breen opened it and stepped outside, Keegan followed with the washtub. Breen stared across the street as Keegan filled the tub by dunking it in a

179

water trough.

"Are ye bloody daft, man?" Keegan said as he brought the overfilled tub up and let it rest on the corner of the trough. "Bringing a fine lass into a place that's likely to be overrun like the damned Alamo was forty years ago?"

Breen smiled. "I figure even the scoundrels that call Purgatory City home will be reluctant to storm a jail with an innocent woman inside."

"Woman . . . a bloody child, man."

Breen shook his head, did not answer, and made a beeline for the nearest livery stable. Child. Sean Keegan hadn't gotten a good look at Ramona Bonderoff lately.

"What I want," Breen told the fat, bald, toothless man working at the livery, "is a horse that can get me to Matt McCulloch's ranch in a hurry, and get me back in a hurry."

The man set his pipe in an ashtray.

"Saddle, blanket and bridle, too," Jed said. He had left his tack on the mule's back in front of the Purgatory City jail.

Breen tossed a gold coin beside the ashtray.

"And I'd like it *muy pronto.*"

The old-timer lifted the coin, smelled it,

twisted it in his fingers, then tried to bend it. Figuring it to be a real double eagle, he let it drop into the bottom pocket of his filthy vest, and hooked a thumb to his right.

"There's a dapple in the corral. But you saddle him yerself. And have it back by day's end." His lips turned upward at the corners. "Else, you pay double."

Breen didn't haggle. Tugging his hat brim, he walked outside, turned, and ducked underneath the railing and into the corral. He spotted the dapple quickly, and felt lucky that the gelding already had a head-stall. The horse didn't run from him, either, letting Breen grab the horsehair headstall and lead it to the fence. After grabbing a bridle and bit, he went to work. He hoped like hell Matt McCulloch was home.

Seeing the dust rising above what passed for McCulloch's home made Breen feel easier, and he wiped the sweat off his brow with the sleeve of his shirt, and kicked the dapple into a trot. The dust had to be coming from the corral, and hearing the pounding hooves and snorting of a mustang told Breen all he needed to know. He reined in by the well, and smiled.

Jed Breen knew about horses, meaning that he knew all he wanted to about horses.

He could ride them, saddle them, run them to death if he had to, and every now and then he liked to bet on one in a race. But Matt McCulloch — he had to be part horse.

He saw the gray stallion that was bucking, and marveled at how McCulloch seemingly anticipated the mustang's every move. When the gray tried to run close to the fence and ram McCulloch's legs against the rails and posts, McCulloch pulled him back to the center. When the horse twisted, McCulloch stuck with him. When the gray arched its back and kicked out his hind legs, McCulloch did not lose his balance.

It was, Breen figured, like watching a brilliant painter at work, or an opera singer performing *The Doctor of Alcantara.*

McCulloch leaped off the bucking horse's back, and somehow managed to keep his feet as he stumbled toward the corral. The horse kept bucking, and McCulloch ducked out of the corral, pulled off his hat and was beating the dust off his chaps as he headed to the water trough.

Slowly, Breen slid out of the uncomfortable and cheaply made saddle, and led the dapple toward Matt McCulloch.

CHAPTER FOURTEEN

It took a while before Matt McCulloch caught his breath. He moved to the water trough where Jed Breen was finally letting a worn-out gelding drink. McCulloch splashed water over his face and head, and untied the bandanna around his neck to towel himself off. Once the hat returned to cover McCulloch's dark head, he pointed at the nag.

"What's that you're riding?" the mustanger asked.

"Horse."

"I'm taking your word for it."

"Got it at a livery in Purgatory City."

McCulloch stretched his legs and rubbed his hindquarters. "How much?"

"Twenty dollars."

"You got robbed."

"That's just for a day."

McCulloch stared hard at the prematurely white-haired marksman. He waited. Jed

Breen usually spoke his mind, but this time the bounty man was stalling. Finally, after wiping his sweaty forehead again, Breen said, "There's a fellow I brought in to the jail at Purgatory City who wants to see you."

Hooking his thumbs in his waistband, Mc-Culloch tried to read Breen's face. "Last report I got," Breen said, "you were chasing after Juan Maldado."

Breen's head bobbed. "Caught him. Collected the bounty in El Paso."

"I never had the dubious pleasure of ever seeing that ugly bandido's face except on a wanted poster," McCulloch said.

"It's not Ugly Juan Maldado that wants to talk to you, Matt," Breen said. "It's Blood Moon."

That made Matt McCulloch forget all about his aching body, chaffed backside and legs. "You brought in Blood Moon?"

Breen nodded.

"Alive."

Another nod.

"How in hell did you manage that?" Mc-Culloch shook his head, then smiled. "That's what . . . twenty thousand dollars?"

"Yeah," Breen said. "Counting what the State of Texas has put up, along with the territories of Arizona and New Mexico."

"How'd you do it?"

Breen's lips almost turned upward into a smile, but he just shook his head and sighed. "It's a long story, Matt, but he did ask to speak to you."

"About what?"

"He didn't say."

"That Apache speaks English?"

Breen nodded again.

"You ain't joshing me, are you, Jed?" McCulloch hooked his thumb toward the corral where the gray stallion snorted and stamped its front hooves, daring, it seemed, for the mustanger to come back for another ride in hell.

"I'm not Sean Keegan, Matt. I don't josh." He cleared his throat. "There's some crowds gathering in town. They might be wanting to string up that Apache."

"Can't blame them for that."

"I left Keegan guarding him."

McCulloch cocked his head again. "Keegan."

"That's a long story, too, and I don't know but half of it, and really don't want to know the other half. But if you want to hear whatever it is that Blood Moon wants to tell you, we'd better get moving."

McCulloch nodded and pointed to another corral. "Saddle up the chestnut for me and that zebra dun for yourself," he said.

"I don't think that glue-bait that you rode in'll get you back to Purgatory City, but you can pull him behind so you don't have to pay another twenty bucks in rental fees." He was already walking to his shack. "I'll fetch my gun belt and Winchester."

It wasn't his birthday, McCulloch thought as he entered his home. And neither Breen nor Keegan were much at coming up with jokes. But Blood Moon. Blood Moon the most desperate Indian in this part of the West. What the hell did he want to talk to McCulloch about?

Breen pulled off at the livery stable when they rode into Purgatory City, and McCulloch kept the chestnut at a lope till he neared the city jail. It had been a long time, McCulloch figured, since he had seen that many horses in front of any saloon in town, and even though The Palace of Purgatory City was a new bucket of blood, McCulloch didn't think most of those customers were testing out their luck at keno or roulette or sampling the imported brandy and champagne. They'd be drinking rotgut and trying to get enough guts to lynch an Indian being held in jail. The crowd that had moved inside the lawyer's office on the other side of the street? Well, that likely held the leading citizens of the town, and they'd be trying to figure out how they could kill an Apache legally, before those pettifogging congressmen and senators and ink-slinging newspaper editors in Austin or the United States Army came in and took all the glory away from this rawhide town in the middle of nowhere.

McCulloch slowed the chestnut to a walk and then reined in the gelding and swung out of the saddle, wrapping the reins around the hitching rail nice and easy, ducking underneath the rail, and grabbing the knob to the door.

Damned thing was locked.

McCulloch stepped back and kicked it three times with his boot. "It's me, Keegan," McCulloch called out. He didn't have to give his name. Keegan's ugly face briefly appeared in the window to McCulloch's left, and a moment later the door opened just enough to let the mustanger slip inside.

The jail was quiet, and filthy, and Keegan laid Jed Breen's Sharps rifle on the desk and motioned at the coffeepot on the potbellied stove.

"I'll take a cup, sure, Sean," McCulloch said as he removed his hat to beat some of the trail dust off his clothes. He found one cell door open, the rest closed, and only one prisoner in one of the locked cages. Mc-Culloch tossed his hat on a rack and let his spurs jingle as he moved to the iron bars.

"I'll be a son of a gun," he whispered. The mangled hand proved beyond any doubt McCulloch had that this big, black-eyed Indian was indeed Blood Moon.

"Mac-Cul-Lock." The Apache nodded.

McCulloch's gut twisted and he wet his dried lips. He stepped just a bit closer to the iron bars. "I'm told you wanted to talk to me."

The Apache's nod was sharp but terse.

"Well." McCulloch hooked his left hand in his waistband, but let the right fall on the butt of the long-barreled single-action Colt holstered on his right hip. "I'm here."

Those cruel black eyes looked over Mc-Culloch's shoulder.

"Sean," McCulloch said. "Why don't you get yourself some supper. Or a whiskey." It wasn't a question, or even a suggestion.

"Well, Matt, me boy," Keegan said gingerly, "the fact of the matter is that I'm supposed to be in that cell over yonder, serving the rest of me sentence."

Which explained what had happened to the saloon and gambling hall across the street.

"I don't think anybody will bother you,"

188

Matt said. "Just give me and Blood Moon five minutes."

"Aye. Sure, laddie, sure. I'll head over to Bondy's gun shop and see how that wee little baby gal is doing."

That caused the Ranger to turn around and stare as the Irishman fetched his campaign hat, pulled it on his head, and brought the cup of coffee over, giving McCulloch the grinning Irishman look, and then turning quickly and moving easily to the door.

McCulloch tried to make sense of what Keegan had just said. But it didn't make any sense at all. Ramona Bonderoff couldn't have had a baby. She wasn't even married. And her pa . . . he would have showed whoever had . . . well, old Bondy knew more than just how to fix firearms.

The door closed behind Keegan, and Mc-Culloch drew in a long breath, held it, exhaled, and looked back at the Apache prisoner.

"All right," McCulloch said. "We're alone. Talk. Sunset's not too far off and I'd like to be back at my ranch before it's dark."

The Indian did not talk. His lips never moved. But his good hand reached into a pouch that hung at his waist, secured around his shoulder by a deerskin strap. The fingers brought out something that his fist closed around, and the arm moved the hand through the iron bars. The fingers opened, spreading out, and something metallic but colorful dropped to the floor. Blood Moon brought his arm back through the bars, and let the arm fall to his side. He said nothing. Just looked.

The coffee cup dropped from McCulloch's hand, spilling the liquid on the hard stone, but running into cracks and not toward the small item the Apache had let fall from his hand.

McCulloch's eyes fell to the floor, but not at the tin cup at his feet. He drew in a breath as he knelt, reached down and picked up the tarnished silver and frayed green and blue ribbon.

"I want a necklace, too, Pa. Like the one you gave Ma."

That started the boys into singsong mockery. "Cynthia wants a necklace . . . Cynthia wants a necklace . . . She thinks she's a woman . . . But she ain't nothin' but a girlie."

"Hush!" McCulloch's wife demanded, and the two boys stopped singing, but they did not stop humming.

McCulloch and his wife had just returned from a barn-raising over at the Jenkins place, and since it was also Rachel's birthday, McCulloch had given her a necklace. Now his daughter was begging for one, too, and, hell, the last thing Matt McCulloch ever wanted was to break his only girl's heart. The boys, Matt Junior, and Michael — he could work them all day and night — and not even thank them for their sweat and hard labor, but Cynthia . . . well . . . she reminded McCulloch too much of Rachel.

So he went to the pewter box on the bureau, opened it and brought the twelve-point star, which hadn't been cleaned in years, the ribbon that held it, and the words in Latin, which translated into something Matt McCulloch had long forgotten. He joked to the boys that he had won it for valor while riding with the Texas cavalry, but Rachel knew that he had won it in a horse race. The loser had bet ten dollars, but it turned out the medal was all he had, and McCulloch didn't think it was worth two bits, even if the loser had said he had fought for the winning side in the War.

McCulloch's wife smiled.

"I reckon you'll be going to barn-raises and dances before you can blink an eye," McCulloch said, and he loved how those eyes brightened, and loved it even more when she reached up and gave him a bear squeeze of a hug.

Later, of course, Rachel McCulloch told her husband that while Cynthia was hugging her proud papa, she was sticking her tongue out at Matt Junior and Michael.

He almost shivered. Then he felt rage like he had not experienced in countless years. Rising back to his full height, McCulloch grimaced. His left hand fisted the worthless necklace — medal — whatever one wanted to call it while his right began pulling the Colt from the holster, the thumb slowly cocking the hammer.

Blood Moon did not smile, did not cower, but said: "Do you wish to see her?"

That . . . that, damn it, stunned McCulloch. The Colt slid back into the holster, and the one-time Ranger's Adam's apple bobbed.

"She's alive?" McCulloch could not comprehend what all was happening. All these years. A vision of the cross he had put up at the graveyard by what had once been his horse ranch flashed before his eyes.

He saw the graveyard at his ranch. He remembered burying his family after the Apache raid. He saw himself placing crosses at the head of the mounds where he had planted his wife and his sons. Eventually, he had put up a cross for Cynthia, too. Over the years, his ranch — or what had remained of it — had fallen into nothing but bad memories. But some citizens had put up a fence around the graveyard. It struck Matthew McCulloch right then that not everyone who called Purgatory City or the surrounding harsh country was a jackal. There were good folks here. Over the years, they had brought cactus blossoms to the graves, and they had been the ones who had replaced the crosses that wind, rain and time had ruined.

"She lives," Blood Moon said.

McCulloch looked at the medal, then tossed it to the floor near the locked door to the Apache's cage.

"How do I know you're telling the truth?" McCulloch spat out angrily. "You could've traded some miserable scum of a Comanchero for this. Or won it off some Apache from another village betting who could drink the most tiswin."

The Apache spoke in his native tongue, then Mexican, and finally English. "Blood Moon is not white eye. Blood Moon does not lie."

McCulloch spit on the floor.

"She your wife now?" He felt cheap and sick to even speak those words aloud, even if the only two men who heard them were the murdering savage and himself. He felt the little coffee he had drank rising up his throat, and wondered if he would puke out his guts here on the floor.

"What would Blood Moon want with a puny white girl with yellow hair and eyes the color of the leaves of cornstalks in the summer?"

Spinning away, McCulloch fought for his breath, spit on the floor, and made himself turn to the hard rock he had been just after discovering what had happened to his family, to himself, all those years ago. Then he picked up the dropped coffee cup and the medal he had given Cynthia and walked across the small room, just to keep moving, to keep thinking, but mostly to get as far away from the Apache prisoner as he could. At the desk, he shoved off papers and ledgers, and sat on the edge.

Blood Moon wasn't lying. McCulloch was sure enough of that now. Blond hair. Green eyes. That was Cynthia. That's all he needed to know. She was alive. *My God,* McCulloch realized, *my daughter is really alive.*

Bitterness followed. Alive as she could be after years with these . . . He tried, but failed, to swallow down his hatred.

"Why?" he finally asked.

"You trade for Litsog," Bloody Moon said.

"Litsog?"

The Apache's head moved up and down just once. He pointed at a yellow-covered book on the shelf behind McCulloch. "Apache name. She wife of Killer of Cougars." Spitting on the floor must have been the Apache's way of saying exactly what he thought of Cynthia's Apache husband.

"All right," McCulloch said. "But what's in this for you? Why would you want to . . . help . . . me?"

"No help you," Blood Moon said. "I just like you," and the Apache laughed. "You want revenge. Blood Moon wants revenge. Three Dogs has become a woman."

Three Dogs. That was an Apache name McCulloch had not heard in years.

Blood Moon then did something that sealed the decision McCulloch knew he had to make. The Apache raised his bad, mangled, pink hand. "You Tejanos think I kill your women and children and cowards of men because of this." He pushed the mangled hand forward, then dropped it. "But it was not white eyes or stupid Mexicans who did this to me. It was my own people."

The door opened, and Sean Keegan returned.

"Want some whiskey, Matt?" the Irishman

195

said as he slid a bottle of Irish on the desk. "You should see that baby, Matt, how Bondy's girl got her all cleaned up and, blessed be the saints, she's so adorable I almost want to dance a jig."

McCulloch ignored his friend. "Keep this Apache buck safe, Sean," he said. "I've got to ride back to my ranch. Tell Breen I'll be back as quickly as I can." But McCulloch was staring at Blood Moon as he spoke.

Then he went through the door, ignoring Keegan's question.

"What did that bloody devil have to tell you?"

CHAPTER FIFTEEN

Outside, McCulloch spotted Jed Breen standing in front of the gun shop, talking to Bondy — or rather getting an earful from the gunsmith. Good, McCulloch thought, that would keep the bounty hunter occupied for a while. Even better, McCulloch when Bonderoff opened the door to the shop and Breen followed him inside.

Then McCulloch checked the cinching on the chestnut, grabbed the reins, and swung into the saddle. He rode the gelding harder than he had when heading into Purgatory City with Breen, but knew the horse would get him to the ranch in good time, and still be healthy enough to fend for himself. Which he'd have to do.

Dusk was coming down hard when Mc-Culloch reached the ranch, showing one of those brilliant sunsets a body rarely saw in Texas, more often seen in the territories of New Mexico and Arizona. This was something to behold, but McCulloch wasn't in any mood to appreciate the beauty of nature. He unsaddled the gelding, removed the bridle, and patted the horse on the rear.

The chestnut moved slowly, heading toward the empty corral, then stopped and turned back, staring at his caregiver, expecting McCulloch to open the corral and maybe rub him down, at least feed him.

Instead McCulloch left the horse in the yard and he moved to the rickety fence — most neighbors had given up taking care of the cemetery some time back, after Matt McCulloch became less known as a man whose family had been wiped out by Indians and more as a marauding jackal who cared about nothing but revenge.

He didn't enter the graveyard, for he figured the gate would collapse and take down half the fence with it if he tried to open it. Rachel's cross was crooked, and Michael's was gone. He looked at Cynthia's, which lay facedown on the ground. Then McCulloch turned and strode away.

He shoved every cartridge he could find into pouches, which he then put in his saddlebags. Thinking of Bonderoff, he cleaned his Colt and his Winchester thoroughly, slicked his holster with bacon grease, and made himself eat leftover soup and drink cold coffee just to have something in his stomach.

The rest of his saddlebags were filled with what little money he could scrape out of the bottom of a coffee can, beef jerky, and stale biscuits. Outside, he picked the pinto, knowing most cowboys would rake a horseman like Matt McCulloch mighty hard for saddling an "Injun pony," but knew this little mustang would outrun a thoroughbred in any race, at any time, and didn't have any quit in him. He saddled the piebald, secured the saddlebags, and strapped on the bedroll, rainslicker and a coat just in case the heat wave snapped.

Besides, the last he heard, those Apaches living mostly in Mexico had taken refuge in the Sierra Madres. With every other wild animal, man and beast. For a place peopled with men and women bound for Hell, it got mighty cold in those hills.

He emptied sacks of grain on the dirt for the chestnut and the other horses he let out. "Go on," he muttered to the animals, but figured they'd eat as long as there was food on the ground and water in the troughs and buckets. After that, they'd wander and graze and drink. Right now, they wore the McCulloch brand, and he didn't think anyone would dare steal a horse. McCulloch had that kind of reputation.

Providing, of course, he got out of Mexico alive. Hell, he might not even get out of Purgatory City in one piece, considering what he knew he had to do.

The roan he saddled, too, knowing it as almost equal to the pinto he had saddled for himself. That horse had gotten McCulloch through that scalawag of a man called Red Nixon and his damned fool horse thieves. Gotten him all the way to this ranch. It would carry an Apache warrior good enough, providing a horse could stomach the smell of an Indian.

He filled three canteens with water for his horse, and two pouches for the roan. Then he walked back into the hovel of a home, built over the ashes of the log cabin the Apaches had torched so many lifetimes ago. He opened a drawer and pulled out an old Manhattan pocket .32, a relic from the War Between the States, one Bonderoff could have easily converted to take brass cartridges, but McCulloch had never brought it in. He found a tin of percussion caps, and a flask of powder, and a pouch of balls. That had to be a miracle.

After lighting a candle, he went to work loading the old relic.

"You know what this is for?" he told Rachel before he left to find mustangs.

"Yes." She smiled. "I won't have to use it, you know." Rachel rubbed her expanding stomach. "I won't have to. You have a daughter to be born."

McCulloch smiled. "You mean another son."

"I think not. Intuition, you understand."

"Maybe so." He nodded at the door. "But there are snakes and critters."

"Which I can chop up with a grubbing hoe."

"Just take care of yourself." He leaned forward and kissed her hard. "And our next boy."

"Our first girl," she said, and, God, how he loved that look in her eyes.

He remembered finding the Manhattan, unfired, in the dirt amid the smoking ruins of his home. He had found that grubbing hoe, too, with blood on a corner and black hair, and he knew Rachel had fought her best — the way she knew how to fight.

It didn't bring an ounce of comfort to him.

■ ■ ■ ■

The street lamps were burning in Purgatory City, and the lights were still on in the windows of the saloon and lawyer's office across the street from the jail. Matt McCulloch reined up in front of the jail, twisted in the saddle, and listened to the noise from the saloon. Shouting. Cussing. Not the usual singing or the clicking of a roulette wheel that one heard at most gambling establishments in Purgatory City. Whatever the folks were talking about in the lawyer's office, they were doing it quietly. Conspiring.

McCulloch spit in the dirt, and slid out of the saddle. He grabbed the lead rope and tied it securely to a crooked wooden column, letting the gray mustang stallion drink. He tied the reins to the roan next to his pinto. For a moment, he considered hobbling the stallion's feet, but quickly dismissed that as unnecessary. And stupid. Barring a miracle, he'd be riding out of this town at a high lope, with no time to mess with the hobbles on a half-broke, mean-eyed mustang with Arab blood coursing through its veins.

He kicked on the door again with his boot,

and stepped back. "It's Matt," he called out, but not too loud, though no one in The Palace of Purgatory City could hear him, and their shouts would prevent anyone still trying to work up nerve to decide something useless in the building across the street.

A lantern was turned up, then McCulloch glimpsed Keegan's face in the window. Wetting his lips, McCulloch waited. The door opened, and McCulloch slipped inside.

"Glad you got back, Matt," Keegan said. "Jed and me been . . ."

McCulloch didn't hear the next words from the Irishman because he was staring at the bounty hunter, cleaning his double-action Colt, while sitting in a chair near the potbellied stove.

The former Ranger nodded and walked over to the cell that housed the Indian, stared briefly at the hard face, then at the mangled hand, and turned quickly and nodded at Jed Breen.

"How 'bout a cup of Keegan's coffee, Jed?" McCulloch said.

"I wouldn't call it coffee," Breen said, "but if you're man enough to drink it . . ." He rose from the chair, and let the Lightning drop into the holster.

"Like anyone who isn't from County Cork knows how to make the best cof—" Sean

Keegan didn't finish because he was looking at McCulloch while he spoke. He saw the mustanger draw the Colt, and thumb back the hammer.

Breen saw it next, but his right hand held the handle on the battered coffeepot, and his left was reaching for a mug.

"What the hell?" both Breen and Keegan said at the same time.

"I hate to do this, boys," McCulloch said, and he waved the barrel just briefly toward the cell that was supposed to be holding Sean Keegan for about a month or so.

"What's this all about?" Keegan said.

"Just get in the cell, gents." McCulloch's voice was firm, and the heavy Colt did not waver in his right hand. "We'll be out of your hair in a jiffy."

Keegan looked past the man holding a gun on him and into the cell. "You can't be serious, Matt. You're breaking this bad apple out of jail?"

"Into the cells, boys," McCulloch said, "but not before you, Jed, unbuckle that rig."

Breen backed away from the stove, leaving the cup and pot where they were. He started to comply with McCulloch's orders.

"Left hand, pard," McCulloch said tightly. "Keep the right one pointed at the ceiling."

The bounty hunter obeyed without a

word, the gun belt dropped to the floor, and Breen kicked it over toward McCulloch's boots.

"Sean." McCulloch pointed with the Colt's barrel.

"Bloody hell. You're worse than an English pig." But Keegan moved to the cell, and Breen followed, though the bounty hunter talked as he walked.

"If you think you can break Blood Moon out of here and turn him over to the Texas Rangers or U.S. marshal are any other of your star-packing compadres, and collect my twenty thousand bucks, Matt, you're gonna be in one rude awakening." By then he was in the jail cell.

"All the way to the back, pards," McCulloch said from outside the door.

The key was still in the lock. The two men walked to the wall, keeping their hands high, and then turned around.

"Have a seat," McCulloch suggested.

They sat on the bunk.

"Sit on your hands," the mustanger said. "It'll keep your hands from sweating."

"Like they ain't already in this furnace," Keegan grumbled, but both men obeyed.

"Now cross your legs at the ankles."

They did that, too.

"Comfortable?" McCulloch said, and he

205

kicked the door shut.

"Don't move just yet," McCulloch said as he used his left hand to turn the key and heard the bolt snap into place. He managed to get the big key out without any difficulty, and then he walked directly to the cell that held Blood Moon. It took a while before he found the right key to that cell, but when he did, when he heard that satisfying metallic sound, he stepped back and aimed the Colt through the bars.

"You try anything, you catch one that won't kill you for a long while."

The Apache said nothing, and walked to the door. McCulloch backed away, and the Apache stopped when he was out of the cell.

"Outside." The Colt waved toward the door. The Indian obeyed.

"The roan's yours," McCulloch said. "Grab the reins, get mounted, and you take the lead rope to the gray stallion." He smiled then for the first time, though he found nothing funny and no pleasure in this situation. "That'll keep your hands full."

When the Apache's hand fell on the door latch, McCulloch spoke again. "You'll ride out first, but the horse I'm on can outrun yours. And I have had plenty of practice shooting, and not missing, in the dark, at a gallop, with the sun in my eyes, or eating dust."

"I hear you, White Eye."

"Good."

The door opened, and both men slipped out, closing the door sharply.

"What in the hell —"

Blood Moon was doing exactly what Mc-Culloch had told him to do, but the voice came from a man in a black hat and brass buttons reflecting off his tunic. There was just enough light for McCulloch to recognize the face, and then the damned Yankee started reaching for the flap that protected his service revolver.

McCulloch stepped forward quickly, and the man turned around to scream. The butt of the Colt slammed downward, knocking off the campaign hat and sending the officer to the boardwalk in front of the jail, knocking loose a few planks and from the way the officer's head struck, probably a few teeth, too.

He knew the man, recognizing him at the last minute. Just by name, though, but from what McCulloch had heard about Second Lieutenant Charles Tibbetts, that was all he wanted to know about him.

Spinning, McCulloch raised the Colt at the Apache, who was stepping into the saddle on the roan with the ease of a cowhand. The Indian had wrapped the lead rope holding the gray stallion around his forearm, for the mangled hand would not be strong enough. That's exactly why Mc-Culloch had thought of this.

"Remember what I said," McCulloch said. He waived the gun ever so slightly, gave the lieutenant another glance but knew that soldier wouldn't be going anywhere for a while, and when he finally could move, he would wish he couldn't with the knot on the skull McCulloch had given him.

Again, McCulloch slipped under the rail, grabbed the reins, and mounted his pinto. Sean Keegan was yelling and cussing from inside the jail, but no one would hear him because of the racket still coming from The Palace of Purgatory City. And a baby was screaming its head off somewhere down the street. The door to what had to be Bondy's gun shop opened, and a woman stepped outside, but McCulloch didn't think she could see him, and, besides, she appeared to have her hands filled with a screaming child.

But now the men began filing out of the lawyer's office, and those men had a clear enough view of what was going on at the jail.

McCulloch was in the saddle now. "Ride!" he yelled at the Apache, and the roan exploded, the snorting, fighting angry stallion followed, and McCulloch fired a round from the Colt that struck the lawyer's shingle above the door. The leading citizens of Purgatory City dropped *en masse.*

The pinto carried McCulloch out of town, past the pretty gal holding the baby in front of Bondy's place.

Two blocks later a gunshot sounded but if the bullet was aimed at McCulloch or Blood Moon, it didn't come close.

McCulloch expected more shots, but Purgatory City's street lamps only went so far, and now he, Blood Moon and the gray stallion had been swallowed by darkness.

McCulloch's bad leg began to hurt, but he bit back the pain, and he kept the Colt trained on where he heard the pounding hooves of the horse carrying the Apache butcher and the great stallion Blood Moon pulled behind him.

If the Indian had any sense, he would have called McCulloch's bluff. Yeah, Matt McCulloch was a fine shot with Winchester or revolver, but right now, even if the dust from the galloping horses ahead of him, hadn't blinded him — it was pitch black now, and McCulloch couldn't see a damned thing.

They turned at the next block.

They spurred their mounts harder.

They thundered on in the total darkness, riding south.

CHAPTER SIXTEEN

Gunshots and curses somehow managed to make their way through the blistering pain that stretched from Second Lieutenant Charles Tibbetts's left ear to his right, and seemed to saw through the top of his skull. His right hand managed to move and find the knot already the size of an apple that seemed to be pushing hair out from the roots. Tears welled in his eyes, and then a voice, much softer than the reports of pistols and the bellowing curses of what had to be a dozen men, reached him.

"Lieutenant, suh, Lieutenant Tibbetts, suh? Are you dead, suh?"

He recognized the Southern accent of one of his troopers, Andy Anderson.

"No," Tibbetts managed to say, and he thought, *But I wish like hell I were.*

Even thinking made his head throb harder.

Other words raced past him, though he only managed to catch about half of them.

"That sneaky snake." . . . "Can you believe what he done?" . . . "Check the jail — it must be some damned trick." . . . "No trick, a-tall, the sumbitch busted that red devil outta the calaboose." . . . "He's a Ranger, by thunder!" . . . "Not in a coupla years. Kicked his sorry arse out." . . . "He's a jackal. Even when he was a Ranger, he was a jackal." . . . "Open the jail." . . . "We gotta form a posse."

Trooper Anderson managed to lift to a half-seated position, and the officer leaned against the rough stone of the Purgatory City jail, using his campaign hat as a pillow. Something wasn't right, though. Tibbetts spit blood out of his mouth, and made his tongue work.

"Gosh, Lieutenant Tibbetts, suh, you have busted out your front two teeth."

The young West Pointer's tongue confirmed the trooper's observation, and now anger caused the lieutenant's face to flush. He started to remember what had happened. He had been making his way to the jail, to demand that the Apache renegade, Blood Moon, be turned over to federal authorities, in particular, Lieutenant Charles Tibbetts, to be transported to the stockade at Fort Spalding, where he would be held until his trial by military tribunal.

212

Tibbetts, of course, had no orders to do that, but he had to guess that would be exactly what the colonel, the Secretary of War, the Secretary of the Interior, and the General of the Army, not to mention the President of the United States would all want. And it would be Lieutenant Charles Tibbetts, certain to be breveted a captain or maybe even jump another grade to Major, would see his name in all the newspapers and illustrated magazines and find himself richer by twenty thousand bucks.

The shouts went on. "McCulloch! It was Matt McCulloch!" . . . "Well, what are we standin' 'round here fer? We oughta be ridin' hard after that swine." . . . "If we'd lynched that red devil as soon as we seen that bounty man bring his sorry arse into the jail, we wouldn't be in this fix." . . . "Homer's right, boys, now Blood Moon's free to be scalpin' and rapin' our wimmenfolks." . . . "We oughta string up Matt McCulloch, the low-down mangy mutt." . . . "Well, what are we standin' 'round here fer?" . . . "Well, who in his right mind would ride after Matt McCulloch and Blood Moon — in the dark?" . . . "Stefan's right, boys, we gotta wait till daylight." . . . "Why don't we check the jail? Maybe this is some joke." . . . "Ain't nobody laughin'." . . .

"Hey, it's the Judge!"

Tibbetts wiped his mouth, spit out blood, wiped his mouth again, and made himself draw a deep breath. "Help me up, Trooper Anderson," he commanded, and felt the strapping Mississippi farm boy ease Tibbetts to his feet. He leaned against the stone wall of the jail as a crowd of ignorant Texans made a path for Judge Harry Fellow. The judge was making a beeline for the door, and Tibbetts whispered to Anderson. "Door," Tibbetts whispered. "Inside."

For a dumb Southerner, Tibbetts thought, Andy Anderson was the best trooper he had under his command. The farm kid moved Tibbetts to the jail door, and opened it, just as the judge arrived.

"You men wait outside," Judge Fellow instructed the crowd of belligerent Texicans, but by then Anderson and Tibbetts were in the jail.

Judge Fellow closed the door behind them.

One jail cell was open. A gun belt was on the floor by the potbellied stove. All the other cells were empty, except one, and that one housed two men Lieutenant Charles Tibbetts knew mostly by reputation.

Sean Keegan, former sergeant at Fort Spalding who, legend had it, murdered a

214

lieutenant in cold blood during some attack against Indians, sat on a bunk beside the white-haired bounty hunter who thought he was going to collect the reward for bringing in Blood Moon. Suddenly, Tibbetts smiled because he realized something. Blood Moon's escape meant Jed Breen had no claim — no claim at all — on that reward. All Tibbetts had to do was find both men. By thunder, the bounty on that Apache butcher might even be upped another thousand dollars or even more, and having helped the most notorious, red-skinned killer on the Texas frontier, there would be a sizable bounty placed on Matt McCulloch's head, too — dead or alive — just the way Tibbetts, and many Texicans, liked it.

"Judge, what's all the fuss about?" Keegan said with a smile. The sergeant — former sergeant, traitor to his uniform, maybe the worst of the jackals, Tibbetts decided, or had been until the former Ranger did this dastardly deed — yawned.

Breen studied his fingernails.

"What happened?" Judge Fellow asked.

The bounty hunter looked up. "What do you mean, Your Honor?"

"You know damned well what I mean!" Judge Fellow roared.

Again, Tibbetts wiped his mouth. "You

answer the Judge, you impudent wharf rats!" Tibbetts said, sending bits of blood and saliva toward the stove.

"Matt McCulloch broke Blood Moon out of jail," the judge said.

The bounty hunter got to his feet, walked to the cell door, put his hands on the bars, and stared at the empty cell. A moment later, he turned back toward the judge and Army officer. "Well, Judge, I guess somebody did."

"We was sleeping, you see, Your Honor," Keegan said, and then he scratched behind his left ear.

"Jackals!" Tibbetts spat out the words, and more saliva, and more blood.

"Why are you in jail, Breen?" Judge Fellow asked.

"Couldn't afford a hotel room, Your Honor."

"You'll both rot in there," Tibbetts let those jackals know.

"I could charge you as accessories," Judge Fellow told them.

Breen shook his head. "My Lightning's on the floor, Your Honor, and my Sharps is leaning against the wall by the gun case." He rattled the doors. "And seeing that Sean and me are locked in this pigsty, I don't think even a jury put together in Purgatory

City would let that indictment hold."

Now it was Judge Fellow's turn to spit on the floor.

The Texas jurist turned to Tibbetts and the trooper, nodded at both men, and turned toward the door they had closed.

"Judge Fellow," Breen called out.

All three men stopped and looked back at the cell.

"I did capture Blood Moon," Breen said with a smile. "You know that. Brought him in, turned him in. That ought to count for something, I mean, not the whole twenty thousand bucks, but maybe a portion of it. Don't you think, Your Honor?"

The judge said: "You brought in Blood Moon."

"That's right." The bounty hunter smiled.

Judge Fellow looked at the empty cell. "Funny, Breen," the jurist said. "I don't see the red devil anywhere."

Lieutenant Charles Tibbetts found much to smile about, to gloat over, from just the look on that jackal of a bounty man's face. The judge opened and left the jail, and Tibbetts followed, and Trooper Andy Anderson closed the door.

"Well?" a blowhard from the crowd of Purgatory City citizens wanting a lynching demanded.

"Blood Moon has broken out of jail," Judge Fellow said, as if that was breaking news.

"With McCulloch's help!" someone shouted.

"That appears to be the case," the judge said.

"I bet those other two jackals, Breen and that drunken Irish louse, helped that no-good Ranger."

Now, Judge Fellow's head shook. "No, no, they had nothing to do with it."

Tibbetts was pressing his tongue at the gap in his front teeth, trying to stop the bleeding, but he looked suspiciously at the jurist. He wasn't so sure that the bounty hunter and especially that traitorous sergeant were completely innocent.

"Breen and Keegan are in jail. Breen's gun belt was on the floor." Judge Fellow's head bobbed as though he were convincing himself. "My theory is that Matt McCulloch acted alone. We saw him." Fellow shot a glance at Tibbetts. "I had sent the lieutenant — we had sent the lieutenant, a citizen's committee that was discussing the matter at Solicitor Van Dyke's offices, to inform Blood Moon that he would be tried tomorrow for murder."

"We don't need no damned trial," a Texan roared.

"Well, you damn sure don't want a lynching," the judge shot back. "You'll have all those Eastern puritans screaming at us, and then Purgatory City would become a blight instead of a beacon. We'd never get the railroad. We'd be scandalized. Lynchings do no good. But a legal trial, and a quick trial, and a swift hanging, that would put this city on the map. That is what we decided across from that den of inequity where you drank whiskey until you found enough courage to try to string up another victim. We are sick of lynchings. We must have justice."

Judge Fellow, Tibbetts figured, was thinking about a federal posting, maybe running for the Senate of the United States.

"There ain't gonna be nothing now, Judge," said a sniffling Texican. "Because McCulloch broke that scalpin', rapin', baby-stealin' rat out of jail."

"And that is why the Citizens Committee of Purgatory City is posting a five hundred dollar reward for the capture and conviction, or death, of Matthew McCulloch," the judge said, and that got a whoop out of the crowd. "And we are adding another five hundred dollars for the capture, conviction or decapitated head — for identification

219

purposes, only — of the Apache terror known as Blood Moon."

Another whoop roared, and the men started talking among themselves, and a few began moving toward the hitching rails in front of The Palace of Purgatory City.

"Wait a minute!" Judge Fellow roared.

The mob stopped moving.

"Don't act like damned fools," Judge Fellow said. "You can't chase those two felons in the dead of night. You can't ride off half-cocked. You'll need supplies. And you'll need a scout. I'd recommend you find Three-Toed Charley. Some of you men should start getting a couple pack mules loaded for a long campaign. Flushing out McCulloch and Blood Moon won't be easy. Wait till daylight. You can't track a man, even two men, when it's a new moon. Find Three-Toed Charley or another scout, maybe two. Clean your weapons. Get as much ammunition as you can at Bonderoff's. And get your whiskey drunk tonight, because you sha'n't have another drop until you have brought in Blood Moon — and Matt McCulloch — dead or alive!"

Now the crowd dispersed, but most of the men headed back to the saloon.

Judge Fellow turned. "I'll be meeting with Van Dyke and the others," he told Tibbetts, "but you should report back to the colonel at Fort Spalding."

Tibbetts nodded firmly.

"And you might wake up Wilson the barber and have him fix that mouth of yours."

The lieutenant nodded again, and watched the judge walk across the street to the lawyer's office. Then he looked back at Trooper Andy Anderson.

"Where are the rest of the troop?" Tibbetts asked.

Anderson tipped his head toward the saloon. "They figgered that while all the Texicans was lynchin' the Injun, they could be drinking whiskey on the house."

"Get them," Tibbetts whispered. "Have them all meet at the edge of town. Ready to ride." The bleeding from his upper gums was slowly stopping. "Is Tiny Olderman with them?"

"He was."

Even better. Like Judge Fellow had suggested, two scouts would be better than just one. Besides, what if Blood Moon or that sharpshooting Texas Ranger killed Three-Toed Charley. "Bring him, too. . . . And do you know where Three-Toed Charley lives?"

"No, suh, but my understandin' is that a night like this one, or any other, he'll be with that hussy in the crib behind the Jack of Diamonds."

"Then I'll get him. I'll see you and the rest of the boys at the edge of town. We're riding hard. In thirty minutes."

"In the dark, suh?"

"Hell, yes. We've got to beat those ignorant Texans to Blood Moon."

The trooper saluted and sprinted.

Tibbetts eased the hat on his head, spit again, and walked to the hitching rail across from the lawyer's office, plotting as he found the reins, and led the horse down the street. He would stop at the telegraph office and instruct the man working to wire the colonel at Fort Spalding that Second Lieutenant Charles Tibbetts was leading his command in pursuit of the hostile Blood Moon and the man who broke the prisoner from the Purgatory City jail, McCulloch. Sure, Tibbetts had no orders to do that, but this is what made a good soldier. Initiative. Even the colonel had told Tibbetts that when he first arrived at Fort Spalding. No one would even suggest reprimand and God forbid a court-martial.

This was Blood Moon. This was the most savage Indian of all the savage races. There had to be initiative. There had to be justice. Blood Moon had to be caught, and so did that jackal McCulloch.

Luck was with Lieutenant Tibbetts. He found Three-Toed Charley at the crib, and the scout was relatively sober, and learning that he'd be tracking down Blood Moon for part of the reward, he had no regrets about leaving the ugly prostitute behind. Tibbetts even paid the woman the dollar Three-Toed Charley did not have. And when his patrol of fifteen soldiers and another tracker and interpreter named Tiny Olderman arrived, they all looked fit for a gallop to glory. Relatively sober, or drunk enough to ride after a butchering Apache savage and one of the worst white men to come out of Texas.

Tibbetts swung into the saddle, raised his hand, and let it fall forward. "Forward," he yelled, "charge!"

They galloped in the darkness, turning south, letting Three-Toed Charley and Tiny Olderman take the point and try to follow the trail. They'd be going to Mexico, Tibbetts knew, so tracking wasn't that necessary right now.

The lieutenant's mouth still hurt, but the pain would pass. And as far as the missing incisors, well, hell, twenty thousand bucks would buy a nice set of whalebone dentures.

CHAPTER SEVENTEEN

"Find Three-Toed Charley or another scout, maybe two. Clean your weapons. Get as much ammunition as you can at Bonderoff's. And get your whiskey drunk tonight, because you sha'n't have another drop until you have brought in Blood Moon — and Matt McCulloch — dead or alive!"

There was more talking outside after Judge Harry Fellow's instructions, but neither Jed Breen nor Sean Keegan could make out the words. Not that it mattered. Nobody would be coming inside the jail for quite a while.

Sounds of boots on the boardwalk faded, as did hoofbeats, and still Keegan and Breen sat on the bunk.

At last, Breen spoke: "Well?"

Keegan had been studying his fingernails. Now he held up his right hand toward Breen and whispered, "Not yet." He looked at his thumb, pondered a bit, and eventually brought the hand back and bit off a hangnail, spit onto the floor, and put his hands on the uncomfortable bunk, stood, listened, and, hearing nothing in the general vicinity of the jail, sat back down.

"Matt and that murdering buck — meaning my twenty thousand bucks — are getting farther away every minute, pal," Breen said.

"We'll catch up," Keegan said.

"Not sitting on our arses locked in this pigpen."

Keegan smiled, and began tugging off his boot. "Laddie, laddie, laddie," he said as he struggled to remove the ancient leather. "Ye needs to put ye faith in the Irish."

The boot came off, flopped to the floor, and the former soldier picked it up by the heel and shook. A key chimed on the stone. Breen instantly moved, and grabbed it as it bounced around, and raced to the cell door while Keegan calmly fetched his boot, then rubbed his calf.

"Nary a thank-yee, Jed?" he said with his eyes bright as though he were in the middle of a weeklong drunkfest. "Do ye have any idea how uncomfortable it is to have that bit of metal wearing a hole in my sock and my limb, me boy?"

Breen was busy trying to get the key into

225

the lock, but he managed to say, "I'll thank you when I have twenty thousand dollars in the bank."

"I wouldn't trust a bank with that kind of money." Keegan grunted as he started pulling on the boot.

The key grated, clicked loudly, and Breen stepped back and pushed the door wide open. He breathed in deeply, like a man tasting fresh air for the first time in months — although nothing in the Purgatory City jail smelled fresh.

Out of the cage, Breen found his gun belt and buckled it on while Keegan went to the window. "We're in luck," the Irishman said. "Some of the boys are still drinking at The Palace of Purgatory City."

Breen checked the Lightning, dropped it back into the holster, and moved to his Sharps. "What makes that lucky for us?"

Leaving the window, Keegan found his Springfield rifle in the gun case. He grabbed his hat, then buckled on his own gun rig. "Lucky for us if some of those boys ride for the Lazy K brand," he said. Now he checked his revolver. "I noticed some of the laddies earlier this evening were Lazy K boys."

Breen now waited by the front door. "I still don't get your meaning."

The former cavalry sergeant had picked

up a couple of canteens. "Jim Kincaid buys most of his cowponies from Matt McCulloch." He nodded, and Breen cracked open the door.

A light still shone inside the lawyer's office, but the shades remained pulled down tight. Just like a lawyer, Keegan figured. Someone had started the self-playing piano inside The Palace of Purgatory City, and farther down the street came the ribald sounds from other saloons.

The rest of the town seemed quiet.

"It ain't likely to get any better," Keegan whispered, and Breen opened the door and stepped outside. Keegan followed and closed the door behind him. They looked down the streets, then stepped off the boardwalk into the dirt and made a beeline for the hitching rails in front of the new, but mangled, saloon.

"Ahhh," Keegan sighed with relief as he fingered the brand on a sorrel's hip. "Blessed be the saints and Jim Kincaid's fine judgment of horse flesh." He carefully slid a heavy rifle from the scabbard. "Tsk, tsk, a Richmond Rifle," he said. "Haven't seen one of these since the Rebellion." He slid his Springfield in the scabbard, and leaned the old Confederate weapon against the rail as he loosened the reins and led the sorrel away.

A horse snorted.

"Shhhhhhh," Breen whispered as he pulled a shotgun from a scabbard, and replaced it with his Sharps. He laid the muzzle loader underneath the rail. "I don't see why anybody would carry a relic like that."

Keegan was letting he sorrel smell his hands, learn his scent. "Laddie," he said softly to the bounty hunter, "when ye make thirty a month you buy what ye can afford. Cowboys ain't professional shootists like we be."

"Don't mention money to me, Sarge," Breen said as he pulled a blood bay gelding out of the dock of horses. "Right now I'm twenty thousand bucks poorer than I was this morn."

They walked their horses down the street, looking straight ahead, not daring to chance a glance back at the saloon, past the closed stores, feeling relieved that even Bonderoff's Gun Shop was closed. A quick look at the window told Breen why.

"Hell, they cleaned Bondy out already."

"Good for the lad. Now maybe that sweet daughter of his won't have to work and can take care of that orphan baby."

They kept walking.

"What the hell do you reckon got into Matt?" Breen asked.

Keegan just shrugged.

"Did you see his eyes?" Breen asked.

"Aye. Like staring into Lucifer at the gate of Hades."

"I've never seen Matt look that way."

They walked another twenty steps before Keegan said: "I have."

A door opened. Both men stopped. They had reached the last street lamp in town. Water splashed down some side alley or narrow street, seconds ticked by, and the door slammed shut.

After both men let out their breath, they walked into the darkness.

"I've known Matt a wee bit longer than ye have, Jed me boy," Keegan said. "Ye didn't know him during those bad years — after . . . after . . . well, ye know the story."

"His family," Breen whispered.

"Aye. He was a terror for a while. A bloody demon. Looking for his daughter. Hating the Indians that took her. Hating himself. Blaming himself for letting it happen, when no one could have stopped it. Had Matt been home, he would've been killed, though I dare say the murdering red devils would have paid dearly for his scalp. He was a mess. I would not have been surprised if he had wound up putting that Colt's barrel in his own mouth and ending his misery. No one would have blamed him, either. The Texas Rangers, me thinks, saved his life. He found a purpose. Or at least put the bad memories behind him. Then he lost that . . ."

"And found us," Breen said.

Keegan laughed. "Bless his heart. We're a pure substitute for a loving family."

"Ain't that the truth."

They turned, began moving south.

"Comanches?" Breen asked.

"How's that?"

They stopped, tightened the cinches in the dark, and swung into the saddles.

"The Indians that massacred Matt's family." Breen tugged on the horn to shift the saddle over to his left. "Were they Comanches?"

Keegan was fiddling with the reins. He opened his mouth, stopped, and turned toward Breen. "Nay," he said and let the word settle before he said it again. Then he said, "They were Apaches."

Both men weighed the word and considered what that meant.

"Apache," Breen said after a long while.

"Aye." Keegan kicked his horse into a walk, and Breen moved his blood bay beside the cavalry man.

"They say it takes an Apache to track an Apache," Breen said.

Keegan's head bobbed. "They say that because there's a great bit of truth in that saying."

"Three-Toed Charley isn't Apache," Breen said.

"That's very true, but he knows them fairly well. And he's the best scout they have working out of Fort Spalding."

"I don't know any Apaches," Breen said.

They rode in silence for half a minute, then Keegan reined in the stolen sorrel. He sat in the saddle for another half a minute, then looked into the blackness where Jed Breen sat on his horse. "I don't, either," Keegan said, and turned his horse around. "But I know one that's close enough."

This time he loped down the Purgatory City road. Breen loped behind him.

The house did not fit in among the false fronts, adobe structures, stone buildings, hovels, *jacales* and picket shacks of Purgatory. This three-story building of white-wash with green trim, complete with shutters, also green, and fancy glass windows looked as if it had been miraculously transported from some genteel Virginia farm, or where the senators, ambassadors from foreign countries in Europe, and presidential staff called home in Washington, D.C. Or out of some storybook. Wooden frame, spotless on the outside, even in the dark, with lamps running by coal oil, not candles. There were two corrals, a barn, a veranda, and cottonwoods had been planted, but, in this part of the country, they were struggling to make a go out of living through the wretched summer, and the wind had blown them pretty much so that the trees were almost parallel with the flat dusty land. They had planted grass, too, and kept throwing sod out every spring, and by every summer, it was deader than John Wilkes Booth.

People never mentioned the house or Maudie in Purgatory City proper. Because Maudie Johnson was anything but proper, and the house she ran and had set up about three years back was anything but respectable. That didn't keep Purgatory City's most respectable men from visiting late at nights, usually riding in from the back way and putting their horses or carriages in the big barn or better corral. The men just never mentioned their visits to anyone, and paid Maudie and her girls quite well to do the exact same.

"What the hell are we doing here?" Breen

asked as he wrapped his reins around a metal ring.

"Trust me, laddie," Keegan said. "I know what I'm doing."

Keegan pulled his hat down tightly, checked his pistol, and climbed up the bricked doorsteps. Breen spit out his disgust and what spit he could work up, frowned, cursed softly, and followed.

The big Negro bouncer named, fittingly, Bouncer Bob, opened the door after Keegan rang the chimes at Maudie's House. Bouncer Bob's dark eyes looked both men over, his lips never moving from the scowl that passed for a frown, and eventually he grunted, and pulled the door open all the way. Keegan removed his hat, Breen did the same, and the door slammed shut, jingling the chimes, and Bouncer Bob grunted: "You know the way, Irish."

"Aye." Breen followed Keegan, though he certainly didn't like the thought of having Bouncer Bob, all of six-foot-seven and some two hundred and ninety pounds of packed muscle, walking behind him. It must have cost a fortune for Maudie when she had that fancy Sunday suit, complete with a black coat with tails and satin collar, made for the doorman and bruising bone-breaker.

Two cowboys — not from the Lazy K, at

least by the brands Keegan had seen hobbled out front — were drinking whiskey and talking to a redhead and a Mexican. Fat Maudie stood behind the bar until her eyes brightened. She slid a glass toward Keegan, and found something fancier and brought it and gently placed it in front of the bounty hunter.

"Well, Jed Breen. I never thought I'd get the pleasure to pleasure you."

Breen tipped his hat. "Ma'am," he said.

Keegan was already pouring Irish whiskey into his shot glass.

Maudie, with rouge maybe an inch deep on her fat face, brought up a bottle of champagne, and poured it until the bubbly spilled over onto the bar. "Drink up, Jed." She laughed. "And tell me exactly what you want from sweet, adorable little Maudie."

Maudie had maybe ten pounds on Bouncer Bob.

"It's me treat," Keegan said. "This being Jeddie me pal's birthday."

"Is that a fact?" Maudie's smile widened revealing gold fillings and one that sparkled like a diamond — or — to Breen's way of thinking — a diamondback rattlesnake's eyes before it struck. "Well, happy birthday, darlin'. We'll give you a birthday you ain't likely to get over."

And a very unpleasant disease to go with it,
Breen thought. Still he smiled, though his
birthday wasn't for seven more months and
nobody knew it, especially Sean Keegan.

Breen raised the flute, made himself smile
at the madam, wished to hell he knew what
Sean Keegan was doing here, and let his
crystal clink against the pewter beer stein
Maudie raised toward him.

"I was thinking about Wildcat Walesja,"
Keegan said after killing his shot and pouring another.

That turned Maudie's face into a hard,
bitter look. "Well, I thought the birthday
boy would like something a little fatter, a
lot more woman, and a fine lady who smells
like lavender and peaches and springtime."
She gulped beer, wiped foam off her painted
lips, and swallowed. "Not that bony bitch."

Breen made himself swallow the flat, god-
awful champagne.

Maudie smiled at Breen. "That hair of
yours," she whispered. "I just want to run
my hands through it, you know? It's so
white and pure. You can run your hands
through mine, too, because mine ain't
white, but it's pure. Just like me." She gig-
gled.

"You'd flatten little Breen like a flapjack,
Maudie," Keegan said and poured his third

235

drink. "It's Wildcat Walesja for Breen or we take our birthday party to Norma Jane's."

Bouncer Bob cleared his throat. It wounded like a battery of cannon firing.

Maudie's eyes turned deadly, and she scowled at Keegan while her right hand dipped underneath the bar, likely, Breen figured, for something other than flat champagne or cheap Mexican beer stolen from a whorehouse on the other side of the Río Grande.

"Wildcat Walesja's busy," one of the cowboys said.

"That's right," his pard said.

Breen turned toward the two cowpokes.

"With Billy," the first waddie said.

"And he paid for all night," his pard whispered.

They let their right hands drop over their holstered revolvers.

CHAPTER EIGHTEEN

"Oh." Keegan turned toward the cowpokes, shook his head, and raised his shot glass. "Well, I hope you boys will join me in wishing Jed Breen a happy fortieth birthday."

Fortieth? Breen scowled.

"Sorry, Jed. No Wildcat Walesja for you. Maybe when you turn fifty. She'll be just as wild." Keegan held the glass higher, and his grin widened. "To Jed Breen."

The cowboys stared at each other. The redhead and the Mexican found the glasses, topped them off, and handed them to the two glassy-eyed cowpokes, then filled their own glasses with forty-rod funneled into Scotch bottles, and raised their glasses, too.

"To Jed Breen," the Mexican said.

"He does have right perty hair," the redhead said.

"Here's how," said one of the waddies.

"How," said Keegan.

Maudie pulled her hand from under the

bar — empty of any weapon — and found her stein.

They drank. Breen breathed easier, and Keegan said. "Wait here, Jed. I gotta visit the privy." He took a few steps from the bar, turned back, and put his hand on Breen's shoulder. "You won't believe this, Jed, but it's the best thing about this place. Maudie, she didn't spare nothing when she built this palace. The privy . . ." Keegan couldn't stifle a drunken snigger. "The privy . . . it's . . . it's . . . it ain't outside the house." He motioned with a crooked thumb. "It's right down the hallway through them curtains and underneath the stairs."

Wiping his nose, refilling the shot glass, he laughed. "I'll be back directly." He winked at Maudie. "Then we'll figure out what Jeddie the birthday boy gets on his fiftieth birthday."

"Thirtieth," the thirty-four-year-old frowned.

He watched Keegan raise the shot glass at the scowling Bouncer Bob, and push his way through the red velvet curtains.

"You need more bubbly," Maudie said, and found the bottle of flat champagne.

Spurs issued by the quartermaster at Fort Spalding did not jingle. That's one thing the U.S. Army got right, and that's why Keegan still wore his Cavalry spurs. The indoor privy was beneath the staircase, but Keegan climbed the stairs, which, because Maudie was such a perfectionist, did not squeak at all.

When he reached the second floor, he paused, listening, and then glanced down the stairs. He stepped up, turned, gripped the balustrade and eased his way on the Persian rug. The gas lamps shown. Keegan moved past the first door, which he knew was the redhead's room. The Mexican's was on the corner, if Keegan's memory was right — he had been pretty much soused that evening. Maudie had the whole third floor, but God only knew how that fat tub of lard managed to go up and down those stairs every morning and night.

Wildcat Walesja's room had the pretty painting over the bookcase. What a banker Keegan had heard one night call a still life, which had caused Keegan to quip: "Fitting, because it's a miracle if you're still living after a night with Wildcat Walesja."

He drew his revolver with his right hand, used his left to grip the door knob, and twisted.

That was another good thing about Maudie. She had ordered no doors of the girls ever be locked after that time Bouncer Bob had to knock one off the hinges to get at and nearly beat some drunk too mean with his fists on one of Maudie's girls. Maudie had to order a replacement door all the way from St. Louis, and she said she'd be good and damned if she ever had to pay that much money for a door. No locks after that.

The door opened, and Keegan rushed inside.

"What the . . . !" The young cowboy threw off the quilt, and tried to reach for the holstered gun in the belt he had tossed over the brass footboard. The butt of Keegan's Remington slammed against the kid's head, and he grunted, and fell in all his pasty white nakedness onto the floor.

Keegan shifted the .44 and aimed it at Wildcat Walesja.

"Be quiet." He ordered.

The dark-skinned, black-haired woman yawned.

Keegan waited, but nothing sounded out of the ordinary downstairs. One of the cowboys had started singing "Lorena," and he sang real loud, and really out of tune. The saints are looking after me, Keegan thought. The noise had drowned out the sound of the waddie hitting the rug.

240

"Get dressed." Keegan ordered.

She didn't. She lunged at Keegan with her talons. Keegan jumped out of her way, and she fell on the bed. Then Keegan sat on her. She tried raising her hands, but couldn't get to them. Keegan had to move fast. He tossed his gun onto the bed, and found the bottle next to an ashtray on the side table. The cowboy's bandanna was next to his shirt, pants, and undergarments — the waddie hadn't bothered taking off his socks — and Keegan grabbed the polka-dotted kerchief and dumped some contents from the bottle onto it. Then he grabbed Wildcat Walesja's black hair, jerked it up, and held the wet bandanna under her nose.

She bit, snapped, snarled, but the laudanum eventually got to her. Her hands dropped. So did her head, and Keegan tossed the bottle and the neckerchief onto the bed.

Maudie was dead right about one thing. This little tigress was bony. Keegan did not know much about how a woman's duds went on, but prostitutes usually didn't wear much clothing. He got something silky over her first, then pulled over the dress. He opened a drawer and found something better — knee-high moccasins, and those he shoved into a pillow case, along with some other items that he didn't know where they went. After that, keeping the pillow case in his left hand, he threw Wildcat Walesja over his left shoulder, grabbed the Remington off the quilt, and moved for the door.

He sighed, turned around, holstered the Remington and returned to the bed, where he picked up the bottle of laudanum, shook it, nodded that there was enough left to be useful, and slid it into a front pocket on his trousers. He might need more of this narcotic. The Remington was drawn again from the holster, and this time Keegan made it out of the door, which he gently closed and then hurried to the stairs.

She was light as a feather, Wildcat Walesja, and the laudanum kept her cold. Keegan didn't know how long she would stay unconscious, and he knew he had to hurry. Bouncer Bob and Maudie weren't patient, and both knew Sean Keegan well enough and his reputation even better. They would be coming to investigate if he wasn't back in the parlor — what Maudie called "the getting to know you better, darlin' room" — soon.

Keegan's luck held. When he stepped into The Getting To Know You Better, Darlin' Room — Bouncer Bob was heading out.

The barrel off the .44 stopped the big

man, and he backed up a few steps.

"What the . . . !" Maudie was reaching underneath the bar the second she saw Keegan and his Army six-shooter. But Jed Breen saw the situation, too, and he dropped the untouched second glass of gut-turning champagne, which tipped over on the bar of engraved cherrywood imported from Liverpool, and palmed his Lightning.

"Leave whatever it is underneath the bar, Maudie," Breen said, cocking the revolver though, it being a self-cocker, he didn't have to. But the sound of any Colt's hammer clicking, Breen had learned in his many years of hunting bad desperadoes, had a stilling effect on some of the hardest customers. Maudie was one hard woman, but she also wasn't an idiot. Nor was she suicidal.

The hands came up empty, fingers spread, and they raised over her head. She even smiled, though her eyes told Breen that he would rue the day he drew down on her.

One of the cowboys, though, was drunk enough to palm his pistol.

The .44 slug from Keegan's Remington struck the holster, ricocheted with a deadly whine, and thudded into a chaise longue, as the cowboy cried out and raised his right hand toward the ceiling, trying to shake some feeling back into his fingers.

His pard's hands were already stretched for the tin-roofed ceiling.

The redhead and the Mexican stepped four or five safer feet away, but continued to sip their drinks.

Jed Breen still had no clue what his pardner was doing or why in hell he had a puny, half-dressed woman of the night hanging over his left shoulder. The girl's black hair fell all the way to the floor.

"Put Wildcat Walesja down!" Maudie roared. But, Breen noticed, her hands remained stretching skyward.

"Jed, me birthday boy, and me," Keegan said, bowing slightly, but keeping the .44 aimed in the general direction of Bouncer Bob and the two waddies. "We will be borrowing this lovely little lass on an important mission."

"You'll leave her here," Maudie barked. "I haven't got my money's worth out of her yet. I paid good hard Yankee dollars for her from Comanchero Jack, and I ain't yet turned a profit in the eighteen months she's been with me. Now you put her down, I say."

"Nay," Keegan said. "We need her."

"Take Bertha." Maudie yelled, motioning at the redhead.

The redhead told Maudie something that made Keegan's eyes widen in appreciation. She could curse with the best man, even a bullwhacker, that Keegan had ever gotten drunk with — and that was saying a lot.

"We'll be taking our leave," Keegan said. "And taking Wildcat Walesja with us. Now, if ye gents, and ye lovely lassies —" here he bowed ever so slightly toward the redhead and the Mexican — "will allow, just stay in here and sample Maudie's finest rotgut and don't dare try to follow us or peek out a window or step onto the front porch. And don't be even more foolish and try to follow us."

Maudie snorted. Bouncer Bob spit into the brass cuspidor.

"I'd pay ye," Keegan said. "But I don't dare reach into my pockets for a coin."

Frowning, Breen used his left hand and fished a couple of greenbacks from his trousers, and dropped those into the spilled champagne.

When Keegan began backing toward the curtain, Breen did the same, but both men stopped when Maudie laughed.

"I got a question for you, Irish?" she said, her hands still held high. "And you, too, Snowflake. How in hell do you think you can get Wildcat Walesja and yourselves onto your mounts and out of my front yard before Bouncer Bob, these two cowpunchers and me don't fill you — and Wildcat Walesja — with about a ton of lead?" She snorted, and spit. "You won't even be able to get her in a saddle before you're barking in hell."

Keegan grinned. "Maudie, Maudie, Maudie. You forget, lassie. I know you all too well. You sha'n't be coming after Jed and me. Because you don't want your lovely palace to be nothing but ashes."

The .44 in Keegan's right hand roared. The gas lamp on the far corner of the fancy-papered wall exploded, and orange flames, fueled by kerosene, leaped up the wallpaper, ignited a cushioned chair, and set the floor on fire.

"Put it out!" Maudie screamed. "Put it out!" She grabbed a bucket and tossed it toward the flames and smoke, but the bucket was filled with corn liquor, and that just fed the wicked flames.

The redhead ran through the door, but Bouncer Bob, the Mexican, and the two cowpokes joined Maudie as they slapped and kicked and beat at the flames.

Keegan, by then, had turned around and pushed through the curtain. Jed Breen quickly followed.

Outside they rushed down the steps. Keegan tossed the unconscious prostitute over the saddle of one of the cowboy's horses, grabbed the reins, and found the stirrups of his stolen horse. Breen moved to the reins of the two other horses belonging to Maudie's paying customers, loosened them. He started to fire a shot from the Lightning, thought better of it, and slapped the nearest mount's rump. Both animals likely could smell the smoke and sense the fire, so when the first horse took off at a lope, the second one followed.

"Hurry." Keegan said, but he didn't wait. He spurred his horse, pulling the gelding carrying Wildcat Walesja behind him.

Jed Breen leaped into the saddle of his purloined pony and followed.

They stopped four hundred yards from the brothel, but just long enough for Breen to dismount, and tie Wildcat Walesja's hands and feet together underneath the cowpony's belly so she wouldn't fall off as they rode hard for Mexico.

Keegan twisted in his saddle and looked back at Maudie's place. He could see the flames, leaping out from one of the windows. "Damn," he said softly. "I hope to bloody hell those cowpokes aren't so drunk they can't put out that little accident."

"Accident." Breen tested the knot.

He wasn't sure the Irishman had heard.

"I'd hate to wear out me welcome at Maudie's." He glanced down at Breen. "Do ye think she'll hold till morning?"

"She won't be out that long," Breen said. "She's already coming to." He stood, and also looked at the flames. "It doesn't look too bad, now," he said softly. "But it'll take a while before they've got it all under control."

"Good. We'll ride hard for an hour. Then check on our scout."

"Scout?" Breen said, and looked down at the moaning little lady of the night — if one dared use the word *lady*.

"She's all I could think of, laddie." Keegan took a sip of water from his canteen, then lowered it. "Best ride. Mexico's still a ways off, and we ain't the only ones riding after Matt and your twenty thousand dollars."

Breen pointed at the dying flames. "They might be joining us."

"Nah." Keegan wiped his lips. "Maudie will be busy fixing up her Getting To Know You Better, Darling Room, and those cowpokes will have an embarrassing walk back to their ranch. By the time anyone there has thoughts about coming after us, we'll be

248

across the Río Grande."

"With a price on our heads as horse thieves."

"Won't be the first time. We'll straighten it all out — even with Maudie — when we get back."

"If we get back."

Keegan was already nudging his horse into a walk.

"I hope to hell you know what you're doing," Breen said as he swung back into the saddle.

"So do I, Jed," Keegan called out gleefully. "So do I."

Both men spurred their mounts and thundered into the blackness.

CHAPTER NINETEEN

Major Block Frazer lowered the binoculars and rubbed the beard that made his face itch.

"Major, suh," Billy Ray Ferguson said behind him.

"What is it?" Frazer brought the spyglass back up and scanned the ridge that rose behind the camp down below.

"I thought the alcalde said we was to meet Santiago Vasquez," Ferguson said.

"We are, boy," Frazer said as he scanned the country for men, women, smoke, dust, anything.

"The alcalde didn't say nothin' 'bout us killin' more bean-eaters, suh."

The binoculars dropped, and Major Block Frazer rolled over, looking up into the sunlight that turned Billy Ray Ferguson into some shaded figure. Frazer couldn't read the boy's face, but the tone of Frazer's Alabama accent had told the major all he needed to know.

"You questionin' my judgment, boy?" Frazer grinned. Once, back when they rode with Forrest, all of Block Frazer's legion would have ridden into Hell or Yankee Gatling guns if their gallant major merely suggested such a thing.

"No, suh," Ferguson said. "I'm just sayin' that we's a long ways from the Dead River, suh, and that I don't trust that scalphuntin' greaser Santiago Vasquez."

Frazer sat up, let the binoculars hang from his neck, and held out both hands. Ferguson grabbed those and pulled Frazer to his feet.

"You've never met Santiago Vasquez," Frazer said as he dusted off his uniform.

"No, suh. Don't reckon I care to, neither, suh. But I'd sure hate to think if he didn't wait on us, and he taken his bunch into Three Dogs's camp, and it was him, that stinkin', no-good Mexican butcher, that got all the praise and glory and gold from them brown-skinned muckety mucks in Mexico City — and not you, suh."

Frazer laughed. "You don't have to worry about that, Billy Ray," he said. "Santiago Vasquez is not in command of the glorious Río Sangrieto Rurales. He commands brigands, not future brigadiers. And he doesn't

251

have the guts to go into the camp of Three Dogs without us to back his play. That's why he asked Blanco, that gutless wonder, to send us to help."

Billy Ray Ferguson nodded. "Yes, suh, I reckon you knows what's right and all, but I just don't trust any greaser, and I trust Vasquez even less." He nodded at the camp of Mexicans below. "But, still, suh, I don't know that us Río Sangrieto Rurales ought to be messin' with them folks down yonder. Ain't hardly worth the effort."

"Don't think we need the practice, is it?" Frazer grinned.

"It ain't that, suh," Ferguson said. He waved his hand in a dismissive gesture. "But that group — wouldn't even be practice. Just tire out our hosses a mite and burn precious powder and lead that we might need when we're at that Dead River." He wiped his nose. "Suh," he added.

But Major Block Frazer wasn't looking at the Alabama trooper anymore. He was staring across the mesa top they were on, at the Río Sangrieto Rurales dust from the west, the dust that moved like a string of mounted horsemen that soon spread into a wider column.

Billy Ray Ferguson saw the change of expression in his commander's face and spun around, his right hand dropping for his holstered revolver. Frazer brought up the binoculars again.

"Major Frazer, suh!" That cry came out from Joseph "Oaxaca Joe" William Henderson III.

"I see them." Frazer replied.

"They could be chargin', suh," Oaxaca Joe said.

"No." Frazer looked above the binoculars. "That would be suicide — for them." He lifted the binoculars. "But be ready just in case. Every fourth man holds the reins to the mounts. All the others be ready to fire."

"Aye, aye," Henderson called out and began issuing orders to the white Rurales.

He found the guidon in the spyglass, brought it into better focus, and frowned, then spit. It was a black flag, dove-tailed, with a scarlet cross painted on the silk. Not the Battle Jack of the Army of the Confederacy, but not the flag of Rurales — real Rurales, either — but it was a battle guidon known across this part of Mexico.

"Billy Ray," Frazer said, as he removed his binoculars and began walking toward his horse, calmly, assured now of who was riding to meet him.

"Suh?" Billy Ray Ferguson hurried to catch up with his commander.

"You want to meet Santiago Vasquez, boy?"

"Not especially, suh," Ferguson answered.

"Well, son, you're about to."

"Hombres," Santiago Vasquez said joyfully as he reined in his high-stepping white stallion, and removed the fringed sombrero from his sweaty, dusty face. He spoke rapidly in Spanish to the fifteen men with him. No, Frazer noticed, two of Vasquez's scalphunters were women, dark-eyed with bandoliers crisscrossing their chests. Their breasts revealed their true sex, but their dark eyes burned with the hatred that filled the eyes of their male companions.

The man carrying the guidon of Vasquez's scalphunters wore a white kepi, or what had once been white but now was stained with years of dust, a green tunic buttoned from his belly to his upturned collar with large brass buttons, gray pants with a red stripe down the sides, tucked inside fine riding boots of black, and short brass spurs. Vasquez's uniform was even sharper, higher boots that came well past his knees, blue britches, and a fancy coat of red, trimmed in white and green with epaulets. He wore gloves. Probably taken off a dead soldier during the days of Maximilian, but Vasquez

254

had doctored his uniform by adding medals. Scalp locks hung from both breasts and others dangled from both shoulders.

One rider wore a ceremonial halberd, but most dressed in white linen or the ragged clothes of ruffians. They were well-armed, and every man and even the two women had knives sheathed on their hips.

A musket's hammer clicked, and Frazer looked away from Vasquez and called out. "Mister Henderson."

"Suh!"

"Have your men stand at ease." He looked back at the Mexican scalphunter. "We have visitors. Guests. Amigos."

Vasquez bowed with mock graciousness.

But then he stood in his stirrups, staring at the encampment below, and sat down, twisted in his saddle, and barked more Spanish. A man rode up to the edge of the mesa, brought up his own pair of binoculars, and took in the scene below, crying out in rushed words that made Major Frazer's ears burn.

"Bueno," Vasquez said, and the rider lowered the cheap binoculars — not the nice Yankee ones Frazer had taken off a dead brigadier at Brice's Crossroads — and returned to the line of Mexicans.

Vasquez issued another order, then dismounted. The Mexicans began tightening their cinches, but Santiago Vasquez left his reins dangling in the dust as he walked to Frazer. A peon went to the fine stallion and worked on his commander's saddle.

Vasquez gestured at the valley. "That, Señor Frazer, appears to be a camp of a peaceful party of my people. Does it not look that way to you?"

"That's the report I got, Vasquez." Frazer wet his dried lips.

"Sí," Vasquez said softly. "Sí, sí, sí, sí. It would be a tragedy, would it not, if such peons, traveling with nothing but goodness in their hearts, traveling in peace for the village market to have been mistaken for an armed camp of . . . *insurrectos* . . . and slaughtered. Is that not so, amigo?"

"I reckon so."

Vasquez laughed. "It would be even worse if such men and women of peace were mistaken for Apaches?" He shook his head, and slapped his sombrero on his pants leg. "Or Comanches."

"It would be a damned shame," Frazer said.

"Sí." Vasquez returned his big hat to his small head. One of the two women walked over and handed Vasquez her canteen.

"Gracias," he said, and drank, smacked

256

his lips, and handed the canteen to the woman, nodded, and the woman held the canteen toward Frazer.

"For you, señor." Frazer did not look at the woman.

"No thanks." The canteen was not lowered. Frazer said: "Water's precious here. And we just stopped to drink. Rest our mounts. Save it. You'll need it before we get to the Dead River."

Vasquez laughed again. "We will need water after we reach the Dead River, mi amigo, for el Río Muerto is dry. It is always dry. That is why we call it dead." He laughed again. "Drink."

"No thanks."

"Drink, amigo. I insist. Besides. It is not water. It is better than water. It is tequila. The finest in the land."

Frazer looked at the canteen, which the woman still had.

"I drank water myself." Vasquez laughed. "It is not poison." He barked in Spanish, and the woman, her cold eyes not moving from Frazer's face, raised the canteen and took a long swallow herself, then once again held the canteen steadily for Frazer to take.

"And surely," Vasquez said, "I would not have my lovely Adelina drink anything but the best."

Sighing, Frazer took the canteen, held it toward Vasquez in a toast that did not hide his mockery, and took a sip. He returned the canteen to the woman, who spun, nodded at Vasquez, and returned to her horse.

"Bueno," Vasquez said. *"Muy bueno."*

"It ain't Kentucky bourbon," Frazer said.

Vasquez grinned, but his eyes turned a shade darker, yet only for a moment. Again he looked at the camp below.

"I say ten men, twelve?" Vasquez said softly.

"Ten," Frazer said. "Two of them are women."

The commander's head nodded.

"I thought we were to meet you at the Dead River," Frazer said. "What brought you here?"

"Women!" Vasquez slapped his thigh. "Cantinas." He ran his red wool sleeve over his long mustache and thin lips. "And we did not wish for you and your soldiers to get lost in the desert. We thought we would celebrate, turn in our scalps for the bounty, and then ride to the camp of the murdering Apache of Three Dogs together. For we are partners, is that not so?"

"I reckon."

Vasquez kept focusing on the camp in the valley.

"How far is it to the Dead River?"

Vasquez did not answer. "Ten men. Two women. But one of the men's hair is silver." He shook his head and crossed himself. "A pity."

"Did you collect your bounties for the bunch of Apaches you did kill?" Frazer asked.

"No." Vasquez drew a nickel-plated revolver from a holster, opened the loading gate, and spun the cylinder on his forearm, checking the rounds. "The village of Camila is north of here. When one of my scouts saw your dust, I guessed it would be you. No one rides atop this mesa unless he is in a hurry." He pointed to the valley. "That is why they ride below. It is cooler. Out of the sun. And no one would be in a hurry, it struck me, to be anywhere in this month at this time of day, except Major Block Frazer and the Río Sangrieto Rurales of legend, fame, and *mucho* glory."

Each drop of sweat made Frazer angrier, but he stood there, ever the Alabama gentleman, waiting for this damned rude guest to get to the point.

"One of them is but a boy." Vasquez shook his head, then laughed. "And one —" Now he pointed, lifted his head upward and laughed heartily. "One . . . just . . ." He could not control his laughter, and turned and yelled at one of his men in Spanish, then, still chuckling looked back at Block Frazer. "One he removed his sombrero to wipe his face and head . . . and he is bald. Bald. We hardly ever see a bald Mexican. It is far too funny."

"Maybe he got scalped," Frazer said.

Which made Vasquez laugh even harder, but the cackling ended, and the scalphunter's face hardened. "Twelve. Minus three. Nine scalps are hardly worth the effort, or the powder, or the lead. Is that not true?"

"Especially when they are not Apaches," Frazer said.

"Yes." Vasquez's head bobbed. "That is why you stopped here, of all places, to rest your horses and drink your water. You did not even notice the poor peons below. You did not even think that you could pass the scalps of poor Mexican people as those of Apaches. You are good hombre. *Muy bueno.*" He called out in Spanish, and a dirty scalphunter, a peon, a mere boy, brought the high-stepping horse to his commander.

Vasquez swung into the fancy saddle without even noticing the boy, who raced back to climb onto his pinto pony. Again, the killer yelled in Spanish, then looked down at Block Frazer.

"To seal our partnership, amigo, this is my gift to you. My men, my two women, and I will kill and scalp those worthless peons below. We will take anything of value — mostly food and water — and we will burn their corpses so no one will ever know what happened here. And the nine scalps we will turn in to the alcalde at Camila. The bounty will hardly buy us a good dinner and good wine, but it is better than nothing. For you and your Rurales, it will be as though you are in the fanciest opera house in . . . oh, Vicksburg . . . that is a *norteamericano* villa, is it not? Watching from the balcony. Enjoy the show, amigo. Watch and see how we work."

It was over quickly. Looking down at the slaughter, Major Block Frazer and most of his command remained silent. From what Frazer could see through the dust and gunsmoke, the travelers were not even armed — at least with firearms. One was shot down trying to use a bullwhip against the charging force of evil, evil men. One raised a spade. Most of them were running when the scalphunters rode over them to save their gunpowder and lead.

Then, the butchery began. Bodies were scalped, then dumped into the biggest of the wagons.

It was one thing, Major Block Frazer thought, for the Río Sangrieto Rurales to murder Mexicans, take their scalps, desecrate their bodies, and turn in the good scalps — the ones that could pass for Indian hair — and collect bounties. Frazer's Rurales were white men, Southerners, not Mexicans. This . . . this . . . this was sickening. Mexicans killing Mexicans. For nothing more than money for liquor and grub, and maybe a woman or two.

Smoke now rose from the burning wagon, but the wind blew from the west, and the scent of burning human flesh would not reach the Río Sangrieto Rurales from their . . . what was it Vasquez had called it? Ah, yes, the balcony of a Vicksburg opera house.

Block Frazer wanted to spit, but his mouth was as dry as the mesa top on which he stood.

Below, Santiago Vasquez wheeled his magnificent stallion, held what had to be a scalp up toward the mesa, and yelled something in Spanish that the wind muffled and Frazer wouldn't have been able to translate even if he had heard the words spoken clearly.

Vasquez spurred his stallion and his men

and women and the boy followed. They pulled the burros and mules behind them, laden with supplies they might need for the journey to the Dead River. They found the switchback that would take them back to the mesa top.

Back to Major Frazer and the Río Sangrieto Rurales.

Frazer turned from the scene of butchery below, and swung into the saddle. "Let's ride," he ordered. "We'll head for that village, Camila."

"What about Vasquez?" someone asked.

"He'll catch up or find us there." Frazer waited till his command was mounted.

He looked at Joseph William Henderson III at his side.

"Well?" Frazer said.

Oaxaca Joe shook his head.

"I asked for your opinion, mister."

Now the Alabaman spit into the sand, wiped his lips, and said. "Well, suh, we can't always pick the men we fight with, Major. And I'll be hogtied and damned if I ever thought I'd be sayin' this, suh, but . . ." He turned his head to spit one more time, then wiped his lips with his sleeve, and let his Southern eyes burn into the major's face. "But, suh, I'd rather ride with a bunch of damned Yankees than be caught dead with them."

264

CHAPTER TWENTY

They had their horses at a slow walk when the eastern skies began turning gray instead of ink black. Matt McCulloch called out to Blood Moon, "Stop." The Apache obeyed and twisted in the saddle. Matt rested the Winchester on his thigh and tilted his head toward the west.

"There's a water hole that way."

The Apache straightened as if insulted. "I not need water."

"Horses do," McCulloch said. "And I bet you'd drink, too, even if you ain't human."

Blood Moon turned to look to the west, but did not kick his horse into a walk. McCulloch thought the renegade was testing the white man to see what he would do, how he could force the Indian to obey. Instead, Blood Moon looked back at McCulloch and asked, "How do you know this water hole?"

McCulloch shifted in the saddle and felt a weary grin crack his face. "You chase mustangs, you learn where most water holes are. Especially in this country."

The Apache did the damnedest thing. He uttered what McCulloch had to take as a grunt of stunned respect.

"I thought no White Eye knew of that watering place," Blood Moon said, his voice almost a whisper.

McCulloch almost chuckled. "Hell," he said, "I'm more mustang than white man anyway." He nodded again in the general direction of the watering hole. "Don't worry. As far as I know, I'm the only white man who knows where that water is." He pointed the rifle barrel toward the southwest. "It's —"

But the Indian was shaking his head. It was light enough now for McCulloch to make that much out.

"One does now," Blood Moon said. "And he will be coming after you . . . and me . . . and the bloody money you *Tejano* dogs put on my head."

McCulloch whispered Jed Breen's name.

"Yes," Blood Moon said, and explained. "The white baby needed water. So did your friend. And the mule we rode."

"So you took them there." McCulloch's head shook. "You could have outlasted them. You left the damned kid out in the

266

sun to die. Breen thought, but he can't go without water as long as you could. Why didn't you just let them die, as much as you hate white people."

The Apache did not look at McCulloch as he answered. "Your friend would not die before I would. He would have put a hole the size of the mule in my belly before he crossed to the other side."

McCulloch felt his head moving up and down. "Yeah." He shoved the Winchester in the scabbard, but moved his right hand toward the holstered Colt. "I reckon he would have at that."

Now he considered the situation in silence. Breen would follow, probably with Keegan. If they could get out of jail, and as well as McCulloch knew those two men, they were likely well on their way south by now. So would a posse or several posses from Purgatory City, and before long, surrounding settlements. Twenty thousand dollars could bring out even town loafers and saloon rats, probably even a struggling businessman or two. The Army from Fort Spalding wouldn't sit still either. Before long, this part of Texas would be crawling with Indian haters, bounty hunters, cowboys, ne'er-do-wells, lawmen and plenty of jaspers just eager to do something to break the damned monotony of living in this hard land.

"All right," McCulloch said, and slowly slid from the saddle. Drawing the Colt, he waved the weapon so that the Apache knew he was to dismount, too.

"There's another watering hole four miles southwest."

"More mud than water," Blood Moon said.

"We can dig it out. Well, you'll dig it out."

"It is a place known to Mexicans and your own people."

"But they won't go there unless they're thirsty," McCulloch said. "Because they don't want to drink mud."

The Apache nodded again. "Yes, you are not a White Eye at all."

"We're gonna do a little finagling." Again, he used the Colt as a finger. "There are rawhide socks in the saddlebag. You'll put them on the two riding horses. I'll put some on the gray. He's tuckered out enough not to want to fight or run. That'll make the tracks harder to follow. Two socks on each hoof. To make it even more difficult."

The Apache nodded again.

"And to make it even more confusing, we'll switch horses. I ride yours. You ride mine. But you still pull the stallion."

Now something that might have passed for a grin appeared on the Indian's face as the sun began to appear over the wasteland.

"Don't worry," McCulloch said, and tapped the stock of the Winchester with the barrel of his Colt. "Yeah, your mount might be faster than mine, but he's also really tired. And it's daylight. I can see pretty well. And you ask any man, white, Mexican or Indian, and they'll tell you that I won't miss with a Winchester when it's sunny."

He pulled his blanket bedroll from behind the saddle. "And I'll use this to wipe out most of the signs we've made here. Then we ride to Muddy Water Spring. We'll rest there all day."

Blood Moon grunted.

"That's the way we do things for the next few days. We ride at night. Rest in the heat."

"It is dangerous."

McCulloch let his head bob. "Yeah, but no Indian scout, nobody at all, can see rising dust when it's dark."

"You are almost Apache."

The white man's eyes hardened. "Don't ever call me that."

Even after Blood Moon used his hands to dig out the mud, the water at Muddy Water Spring hardly looked fitting for a man to drink. The three horses didn't mind, and McCulloch used two bandannas from his saddlebags to filter out much of the filth as he strained water into one canteen. He splashed more of the water, of a reddish-brown tint, over his face and head. With the sun where it was now, even the water felt hot, and no wind blew to cool him off.

Even the seconds crept along like hours. McCulloch longed for a cup of coffee, hot coffee, even in this furnace, but did not build a fire. There was hardly enough scrub in this hellish environment to get a fire going long enough to light a cigarette, and McCulloch didn't want to risk anyone seeing smoke, either.

He could see the dust, especially from his perch on a slab of rock so that he could look down on Blood Moon, who sat in the sun, utterly oblivious to the burning heat and stinking mud.

"Three trails," Blood Moon said without raising his head.

McCulloch nodded in reply. He wasn't going to waste his breath with words. Plumes of dust rose in the distance, but one McCulloch guessed had to be coming from the stagecoach heading from Purgatory City to El Paso. That's where it would be if it were running on schedule, and the new operator demanded that all drivers kept right on schedule. The other two spots just told McCulloch where idiots rode south. The smart men, the real posses, the men that posed the biggest threat to McCulloch and Blood Moon would not be riding hard enough to kick up dust that could be seen from McCulloch's perch. As hot as it was, they would be riding slowly, trying to find tracks or horse apples, something that would tell them they were on the right trail.

But the men looking for McCulloch and the Apache would not just be coming from the north. Telegraph wires likely had been singing all night and most of this morning, so that meant Army patrols and lawmen would be patrolling the river that separated Texas from Mexico.

It would take some doing to get across the border. And then? Rurales. Mexican bandits. Scalphunters. Maybe even some Comanches following the Great War Trail.

Damn it all to hell, McCulloch thought, *I really want some coffee.* He was tired, and sweat burned his eyes, yet that pleased him. It kept him from growing even wearier, or falling asleep. Coffee could wait. It would have to wait. Besides, he knew coffee and sleep were nothing. He wanted his daughter even more.

"Hombre, do not move."

The words came from behind McCulloch, just as a pebble rolled down the incline past the mustanger.

McCulloch did not move. The accent was heavily Spanish, and now a chuckle followed. Rapid Spanish followed, and McCulloch saw another man, wearing a beaded sugarloaf sombrero and the Mexican-style pants with conchos and studs down the legs. The man aimed a sawed-off shotgun at Blood Moon, who did not appear to even notice him. The Apache could have been asleep.

"Amigo," the Mexican behind McCulloch said. "Your quick-shooting rifle, *por favor.* Pleeeze. Let it slide down this rock just a little. So you do not use it on Juan." He let out a gleeful laugh. "Or me."

McCulloch had been holding the rifle all this time, butted against the hot stone he sat on. His thumb moved to the hammer, and his finger tightened against the trigger, as the bandit said. "Do not make me shoot you, amigo. Not yet, anyway."

"I just don't want this .44-40 to go off by accident," McCulloch said, adding "amigo" at the end, but spitting out that word.

"Bueno, bueno, bueno," the bandit said and cackled again. Once the hammer was lowered, McCulloch laid the rifle at his side, then shoved it slightly. It slid maybe ten feet past him, stopping just at the edge where the slab entered.

"You listen *muy* good," the bandit said. "Now listen to this *muy* good and you will live a short while longer. The revolver in your holster. Do the same. Draw it — no, no, no, señor, let me finish. Draw it with your left hand, *por favor.* Using only your thumb and forefinger. The other fingers, they need to be extended as if you were showing me how clean your nails are before you eat your tortilla. *Bueno. Muy bueno.* I like how you follow my directions, amigo."

The heavy Colt rested on the stone.

"Let it slide, hombre. To join its friend the fast-shooting repeating gun below."

The bandit with the fancy britches stood in front of Blood Moon, who still did not look up. In fact, the Indian hardly even breathed. The bandit said something in rapid Spanish that McCulloch thought translated as, *I believe this blankethead is dead.*

The man behind McCulloch answered in Spanish, and the man holding his scatter-gun at Blood Moon laughed.

"Amigo," the bandit behind McCulloch said. "*Por favor,* one more request, señor.

273

Stand up. And slowly turn around. I like to be looking into the eyes of the man I kill. *Por favor.* I do not wish to shoot you in your back, amigo."

McCulloch let out a weary sigh. He turned, ever so slowly at first, and then shot the bearded bandit in the belly with the .32-caliber Manhattan he had stuck inside his waistband.

The man screamed in agony, dropping an old Dragoon .44, and clutched at his belly. McCulloch turned to chance a shot at the one wearing the fancy britches, but saw that Blood Moon had moved at lightning speed. The best McCulloch could figure was that the Apache had thrown a rock that he clutched in his good hand, and that had caught the bandit's jaw as he turned upon hearing the soft report of McCulloch's hideaway gun. The bandit had dropped the shotgun, and was clutching his bleeding hand, when Blood Moon tackled him from behind, driving him into the muddy spring. Now the Apache held the man's head under the hot, dirty water.

McCulloch spun around. The Mexican lay on his back, still clutching his stomach, groaning pitifully. Leveling the Manhattan, McCulloch reconsidered, lowered the hammer, and slid the .32 into his pocket. He doubted if anyone from the road had heard the report of his weapon, but he didn't want to risk firing another shot. Shoving the Manhattan into his trousers pocket, he hurried up the hill the few yards.

The gut-shot thief and killer let one hand fall to the belted knife at his side. The other hand clutched the bloody hole in his stomach. The bearded man had the knife up and was raising it when McCulloch reached him.

That made everything a whole lot easier. McCulloch used both hands to grab the dying killer's arm. His right foot kicked the man in the groin.

"Aiyyeeee," the man said in the whisper of a dying man, and then McCulloch used his weight and muscle to drive the knife in the bandit's hand straight into his chest.

Turning before the death rattle in the bandit's throat escaped, McCulloch drew the .32, and let his feet and momentum carry him to the side of the rock.

"Hold it!"

Blood Moon looked up. He was reaching down for the scattergun. The other bandit had been dragged just far enough from the muddy spring so that he wouldn't pollute what passed for water.

The Apache looked up, then straightened.

"You work fast," Blood Moon said.

"You do, too."

The Indian bowed as if he liked the compliment. Then he turned and stared at the dust.

"Your shot might have been heard," he said, still scanning the country.

"Maybe. Probably not," McCulloch said. "But we can't risk it. We'll move out of here. Horses have had enough to drink. We'll spend the rest of the day in some shade."

First, they had to tidy things up. The shotgun McCulloch stuck in his saddlebags. It might come in handy. The knife pulled from the dead man's chest, he tossed into the dirt, along with his pathetic Mexican copy of a Colt.

They found the two horses hobbled in a draw about three hundred yards southwest, brought the animals back, let them drink the muddy water. McCulloch took the canteens, and a pouch of beef jerky. Then he had Blood Moon tie the dead men to the saddles. After that, he slapped the rumps of both mounts. The horses took off running southeast.

"There's a chance a posse will follow the buzzards who follow the horses," McCulloch said. "One less problem we'll have to deal with. We'll find shade southwest of here."

Again, Blood Moon said: "You are not *almost* Apache. You *are* Apache."

"I've warned you once. Call me that again," McCulloch said. "And I'll cut out your tongue."

CHAPTER TWENTY-ONE

"Your leg hurts, White Eye."

Ignoring Blood Moon's comment, McCulloch limped as he carried the saddle from the picket line, and laid it on the ground to dry. The way the sun blazed, it wouldn't take long to dry the saddle or the blanket. Then he favored his left leg and he headed back to the horses to rub them down.

"Bullet wound?"

McCulloch grunted. He didn't know what made the damned Apache so talkative, but the weary Ranger decided to answer. "Horse fall." Which happened in a gunfight, but he didn't want to engage the Indian in conversation.

"Ahh."

The Apache found a spot in the sun, sat down, Indian style, legs folded in a way Matt McCulloch could never twist his even before horse wrecks and gun battles had taken their toll. McCulloch wiped his forehead, ran fingers through his soaking hair, and then ambled toward the rocks. He dipped his hand in the tepid water, held it under his nose, then drank.

The horses drank from the spring, but McCulloch found fresher water in the rocks, which collected rainwater. Not much. But a thunderhead must have rolled through here — this was the season for storms that blew in quickly, dumped water into the desert, then blew out just as fast. The spring here usually held some water, but finding water in the rocks was always a gamble. He splashed more water on his face, then grabbed the canteens he had taken from the two dead bandits.

He pitched one to Blood Moon, and opened the second for himself. Smelled it. Took a swallow, then brought it to the dip in the rocks. It wasn't deep enough to submerge the canteen, so McCulloch used his bandanna, let the piece of fabric soak up the water, then he squeezed it while holding it in a ball over the canteen's opening. He waited for that damned Indian to tell him again he was doing something only an Apache would do. Which was a damned lie. Any man with any brains would have done the same thing. They would cross the

Río Grande if not tonight then tomorrow night, and could fill canteens when they reached the border. But a smart man — even a damned fool — would know that any time you found water in this country, you made sure you drank your fill and filled your canteens.

But Blood Moon kept his trap shut.

Which pleased McCulloch just fine.

Canteen filled, he tied the bandanna around his neck, letting the wetness cool him more. They were in a rocky place in an arroyo, a good place to hide but far from a good site to scout the country. And it would be damned easy to get caught in an ambush, so McCulloch took the saddlebags with the scattergun, his Winchester and his sidearms with him when he climbed up the embankment and sat on the edge. He wasn't going to leave any weapon that the Apache could get to first. No wind blew up here, and the view didn't offer much. He saw no dust, but as still as this place had become, he had not expected to see much of anything.

Below, the gray snorted, and McCulloch looked back quickly, bringing the Winchester up to his shoulder. Blood Moon still sat, cross-legged, staring at nothing, a statue of copper stone. The gray stallion had rammed its forefeet into the spring, splashing water, causing the other two horses to snort, and step back. The horse neighed, shook its head, and rammed its feet into the water again, spraying the roan. The gelding snorted. The pinto backed away. The stallion reared and seemingly laughed. The Apache did not care.

And for a moment — McCulloch blamed the sun and his mostly empty belly — the former Ranger did not see horses playing in the water, but Cynthia and her brothers.

Just after the War. He had just made it home, traveling mostly by foot after the Surrender. Just after the War? How long had it taken him to walk all the way from Virginia to Texas? That had been his luck. He had joined the infantry, marched to the train station, marched to battle after battle, just walked and walked and walked across pretty much the entire southern United States. Marched till his socks wore out, marched till his brogans wore out, marched until his feet wore out. Then walked up to sign his paper and take the oath to the Union and marched, walked, and sometimes even crawled all the way from Virginia back to Texas, home, sweet home.

Well . . . Cynthia would have been, what, six years old? Seven? Hell, now McCulloch couldn't even remember her birthday.

They were down in the Hill Country, in the pretty but rocky little stream. Cynthia splashed in the water, laughing with girlish glee as her brothers ducked. Matt Junior even screeched, "Stop blindin' me." She just kept splashing.

"Is itgood to be home?" McCulloch's wife asked. She handed him a chicken leg, and he took it and brought it to his mouth, and then looked at the warm drumstick, fried crispy, and he had to think how many years had gone by since he had eaten chicken. Too long. He almost cried staring at the meat in his hand, smelling the grease, when most of what he had been eating for the past few years had been cornmeal soaked in water, or raw corn, sometimes even rats.

"It's good," he said at last but did not want to bite into the chicken. Wanted to just savor it. He felt his wife's arm come over his shoulder.

"It is good to have you home," she said.

Her hand squeezed his shoulder.

Their children laughed and splashed and screamed.

And he made himself eat the drumstick, savoring every bite, then gnawing on the bone for any remnants like some half-starved dog. The water from the stream slaked his thirst, and still the children played. Like ducks. Maybe even fish.

He thought that if he could just spend the rest of his life in this moment, right here, with no one around for a mile or two, that would suit him right down to the ground.

But he had this dream in the back of his head. A dream for something different. He wanted something new, something for himself. And he dropped the chicken bone onto the blanket upon which he and his wife sat, and he turned and said to her:

"I've been thinking. About . . . about . . . moving."

"Moving, my husband?" she said.

His head bobbed. "West."

"California?"

He laughed. "Not that far west. Not even out of Texas. I hear there are wild horses, plenty of mustangs, that can be rounded up. I can catch them. Break them. Train them. Sell them."

"Who would you sell them to?"

"Express men. Livery stables. Ranchers. Beef is becoming a big business, I hear, and ranchers have been driving cattle to Missouri, and there's talk that they'll be finding new markets in Kansas. They need horses for those drives. Lots of horses. And ranchers have to give their cowhands something to ride."

He smiled. "If there's one thing I missed — other than you and the kids — it was horses. I must have been drunk joining the Texas infantry instead of a horse regiment."

She smiled. "You are a *caballero.*" And she kissed his forehead. "What about the Indians? Are they not many farther west?"

"I reckon they are," he said. "And that means I'd have another market to sell the horses I catch. Army posts are sprouting up all over the place. I just read in the *Gazette* and *Texas Banner* that the Yankees just approved a new post going up somewhere east and north of El Paso called Spelling or Spawning — Spalding."

"You would sell horses to the Yankees?"

He smiled. "War's over. And Yankees pay in gold, I hear, not state script."

The children splashed and a moment later, Cynthia was crying. Matt Junior had splashed too much water into her face, and his brother had sneaked up from behind and dunked her head. The blonde hair lashed out as she tossed her head back and forth, wailing, spitting out water, angry as a hooked bass.

McCulloch had to wade into the stream in his new boots, and the boys cowered, but he just told them, "Not so rough, boys.

Remember she's your sister, a girl." He held her against his shoulder. "It's all right, Cynthia. They were just playing."

"I want to go home, Papa!" she cried.

"We're going home in a jiffy. You can eat some chicken and dry off." He gave his sons the stern look, then waded back to shore and handed the soaking little tigress to her mother.

"Fact is, we might be finding us a new home," McCulloch said.

His wife nodded.

"I want to go to our new home, Papa," Cynthia said.

"We will directly. It'll be the best home you ever had. I promise."

What would have happened, he often wondered, if he hadn't been so damned determined to catch horses, to uproot his family, to try to start a new life, a better life, in a lawless, vulgar, cruel part of the state that was filled with red-skinned butchers and white men just as cruel, just as violent, just as deadly?

He was sweating now, hard, his vision blurred, his eyes stinging so badly he couldn't see. McCulloch loosened the bandanna, which had briefly dried out but now was wet from perspiration. He mopped his face with the rag, then wiped his forehead and cheeks dry as best he could with his shirtsleeve.

It hurt to swallow. He made himself drink more water, and that burned the back of his mouth and all the way down until it exploded in his guts.

He slid down the embankment, worrying now. His lips felt dry, but his hands were clammy, and now, suddenly, without any control, he began to shiver. The horses shied away from him, and he paused, backed up, circled around them. They must have caught his scent, and something about the way he smelled must have made the animals fearful.

Well, he tried to tell himself, *as bad as you stink right about now, you'd scare a wolf dog off a wagon filled with buffalo guts.*

The Apache had not moved. McCulloch looked at the water hole in the rocks. Rainwater did not turn bad. It might not taste good all the time, but this spring was known for having good water. That couldn't be the cause of how weak he felt, the dizziness, the roaring in his belly. Besides.

Again he tried to swallow but couldn't. He brought up the canteen again, drank, but most of the water spilled down his shirtfront, though some trickled through

286

some passage in his swollen throat.

He stared at the murdering Apache butcher, but didn't see him. He saw . . .

"I don't . . . want . . . to . . . die . . . Papa." Cynthia struggled just to say those six words, words that came out as a mere whisper. She tugged at the binding over her throat, the one that stank to high heaven, but McCulloch reached over, took her hand, and pulled it away.

"It . . . smells . . ." she said.

He kept her tiny, cold hand in his big, burly one, and raised a finger on the other hand to his lip and asked her to stay quiet.

"It's good for you," he told her.

Tears streamed down her cheeks, breaking McCulloch's heart, and she again pleaded for her brave papa not to let her die.

"You're gonna be fine, Cynthia," he told her. "Just fine. If you leave that wrapping over your throat. It's just your tonsils. The old sawbones said there's nothing to worry about. It'll pass, the swelling will go down, and you'll be back in school in no time. Terrorizing your brothers, too."

"Promise," she whispered. "Promise you won't let me die."

"You won't die, darling. Trust me. I'll never let you die — as long as I'm alive."

■ ■ ■ ■

The scene changed, but it took a while before he could see through the sweat — or were tears blinding him. It took even longer before the world around him stopped spinning.

Cynthia was gone.

Blood Moon's eyes had opened.

"What is the matter, White Eye?"

It sounded like Cynthia. And that scared Matt McCulloch, a man who had never known fear, not even at Sharpsburg or Gettysburg or waving the white flag tied to his musket when he led what remained of the boys up to the line of bluecoats, surrendering after four miserably bitter years.

"I ask are you sick, White Eye?"

Better. That sounded like Blood Moon. The words, though, came as though they had been spoken over in La Mesilla in New Mexico Territory, not ten or twenty yards away from him.

"Hell, no," McCulloch made himself say — or at least, he thought he had spoken those words. "Get up. It's time we rode out. It's dusk already."

He began backing up a few feet, then paused until the ground stopped spinning and until Blood Moon came into a sharper focus.

"Get up, I say."

"The sun will not sink for another three of what you White Eyes call . . . *a horas* . . . hours."

"That's a damned lie. Get up. Or I'll plug you where you sit."

He couldn't see him now. The damned sweat was blinding him, and for a man who kept sweating like a sieve, he tried to figure out why he felt so cold.

Then, his vision cleared, and he stared up into the face of the pinto gelding. He frowned. Above the pinto's ears, he saw the pale, hot, burning sky.

"Damn," he tried to whisper. He had fallen onto his back. He balled his fingers, relaxed them, tried to push himself to a seated position. When his hands and arms failed him, he dragged the right hand to his holster. Swallowing again, though that hurt like blazes and accomplished nothing else but making him gag, he finally felt the burning of the hot backstrap of the Colt. His fingers reached around the walnut grip, and he tugged.

Tugged.

Tugged again.

The damn revolver felt heavier than a

railroad tie. The Colt would not budge one inch. Someone — perhaps that sneaking, conniving, murdering buck of an Apache — had glued the pistol in the leather.

So he looked for the saddlebags. The shotgun. That would do the job. He'd blow the Apache to Kingdom Come. But the scattergun . . . the saddlebags . . . where had he left them.

And his Winchester? He could not find it.

The Manhattan. He was patting his belly for the hideaway pistol. At least he thought he was, but when the shadow crossed his face, offering a refreshing coolness, he realized his hands remained on the hot ground. The horse above him snorted.

The man standing above him grunted.

Then Blood Moon lowered himself onto the ground, and his right hand reached toward Matt McCulloch's throat. The last thing McCulloch felt was the hand on his windpipe.

After that, the cruel world of the Texas desert turned completely black.

CHAPTER TWENTY-TWO

Wildcat Walesja did not move at all when Jed Breen cut loose the bindings underneath the horse's belly, lifted her off the saddle — she weighed lighter than a quail's feather — and laid her on the sand by the water hole. After riding most of the night, and into the day, Breen feared the woman might be dead.

Well, he soon learned, she was far from barking in hell, but she barked. She barked and cussed and then the hard bone in the bottom of her right foot slammed into the bounty hunter's left shin just above his boot top. After that, for the next ten or fifteen seconds, it was Jed Breen who was barking and cussing, only he had to keep hopping as he did some circular dance.

"Stop that racket," Sean Keegan barked, "before you scare off our horses, ye bloody idiots."

Breen had to hop around a few more seconds before he dared test his leg to see if

291

it would support his weight.

When he was standing, still for the moment, and his breath had resumed to something slightly more natural, Wildcat Walesja was sitting up, and still screaming.

"You gringo pigs. You Irish moon-calf. You white-headed freak of nature. You think you can take me in the night, have your way with me without paying the gringo dollar. You think you can have your pleasure, but the pleasure will be mine, you stinking, sniveling cowards. For it will pleasure me greatly to cut off your *pelotas,* your *cojones.* I will slice off your manhood, Irish dog, and feed it to the pigs. And you, you white-haired fool, you I will take great pleasure in making you suffer."

"This wasn't my idea," Breen said. "Hell, I still don't even know what that Irish dog was thinking."

Keegan opened his mouth as if to solve that mystery, but the prostitute from Maudie's kept right on cussing, and every few words, saying something both men could understand.

"That is why you will suffer. Because you did nothing. You let the Irish dog take me away. I rode at a gallop or hard trot on my belly, when I can ride better than either of you fools. So, yes, you will die. And when you die, you will be thankful that you are dead, but death . . . death . . . welcomed death will be so long in coming, you will be blubbering worse than the fool assistant teller at the Purgatory City bank when he shows up at Maudie's."

"Are you done?" Keegan asked.

"She damned near broke my leg," Breen fired back.

"I'm not talking to you, Jed. I'm talking to this Yaqui"

She spit at him. Then she spit again, picked up a handful of sand, and hurled it at Keegan, but the wind blew it into Breen's face, causing him to duck and curse and swear savagely.

"Listen . . ." Keegan was lucky to get that much out.

"You piece of slime. That's right, I am Yaqui. Yes, Yaqui. Some pigs — though they did not stink as much as you two stink — captured me when they raided our camp three years ago. They sold me to Maudie. Hell, you fiends and dogs and demons, I was better off when those renegade Mexicans took me, when they did what they wanted, but they fed me better, and did not charge me for the liquor I drank. Maudie. She does. Half of what I earn for whoever I entertain, and just fifty percent off whatever she charges you real men for the liquor she waters down."

"Will you shut the hell up?" Keegan barked.

"Why should I? After I was nothing more than a saddlebag or bedroll on a hard ride."

"Because I got a proposition."

"Which is better than a proposal, I presume! Proposition?" She spit.

The horses snorted, then moved to the spring to drink.

Breen hopped over to them to make sure they went no farther than the water.

The Yaqui kidnapped out of Maudie's place kept right on ranting.

"How many propositions have I had since I was taken from my people? You gringos think of . . . I believe the word is . . . dee-vee-ant. The cost is extra, but proposition me, you rat. Propose to me. I bet it is nothing I have not been asked to do before. And likely is nothing that I have never done before — in my two and a half long years working for that —"

"Enough!" Keegan's shout had Breen urgently grabbing a rein to the most frightened horse, and it also caused Wildcat Walesja to stop. She probably needed to catch her breath anyway, Breen figured.

"I figured that it takes an Apache to trail

an Apache," Keegan said.

"Have you not listened to me? Are you deaf? Or are you just a dumb Irish pig? I am not Apache. I am Yaqui."

"I heard you, woman," the old cavalry trooper barked back. "But the way it is, I figure, you're close enough. I figure a Yaqui is just as good as tracking an Apache as an Apache is."

"Have you lost your bloody mind?" It was Breen who spoke.

"No," Keegan barked. "I ain't sunstroke or nothing like it. She's Yaqui, and I bet she can figure out where the Apaches are hiding out. That's gotta be where Blood Moon is heading."

"Blood Moon." Wildcat Walesja tested the name. And she tested it in a soft, almost feminine voice.

"You know him, I take it," Keegan said.

She didn't answer, at least, not verbally, but her head nodded ever so slightly.

Keegan wiped sweat from his brow. He let out a sigh of relief.

"Do you know where he'd be headed for?" Breen heard himself ask.

"I have been away from my people for three years," Wildcat Walesja said. "And Apaches, like most smart Indians, move their camps."

"We just need a general direction, place where . . . you . . . could pick up the trail."

"They will change horses," she said.

"Not one of them," Breen said. "Maybe not any of them. They're good horses."

"McCulloch horses," Keegan said with a nod.

A slight breeze picked up, but didn't last very long. It was too hot, Breen figured, for the wind to blow.

Wildcat Walesja snapped her fingers and held out her hand. *"Agua,"* she demanded. "Water."

Finding a canteen on the nearest saddle, Breen brought the container over to her, keeping a respectful distance from Wildcat Walesja's feet, then tossed it to the Yaqui woman.

She drank, not much, hardly even what Breen would call a swallow, before closing the cap tightly. After placing the canteen at her side, her eyes bore into Keegan.

"I will hear your proposition now, you Irish piece of rancid meat."

Keegan cleared his throat. "You help us find Blood Moon. You lead us to him. Jed and me . . . we'll do the rest."

She snorted. "The rest? Meaning you will get yourselves killed."

"That's a possibility, but if you've been at

Maudie's place for three years, you've been around long enough to learn that Jed Breen and Sean Keegan don't die all that easy."

She began looking at the fingernails on her right hand. "Go on," she said.

"There's a reward of twenty thousand dollars — American dollars, too — for the capture, dead or alive, of Blood Moon. All we want is Blood Moon –"

"And to get Matt back," Breen put in.

"And to get Matt back. Matt McCulloch. He's our pard."

"A jackal."

"You ain't far from being a jackal yourself, gal," Keegan said.

Breen swore he thought Wildcat Walesja smiled then, but it was fleeting, and, most likely, nothing more than a mirage.

Wildcat Walesja studied the fingernails on her other hand.

"Continue, stupid mick."

"We get Blood Moon. Dead or alive. We get our pard McCulloch out of whatever hell he's gotten himself into. We collect the bounty. And you get a quarter of that reward."

"Now," Breen interjected, "just wait a damned minute, Sean. I brought Blood Moon in myself and . . ."

"What is a quarter of that reward?" Wildcat Walesja asked.

Keegan frowned. He brought up both hands, began counting fingers, but did not finish one hand before he had turned and stared pleadingly at the bounty hunter with the stark white hair.

"Five thousand dollars," Breen said with a sigh.

"You heard the man," Keegan said. "Five thousand bucks. That'd take you a damned long time to earn at Maudie's, even if she give you a raise and let you drink whiskey for free."

The Yaqui soiled dove picked up the canteen, had another drink, and wiped her lips with her arm.

"I need clothes," she said. "Something I can ride a horse in. Seated in the saddle. Not riding with my guts on the leather."

"I packed a pillowcase with some of your items," Keegan said, and hurried to his horse.

The woman sniffed the air, then studied the countryside. "Where are we?" she asked. "Exactly."

That let out a rough curse from Breen's lips. "Hell's bells," he said after the first blast of profanity. "Some scout and guide she's gonna make for us, Sean. She doesn't even know where we are."

"That is because this is not my country. That white hair must be because you are old. Your brain is turning into mush. You belong on a rocking chair, or in a casket six feet under Texas dirt." Then she kicked Texas dirt in Breen's direction. "We are in Texas, fool. I had never seen this part of hell until the Mexicans brought me here. But on the other side of the river." And she pointed south. "That is the country of my people. The Yaqui. I know every inch of it. And I know where the Apaches always go when they wish to camp in the land on the other side of that river. So keep your mouth closed, Old One, and you will, perhaps, live to collect the quarter of the reward that Blood Moon's head will bring you."

"Three-quarters," Breen said.

"Half," Keegan corrected.

Breen turned, cursed softly, and shook his head.

"Perhaps none," Wildcat Walesja said. She was pointed at the rising dust.

There were three of them. That was the good news. Just three. The Comanche warriors came into view as their ponies climbed out of the depression. A hundred yards away. Breen heard their yips and Indian war songs as he pulled closer to the saddle, drew the Sharps from the scabbard.

But that's as far as he got.

"Damn it!" Breen dropped the rein to the horse he had been holding, and reached for the reins to the mount that was shying away, about to run. Keegan was turning, dropping to his left knee and drawing his revolver.

There were times when a man could think, Breen knew, and there were times when thinking would get a body killed. That's when a smart man, a savvy Westerner knew not to think, but to react.

Wildcat Walesja was running toward him, so Breen threw her the Sharps.

Quickly, he was turning as an arrow whipped over his head. He snagged the reins to the horse Keegan had stolen for Wildcat Walesja, put it in the hand that held the reins to Keegan's mount. His left had reached down and just managed to get a firm hold on the reins of his stolen horse. The leather burned his palm as the gelding tried to run. Breen fell into the muddy water on his knees. Another arrow smacked, and one of the horses kicked out, jerking Breen down onto his back. But he would not loosen his grip on the reins.

If the braves killed him, that would be one thing. But Breen knew he could not lose their horses. Being afoot? In this country.

That could kill a man a lot slower that a Comanche would.

The Sharps roared. Breen saw a horse somersault, throwing the Comanche with the buffalo headdress hard into the ground. The horse didn't get up. The warrior might have, but Wildcat Walesja ran over to him and began bashing in the man's skull with the stock of Breen's heavy rifle.

She was smart, Wildcat Walesja. Breen knew that. Most people would have tried to shoot the rider, but she killed the horse.

Breen was dragged deeper into water, then into the shallows. He blinked out water and saw another horse go down. Keegan rose then, thumbed back the hammer of his Remington. What looked like a spear flew between the Irishman's legs. The .44 Keegan held barked, and the Comanche somersaulted over the pony's back. Keegan leaped out of the way as the riderless pony thundered past him, and after that Breen couldn't see anything, for the horses were dragging him after the runaway mount. Yet Breen had a firm grip on those reins, no matter how hard the horses pulled, and no matter how deep the reins burned into his palms, he refused to let go.

At least the horses weren't running. Too bloated from the water he thought, and he saw the patch of prickly pear coming right at him.

He closed his eyes. Then the horses stopped.

"Easy boys, easy boys, easy now. Don't ye worry ye bloody heads off. It's over now, gents. Rest easy. Rest easy."

Breen lifted his head. Keegan stood in front of the horses, and he reached down and took reins.

The bounty hunter rolled over, stared at the welts on his palms — wished he had thought to have pulled on gloves — but remembered that Wildcat Walesja had shot another Indian's horse. She hadn't hit the brave riding it.

Sensing danger, Breen drew the Lightning .38, grimacing at the burning in his right hand, and he made himself stand. He stepped away from the horses, but stopped.

His breath slowed just slightly, though his stomach twisted. The spirit of that third Comanche was already in the happy hunting ground, not that he would be too happy.

Wildcat Walesja stood over his body, hammering his face into a pulp with the stock of Breen's Sharps.

It would take some cleaning, Breen thought, to get that weapon clean again.

Gingerly, he dropped the Lightning back

into the holster, and moved to help Keegan hold the horses.

A strange noise came from Wildcat Walesja. Breen turned. The woman had stopped crushing the Indian's face, and held the Sharps over her head, dancing around the corpse.

"What's she doing?" Breen asked.

"By my guessing, it be her victory song," Keegan said.

The Irishman looked at Breen.

"How's them hands feel, me boy?" he asked.

The woman kept singing. "Right now," Breen said, "better than my belly does."

CHAPTER TWENTY-THREE

The soulless black eyes of Satan himself stared down at him, and Matt McCulloch readied himself for the first pains of hell.

Instead, Lucifer asked, "How White Eye feel?"

McCulloch frowned, raised his head slightly off whatever his head rested against — most likely a sandstone rock, since all around him he saw the rugged, dry hell that he knew had to be either Hell itself — or the Big Bend of West Texas.

"Hell," he said at last, but not an answer, and not a location, just an oath he had been pretty good at using since before he found himself in the Confederate infantry . . . breaking mustangs he had captured . . . serving in the Texas Rangers . . . and on and on and on. "Why didn't you kill me when you had your chance?"

The Indian knelt, put the back of his good hand on McCulloch's forehead and nodded. "Not no more. You live. Maybe. For a while."

"You didn't answer my question."

Blood Moon's head shook. "I hear you smart man. But you talk like fool. Why would Blood Moon bring you to see daughter, to take daughter from her Apache family?"

McCulloch tried to sit up, but that wasn't happening any time in the foreseeable future. Sighing, he let his head rest back, gently, on the hard stone. "Her family isn't Apache." The words came out in a low whisper. Then he groaned. His eyes closed.

When they opened an eternity later, the Apache's savage face again greeted him, and the scenery was different. He was in the shade of green-branched trees, and water rippled by. He could figure out where he was this time, too, and it wasn't — at least from where the sun was sinking — in Texas. The water he heard running was north of him.

"Mexico."

Blood Moon nodded.

McCulloch managed to sit up this time, and he turned and spit out whatever moisture he could bring to his mouth, which felt as dried out as a failed sodbuster's well. The Indian's good hand reached out, holding

305

something.

"Chew root," the Apache ordered.

McCulloch found it, felt it, sniffed it. He thought how much he would rather have some apple-cured chewing tobacco brought in by stagecoach from Virginia. But the root went into his mouth, and moisture, blessed spit, began reducing the size of his tongue.

The Indian disappeared, returned a few minutes later, and held out a canteen.

McCulloch hesitated, then asked, "How come the bad water at the spring didn't make you sick?"

The canteen did not budge, and Blood Moon did not seem inclined to answer, so the former Ranger took the canteen, pulled out the stopper, and drank.

"Not much," Blood Moon ordered. "Stomach not ready yet."

For an Indian, he was a damned good doctor. McCulloch turned to his left and vomited.

"Good," the Apache said when McCulloch was wiping his mouth with a filthy shirt sleeve. "Clean out inside. Make better."

"I don't feel much better," McCulloch said, but he knew he was lying. The retching had been like medicine to his gut and bowels. He slid himself into a sitting position, braced his back against a tree, and wiped his mouth with his hand. He turned, spit, and again faced the Indian.

"Your stomach cast iron? That how you weren't poisoned at the well."

For a moment, Blood Moon appeared to smile. But that had to be a mirage, a product of the bad water still playing with his mind, his vision, and his entire body. The Apache's head shook, and he squatted next to McCulloch, picking up the canteen, securing the cap, and folding his arms across his chest. "Water at spring good," he said. "Water in dead man's canteen not good."

He had consumed water from both of the springs — the one where they had been attacked by the two Mexican bandidos, and the one where the boulders and lava held rainwater. But McCulloch had also used water from one of the bandits' canteens. That's what had damned near sent him to the bowels of hell.

Suddenly, Blood Moon laughed. He pointed at McCulloch, and then tapped his chest. "You. Me. We do Mexicans favor. At least, one of them." He shrugged, as though considering. "Maybe both. They die quickly. No suffer. We no kill them, one, maybe both, die throwing up blood and the lining of his stomach." His head bobbed up and down. "Good thing. We work good . . .

together. Mexican thank us."

That had to be the longest speech McCulloch had ever heard not only from Blood Moon, but any Apache Indian he had talked to.

"You could have killed me," McCulloch said.

"Many times." Now the Apache smiled. "Even before friend you have, with snow hair and big, far-shooting long gun, bring me in."

"Lucky he caught you."

The Indian's head shook. "Good luck? No. Bad luck?" The head moved up, then down. "Blood Moon ride to find Mac-Cul-Lock."

He was gone, though, before he could explain, and McCulloch figured he damned sure didn't have enough strength to go chasing after that renegade butcher. He had another root to chew, and he sat up, feeling cool for the first time in days. His bum leg didn't hurt too bad, and he tried to reach into his memories to figure out how Blood Moon had managed to get him across the hell that was Texas, into the Big Bend, and then across the Río Grande into Mexico. He tried, but his memories had blocked out whatever hell McCulloch had endured.

He rubbed the scrub of beard that itched

his face. Not that long, he could tell by the length of the stubble. And he remembered something that scout, Three-Toed Charley, had told McCulloch one time when riding with the Texas Rangers. "Never underestimate an Apache buck. Or an Apache squaw. Even when they's dead, don't underestimate 'em. They ain't human. That's what makes 'em tough to kill."

When Blood Moon returned, he held a hollowed out gourd that contained a steaming liquid. McCulloch didn't know how the Apache had managed to brew up something warm for he smelled no smoke, saw no smoke, but the gourd was indeed hot, and the tan liquid it held smelled like. . . .

"Tea?" he asked.

The Indian shrugged. "Medicine. Taste good." He turned and spit. "For White Eye, taste good. Apache."

"I guess it ain't tiswin," McCulloch said, blew over the makeshift cup, and took a taste. Over the gourd he could see a faint trace of a smile on the brave's face.

The tea made McCulloch's stomach stop growling. It was some type of drug, McCulloch figured, that diminished the hunger and the sickness in his gut, and made him feel somewhat stronger. Hell, another cup of this liquor, he thought, and he might feel like forking a saddle.

When he was finished, Blood Moon took the gourd and tossed it over brush and rocks. It splashed.

"We're that close to the river?" McCulloch asked.

The Apache nodded.

"We should go," McCulloch said, then looked at the Indian. "How far?"

"Seven suns. Eight. Hard ride."

"I can ride."

"We wait."

McCulloch's eyes closed, though he did not feel tired, and when they opened, he knew he had slept without dreams. Birds sang in the trees, the Río Grande rippled, and it was morning.

This time, he made himself stand, and gingerly, using tree branches and boulders for support, made his way from the camp. He saw the horses, picketed Apache style, and they snorted and considered McCulloch briefly, before he disappeared and found a place to relieve his bladder and bowels. It took him longer to inch his way back to his sickbed. As soon as he sat, the Apache brave came back and handed him another makeshift cup of tea.

"Is my daughter your wife?" How he had found the courage to ask that question, Mc-

310

Culloch could not figure out. Hell, he did not even know why he had asked the butcher of scores of Texas settlers — and more Mexicans, and settlers in New Mexico and Arizona territories. Or other Indians. But there it was. The question was out there, and McCulloch steeled himself for the answer.

"White Eye fool," Blood Moon said. He shook his head, then dipped it and spit between his knees. "What Blood Moon want with puny white girl with sick eyes and hair no black, not even dark? Blood Moon say white women not even worth . . . how you say . . . *raping*?"

"And scalping?" McCulloch asked bitterly.

"Mac-Cul-Lock know better. Apaches no take scalp."

McCulloch knew the truth of that statement.

"I want to know why the hell you're taking me to see her?" A sudden fear seized him. "Is she . . . sick?"

"Not when last seen. *¿Quién sabe?* Not know. Not now. You learn when get there."

McCulloch drank the tea. "Well," he said, just to say something, maybe to get some kind of response from the Apache. "You're a good medicine man. I ought to thank you for saving my life."

311

The Indian's good hand reached and jerked the gourd away, which he turned and smashed against a rock. When he looked back into McCulloch's eyes, the face was masked with rage, and the eyes blacker than coal.

"Blood Moon no holy man. Only medicine Blood Moon practice is death." He spit and the good hand clenched tightly into a fist that shook. "Once. Once. Yes. Blood Moon practice healing. Helping. Once Blood Moon speak, and Apaches listen. Once. But no more. No more. Blood Moon great holy man. Long ago. No more. No more."

He frowned. A long silence filled the miles between McCulloch and this Apache warrior, driven by hate.

"So Blood Moon give up medicine. And I kill. Kill and kill and kill." He raised his bad hand. "Do you know who give this to me?"

"Texans?" It was a guess.

"The people of Blood Moon," the Apache said. "The chief you call Three Dogs."

A sickness came to the people of Blood Moon's village. At the time, the best McCulloch could make out from the Apache's pidgin English, sometimes blended with the Spanish of the Texas–Mexico border, Blood Moon was known as Healer. Just plain

Healer. Like his father, a holy man of the Apache village. And Blood Moon had healed. Till the white men, or the Mexicans, or someone brought in the sickness. The sickness that rotted faces. The spotted death.

Smallpox.

McCulloch had seen cases of that across Texas, but smallpox didn't ravage white men the way it did Indian nations. Comanches, Kiowas, and even tribes no longer in existence, had been almost wiped out by the disease. The deadly, fast-spreading killer called smallpox. It swept through the village where Three Dogs and Blood Moon lived. It killed many. Killed them while Blood Moon's father was gone to another camp, to help that village's holy man deal with a sickness. Others were horribly disfigured. But that spotted death that rotted the faces and figures of many Apaches did not turn Healer into Blood Moon. No, that came from Three Dogs, who blamed the village medicine man for the deaths of his family, and the horrible way they had died.

Three Dogs attacked Blood Moon, and in the struggle, put the holy man's hand over the hot coals. The flesh burned. And burned. And afterward — because other warriors pulled the enraged Three Dogs off Healer's body — the medicine man tried to

313

heal his ruined hand and arm.

"But my medicine," Blood Moon said, raising his disfigured arm. "Was gone."

"But you rode with Three Dogs when he became chief," McCulloch pointed out. "You rode with him for a long time."

The head did its one-bob nod. "We found a reason to fight."

McCulloch understood. The two feuding Indians found a common enemy in the Mexicans and the settlers and soldiers of the United States.

"The *Tejanos,*" Blood Moon said. He stopped, and spit at McCulloch's boots. "Killed my sons."

He turned to walk away, but that statement caused McCulloch's hands to clench, and he could not hold back the words.

"The Apaches," McCulloch said. "Killed mine."

The former holy man, now a murdering butcher on two sides of the river that flowed just yards from McCulloch, returned an hour later. But this time he held horses.

"Three Dogs is now a woman," he said. "He wants to fight no more. So he drove Blood Moon from village."

Now McCulloch understood. Apaches weren't that much different than white men, either. Some perceived slight. Some insult. Disrespect. The bruised ego or whatever callous remark, and no apology, or just a building up of years of anger and resentment. And Blood Moon wanted revenge.

"My daughter is Three Dogs's wife?" McCulloch said.

"No. But soon. Girl's husband dead now."

"How did he die?"

"Scalphunters killed him," Blood Moon said. "But only because I left him to die." The killer grinned. "Killer of Cougars was favorite son to Three Dogs."

The Indian, the former medicine man of an Apache who had saved Matt McCulloch's life, was mad. Stark raving mad. But he was the only person who could bring McCulloch to his precious Cynthia, the daughter he had thought dead for years now.

"We go."

Matt McCulloch pushed himself to his feet. He found his hat. The Apache disappeared for a moment, then returned, and tossed the gun belt to the former Ranger. McCulloch caught it, and then buckled it around his waist.

"I pull gray behind me," the Indian said. "Like old times. Long gun in leather pouch." He gestured to the scabbard, and McCulloch spotted the stock of the Winchester on his pinto.

The Apache said: "Like old times."

McCulloch tightened the hat on his head and eased toward his horse.

"Ride hard," Blood Moon said as he climbed into the saddle on his horse.

"We'll walk them first, let them get used to us. Been a while since they've ridden hard, and —" His head tilted at the gray mustang stallion. "We don't want to spook him."

McCulloch had figured he'd trade the gray for his daughter, but now he realized Blood Moon probably wanted to kill Three Dogs, and maybe kill Cynthia, too. He might just want McCulloch to take the white girl away from the Apache chief, thinking that would bring pain and embarrassment and probably a great deal of disrespect. But McCulloch had lived long enough to know that a smart man never trusted anyone driven crazy with rage.

"No," Blood Moon said. "We ride. And we ride hard." He pointed his good hand across the river. "Bluecoats come."

"They can't cross the Río Grande," McCulloch said.

The Indian's head shook. "You bet golden-hair daughter's life on that? You bet chance to get puny white girl back to your

316

own people?"

McCulloch found the reins. The Indian kicked his gelding and took off at a walk, but only until the brush and rocks had been cleared. Then he pushed the animals into a gallop.

The pinto galloped after them, and Matt McCulloch gave the gelding plenty of rein.

He did not look over his shoulder at the Army patrol as it neared the river.

CHAPTER TWENTY-FOUR

Second Lieutenant Charles Tibbetts, Eighth United States Cavalry, ground his teeth, clenched his fist, and tried not to lose his temper. His butt hurt, and so did his thighs. The McClellan saddles issued by the Army quartermaster were not fit for riding, and he had been riding a damned long time. On hot days like this one, he wished he had used his Uncle McCaslin's influence to hold out for an artillery assignment, but Rister Tibbetts, that arrogant father who knew everything, told him that soldiers accept their assignments, and orders, without question. Which might have been worth something had Rister Tibbetts actually served in the Army during the Rebellion instead of following the troops from New Hampshire to Virginia as a sutler.

His horse urinated for the second time since they had stopped. That was the proverbial straw that broke the camel's back.

"How long are we just going to sit here, Three Toes?" The venom in his voice caused his horse to turn its head slightly and stare. Damned piece of glue bait likely thought a cougar had jumped on its back.

The rugged, stinking, scout with dirty hair that hung knotted by the wind and likely had not felt soap or a brush in decades, kept breaking open horse apples, then sniffing his fingers and rubbing them together. He did not even look up.

Tibbetts's face flushed — and not because the sun was blasting him with the intensity of hell.

"Three-Toes."

The miserable cretin pitched the remnants of dung into the sand, did not even wipe his fingers, and stared off into the desert.

Tibbetts steamed, almost literally.

Then the wretched, stinking man spoke.

"Toed."

The young lieutenant stopped gnashing his teeth, and tilted his head. "What's that?"

"You got my name wrong, Tibbetts." The scout pushed his hat, which had been battered into some senseless shape and was so filthy one could not tell where the fur felt began and the dirt and stains ended. He studied the land to the southeast.

Tibbetts held his temper, waiting, and

when two minutes passed, and the scout had not spoken, he stood in the stirrups, and opened his mouth.

But the tramp said something first. "Three-Toed Charley's the name. Toed. Not Toes. I don't rightly recall how that handle got laid upon me, neither." He reached down and rubbed the scuffed toes of his Apache-style moccasins. "Last time I took a bath, I still had all ten of 'em." He rose, spit in the sand, and turned to face Tibbetts and the command. "Want to count 'em yourself?"

The troopers behind Tibbetts chuckled, but that stopped when the lieutenant turned sharply and stared at them as hard as he could. Then, after sinking back into the saddle, he faced the scout again. "How long are we just going to sit here, Three-*Toed* Charley?" he said, emphasizing the body parts with icy sarcasm. Finding a handkerchief in his tunic, he mopped his face, and frowned when he looked at how filthy the piece of silk had become.

How long had they been riding in this barren blight of what some people would call land? He realized how reckless he had been, charging out of Purgatory City in the middle of the night, not thinking about provisions. They had been living off the land, but mostly on water, hardtack and beef jerky. Two days? Three? By now forts from all across West Texas, and likely into the southern part of New Mexico Territory, had patrols out. And that martinet of a commanding officer at Fort Spalding had undoubtedly sent word to Mexico. Twenty thousand dollars for Tibbetts's taking and here he was waiting for a bearded man in greasy buckskins to get his corncob pipe lighted as he kicked around the sand near the pile of horse droppings.

After the jackal named McCulloch and the most savage of all the Southwestern Indians had covered another mile or two, Three-Toed Charley withdrew the pipe from his mouth, pointed it southeast, and said: "They lit out that-away."

Tibbetts exhaled, and then drew in a deep breath. *Finally,* he thought.

But then the scout's pipe changed directions and started pointing southwest. "But they'll turn back in a few miles, and move to the west."

"How do you know?"

"I don't. We'll wait till Tiny comes back to make sure."

"Wait?" Tibbetts spit out the word. His heart pounded against his ribs. "Wait? Wait for that fat, slow tub of molasses and iron?"

Three-Toed Charley had sent Tiny Older-man, the worthless brute, into an arroyo thirty minutes ago. Maybe longer.

"Maybe," came a Southern voice behind Tibbetts, a voice the officer recognized as that of Trooper Anderson. "Maybe we ought to ride straight to the river, patrol it up and down till someone finds where they crossed."

The logic of that thought numbed Tibbetts. He cursed himself for not thinking of it himself, and then he cursed Trooper Anderson for not mentioning it until this moment, after countless miles, and agonizing saddle sores, on the trail, night and day.

"That'd be one way of doin' it," Three-Toed Charley said, then puffed on his pipe.

"Then, by God, why don't we do it?" Tibbetts roared so hard he had to grab the reins to keep his horse under control.

Three-Toed Charley smoked his pipe some more, then removed it and tapped the cob on the butt of his holstered Dragoon .44. Eventually, he turned the bowl over and dumped the contents into the sand, before slipping the pipe into a leather pouch that hung from a rawhide thong over his neck.

"Well." The scout stifled a yawn. "We're following three horses. One ain't shod. That one ain't carrying no man. Stallion. The one lots of folks been talkin' 'bout. All three are mustangs. McCulloch hosses, no doubt. There's a twist in the shoe on the right forefoot of one of them saddle mounts. And the other's got a particular gait, kinda left-leanin'. Trail's right easy to read. That's why I sent Olderman yonder way. Y'all might be payin' me too much money for this job." He laughed, shook his head, and spit. "Damn. I could use a jug of mescal right 'bout now."

"If the trail's so damned easy to follow, why don't we just follow it and catch up with those sons of bitches?" Tibbetts barked. "Or do what Trooper Anderson suggested. Ride to the Río Grande and patrol it till we see where they crossed. Hell, I bet a lot of men, bounty hunters, are already doing that."

"And," Three-Toed Charley said quickly, "wearin' out their mounts for nothin'."

Tibbetts started to snap, but, in one of the rare occasions, held his tongue.

"What," the scout said as though he were talking to a schoolhouse filled with young boys and girls, "if they change hosses? Or what if they ain't goin' to Mexico? Just makin' us think they's headin' that-away afore they turn 'round and light out for . . ." He shrugged. "New Mexico Territory? Ride up no'th to see Blood Moon's Jicarilla kinfolk? Or jes turn west and cross over the border down south of Las Cruces? The way I hear things, 'em Apaches under Three Dogs has been hidin' in the Sierra Madres — 'em Ox-si-dent'l ones. That's farther west."

The clopping of hooves caused everyone to look toward the arroyo. Three-Toed Charley must have caught the whiff of Tiny Olderman — though how he could smell anything over his own filth was something Tibbetts could not fathom. The scout moved toward his horse, but kept talking. " 'Course, I figger that stallion they'd keep, so that's the only track I really need to foller, but, hell, a hoss like that could break away from 'em ol' boys. So best way I know to catch 'em mangy dawgs is to follow the trail. That's what I do. I follow the trail." He swung into the saddle. "I don't guess. Might take us a whilst longer, but . . . I ain't so green I'd try to guess what an Apache's doin'."

"It's not an Apache you're following," Tibbetts barked. "It's the Ranger . . . McCulloch. He's the one who's responsible for all this."

Massive, bruised, sweating, panting Tiny Olderman rode his big horse out of the arroyo, reined to a stop, and wiped his face.

"Well," Three-Toed Charley said.

A big thumb hooked toward the southeast. "Turned west. Before the rocky country."

"What I expected," Three-Toed Charley said and then looked at Tibbetts. "Figured some greenhorns would head into the rocks. Good way to cripple hosses and men." He looked back at the ugly Olderman. "How far did you follow the tracks east?"

A big thumb pointed. "Till they turned south. Easier to come up here, ride that way. We can pick up the trail there."

Three-Toed Charley found his canteen, took enough water to gargle and spit out, then wiped his mouth. "You ain't as dumb as I thought, Tiny." He corked the canteen and then faced the lieutenant. "Can't say that 'bout ever'-body." Grabbing the reins, he turned his horse and rode off a few yards, but quickly stopped, and twisted in the saddle.

"Oh, there's somethin' you might oughta know, Lieutenant. That Ranger . . . he ain't in charge no more. Not for a while, I mean. Maybe permanent."

Tibbetts frowned.

"The big Apache's got him belly down over a hoss. I imagine he's still alive, though. Apaches are scared to death of dead folks."

He chuckled. "Funny, ain't it. Murderin', torturin', savage as they come, but they won't even hardly touch a dead body except to put it under the sod. So, like I said. I ain't gonna try to guess what some Apache is thinkin'. We'll follow the trail. See what happens."

He turned back, kicked the horse, and rode into the endless country.

The holy man of the Apache village, Yo-íí, entered the wickiup of Litsog, and grunted. The white woman with the yellow hair, now cropped closely to her scalp, barely hanging over her ears, looked up from where she sat stitching a deerskin dress with sinew.

"You will go home," Yo-íí said gruffly. His face showed a frown. But his eyes told her something disturbed him.

She chose her words carefully. All these years with Three Dogs, all these years after beatings and worse, until the people had finally accepted her, with some reservations, she knew her place. She knew that life in an Apache village for a girl from Texas was tenuous on the best of days.

"I am home," she said.

The old man's head shook slightly. "No. This is the home we made for you, that you made for yourself. But the days of the

Apaches are ending. This I have seen. And I have seen you . . . and you will go home. To the place of your own kind."

Her stomach churned. The fear she could taste on her tongue. Home? She dared not think of that, because she remembered the flames of her home. She remembered her mother's screams before the Apaches ended her suffering. She remembered the bodies of her brothers. And she could not forget the countless nightmares when she would awaken in the dead of the night, in a cold sweat, screaming, "Papa! Papa! Where are you?"

Which would cause Killer of Cougars to grab her by her blonde hair, jerk her onto the bear robe, and put both hands over her throat until she could not breathe. "Speak the tongue of your husband, woman!" the warrior would snap. "And be quiet. Never scream in the night. Screams can bring our enemies to our camp. Screams can bring death to our people. And I can bring death to you."

She realized she was rubbing her throat.

"This is . . . home . . . to me . . . now." She did not know how she ever managed to say those words.

Yo-íí shook his powerful head.

"This home will be no more." He raised

his hand. "You will not speak of this to anyone, not even Three Dogs. I tell you because the Spirit told me that you must know this. The village is no longer safe."

She gasped. "You must tell Three-"

"No!" Yo-íí's face made Litsog hang her head in shame, and fear.

"I must stay silent. That was in my vision, too." When Litsog raised her head, she saw tears disappearing into the heavy, deep wrinkles of the holy man's old face. "But I do not know if I can not speak of what I know. And that is why I am leaving the village."

"Leaving?" Litsog said.

The old man let his head move once down, and then up. "Yes. I am an old man. I have not many moons left to live. Therefore, I must go. Do not worry, child. I have had a good life, but all lives must end. My time is coming. So I go."

He swallowed. "We . . . the Apaches . . . are all dead."

"Dead?" Litsog trembled.

"We are dead," the holy man said. "Dead but we do not yet know it. And you will go home."

"I cannot . . ."

"You will go home, child. The spirit has ordained it. You will go home. But here is what I do not know, for I could not see."

She waited.

"When you are carried home — for this I saw . . . you were in the arms of a great beast. The beast that will carry you home. But I do not know, Litsog, if when you leave here for home." He swallowed, and his voice dropped to a whisper. "I cannot say if you will be alive . . . or dead."

Yo-íí turned and left without another word, or another tear.

The country was cooler here, this close to the river, shaded by the mountains of the Big Bend of the Río Grande. Cooler, Lieutenant Charles Tibbetts thought, but no less deadly.

Three-Toed Charley's horse splashed across the river from the Mexican side, and he reined up. "They camped over yonder." His filthy arm and even dirtier fingers pointed to a shady patch of boulders and scrub on the Mexican side. "Rode out. Not too long ago."

"We can catch 'em!" Trooper Anderson shouted with eagerness and greed.

The scout shook his head. "That's Mexico, boys. And even if we could cross the border, we ain't catchin' 'em no time soon. Their hosses are well rested. Ours be tuckered out. And the Ranger . . . he's still alive. Riding upright now. You won't find a better rider in Texas than McCulloch. Or a man who can get more out of a rangy little mustang."

Lieutenant Charles Tibbetts had found his Rubicon. "Who says we can't cross the river?" he asked, and smiled when he heard his own words.

It was the big brute, Tiny Olderman, who answered. "That hoss soldier ridin' up might be the one, suh."

Twisting in the saddle, Tibbetts spotted a blue-coated soldier in campaign hat riding hard on the United States side of the river from the west. When the face was recognizable, Tibbetts knew the rider was from Fort Spalding.

CHAPTER TWENTY-FIVE

The Army soldier reined in, and saluted. "Lieutenant Tibbetts, sir," he said sharply. "Corporal Grant from Troop B." He was already reaching inside his tunic and withdrawing the orders from the mealy-mouthed commander. "This is from —"

"Forget the formalities, soldier," Tibbetts barked. "Just tell me what the colonel says."

But the white envelope was already being extended. With great reluctance, Tibbetts took it, but did not open it.

"The colonel instructs you to follow Blood Moon and McCulloch and apprehend if possible, but on no condition are you and your men to leave the United States, sir." The soldier then relaxed, and wiped his face. "You boys were sure hard to find. I've been riding up and down this side of the river since yesterday morning."

Tibbetts let the orders fall to the ground. He wet his lips and saw the look on the faces of his men.

"Your orders never reached us, Corporal," Tibbetts said.

The trooper's face paled.

Tibbetts looked at his soldiers, and knew they wanted that reward. When he looked again into the corporal's eyes, he smiled.

"There's twenty thousand dollars in this for us, Corporal. And our scout here —" he nodded at Three-Toed Charley — "he says we can catch up with that money. They just rode out of here."

"Sir," the corporal said nervously, and pointed at the river. "That is Mexico, sir. And the colonel —"

"You can ride with us, Corporal," Tibbetts said. "Or you can ride back and tell the colonel that you did not find us before we crossed the river."

The young trooper's face changed. He seemed older, no longer tired, and like a man who would make sergeant before too long. If he lived. "Lieutenant, if you cross that river, you could risk starting another war with Mexico."

"Twenty . . . thousand . . . dollars." Tibbetts grinned. "It's within our reach, soldier. And the glory that comes to the men who bring in Blood Moon . . . dead."

The head shook. "I am a soldier, Lieutenant. And I have my orders." He pointed to the paper that Tibbetts's horse was now eating.

"Then just keep your mouth shut," Tibbetts said. "We'll pay you for that when we come back and collect the reward."

The trooper did not answer. He turned his horse, and put it into a trot as he rode toward the high walls of the Big Bend.

"Tiny." Tibbetts ordered.

The scout understood, slid the Henry .44 repeater from his scabbard. A moment later, the gun roared, the corporal fell to the ground, and the horse loped away.

"Make sure he's dead," Tibbetts ordered, and Tiny Olderman put his horse into a slow walk, levering another round into the repeater as he approached the unmoving body.

Tibbetts looked at his men, making eye contact with all fifteen riders. He did not look at Three-Toed Charley, but the scout was being well paid, and, most likely, he wouldn't put up a fight. He might be a Southerner, but he had fought his last Lost Cause. And . . . well . . . even twenty thousand bucks split eighteen ways went quite a far piece.

The men were game. Tibbetts grinned, turned his horse, and rode into the Río

Grande.

"Here's for a brevet," he said happily.

He did not hear Three-Toed Charley's addition: "Or a coffin."

"Did you hear that?" Breen reined in his horse, turned in the saddle, and looked northeast.

"Hold up there, Injun!" Sean Keegan called out, stopping his horse, but not turning around toward Breen until that ninety-nine pounds of Yaqui nitroglycerine stopped her horse, and spit in the dirt.

"Rifle shot," Keegan said.

"Not a Sharps," Breen said.

"Well, Jed, there ain't that many of them big guns down this way. Buffalo don't get into Mexico, is my way of thinking." He sniffed, looked again at Wildcat Walesja, and said. "Light gun. Carbine. Winchester or something like it."

"Matt's?"

Keegan shook his head, but wasn't convincing himself, or Breen. There was another report, but this one was different, muffled.

"No." That was enough to convince Keegan. "That be a make-certain shot. Put on a body's head. Hell, even as far away as we are, even I can hear that good enough. And

334

you know Matt McColloch. He don't need no make-certain shot. 'Cause he makes his first shot certain."

"Somebody shoot rabbit," Wildcat Walesja barked. "You want to steal man's supper, ride back. I go west."

Keegan and Breen studied one another. They had seen no sign of the stallion, no tracks, nothing. Sean Keegan's idea of finding a scout in the Yaqui captive who had been sold into prostitution was beginning to seem like the hare-brained idea it had always been. She was just guessing that Blood Moon and Matt McCulloch would be heading for an Apache camp in the Sierra Madres Occidentals. But Breen sighed and kicked his horse into a walk. He rode alongside Keegan, letting their scout, their guide, the woman they had kidnapped, keep about twenty or thirty feet in front of them.

"This is crazy," Breen said. "You know that, don't you?"

"Everything that has happened so far has been crazy, Jed. Matt busting an Apache out of the calaboose. Not just any, Apache, but Blood Moon himself."

"Don't remind me. I'm twenty thousand bucks poorer."

"Taking a rank mustang stallion with him," Keegan said. "And —"

Breen interrupted. "We don't even know if they crossed the border."

"They had to cross the border," Keegan said. "Blood Moon and his band has been hiding in Mexico for some time now. They only ride north to trade, kill or steal."

"I'm just not sure," Breen said.

"You're sure enough to ride with me."

Breen let out a laugh that held little, if any, humor. "I'm crazy enough to ride with you."

"Because everything's crazy," Keegan said, as he tipped his hat up. "Crazy that Matt's daughter could still be alive after all these years. Crazy enough that Blood Moon would let Matt hear that. But that's the only thing that could drive Matt crazy enough to bust that right hand of the Devil himself. Bust him out of jail, put us in jail, and ride south."

Breen just sighed.

"Listen, pard. We can ride slow and careful, let that little she-devil play scout and try to pick up a sign, try to find a trail to follow. Or we can outguess them. Get to the mountains. Wait on Matt and the Apache. I'd rather be ahead of them than behind them. Ahead of them, we can pitch in and help Matt if he gets into a jam. Behind . . . well . . . we might not get there to help him in time."

"All right," Breen said, but he twisted to look back just the same.

When he turned back, he saw that Wildcat Walesja had stopped her horse, and that Sean Keegan had slowed his. He also saw why, and reined his mount in beside Keegan.

"Hombres," a Mexican called out, and gestured them forward. Sunlight reflected the silver fillings in his teeth. "Join us."

Keegan and Breen nudged their horses forward.

"But, *por favor,*" the bandit said, raising a Spencer carbine. "Let us see your hands."

Breen draped the reins over his horse's neck. Keegan did the same.

The horses clopped slowly.

There were three of them. The speaker who now brought the carbine to his shoulder and drew a bead in the general direction of the riders, somewhere between Breen and Keegan. Another held a pistol pointed at Wildcat Walesja with his left hand while his right fisted the reins of the Yaqui's horse.

The third, who appeared to be barely into his teens, held the reins to the horses of the bandits.

"Just three," Keegan whispered.

Breen just let his head bob, but he looked around the country, shifting left and right in the saddle as though he had a hard time keeping his balance without having the reins in his hands.

The Mexican with the fillings, obviously the leader, laughed and fired off something at his compadres, who also laughed.

As they drew closer, Breen made the decision that there were only these three. There just was no place for anyone to hide in this desert, and from the way these road agents looked — not that there was a road anywhere near here — they couldn't afford to split more than three ways.

But there were those shiny fillings. That cost money. Even in Mexico.

Well, Breen decided, if everything in the world and everyone in Texas and Mexico had gone crazy, he might as well join the party. He brushed his spurs against the horse's flank and let the mount carry him a bit faster.

"I can't . . ." he tried to explain, looking nervous, his hands flailing over his head. "Control . . . him . . ."

He was ahead of Keegan now, coming closer to the leader, who moved his gun-sights on Breen, then thought better and trained the barrel on Keegan.

That's when Breen cried out and fell out of the saddle.

Or so it seemed to the thieves.

The man holding the reins of Wildcat Walesja's horse, lifted his head back and laughed with glee. An instant later, though, his was gargling with the blood in his throat for the Yaqui had produced her knife and plunged it deep.

That caused the boy holding the horses to drop the reins and palm a revolver. He wasn't, it appeared, as young, scared and inexperienced as Breen had first thought.

Breen was on the dirt then, and before the prairie rat with the glittering teeth had heard his partner choking on his own blood, Breen was coming up to his knees with the Colt Lightning in his right hand.

He fired twice. The first round went high. The second tore off the man's right ear.

By then, Keegan had jerked the Springfield out of the scabbard.

Breen calmed his breathing, steadied the Colt by letting his left hand grip his right wrist. He let out a breath. The Mexican was twisting one way and the other, trying to guess who posed the bigger threat, Breen with the handgun or Keegan with the rifle.

He chose Breen. Which wasn't crazy at all. Keegan had only one shot in the Springfield, and Breen had four more in the chambers of the .38. And the bandit's horse holder and a gun now, and he was about to use it.

The shot from Keegan's Springfield drowned out the report of Breen's Colt. Both bullets found the marks. The kid who had been holding the horses let his pistol echo the twin shots from the two jackals, but he was shooting skyward, likely already dead, being lifted off his feet and driven back ten feet from the .45-70 round of Keegan's long gun. Breen's .38 slug caught the man in the chest. The Mexican spun around, dropped to his knees, dropped his heavy rifle, and looked for just a moment at the terrible sight of Wildcat Walesja.

Most likely, Breen figured, he was praying his fate would not be the same of his partner's. The Yaqui woman was screaming and singing as she plunged the knife countless times into the body of the bandit who lay on the ground, no longer choking to death on his own blood.

The leader, still on his knees, was still for a moment, then crashed forward into the ground.

The next shot tore off Sean Keegan's hat.

"Sweet Mother of God!" Keegan dived off the horse.

So, Breen decided, these bandits weren't so stupid. They had a fourth man, hiding somewhere on the ground with a long gun. Breen shifted the pistol to his left hand and ran after his horse, still trotting as though the bounty hunter remained in the saddle, still trotting as though three men weren't dead in the desert. Still trotting as another bullet whistled over Breen's head.

He reached the horse, found the stock of his Sharps, and fell to the ground as the next bullet must have torn over the gelding's back. Because while Breen was hitting the ground, the horse was galloping away.

Breen rolled onto his stomach, and readied the Sharps.

Wildcat Walesja sang. Her horse went loping after Breen's, as did Keegan's and the other horses of the bandits. Another, three hundred yards southwest, suddenly appeared and also galloped, raising dust.

A voice cried out maybe two hundred yards southwest. It was hard to hear because Wildcat Walesja kept singing and stabbing, but Breen figured it was a savage curse or a cry for help.

Then a shot whined off a stone near Wildcat Walesja, who did not stop her butchery.

"I see him," Keegan yelled. He returned a

shot from his Springfield.

Breen blinked away sweat. He breathed easy now, in control, and looked through the brass telescopic sight on the Sharps. Two hundred yards, he figured, and moved the barrel toward where white smoke was slowly vanishing.

Wildcat Walesja sang and stabbed.

"Hell, I must be crazy," Sean Keegan said. And the Irishman stood up, fired and yelled, "Charge!" He ran toward where the fourth assassin must have been hiding, fumbling with the heavy Springfield to unload the spent shell and replace it with another .45-70 round.

Wildcat Walesja stabbed and sang.

Gunsmoke appeared just above the ground, and the report followed.

"God Almighty," Keegan yelled. "That burned my ear." But his rifle was loaded now, and the crazy fool kept running.

Through the brass scope, Breen spotted the movement. A man on his back, loading a rifle, from the sound of the gunshots, a Sharps just like Breen's.

Breen's big rifle roared. He did not hear the man cry out, but saw him as he sat up, and fired. He must have rushed his shot because Breen did hear the bullet whistle by. Keegan's Springfield barked, but he definitely rushed his aim. Keegan kept running, trying to reload. Breen came to his knees, rushing while watching the assassin work to get a fresh load into his rifle.

It was going to be a race. One man was going to die with the next shot. Breen figured Keegan would not be able to shoot cleanly, not if he kept running like the crazy Irish fool he was. The gunman likely knew that. So the next man to die was going to be . . .

Hell, Breen thought, *me.* He couldn't finger a shell out of his pocket. And the man two hundred yards away was leveling his rifle.

Another gunshot roared. Breen blinked, turned, heard the bark of a carbine again. The man with the long gun spun and stood up, dropping his gun, and holding his arm. Then a pink mist came out of the back of his head, and he dropped.

Breen turned, and saw Wildcat Walesja working the Spencer carbine the bandit leader had been holding. She had left the man she had hacked to pieces, calmly picked up the Spencer, and cut loose.

He was still a bit wobbly when Keegan, out of breath, reached him.

"Well," Keegan finally managed.

Breen could only nod. He saw Wildcat

Walesja walking to the assassin she had killed, wiping the blood off the knife she planned to use again.

Using the Sharps, Breen pushed himself to his feet. He looked at the dust.

"Guess . . . guess . . . I'll round up . . . the . . . horses." He was as out of breath as the panting old horse soldier. Breen found his hat and started walking west.

Sean Keegan looked over at Wildcat Walesja, who had reached the last man to die. She raised her knife, and brought it down. Raised it again, slammed it down. And repeated while she sang gleefully.

"Yeah." The Irishman swallowed. "Me thinks . . . I'll . . . help you . . . Jed."

CHAPTER TWENTY-SIX

From atop the lone butte, Matt McCulloch studied the dust rising from the north. He spit out contempt and rolled over on his back, looking up at Blood Moon. The Apache held reins to both horses and the lead rope to the gray stallion in his good hand. His grin was the kind that made McCulloch want to wipe it off the ugly copper face.

"You were right," McCulloch conceded. "The Río Grande did not stop those savages."

The shoulders that supported the ugly head shrugged. "It never much river."

Grunting, McCulloch pushed himself to his feet. "I didn't think any Apache had a sense of humor."

"Only when make fun of White Eye."

McCulloch took the reins to his horse, but looked back at the dust. "I wonder what those shots were." He wiped his face.

"Signal?" He shook his head, dismissing that idea. "Well, our horses are fresh — thanks to that damned scalphunter's canteen filled with bad water. I don't think they can outrun us."

"Maybe so. But they might."

The Apache's bad hand pointed to the south.

McCulloch looked over the saddle and frowned again.

The view from the butte let him see for miles in all directions, and the dust rising from the south came from La Aldea de las Siete Hermanas de la Fe — The Village of the Seven Sisters of Faith. From here, McCulloch could even see the faint outlines of the cathedral and the *jacales* where the villagers lived, worked, and died. The riders were a lot closer, and the flapping piece of cloth would be a guidon.

"Rurales," McCulloch whispered.

He looked back at the bluecoats riding south. The butte, he realized, would prevent the Rurales from seeing the American soldiers riding north, just as it would stop the cavalry troopers from seeing the Rurales trotting south. The wind was blowing now, and taking the dust back to the ground with it.

"We stuck on hill," Blood Moon said. "We

ride down, east or west, both will see us."

"Yeah."

"I sing Death Song. Too bad no Litsog you see. But we take many lives with us. White Eyes. And Mexicans."

McCulloch shook his head. "Maybe not." He looked south, then north, and smiled. "You ever hear what the Sioux did to some bluecoats up in Wyoming Territory maybe a year or two after the War ended?"

That was too much for the Apache butcher to comprehend.

"Fort Phil Kearney," McCulloch said. On the Bozeman Trail."

"Who cares about Sioux? They no Apache."

McCulloch slid the Winchester from the scabbard, worked the lever just enough to make sure a cartridge was already chambered, and kept looking over the saddle at the approaching Rurales. Satisfied, he returned the .44-40 into the stained leather holder. He spoke quickly now, trying to convince himself that this plan forming in his head would work.

"Soldiers were at a fort. The Sioux harassed them —" He stopped, deciding that Blood Moon would not know the meaning of the word harassed, so he said: "Bothered them with quick raids, taking pot shots, stealing a pony or two, killing one or two men who got caught alone, too far from help."

Blood Moon waited.

"Then one time, a few of their braves rode toward a pretty big size patrol. Seventy men. No, I think it was eighty. And they mocked the bluecoats, hurled insults at them. Remember, it was just a handful of Indians, and eighty bluebellies. The big chief of the patrol went after them."

McCulloch pulled his hat down tightly. "Problem was, there were a hell of a lot more Sioux warriors waiting. The Yankees rode right into them, and the Indians cut them down to a man." He tightened the cinch of his saddle. "Deception. Tomfoolery. It caused quite a stir. Red Cloud was the big chief."

That caused Blood Moon to raise his head. "His name I hear."

"The decoys worked. Lured the Yanks into an ambush. One of the big victories for the Sioux."

"Sioux not dumb as Apache thought."

McCulloch smiled. "Well, how about if you and me play decoy? We lead the Rurales" — he pointed south — "and the Yankees" — pointed north — "into an ambush." He swung onto his horse. "Just like Red Cloud did."

Now Blood Moon's head cocked to one side. "But just you. Me. No one to ambush."

The smile stretched across McCulloch's face, and he pointed south again, and north again. And the Apache understood.

"I will take Mexicans."

McCulloch shook his head. "You'll be pulling the stallion. That'll slow you down. I'll take the Rurales. You take the bluecoats." He rushed the next words. "And there really ain't no time for debating."

Blood Moon wrapped the lead rope around the forearm of the mangled hand, and moved gracefully into the saddle. He kicked the gelding and loped down the butte toward the approaching Army patrol from Fort Spalding. McCulloch stepped into the saddle, and spurred his mount down the southern side of the butte. He was raising dust toward La Aldea de las Siete Hermanas de la Fe.

No one would have guessed that for a few days he had been if not close to death's door, at least sick as the sickest dog in the state of Texas. But he was in a saddle, on a good horse, and the rush of air as he trotted down the incline refreshed him even more. He cut loose with a Rebel yell, spurring the mount harder, and had to remind himself not to draw his Colt.

Hooves pounded, and he felt good again, felt alive. The patrol stopped. He caught the reflection of sunlight on someone's pair of binoculars. A rifle pointed in his direction — at least McCulloch guessed it had to be a rifle, musket or whatever these Rurales had managed to buy, barter or steal. He could see the guidon a bit clearer now, and he jerked the Winchester from the scabbard, thumbed back the hammer, and, resting the stock against his thigh, touched the trigger.

The shot caused his mount to pick up the pace. Horses among the Rurales danced. One rider was tossed into the dirt. Smoke rushed from one of the Mexican's guns, and McCulloch turned his horse, and galloped west. Another bullet rang out. The former Ranger leaned lower in the saddle, and used the barrel of the Winchester as a whip, letting the warm barrel touch his horse's hip.

Another shot. Then more.

McCulloch turned his horse south. Now he looked back and saw the dust.

The Rurales had taken the bait. They were galloping south. A trumpet blared. McCulloch wanted to laugh, but now he had to set his jaw tight. He was almost to the butte.

Where the hell is Blood Moon and my stallion?

Then he saw them both, two hundred, maybe three hundred yards south of the butte. The Apache was leaning low, almost it appeared, to the gelding's withers, galloping hard with the gray mustang stud riding right alongside him, then pulling ahead.

For a few strides, McCulloch could only marvel at that horse, how fine it ran. A horse like that could buy every white captive the Apaches had, but he wanted to trade it for just one.

If he could breathe now, he would have caught his breath. He saw dust, and the thundering horses of maybe a dozen or so horses chasing after the Apache and the stallion. A few of them must have seen McCulloch because he saw dust flying off the ground maybe twenty yards to his right.

He kept the horse angling south, drawing closer to the bluebellies. Another shot zipped past him. He heard the bullet's whine. His eyes jerked westward, and he knew Blood Moon would outrun everyone here — including himself. So he pulled on the reins, leaned in the saddle, and put his horse into a lope after the dust Blood Moon was raising.

Another shot rang off a rock somewhere. McCulloch looked back at the bluecoats, saw them slowing a bit, confused. By now they had spotted the dust from the Rurales, and by now both the Mexican soldiers and the United States cavalrymen could see each other. Most likely, the Americans could even see the guidon of the Mexican troopers. The troopers from Fort Spalding carried no guidon.

Another shot tugged on the flapping chaps McCulloch wore.

His horse found another gear, and McCulloch looked south.

The Rurales were no longer riding after him. They had stopped their horses and began milling about, wondering at these strangers who had appeared from the southern side of the lone butte.

Through the wind in his ears, he managed to make out a trumpet call. It ended. Blared out again. McCulloch glanced back at the Americans. Only a few were still riding after him, and one of those slowed and looked at the Rurales. McCulloch again studied the Mexicans. They were riding again, but this time, they were not coming after McCulloch.

Nobody was shooting anymore, either, but McCulloch gave the gelding all the rein it wanted. He had the wind rushing past him, and his body became one with the galloping horse. He glanced back now, north and east.

The two cavalrymen were trotting back to the rest of the command.

McCulloch smiled. His duplicity had worked after all. Rurales were riding toward American soldiers. The Americans were waiting, uncertain. They would have a lot of explaining to do, and, if everything worked out the way McCulloch hoped, they might even be on their way south to a dungeon in Mexico City.

He frowned then, and kept riding. He rode after the dust that was trailing a long ways ahead of him. McCulloch kept his horse galloping after Blood Moon and the gray mustang stallion.

And once again, somehow, some way, he found himself riding somewhere else, on another horse, chasing after another rider, a damn long time ago.

There was nothing like this feeling. That's what McCulloch had always believed. Feeling the horse beneath you. Riding with the wind at your back, but also at your face. Low in the saddle, looking ahead, grinning wide. Feeling your heart pound with every jump the horse made.

Usually.

But not today.

On this morning, Matt McCulloch rode

in fear. He spurred his mustang, biting his lip, praying for one of the few times in his life, and let the horse chase after the dust a hundred yards ahead of him.

He was sweating, and the temperature had to be in the forties. It was December, just a few days after Christmas, and McCulloch cussed himself for being a damned fool.

Cynthia was ten years old. Just ten. She wasn't the rider McCulloch's sons were. Hell, she was just a little girl. Ten years old, but McCulloch still saw her as three years old, maybe four, sometimes just that little bundle of pink that the midwife had put in his arms while his wife slept.

He could see her tumbling, the horse falling, rolling over her.

Again, he cursed himself, and raked the spurs harder. He had to catch up. Had to stop her. He was stupid. That horse wasn't fully broken. The crazy little mare must have been spooked and now was running away. He could hear Cynthia screaming. If she was hurt, or even killed, McCulloch would take his revolver and blow his brains out.

He rode hard. Rode harder. Then, Cynthia and the mare disappeared in an arroyo. The December wind blew the dust away. McCulloch waited to spot more dust, but there was none.

His heart skipped. The horse must have stumbled, fallen. The edge of the arroyo came closer, and still he saw no sign of his precious baby girl or the mare he thought he had gentled.

Now, McCulloch prayed. He had to slow his gelding. He couldn't plunge into the dip. He steeled himself, and wondered if his eyes were filled with tears or sweat. Sweat when it wasn't even forty-five degrees.

A moment later, the mare lunged forward. Cynthia was still in the saddle. She reined in and waved her arms wildly.

"Thank you, God." McCulloch couldn't remember the last time he had uttered that phrase aloud.

Pulling on the reins, easing off with the spurs, McCulloch slowed the gelding and felt his life's blood pumping through his heart one more time. Cynthia wave gleefully again, and McCulloch had his horse at a walk when he approached her.

"Papa!" the little girl said, trying to stand in the stirrups. "Papa, oh, Papa. Thank you. Thank you. Thank you!" She blew him a kiss, and leaned forward and whispered, "I love you," into the mare's ear.

Loved filled her eyes. Or maybe that was a bit of mischievousness.

"Papa," Cynthia practically squealed.

"Can we do this every day?"

The dust had stopped, and McCulloch slowed the gelding. Both rider and horse were sweating. White lather foamed on the pinto's neck, and McCulloch took a quick glance behind him, but saw no dust.

When he dipped into an arroyo, he saw Blood Moon, holding the reins and lead rope, letting both horses drink from a shallow pool of water.

"I hope you let them cool off first," McCulloch said, reining in his horse, which desperately wanted to drink before the water was slopped up.

"Blood Moon not fool."

McCulloch removed his hat and wiped his sweaty forehead.

"Your plan good." The Apache even nodded his approval.

"Now and then . . ." McCulloch stopped to catch his breath. His bad leg began to throb, and he could not block that memory of chasing after Cynthia from his mind. "Now and then," he said at last, "something I think of works."

"Maybe so."

Maybe so was right. It might not work out the way McCulloch planned. There was more than a fair to middling chance that the Army patrol, in Mexico without permission, would join up with the Rurales. Twenty thousand dollars could make many an officer forget about little things such as international boundaries. Or, for all McCulloch knew, the president of the United States and whoever was running the country down in Mexico City these days had reached a deal, allowing U.S. Army troops, in pursuit of an Indian like Blood Moon, to cross the border.

And right now, McCulloch knew, the horses he and the Apache had wouldn't be riding hard for at least a day or two.

He found the canteen and drank. The horse protested.

"In a bit, boy," McCulloch said.

Then came the gunshots from the east.

McCulloch turned in the saddle. Blood Moon raised his head.

It sounded like a pitched battle.

The Apache spit, nodded, and said, "Plan work damn good. Me think."

CHAPTER TWENTY-SEVEN

There was one thing Second Lieutenant Charles Tibbetts, Eighth United States Cavalry, had learned during his few months on the Texas frontier. He could not outride anyone in his command. And there was one thing he had learned from Three-Toed Charley.

Six weeks back, the patrol Tibbetts was commanding had come across a couple of Mexican muleskinners who had been ambushed by Comanches. One of them had died game, and the Comanches had treated his body with high respect, although they had scalped him. The other had been captured alive, dragged back to the wagon, where he had been tied to the wagon tongue and then roasted alive over a fire. Somehow, Tibbetts had managed not to throw up his breakfast, but he was breathing hard and sweating when Tiny Olderman rode up and pointed east toward the trail to Fort

Stockton.

"The other one got away," Olderman said, pointing down the road.

In a shaky voice, Tibbetts asked, "Other one?"

Three-Toed Charley turned toward Tibbetts and explained, "The third freight man." The scout looked at the giant Olderman and said, "What was he ridin'? A mule?"

Olderman's head bobbed slightly.

Three-Toed Charley nodded. "Well, Comanches ain't all that partial for mule meat. Smart fellow. That's why he lived. Imagine he'll make a report at Stockton and they'll send some troopers out to join us. Not that we'll ever find hide nor hair of the bucks that done this fine job of butchery."

But Tibbetts was having a hard time figuring out what had happened here.

"You mean . . . ?" He shook his head. "Do you mean one of these men employed by the freighting company ran? Abandoned his post?"

"That's right," Three-Toed Charley said.

"But . . . he could've been killed, too. Captured alive like this poor soul." Tibbetts shook his head. "Or died game like that brave man over there."

"He sure could've, Lieutenant." Three-

Toed Charley's head bobbed.

"Comanches on Comanche horses could certainly outrun a mule," Tibbetts added.

"Yup. Ain't no doubt about it." A smile cracked through the scout's beard-stubbled face. "But the thing is, Lieutenant, in a situation like this. Well, Lieutenant, it's like the two men bein' chased by the silvertip grizzly. You ain't gotta be faster than the bear. You just gotta be faster than your pard."

Now Tibbetts could see the guidon flapping in the wind that picked up, and he knew the men riding to him were Mexican Rurales.

"What's the nearest village, Tiny?" Tibbetts asked.

"Village of the Seven Bitches," Olderman said.

Three-Toed Charley took out his pipe and began stuffing the cob with tobacco. "La Aldea de las Siete Hermanas de la Fe," he said sweetly in Spanish, then repeated it in gruff English. "The Village of the Seven Sitters of Faith."

"Is that where the Rurales are based?"

"It's not much of a village, four kilometers from here, suh," the scout said, and stuck the pipe's stem in his mouth as he sought for a match. "They usually stop there for Mass or goat meat."

"How many people?"

"A dozen. Counting farmers and goat tenders in the area, two dozen."

"And no . . . jail?"

"Nope. Nobody there ever goes to jail. Even Comanches leave the place alone when they're raiding on this side of the river. Ain't worth the trouble."

Olderman laughed. "Greasers will send us to The Dungeon of Death."

Three-Toe Charley got his pipe lighted, and said, "Yep. *La Mazmorra de la Muerte.*" The words sounded so sweet in Spanish.

"We ought to make a run for it, Lieutenant," Trooper Anderson cried out.

Another panicked voice sang: "The river ain't but some miles north, sir!"

"Steady, men," Tibbetts said. "Steady." He wasn't about to run. For if they retreated, he would surely be the first one to catch a bullet between his shoulder blades.

There weren't more than a dozen, Tibbetts realized. And the town on the other side of the butte had no more than that. Tibbetts had fifteen troopers, plus the two scouts. But the soldiers, at least nine of them, were as green as Charles Tibbetts. They just knew how to ride a hell of a lot better. And a hell of a lot faster.

"Stand your ground, men," Tibbetts said,

hating it when his voice cracked. "We have nothing to fear. We represent the United States."

A trumpet blew, and Tibbetts started to say, "Trumpeter." Only he realized that he had no musician in his command. Hell, he didn't really have a command. They had been drinking in The Palace of Purgatory City when Blood Moon had been broken out of the jail.

"Should we raise a white flag?" a trooper named Hulse said.

"No. Let them come. But we are not surrendering."

Three minutes later, the Rurales halted their horses. The man with the guidon and two others spurred their mounts and trotted in front of the shaking group of American soldiers. The riders reined up ten yards in front of the line of cavalrymen.

A man wearing a blue kepi with a long white piece of cotton hanging from the back saluted and spoke in rapid Spanish, only his voice did not have the musical rhythm of the usually gruff Three-Toed Charley.

"He's askin' who be in command, Lieutenant," the scout translated.

Tibbetts drew in a deep breath, held it, finally exhaled and tried to steady his resolve, but mostly, his voice.

"I am," he said, much too softly, but then coughed and spoke louder. "Charles Tibbetts, Second Lieutenant, Eighth United States Cavalry." The man in the kepi looked at the taller Rurale carrying the guidon. The two men spoke in quick Spanish, while the third man, holding a carbine across his thighs, studied Tibbetts's command.

The Rurale leader spoke again.

"He asks us why ain't we on our side of the river," Three-Toed Charley said.

"Tell him . . ." Here, Tibbetts paused. He was sweating harder now, and his hands had turned clammy. He bit his bottom lip, felt his Adam's apple bob, and wished he had tried for an appointment at Annapolis instead. "Tell him we were pursuing a hostile Apache. A butcher of his people as well as ours."

The scout spoke, but the Rurale commander's face did not change. When Three-Toed Charley had finished, the Rurale barked out something sharp.

Three-Toed Charley took time to remove his pipe, empty the cob of ash, and stuff it into his pouch. "He says our pursuit should have ended on our side of the Río Grande."

"Tell him that the savage we were chasing was Blood Moon."

He waited, sure that knowledge of the

proximity of such a notorious red savage would change the entire tone of this conversation. The Rurales would offer to serve under Tibbetts's command. Maybe Tibbetts would resign his commission and accept an appointment in Mexico City. He had heard the Mexican women were lovely, especially farther south.

The name changed nothing.

"He says when they chase Blood Moon into Texas, they stay in Mexico."

This was not going the way Tibbetts wanted it to go. He decided on another tack, and pointed his gauntlet west. "Tell him Blood Moon and a Texas traitor are getting away as we speak. Tell him that we will put ourselves under his command. That we will ride with him after that butcher." His voice picked up speed. It cracked, sure, it always cracked, but he felt he spoke with such passion, with such truth, that the Rurales had to listen. They would ride together. Catch Blood Moon and that arrogant Texas dog. And then . . . then . . . hell, Mexicans could not outfight American soldiers, even the green peas that rode with Lieutenant Charles Tibbetts.

"Tell him . . ."

The leader of the Rurales held out his hand. "I hear what you say."

Damn it all, Tibbetts thought. The man spoke English. And a hell of a lot better than either of the two scouts riding with Tibbetts.

The officer turned to the one cradling the carbine, spoke, and that man turned in his saddle and shouted out at the men waiting patiently behind them.

A chorus of laughter rippled to those Mexicans.

When the officer in charge of the Mexicans looked at Tibbetts, he reached for his sidearm, pulled it, and held it with the barrel facing skyward. "Your men," he said, slower now, stressing each and every word, and behind him, the other Mexican riders drew their revolvers. "Your men will surrender their arms and they will follow me. We will ride to Dieciséis Cabras. We will telegraph the general in Ciudad de México, and he and El Presidente will determine your fate. You will surrender your firearms. *Por favor.*"

Tibbetts leaned forward in his saddle and looked west. The dust had faded. Blood Moon and that Texas jackal named McCulloch were long out of sight. This close to twenty thousand dollars and glory, and now. He straightened.

"Where are we riding to?" he asked Three-Toed Charley.

"Biggest town in these parts. Seventeen Goats."

That almost made Tibbetts laugh. Here he was, commissioned officer in the Army of the United States, and he was surrendering to a bunch of Mexican rubes to be taken to a city that was called Seventeen Goats. His classmates at West Point would never let him live this down.

"Your weapons, señor," the officer commanded.

Straightening, Tibbetts knew what he had to do, and he summoned the resolve. "Indeed." He kicked his horse forward, walking the mount toward the three men.

"I understand," he said, and pulled open the flap that protected his revolver, drew it, and shot the Mexican out of the saddle.

The horse Tibbetts rode had to be played out from the hard ride. That's the only reason it did not panic and toss Tibbetts to the ground. Tibbetts had nothing more to do than just turn his arm a few inches to the right. His thumb worked the hammer, his pointer finger touched the trigger, and the man with the rifle was clutching his face, and falling to the earth. His horse bolted, dragging the man behind him, galloping back to that village of whoever men

366

and women had to live in such a manure heap.

But the Mexican with the guidon was smart. For as Tibbetts turned, uttering what he thought were orders, and tried to shoot the flag-carrying greaser, the brass tip of the guidon pole slammed into Tibbetts's head.

That was enough to — finally — bring Tibbetts's horse back to life. Tibbetts crashed to the dirt, and his horse trotted after the horse that was now dragging the Mexican's body back toward The Village of the Seven Sisters of Faith.

Tibbetts rolled over, cocking his pistol, but saw the Rurale preparing to drive the tip of the guidon pole into Tibbetts's own belly. And he would have, likely giving Tibbetts a mortal wound, an agonizing belly wound that would take a long time before death came. Then the face of the angry Mexican exploded in a geyser of crimson, and that man was falling off his horse, and his horse was turning and running in an easterly direction.

"Give them greasers hell!" came a shout.

The Rurales charged. Tibbetts rolled over on his belly. He had four shots left. Three. He used both hands. Tried to find a likely target.

He felt the kick of the revolver in his hand,

but heard no shot. Was this always the case in battle? He thought about that, but then thought about nothing but killing as many of these Rurales as he could. The gun kicked again. Then he saw nothing but dust. He heard the battle behind him, and rolled onto his back. A horse jumped over him and almost caused him to soil his britches. He cocked the hammer, pulled the trigger and felt and heard nothing. He knew his revolver was empty. He started to reload it, then saw the Rurale commander's Colt in the dirt.

That was better. Tibbetts rolled onto his stomach and crawled on hands and knees. He lunged the last few feet, and his right hand found the grip. Now he was sitting, and a man rushed out through the dust, yelling, his face disheveled and clutching a carbine in his hands.

"Lieutenant!" the man shouted.

And Tibbetts shot the man in the throat.

He rose, thumbed the hammer, and stepped to the man.

The boy clutched his throat, and blood poured out of his mouth.

"Anderson," Tibbetts said, and watched the trooper's eyes glaze over.

Tibbetts bent over, grabbed the Spring-field carbine, and ran into the dust. He did not look back at the soldier, his own man, that he had just killed.

"Well, Lieutenant," Three-Toed Charley said softly as he tightened the cinch of his saddle. "If you didn't cause no international incident by crossin' the river, suh, you sure have started the ball now."

A few yards away, Tiny Olderman stopped over a fallen Rurale and called out, "Lieutenant. This greaser's still alive." Then he lowered the barrel of his revolver and let the pistol bark. "But not no more, he ain't."

Three-Toed Charley moved to his saddlebags, opened the nearest one, and fished out a rag that he started wrapping over the buckskins just above his left boot.

"You hit, Scout?" Tibbetts asked.

"It ain't much." Three-Toed Charley tied a knot, scratched his stubble and looked around. "Them Rurales put up a good fight."

"How many do we have left?" Tibbetts asked.

"Five of your soldier-boys," the scout answered. "Hulse, McAdam, Lincoln, Younger, Baxter. Plus Tiny and me. We ain't found Anderson yet, alive, dead or wounded."

Tibbetts tried not to think of Trooper Anderson.

369

"Lieutenant!" Hulse called out several yards south, and Tibbetts knew what the trooper had found.

"It's Anderson, sir. He's dead." The last word seemed to echo.

Trooper Younger was gathering the horses. Now he reined his bay in and pointed south. "Sir. Them Meskins is walkin' this-away. Bringin' asses with 'em. Looks like a priest is leadin' 'em."

Three-Toed Charley mounted his horse. "Lieutenant," he said. "It's time we rode back to Texas."

The officer realized he still held the Rurale commander's pistol. Now he cocked it, and aimed it at the scout's chest. "No. We ride. But we ride west." He smiled. "There's twenty thousand dollars waiting for us there. And now we only have to split it eight ways."

But he was thinking that by the time they had Blood Moon's scalp, that split would be down quite a bit more.

"We'll need that money, Scout," Tibbetts said with a wry smile. "To get us as far away as we can from the Mexican and American law."

"How you plan on collectin' that reward — if you was lucky enough to catch Blood Moon — from the American law?" Three-

370

Toed Charley asked. "If you was somehow to catch the dirty dog."

"You leave that to me."

The scout's head shook, but he smiled. "All right, Lieutenant. But we best ride."

CHAPTER TWENTY-EIGHT

"You do not want to go to that town,"
Wildcat Walesja said.

Jed Breen lost his cool. "What would you
know about a little village in the middle of
nowhere somewhere in Chihuahua?"

He had lost track of the days. Hell, it took
them a day to catch the horses after that
little gunfight with four bandidos. Breen had
worn holes in the soles of both boots, and
Sean Keegan had not fared much better.
They had been walking and riding for what
seemed to be years, and had not even seen
a sign of life in the past five days. The town
in the distance did not look like much, but
it would have something to eat, and maybe
provisions to buy. Right now, Jed Breen did
not even care if the town didn't have a
cantina.

"There is nothing in that town for us?"
the Yaqui woman said.

"There's shade," Breen barked. That's

what he wanted most. Just to get out of the sun, even for ten minutes. Well, maybe fifteen.

"Shade," Wildcat Walesja said, "is there." She pointed.

They could see the purple outline of the Sierra Madre Occidental range now, distant in the haze as the sun started its descent toward them, but visible. Yet for all Jed Breen knew, those rising peaks were nothing more than a mirage.

"Those mountains, dearie," Keegan said, "do appear to be quite a ways off."

The Yaqui repeated: "There is nothing in that town for you."

Breen barked: "Is there a blacksmith?"

That made the woman's scowl turn even harder. Breen's horse had lost a shoe. That's why he had been walking so much. And Keegan's was limping. Wildcat Walesja's gelding had fared a little better, because, well, it was nothing but a damned cowpony, but mostly because all it had to carry was the little Yaqui girl, and not two men packing hard muscle and plenty of iron and lead.

She did not answer, and that told the two men what they needed to know.

"Lassie," Keegan said, having not been walking as long, and having not lost a fortune in bounty money, as Breen had. The

Irishman even smiled as he pointed at the buildings that rose in the vast desert. "We need horses, fresh ones, or we need water and care for these. A smithy to put on a shoe. Maybe some grub and supplies."

"I'd take a bath and a shave and a bed," Breen said. "But there's no time for that."

"And a whiskey," Breen said longingly. "Even a shot of tequila instead of me blessed Irish. But water will suit me right down to the ground."

"The point is . . . we don't get to those mountains," Breen said, pointing west, "if we don't have good horses."

"If you set foot in that town," the Yaqui said, "we will all die."

Breen blinked. He glanced at Keegan, who cocked his head in that curious way, and ran his tongue over his cracked lips.

"How's that, lassie?" Keegan asked.

Breen looked back at Wildcat Walesja and waited for her answer.

"That village," she said, "is El Lugar Donde Los Hombres que Toman Cueros Cabelludos Se Juntan para Emborracharse."

"That's a passel of words for such a tiny little village," Keegan said, shaking his head.

But Breen had stiffened. "I thought that was just a myth."

"It," the Yaqui woman said bitterly, "is no

myth." She pointed, and spit. "It is real. And it is deadly."

"What is it?" Keegan asked, and turned to face the bounty hunter. "Only words I savvied was *Los Hombres.*"

The woman snorted. "Not *Emborracharse,* you stinking Irish pig?"

In better spirits, Jed Breen might have chuckled. He just said, "That mean's 'get drunk.' " Too tired to raise his arm and extend a finger to point, he nodded at the village instead. "It's a place for only scalphunters. It's where they go to get drunk, brag, buy supplies, women."

"The Place Where Scalp Men Hang Out To Get Drunk," Wildcat Walesja said.

"I'll be damned." Keegan shook his head. "I read that in a dime novel. Figured it was just a fancy idea for some dumb-arse scribbler."

"It is real," the Yaqui said, repeating her warning. "If we go there, they will kill us. They will take my scalp. You." She spit again. "You they will just drag into the desert to feed the buzzards and coyotes."

"How many men?" asked Breen, drawing his Colt and checking the cartridges.

Wildcat Walesja shrugged. "It depends." She looked at the adobe and sod structures. "Usually just a few. Sometimes none. But even if only the men who run the stores are there, they will be enough to kill us all."

"Maybe we sneak in at night," Keegan said. "Steal three fresh horses."

"You steal a man's horse in this country, or anywhere in the Southwest, and they'll run you down and kill you on the spot," Breen pointed out as he holstered his Colt.

"Well?" Keegan drew his Remington, blew off the dust, opened the gate, and rotated the cylinder to check his rounds.

"What's the nearest town?" Breen asked.

"Chihuahua," she said, and made a vague gesture with her head.

"That's no good," Breen said. "Too big. We'd be arrested." He looked at the Yaqui. "And Maudie treated you better than they'd treat you there."

He swore briefly, looked at their mounts, then at the Sierra Madre range, and shook his head. "These horses will be dead before we reach those mountains."

"Which means we'll be dead, too," Keegan holstered the revolver.

"Maybe no scalphunters are there," Breen said. He looked at the woman.

"You can go," he said. "Keegan's idea was stupid to begin with. We're sorry we got you this far, but we thank you for helping us get this far. We'll see what happens in that village of scalphunters." He pointed at the faraway mountain range. "Follow that northwest, it'll get you right to Arizona Territory. Tucson . . . it's a good place to start over."

He went to his horse, took a swallow of hot water from the canteen, and taking the reins began walking toward El Lugar Donde Los Hombres que Toman Cueros Cabelludos Se Juntan para Emborracharse . . . The Place Where Scalp Men Hang Out To Get Drunk.

Keegan caught up with him after only a few yards, holding the reins in his left hand, and the Springfield in his right.

Fifty yards later, Wildcat Walesja rode up beside them on the gelding.

"I have lived too long already," she said.

Breen stopped, and pointed at his saddlebags. "Get the Dragoon we took off those ambushers. And don't shoot your foot off."

She turned the gelding, stopped it and leaned down from the saddle to unfasten the straps and pull out the massive .44. "Gracias," she said. "I will also try not to shoot your fool head off."

They had to walk better than three-quarters of a mile to reach The Place Where Scalp Men Hang Out To Get Drunk. That was the way of this country. You could see forever, and it took forever to get wherever the hell you were going. After riding for a hundred yards, Wildcat Walesja dismounted and walked with the others. She probably figured she made a smaller target walking, and, Breen figured she was right about that.

About three hundred yards from what passed, at least for scalphunters, as a village, Jed Breen whispered: "It ain't empty."

"Yeah." Sean Keegan spit. "About as empty as Maudie's on the Saturday night after payday."

Fifty yards from The Place Where Scalp Men Hang Out To Get Drunk, Sean Keegan said: "Mother Mary and Joseph, I didn't know there was this many bloody scalphunters in the entire West."

El Lugar Donde Los Hombres que Toman Cueros Cabelludos Se Juntan para Emborracharse was a village, if one could call it that, of six buildings, not including the privies, and two of the buildings, likely the cribs for the prostitutes, were not much larger than the four-seater behind what had to be the saloon. No signs advertised what could be found inside the buildings.

The livery stable, naturally, needed no sign. The racket of an out-of-tune self-playing piano was all one needed to figure out was the saloon, and, probably, a gambling hall. The scalphunter playing the accordion did nothing to make the song sound any better. The cantina also had the most horses tethered out front. Shouts, curses and the pounding of glasses and bottles on a bar accompanied the song.

Across the street stood a worn-down adobe that probably served as an inn. In the shade on the eastern side of that structure, a man slept on a long bench, his head covered with a sombrero. Must be full up, Breen thought, and studied the last building.

That would be the general store. But what would a couple of gringos like Jed Breen and Sean Keegan find in such a place? Whetstones to sharpen scalping knives? Scalping knives? Bullets, powder, lead, parts of guns for quick fixes? Latigos to tie the scalps together?

There was no café that Breen could see. No smoke rose from the chimneys, but even though the sun was starting to set, it was still hotter here than at the hinges of hell.

"Well, laddie," Keegan whispered, "what do ye think?"

"No guards," Breen whispered back, though he doubted if anyone could hear above the racket in the saloon.

"What's there to guard?" Keegan said, and he turned to the Yaqui. "Is it always this crowded?"

Wildcat Walesja was still blinking away her own shock. "Never have I heard of this many people at this place at the same time."

"Must be a soiree of damned scalphunters," Breen said. When he turned, he saw Keegan moving toward the saloon's nearest window.

He almost barked out the Irishman's name, but stopped.

There were no glass windows, not in this hellhole. Keegan removed his hat, knelt and peered inside. Jed Breen held his breath. The woman beside him started humming what the bounty hunter guessed to be her death song.

"Quiet," he whispered. The death chant stopped.

Slowly Keegan began backing away, but did not stand to his full height until he held the reins to his worn-down horse.

"What were you doing?" Breen whispered. "Trying to steal a mug of beer?"

"Seeing what we're up against."

Breen waited.

"Mexicans and white men, but a bunch of the white men are dressed like Rurales."

"White Rurales?" Breen wet his lips.

380

"And there's a Rebel battle flag tacked up on the wall above the bar — well, it ain't much of a bar."

Keegan swallowed. "I recollect after the Rebellion that a bunch of Rebs didn't want to take the oath of allegiance, so they headed down south to serve with that dumb, arrogant Austrian runnin' the country back then."

Breen was thinking the same thing, but he knew where those white Rurales came from or what they were doing in a haven for scalphunters did not matter. "How many?" he asked.

"Mexicans or the gringos?"

"Both!" That came out louder than Breen meant.

"Too damned many to count."

Breen looked down what passed for a street at the livery, sighed again, and nodded at the big structure of thick adobe and the three corrals filled with horses, mules and burros. "Let's trade for three fresh horses."

"Aye," Keegan said. "Though I doubt the saints will bless us enough to find some Matt McCulloch mounts here."

"I'd rather the saints bless us by letting us get out of this place alive."

Nervously, they walked toward the mas-

381

sive livery, their tired mounts hanging their heads as they moved east. Breen kept his eyes on the inn, hoping the snoring man on the bench did not wake up. Keegan looked ahead at the livery, waiting for some scalp-hunter or even worse — some hombre who made money off scalphunters — showed his face. The Yaqui kept her eyes behind them, staring at the cribs, the mercantile, and the rowdy saloon.

Two long-lasting minutes later, they walked through the open door and into the darkness of the livery. The office was empty, but there was a pot of coffee on the hearth of the fireplace. The two men shoved their long guns into the scabbards on their saddles. "You pick the horses," Breen told Keegan. "But from what they have in the stalls. Not in the corrals." Keegan gave him the Irish glare that meant Sean Keegan was no bloody idiot and he had lived this long to know that the inside stalls held the best horses and that stealing horses inside the livery would be less likely to be seen from some drunken scalphunter crossing the street from the cantina to the hotel.

"I'll see if there's anything in that office that we can use." Breen spun around and told the Yaqui to unsaddle their mounts.

"And be quick."

They moved as if their lives depended on it. Which they did. In the office, Breen found a Remington over-and-under derringer, checked it, saw it held .41-calber shells in each barrel, and slipped it into his trousers pocket. He lifted the canteen, half full, and filled an empty canteen in the corner with the liquid.

There were a few tortillas, covered with flies, but Breen wasn't that particular at this stage of the game, so he shoved those into a sack, and threw the sack over his shoulder. He even found a bottle, about one-quarter full, of tequila. That, he left untouched and even dropped it in a wastebasket so Sean Keegan would not be likely to find it.

Liquor would have tasted mighty fine. But liquor was one thing a body did not need in the desert.

He came out of the office, saw Keegan and Wildcat Walesja busy at work on three bay geldings, and moved to the entryway. Everything still looked quiet, so he turned around, and picked up a relatively clean saddle blanket from a rack, and threw it on the third gelding's back.

Wildcat Walesja stopped to wipe the sweat pouring down her forehead. Breen removed the derringer from his pocket and handed it to her. "It's not much," he said. "But it's not as ancient or as rusty as that old Dragoon."

She took it, and slipped it into a pocket. The Dragoon, that massive horse pistol, looked ridiculous sticking out of her waistband.

"There's . . . ummm . . ." Breen struggled to find the words.

"Please," the Yaqui said. "Spare me that garbage about saving the last damned bullet for myself."

The saddles went on quickly. "Don't bother with the bridles," Breen told the Yaqui. "We'll use what's already on them."

Time was of the essence.

And time had just ran out.

"Well, well, well, well," a Southern accent called out from behind them. "Look what has come callin' on us. Horse thieves. Yankees by the looks of 'em. And, my, oh, my, a lovely squaw with a fine head of hair that'll bring us fifty pesos in Chihuahua. Or more . . . if we sell her as a whore."

CHAPTER TWENTY-NINE

Litsog woke from more bad dreams. She sat up, sweating despite the coolness of the mountain air, and waited until her heart stopped pounding and her breath returned to normal. The darkness told her nothing, but the silence told her that she had not screamed in her sleep.

She thought about the holy man.

Then she thought about other men . . . white men . . . a deep in her memories. Again, she practiced, and prayed, not the prayers of the Apache, but prayers to the God she remembered from so many lifetimes ago.

"My . . . name . . . is . . . Lit . . ."

She stopped, exasperated, and waited till she had stopped shaking. Then she had a vision.

The handsome man with the leathery face laughed. He walked to the white child and helped her up, picked her up, and sat her on the top rail of a circular corral.

"You all right?" he said. His voice had this soothing drawl.

The white girl with the golden hair, such a tiny little thing, frowned, and the green eyes glowed with intensity. "You know," the white man said easily, "your eyes are really pretty when you're happy. They look like . . . oh . . . I don't know. They look like the first grass of spring."

He took her right arm and removed his bandanna, then wiped off the dirt from the scratch.

His eyes lifted, caught her stare. He said, "Want me to spit on it?"

"Spit's nasty."

"Not Papa spit. Papa spit cures everything."

"It's nasty."

He laughed. "All right. No spit. But you can yell if this hurts."

It didn't hurt. Calouses covered his hands, and she could see the crooked fingers from bones broken that never healed quite the way they should have. His hands were hard from hard work, but he could make them so gentle.

"What about my eyes, Papa?" the little girl asked.

He smiled, but did not look up, just worked cleaning the scratch she had taken when she fell.

"Oh, yeah." He stopped cleaning, looked at his doctoring job, and said: "You sure you don't want spit?"

Her head shook quickly. "What about my eyes?"

"Well, most times, like I said." He was tying the bandanna back over his neck. "They're right pretty. Green like new grass. But I don't know. You get this look sometimes, like when one of your brothers pushed you down."

"I'm gonna rip off Matthew's face when I catch him."

"Oh, don't do that."

"I'll claw his eyes out."

"Oh, that would be too much. I'm thinking your ma will be hiding him for being too rough with you."

"He ain't too rough." She saw the way his head cocked to one side, and sighed. "He *isn't* too rough — *wasn't* . . . too rough. I just slipped. That's all."

"I see." He examined her arm. "I reckon that'll hold. Till your ma sees it. She's had more practice being a nurse than me."

"What . . . about . . . my . . . eyes?" Enunciating each word.

"When you get mad," he said, and helped her down off the top rail. "Those pretty eyes that look like good grass, they turn to . . . moss on a pond." He thought about that for a moment, shook his head. "Moss on a rock?" The head shook again. "You ever seen an alligator?"

"Just in a storybook."

"Well, you don't have to worry about seeing an alligator." He laughed out loud. "Not out here. Not unless some dog and pony comes to Purgatory City."

"I like dogs and ponies," she said.

"Well, an alligator is sort of like a rattlesnake, only it's wet, and mostly green. And it's sort of like a badger. Remember when we saw that badger —"

"It scared me!" she said.

"Scared me, too."

He laughed. "No, those eyes, they don't turn to something like a gator. They turn something worse. They are like . . . turnip greens."

She gagged. "I hate turnip greens."

"I know. And don't tell your ma, but I can't stand them myself."

"My eyes look like turnip greens?"

He nodded. "When you're mad."

"Well," she said, pouting. "I'll try not to be mad . . . for a while . . . But one of these days, I'll claw out Matthew's eyes."

He swatted her backside as she ran off to find her brothers.

A dog growled outside of the wickiup, and Litsog lost the memory, the gentle face on the hard man. Horses picketed near the wickiups of the bravest warriors and began snorting. Something, she knew was wrong.

She rose, grabbed a tomahawk, and started to the opening. But she stopped, catching one more moment, one more memory, and heard the voice of a young boy.

"Cyn-thi-a!"

The young girl with the sore arm and golden hair runs from the corral and finds a tall, gangling boy rubbing his hindquarters with both hands. She sees the woman standing in front of the summer kitchen, hands on her hips, the apron flapping in the wind. The woman is glaring at the young boy with curly hair and red-rimmed eyes. She also sees the switch lying at the stern, but beautiful, woman's feet.

She has felt that switch before. She knew exactly why the boy was rubbing his buttocks.

And she felt the cold green of her eyes,

the color of turnip greens, softening, becoming more gentle, like new grass after a spring rain. She felt sorry for the poor boy.

"I'm sorry . . ." the tall kid said. "Sorry that . . . I pushed you . . . down."

She saw another boy coming out of what looks like a dugout of some kind, holding potatoes in his arms. He brought them to the woman with the stern look, and she nodded, and the boy dropped them into a silver tub.

The woman spoke to the second boy, and his head bobbed with enthusiasm, and then he ran toward the golden-haired girl and the tall boy.

The eyes now sparkled with gentleness, and when the boy joined the taller boy, she laughed.

"Let's go play!" she screamed with girlish delight, and the boys chased after her as she raced past the laughing man who thought that his spit was like medicine, as a horse nuzzled up to him as though begging for the apple he had picked off the top of a corral post and was rubbing against his tan britches.

She says . . . "I . . . am . . . Si-si-Sin . . . Cyn-theee . . . I am . . . Cynthia."

She has to breathe in deeply, and after

slowly exhaling, she starts the second part of the puzzle.

"Mmmmm. . . . Mmmmmm. M . . ."

Voices are shouting now in the darkness. There is danger. These are the voices of her people. She knows some of their shouts. A fire begins to glow.

"Litsog!" calls an Apache warrior.

Moccasins sound softly, but she knows they come from her.

Time. She has such little time. But she must finish. She must . . .

. . . Remember!

"Mac . . . Ma . . . Mi . . . Mac-Cuhhhh." It comes out in a rush. "McCulloch."

The tanned skin pushes open, and the head of an Apache man, silhouetted from the growing campfires, appeared. The warrior said: "Litsog. You are needed." The words were not in the same language that Litsog had just spoken, but the words were familiar to her. They were the words of the language she used every day. Cynthia . . . McCulloch . . . Those were words she knew she must only speak at night, and only when she was alone.

An Apache woman turned, and beckoned for Litsog to join the crowd by the fire. Behind her people — or the people she had

391

lived with for many long summers — came a scream of agony, and fear.

Frowning, she found the resolve she had needed for all these years with these people. Now she was no longer Cynthia McCulloch. She was Litsog. The people parted for her, and she stepped into the circle.

The man on the ground was not Mexican. His face was tan, but not that dark. His eyes were closed, so she could not see the color. His teeth were clenched, and when they unclenched, she saw their blackness, except for one that sparkled with a gold filling. He spit out blood, and blood poured from his nose. He screamed.

Hawk's Talons, the Apache warrior, had his moccasin planted on the white man's left arm. The white man's hand burned and sizzled on the coals from the fire.

"For . . . God . . . God's . . . Oh, God . . . MERCY!" the white man screamed.

Another warrior, Spotted Dog, jerked the man's buckskin britches off, then pulled down his faded underwear until his nakedness showed. Another warrior, Ten Horses, scooped up more embers from the fire. He used a clay pot. Smiling, he brought them over as Spotted Dog got out of the way. The coals dumped onto the man's exposed groin.

Now, he screamed and cried and begged for mercy.

There was never mercy for a white man in the camp of an Apache.

"Enough!"

The words stopped all chatter, stopped all talk, stopped everything but the screams of the white man.

Three Dogs strode to the torture site. Spotted Dog and Ten Horses kicked sand onto the man's scalded groin. Hawk's Talons removed his foot from the man's forehead. The white man curled into a ball, and whimpered.

"What is this?" Three Dogs said.

"This man has killed Yo-íí," Hawk's Talons answered.

Now the silence, except for the gasp that escaped Litsog's throat, rushed through the camp like the wind.

"Yo-íí?" Three Dogs seemed shocked to his very core.

"No . . ." The white man, using his good hand to cover his burned manhood, shook his head. "No . . ." The words were not spoken in the language that Litsog so often tried to remember at night.

Three Dogs knelt near the white man. "You speak Apache?" he said.

The man's sweating but pale face nodded.

Three Dogs raised his head and looked at Hawk's Talons. "Tell me," he ordered.

"Yo-íí was riding with the three men this man had with him," the Apache warrior said. He rode between two of them. The other rode behind him."

"That is not dead," Three Dogs said.

"He is as good as dead," Spotted Dog said. "The Mexicans captured him. They took him away. They will kill him."

"You were there?" Three Dogs asked.

"I saw it with my own eyes." Spotted Dog then spit on the white captive's privates.

Litsog remembered her last talk with the great Apache holy man. She recalled the tears that fell from his old rheumy eyes. She recalled what he had said about dying. Maybe that was Yo-íí's vision. He knew he was going to die, and, brave man that he was, he rode out to meet his death.

But she also remembered the rest of his vision. That this village, that the Apaches, that they would soon be dead. And Litsog? Her fate was not known to the much lauded holy man of this village. Litsog would leave to return to the white men . . . the McCullochs . . . but . . . alive? Dead? Even the great holy man had no answer.

Three Dogs looked at Ten Horses.

"And you? Were you there when they took

the great Yo-íí away to the rising sun?"

Ten Horses shook his head and dropped his gaze.

"Then by what right do you have to torture this man?" Three Dogs looked at the man whose body trembled and whose face turned whiter and whiter. "Speak," the chief commanded. "Speak and your death will be quick."

"You . . . can't . . . kill . . . me . . ." the man whined.

"You know where we camp," Three Dogs spoke calmly. "You cannot live with such knowledge."

"But . . . God!" He spoke English again. "Please. You can move camp. You can leave here. But you do not have much time."

Three Dogs turned, found Litsog, motioned her forward. When she did not move, a hand shoved her from behind.

"Enough!" Three Dogs said.

Litsog did not look at the old hag who had shoved her. She had just been shamed enough by the chief's rebuke. She walked to Three Dogs and turned and looked at the white man. After wetting her lips, she knelt beside the man, looking into his face, not his mangled body. But his face was sickening enough.

"Say what you just told me to this Apache

woman," Three Dogs commanded the prisoner.

Litsog's shoulders straightened. Three Dogs had called her Apache.

"Apache!" the man gasped. "Her . . . she . . . blonde hair." That was said in Apache, too.

"And I have seen Mexicans with hair the color of corn. And eyes the color of the sky." Three Dogs folded his arms over his chest. "Speak now. Or I turn you over to the squaws." The last two sentences were spoken in English.

Litsog tried to remember the words, understand them. Then she waited for the white man to speak.

"We got word . . . to . . . I don't know."

Litsog shook her head. "His mind is leaving him," she told Three Dogs in Apache.

"No." The man gasped, groaned, turned his head and vomited slightly. "No," he sighed.

Litsog wet her lips. "Speak." She could not believe how the word sounded. "Slowly."

Tears poured from the captive's eyes. "Mercy, child. Have mercy on a poor sinner, sweet angel. Please. That . . . oh, God, sweet girl, you can speak English. You can save me. You can . . ." The words came too fast. She could only make out and remember what a handful of them meant. "I . . . ain't . . . done nothing. I'm just a . . . a gold miner. Looking . . . You know. For the mother lode. That old Apache. We didn't take him. I didn't. Don't you see. It was just. . . . It was a deal. You see. Do you savvy that, girl. Please, oh my God, please, pretty little girl. I ain't never done no harm to no one. I'm just a . . ."

He stopped, and looked up at Hawk's Talons, who was reaching into a hideous looking lady's handbag.

A lady's handbag. Litsog thought. *How do I know that?*

Hawk's Talons frowned. He cringed as he withdrew the lock of glistening black hair. Women behind Litsog screamed. Others began singing songs of mourning. The scalp fell to the ground. Hawk's Talons brought out another. Then he dropped it and the handbag and stepped several steps away from the . . . ugliness . . . the trophies taken off the Apache dead.

"Where did you find the white eye pouch?" Three Dogs demanded.

"Around this man's shoulder," Hawk's Talons said.

"No," the man cried out. He started blubbering. "It ain't . . . mine . . . I swear . . .

On, please, Golden Hair. Please." The words were broken Apache and English.

"Litsog?" Three Dogs commanded.

She looked at him, feeling sad that she could not help her people.

"What did he say?" the Apache chief asked.

Her head shook. "He talks crazy. Most words I don't remember. He makes no sense. I . . ."

No. She closed her lips tight. Apaches do not apologize.

Three Dogs pointed to the handbag and the Apache scalps. "Bury those," he ordered. "Far from our village."

He turned, and the crowd parted. He said three more words before he was back inside his wickiup.

"Kill him . . . slowly."

CHAPTER THIRTY

Block Frazer hated being here. El Lugar Donde Los Hombres que Toman Cueros Cabelludos Se Juntan para Emborracharse. A passel of words to describe nothing of a town. Hell, Frazer's slaves had better quarters than this dusty piece of filth in the middle of nowhere. No bourbon to be found in this den of inequity, and the water tasted like the iron hooves on the horses in the corrals and stables. The heat here sucked the soul out of everyone, and the commander of the Río Sangrieto Rurales loathed Santiago Vasquez and his dark-skinned scalphunters.

For three days, Frazer and his men had been waiting in this miserable place, waiting for some of Vasquez's men to return with what the untrustworthy Mexican said was the key to finding the camp of Three Dogs and his Apaches. Three days felt like three months, but the lodging was free, and so was the stabling of their livestock. The only thing that cost money were the women — and Frazer had no interest in any of those vermin — and the liquor. The tortillas and the beans were free, providing you drank, and the owner of this bucket of blood took his payment in scalps. Scalps, Block Frazer figured, weren't script, coin, gold. Besides, scalps could be easily replaced.

A shadow appeared in the doorway, nothing but a silhouette, but one of the drunken Mexican riders for Vasquez lifted his filthy shot glass and yelled out, "Oaxaca!" And the man standing beside him turned, smiled, and called out, "José. ¿*Qué pasa?*"

Joseph William Henderson III entered, and the Mexicans waved at him to join. Henderson spoke to the lean, leathery men in the tongue he had grown accustomed to speaking. Not a damned trace of Alabama could be heard these days, which caused Frazer to shake his head. He had been here too damned long. He should have done what Joe Shelby and all the others — practically all the others, anyway — had done. Tucked their tails up between their legs and slinked on home, across the Río Grande in Texas, and then east through Louisiana and north to his home in Alabama.

Henderson kept his conversation brief,

removed his hat, and walked to the table in the corner where Major Frazer sat by himself.

"Major." Henderson lowered his hat to his thigh and saluted with his right hand.

Frazer did not return the salute. Formalities, he thought, should have been dropped years earlier, but he waved his tumbler at the empty chair.

The Alabaman did not sit at first. His lips parted, but he spoke not a word, looked over his shoulder, sighed, and at last dragged the chair across the floor of dirt and sat down.

"Have a drink," Frazer said.

"No thank you, sir." The eruption of voices at the bar caused both men to turn and look, but it was only Santiago Vasquez walking inside, and making his way to the bar, holding one of those scantily dressed chirpies close to him.

"How long are we to stay here, Major?" Henderson asked.

With a heavy sigh, Frazer tipped his head toward the Mexican scalphunter. "Ask Vasquez," he said. Then he shook his head and killed the disgusting, throat-burning, tongue-melting tequila. "Maybe not long." He considered refilling his glass, but he knew he had consumed enough tequila for one day.

Henderson leaned forward, and said in a whisper just loud enough to be heard over the cackling of Mexican voices at the bar. "Some of the boys have been doin' some figurin', suh."

"What kind of figurin'?"

"That it's maybe three hundred kilometers to El Paso."

"Put that in English, bub."

"Less than two hundred miles. 'Bout one hundred eighty-five, eighty-six."

"That's still a right fer piece." Maybe, Frazer figured, he ought to have one more shot. His hand gripped the bottle, and he decided why waste time pouring the clear coal oil into a glass. He drank straight from the bottle.

"A week's hard ride," Henderson said.

"And what's in El Paso?" Frazer made himself drink again. "More greasers like these swine? Maybe tequila that's a grade better than this liver-rotter?" He pitched the bottle across the room, where it smashed against the west wall to add to the pile of shards. No one paid any attention. Frazer laughed, and tried to find a plug of tobacco, but he gave up after half a minute. He had been out of tobacco for weeks.

"America," Henderson answered.

Frazer frowned.

"That's what's north of here," Henderson said. "Some of the boys think it's as close as we've been since we come down here all them years ago."

A chill raced up Frazer's backbone. He frowned, suddenly sobered by the thought, the understanding of what he had just been told. And the fire in young Henderson's eyes told Frazer something else.

"El Paso is not our America, boy," Frazer said.

"Maybe not, suh, but the boys figure they can see home from there."

"Desert?" Frazer shook his head. "You'd quit the cause. Go back to live with Yankees."

"Seems I recollect seein' Lone Star flags aplenty when we was marchin' ag'in the bluebellies. Buried Texicans a plenty beside our own Alabama boys."

"Maybe so, but it's under Yankee rule now, son." He hoped the son would tame this kid's insolence.

"Well, the boys figure they could see Alabama from there, suh."

"Only if they got exceptional eyesight, boy. Alabama's a damned long ways from El Paso."

"But it's close enough. Closer than we've

ever been."

Frazer shook his head, and started to laugh, but the words Henderson had said slowly struck him. "*We've* ever been?" the major asked.

Joseph William Henderson III did not blink or even turn his head.

"This talkin' you've heard some of the boys a-sayin' . . . was most of this talkin' comin' out of your sweet mouth, *Oaxaca José*?" He emphasized the boy's Mexican nickname.

"I let the boys talk, suh. I just listen. Like I been listenin' to you for a coon's age. But what the boys have been sayin', suh, makes a lot of sense. And we figure, well, suh, we'd surely like for you to lead us back home. To Alabama."

"The damned Yanks took our home away from us, son."

"No, suh. You took us away from home. Suh. Time we went back home."

He hadn't felt that dagger in his belly since word came of Appomattox. He hadn't felt that chill since he had seen the flames and smoke of his home. Which reminded Major Block Frazer of why he was sitting in a hovel in the worst patch of land on the globe. He leaned forward and said in a hoarse but strong whisper.

"Let me remind you, Mistah Henderson, that we are here with these swine, these filthy bean-eaters, because by all the reports we have heard, and all the evidence that we have uncovered, that the demon red savage responsible for the lives of my family — and yours — and the friends and soldiers that fought alongside us during that lost but glorious cause — that that murderin' dog was Three Dogs and his infernal Apaches. And that vengeance is finally within our grasp. That we can avenge the slaughter and the inhumanity."

He pushed himself back, and lowered his hands, gripping the arms of the rickety chair, to keep his whole body from shaking. He thought he might break the dried-out wood in two.

For a moment, he could not see. It had to be sweat, he told himself, dripping into his eyes, but when the vision returned, he saw the same look on Henderson's face. Nothing had changed. His speech had fallen upon deaf ears.

That boy with the head of a mule simply asked: "And how much longer do you reckon we'll have to wait before you can get your vengeance, suh?"

Frazer had no answer. He reached for the bottle only to realize he had hurled it into the trash heap inside the cantina. Then he found the glass and tried to taste the last drop or two. He thought Henderson would stand up and leave, leave him alone, leave with all his glorious Alabama boys . . . to ride away, back to Texas, back to whatever homes they might have. And they probably would have.

But Providence entered the cantina.

He heard the hooves of horses, first, then one of Vasquez's men dashed through the opening, spewing out Spanish words that excited all the Mexicans. Even Joseph William Henderson III spun in his seat, and rose.

The rider finished talking, then hurried outside.

Henderson turned, the rigidness gone from his body, his face. His eyes were wide. He turned slightly and stared down at Frazer.

"What did that greaser say, boy?" Frazer demanded.

"They are back," Henderson said. "They have . . ."

He didn't finish. The dust-caked rider returned, followed by another man, and then the third.

It was the sight of the third man that made Major Block Frazer leap to his feet, knocking the lousy chair into the dirt behind him. He had reached for his revolver, but one of Santiago's men grabbed the forearm like a vise and held it.

"No, Major," Henderson whispered.

The third man was an Apache.

Santiago Vasquez laughed and rushed toward the old Indian, weathered by time and hardships and all the white people — children, women, men, old folks, even dogs — he had murdered.

He clapped both hands on the old Apache's shoulders, then fired out Spanish at the first rider.

The Mexican scalphunter answered.

Henderson stared ahead, but translated for Frazer.

"Has the Apache been paid?"

The man answered, and again, Henderson translated. "Only half of his thirty pieces of silver."

Vasquez let out a whoop, glanced at Henderson and Frazer, and then spoke in the guttural grunts of the Indian at the old killer.

Henderson could not translate the Apache, but when Vasquez shouted to his men, the Alabaman looked back at Frazer and spoke loudly, because the room was filled with excited chatter. "The Indian has agreed to lead us to his camp. There he will be paid the rest of the money he is owed. It is . . ." Henderson had to swallow before he could finish. ". . . the camp of Three Dogs."

There was another question that Vasquez directed at the rider, who answered and then made the sign of the cross.

"He asked about a man named Diego," Henderson translated, "and was told that Diego, if he is lucky, is dead. They had to leave him behind, as a sacrifice, otherwise they all might have been killed."

Vasquez almost shouted: *"¿Moverán su aldea?"*

The scalphunter shook his head, and pointed at the Apache, saying: *"Dice que no es probable."*

Again, Henderson translated rapidly. " 'Will they move their village?' The Apache says it ain't likely."

Putting his left arm around the old Apache's shoulders, Vasquez turned the warrior around, and called out in Spanish at Frazer: *"La llave de la cerradura."*

Frazer looked again at Henderson, who translated: "The key to the lock."

Men began opening new bottles of tequila. Others broke into songs, and Henderson looked at Frazer, who said, "Tell the boys that we'll be riding into one final battle. Tell

408

them that when we have killed Three Dogs and all of his men, women, dogs and kids . . . tell them . . . that . . . their service to the Confederacy will no longer be needed. Y'all can go home, if that's what y'all want."

"And you, suh?" Henderson asked.

Frazer shook his head. "I ain't got no home, boy, not in Alabama, no more. Not even here, no more. But all I want from you and the boys is to give me one last good fight. One victory that'll make up for all 'em heartaches and defeats we've had to live through."

The boy's eyes brightened, his hat returned snugly to his head, and he saluted.

He turned to go, but that's when Billy Ray Ferguson rushed into the cantina. Frazer and Henderson both saw him, and at first figured Ferguson had come in to see what had started all the excitement, but he looked at the Apache and Santiago Vasquez only for a moment, then glanced at the bar, then turned and saw the two Alabamans. He rushed forward, saluted, and said, his breath short, but the words clear. "Major, we got visitors."

Frazer's head tilted.

"Spies, suh. Tobey seen 'em. Hoss thieves, it appears to be."

"How many?" Frazer asked.

The boy held out his hand and raised three fingers. "One of 'em's tiny. Either a boy or maybe a gal." He cleared his throat. "And one of 'em's, this is what Tobey says, is wearin' the patched britches of a gol-durned Yankee, suh."

"Where are they?" Henderson barked.

Ferguson's head tilted toward the livery.

"Inside, suh," the boy said. "Got a detail in case they come out first."

"Well." Major Block Frazer had sobered up quickly. It was shaping up to be a fine day, he thought, after all. He might get to kill himself a Yankee, and then ride off to end his long quest at revenge and take the scalp of Three Dogs and as many Apaches as he could.

"Vasquez!" he barked. The Mexican turned around. Frazer looked at Ferguson, ordering him to place squads at positions so that they would have the horse thieves caught in an enfilade, and then he told Vasquez what was going on while his Mexicans were getting roostered instead of watching their horses.

A few minutes later, Major Block Frazer was standing in the doorway to the livery stable, feeling like he often had before putting some Yankee prisoners before a firing squad, and saying:

"Well, well, well, well. Look what has come callin' on us. Horse thieves. Yankees by the looks of 'em. And, my, oh my, a lovely squaw with a fine head of hair that'll bring us fifty pesos in Chihuahua. Or more . . . if we sell her as a whore."

CHAPTER THIRTY-ONE

Sean Keegan cursed his luck. He had just leaned his Springfield against the stall to grab the reins to a finicky horse that the Yaqui wench was having trouble getting saddled. So here he was with both hands wrapped around the leather headstall, staring into the mean eyes of the horse he figured would be ridden by Jed Breen, and in walks a bunch of Rurales who weren't Mexicans at all. Sean Keegan had heard that accent enough during the Rebellion.

Jed Breen had come over and was tightening the cinch on one side of the saddle. Wildcat Walesja turned around, the only one of the three with both hands freed. Jed Breen had already shoved his Sharps into the scabbard.

"Where you boys from?" the leader of the Southern Rurales said. His grin stretched from one ugly ear to one cauliflower ear. The man was having fun with this, and his eyes explained to Keegan why. That drunken sot was full of tequila.

"Major Frazer," one of the Rebs said. "Let's just shoot these thievin' curs and be done with it."

"We will, boy, we most certainly will, but that fella yonder, the one trying to kiss that gelding, why he's dressed up as a Yank. And we must have the courtesy and grace to put him afor' a firin' squad."

"I say we shoot 'em now, Major," a leathery man in a Mexican sombrero said in an accent as deeply Southern as this major's.

"And risk killin' my hoss, Billy Ray? I don't think so, boy. I don't think so a-tall."

The man smiled again. Then he said, "Tobey, relieve my hoss from these miscreants and put him back in the stall."

A pockmarked punk wearing one of those bummer caps of the Secessionists that was stained and torn with a brim that was pretty much chewed up walked toward them casually, holding an old horse pistol with the barrel pointed at the ground. Walking right behind the horse. Jed Breen turned toward Keegan, and the bounty hunter had to have read the Irishman's mind, because he was standing and walking toward Keegan, and unbuckling his gun belt. Keegan did not have any time to consider Wildcat Walesja.

He just waited and then twisted the head-stall as tightly as he could, stepped back after freeing his hands from the leather and cut loose with his best imitation of a Rebel yell.

The gelding snorted and kicked, and its rear hooves caught the stupid Confederate jackass full in the chest, sending him flying backward and scattering the other Rebs.

By then, Breen himself was screeching, and the other two horses they had saddled for themselves, turned and raced through the handful of Rebs at the doorway.

One didn't. He managed to avoid the gelding Keegan had scared the devil out of, and started to level his six-shooter when Breen put a .38 slug into his gut.

That made the other horses that remained in their stalls start up a cacophony of screams as their hooves smashed against the stalls. Dust and hay filled the air.

Keegan found his Springfield and slipped into an empty stall. Out of the corner of his eye, he saw the Yaqui woman pulling that massive horse pistol and jerking the trigger. The upper half of her body vanished in a cloud of white smoke. And Keegan thought, though he wouldn't swear to it, that he heard a high-pitched shriek from the Confederate line.

Two more rounds barked. Keegan fell to his belly, and brought the Springfield up. He found two of the Rebs, lined up like passenger pigeons, ready to die. The .45-70 roared, and Keegan laid it on the hay, then found his Remington. Breen was atop the railing, then dived into the horse manure and hay beside the Irishman just moments before bullets riddled the plank where the bounty hunter had been perched.

Bullets continued to chew up the wood, pound into the adobe, and send more horses screaming and stamping.

Keegan looked underneath the rails, and saw the Yaqui. She had found cover behind a water barrel. He watched her aim, then lower the .44, and make herself into as small as a target as she could. Bullets carved the side of the water barrel. A few others punched the gate of the stall in which Breen and Keegan hid.

Through the smoke, Keegan made out the two men his .45-70 had cut in half. Idiots. That would teach them to line up in single file during a gunfight. The man the horse had kicked lay spread-eagled, and Keegan could not see if the punk's shell jacket was rising and falling like a man knocked senseless or as still as a dumb peckerwood without sense enough to walk around, not behind, any horse.

Just then a figure appeared to Keegan's left. Damn if that Reb wasn't quiet, just like an Apache. He had used the roaring cannonade of gunfire to sneak up the adobe wall that separated two stalls. He had the drop on both Keegan and Breen, and his finger was tightening on the trigger with a blood shot through his dirty muslin shirt, the Colt fell unfired to the straw and the man folded over the adobe like a pair of saddlebags.

Wildcat Walesja let out a triumphant war cry.

Jed Breen turned around and shot another man off his perch, then crawled quickly toward the water trough.

"Hold your fire!" called the Southern leader. "Hold your fire! Hold your fire! You might hit Timmy."

"Timmy's done fer, Major Frazer!" came a cry from Keegan's right. "That damned bitch shot Timmy."

The ringing left Keegan's ears. Breen pulled the dead Reb's revolver from the trough, looked at it, cursed, then aimed through a crack in the rails and squeezed the trigger. The report was a metallic snap.

"Damned Johnny Rebs," Breen said hoarsely. "Still using cap and ball like it was

Eighteen and Sixty-two." He flung the revolver against the adobe.

Keegan's eyes moved to the upper torso of the dead man, whose arms stretched toward the water trough and the feed bucket.

"Jed," Keegan whispered.

The Irishman's head tilted toward the corpse, and Breen turned. It took him only a few seconds to realize what had caught Sean Keegan's eye. The white-haired bounty hunter reached up and fingered a glistening black trophy tied to the Reb's left sleeve. Breen released it, wiped his fingertips on his trousers, and used the barrel of his lightning to push away another long piece of cured black hair.

When the bounty hunter looked at Keegan, he whispered, "The Place Where Scalp Men Hang Out To Get Drunk."

Of course, Keegan thought, who else would be in this hellhole other than scalp-hunting trash. It gave Keegan an idea.

"Hey, Major!" he shouted, then cleared his throat and tried again.

"What is it, Yank?" the Southerner drawled.

"We seem to be getting off on the wrong foot here, Major." Keegan busied himself reloading the Remington. "See, I do believe we happen to be in the same type of business."

There was no response except for nervous horses stomping around on the inside and outside. Then several Mexicans began hollering outside, and a Hispanic voice called out, "Amigo . . . ?" The rest of the Spanish went way too fast for Keegan, his ears still pounding from the pitched battle, to comprehend.

A Southern accent answered the query from inside the livery, but that voice was not from this Major Frazer.

"And what business is yours?" the major said after a long silence.

"We're after an Apache scalp." Keegan wet his lips.

"One scalp. A hundred pesos? That is not much of a business. Did no one at the border tell you that The Place Where Scalp Men Hang Out To Get Drunk is where scalphunters go to celebrate, not where men go to take scalps?"

"Major," Keegan said, and this time he smiled. "We're after Blood Moon himself."

There was a pause, but not for long.

"Alas, Yank, you did not find that Apache butcher here. But we will mark your grave accordingly that you died seekin' Blood Moon."

"Well," Keegan said, "the thing is, Major, we know where Blood Moon is camped."

Breen gave Keegan one of those looks, and Keegan tried to stare back at him, though he could understand the bounty hunter's position. Sean Keegan had not had enough Irish whiskey or cold porter to come up with a brilliant plan.

More Spanish came from the outside, and some talk answered from the inside. Then the major said, "What is your proposition?"

"Partners. Fifty-fifty. You get half the reward for Blood Moon. My pard and me take the other half. But all the other scalps, those will be for your boys only. My pard and me. Ten thousand dollars will suit us just fine."

"Well," the Southerner said, "I think my Rurales will keep with our current partnership. With Santiago Vasquez."

"But can this Santiago Vasquez take you right smack to Blood Moon and . . ." He turned quickly to Breen, mouthing, "What's that Apache chief's name?" Reading Breen's lip, Keegan called out, "Three Dogs' wickiups?"

Breen started muttering curses while shaking his head.

"I think we'll just kill you, the red-skinned bitch, and your pard," Major Frazer said.

"Yeah, but then you won't have enough men to wipe out Three Dogs and all those Apaches," Keegan said.

By now, the Yaqui woman had started her death song.

"You can't kill us all," the major said.

"But we can sure put a big hurt on you. Hell, Major, we've already killed six."

"Seven," the major corrected. "A busted rib must have punctured poor Tobey's heart."

"And we're just getting started," Keegan said.

The major laughed. "Yank." The pause stretched as Keegan heard whispers. Spirited whispers. "Yank," the major resumed after the quiet discussion. "We can wait you out. Starve you out. Burn you out."

"You won't burn us out, Major."

"Why not?"

" 'Cause you got too much prime horse-flesh in this livery. Burn us out, your horses fry like steaks."

"Fry like you and your low-down Yankee friend of dog dung."

"And you can't afford to starve us out."

"Why not?"

" 'Cause if we don't start raising dust, Three Dogs and Blood Moon won't be around for you or me or any other scalphunter in this part of Mexico."

Breen mouthed: *Do you know what you're talking about?*

Keegan answered in kind: *Of course not.*

"How do you know where Blood Moon and Three Dogs are?"

Keegan let out a sigh of relief. "That Yaqui with us. She knows."

A minute passed, followed by another, but this time Keegan heard no whispers. Even the Spanish-speaking scalphunters outside remained quiet. Finally the major said, "How can we trust y'all?"

"That ain't the question, Major," Keegan shot back. "The question is: How can we trust you?"

"So we're back to that . . . Mexican standoff." He chuckled at his joke. Then he said, "All right. I will step out. If my men start shooting, you no doubt will take me to Hell with you. Then we will discuss your proposition with Santiago Vasquez." Another long silence followed. "You men keep your guns out. My men will lower theirs." He barked a brusque order.

"You have my word, as a Southern officer who served under General Forrest."

Keegan did not even look at Breen. He stood quickly, using his hat to beat off the straw and dust from his outfit. He figured he'd get his head blown off, and if that were to be his end, he didn't want to die dirty and covered with hay. He stepped to the gate, pushed it open, careful not to get splinters from gunshots in his hand. He stepped into the main area, staring at the dead and the living, then at the Yaqui.

Her face had become a statue, but her eyes burned with hatred at Keegan. Still she moved toward him, holding the smoking Dragoon, which she dropped into the straw.

"Empty," she said, and raised her hands.

"There's no need for that, child," the major said as he approached the three horse thieves. "At least not until we work out a few details." He removed his hat and bowed. "I am Major Block Frazer of the sovereign Confederate state of Alabama."

They left the dead in the barn for the time being, stepping out into the bright sun, where Keegan saw just how many scalp-hunters happened to be in this small, dirty outpost that no one even in West Texas would call a village.

The Rebels and the Mexicans formed a wide circle, and Keegan figured this was how he died. With a half-baked plan in the biggest wasteland he had ever seen. He hoped Matt McCulloch was having better luck.

The major talked quickly with the Mexican butcher Keegan figured had to be Santiago Vasquez, and then an ex-Rebel soldier was ordered through the lines. He appeared to be heading toward the cantina. A few minutes later, he returned. This time an Indian came with him.

When the line parted and the two men entered, Keegan heard the Yaqui woman hiss. "Yo-íi." He had no idea what that meant.

But the look on Major Block Frazer's face told Keegan that he, Jed Breen and Wildcat Walesja were about to be cut down in the prime of their lives.

"Yank," the major said, and he waved his left hand at the ancient Indian. "This is our own guide. Our Apache Judas. This old codger is gonna lead us to the camp of Three Dogs. And we shall kill everyone in camp. If Blood Moon is there, so be it. If not, I don't rightly give a damn."

The Mexican leader came forward, grinning a sickening smile and saying in decent English. "So you see, your guide and your proposition are worthless to us. Drop your guns."

Too many cocking guns punctuated the statement.

"We'll give you time to make your peace,

and you will be executed with honor —
though you deserve none of this — by firin'
squad," Major Frazer said.

Keegan knew he had no choice. His gun
belt dropped at his feet.

"Nice plan," Breen said sarcastically, and
let his gun rig fall to the dust, too.

Major Frazer and Santiago Vasquez were
enjoying themselves when Wildcat Walesja
brought up the Remington derringer and
shot the old Apache right between his eyes.

Chapter Thirty-Two

The grizzled old Apache medicine man dropped like a stone. The Mexicans trained their revolvers and rifles on Wildcat Walesja. That's when Jed Breen took five quick steps and dived. His right shoulder caught the bony Yaqui woman at her waist, and he drove her to the hard dirt as bullets whined over them. He landed with a thud, felt a bullet scorch the nape of his neck, and another tear through the back of his left thigh. The woman fought him, like he was trying to rape her, but Breen managed to cover her, and figured this was how his end would come. Atop a feisty, crazed woman, riddled by bullets from scalphunters, and not even getting a chance to tell Matt McCulloch exactly what he thought of him.

Well, Breen thought as he closed his eyes and felt another bullet kick sand into his ear, *maybe I'll get a chance to give that unholy devil a piece of my mind in Hell.*

Wildcat Walesja screamed as another bullet slammed into her balled fist just before she brought it down on Breen's back.

Then, in this hellish maelstrom, Jed Breen heard something that sounded just downright heavenly.

"Hold your fire!"

"*¡Deja de disparar! ¡Detener!*"

"Hold your fire!"

"*¡Detener!*"

"Stop shooting, or ye'll never get to see Three Dogs and all them Apache scalps!"

"*¡Dejen de disparar, imbéciles!*"

"Hold your fire!"

"Cease fire! Cease fire!"

The ringing left Breen's ears, and the gunfire faded. He rolled off the Yaqui, and unknotted the bandanna around his neck. Mexicans and Alabamans circled them, with more than a few keeping their smoking weapons trained at Breen and the squaw. Sliding over, Breen took Wildcat Walesja's bloody hand, and wrapped the bandanna around the wound. He gritted his teeth and watched Sean Keegan slip through the circle of guards and kneel beside him.

"How bad ye hit, bub?"

Through clenched teeth, Breen said, "I think it just tore through the flesh a bit."

"I'll have to pull down ye britches."

"I do it," the Yaqui said, then tied off Breen's bandanna over her own wound, using her teeth.

"The hell you will," Breen said.

"Laddie," Keegan said with that vindictive Irish look of glee in his eyes, "it's not like a woman from Maudie's has never seen a man's limbs before."

Suddenly, two men stood over the jackals and the woman.

Breen and Keegan both looked up at Major Block Frazer and Santiago Vasquez.

"The Apaches are known to bury a man up to his head, then pour honey over him, and watch the ants come," the former Rebel officer said. "We have our own methods that make the Apache way seem . . . civilized."

The fierce Mexican barked something in Spanish, but all Breen recognized were the curse words.

"You want those Apaches," Keegan said. "You'll deal with us."

"Mistah Henderson!" the Johnny Reb called out. "How is that Apache?"

A moment later, another Southern voice called from beyond the circle of scalphunters. "He's barking in Apache hell, suh!"

The Mexican and Reb exchanged a glance, then the Mexican, this Santiago Vasquez, knelt, pushed back his sombrero and grinned. "You have cost us much time and men, amigos." He lifted his chin at Wildcat Walesja. "How can she have knowledge of the Apache camp? A Yaqui does —"

"I am not a Yaqui, you piece of Mexican dung," Wildcat Walesja snapped. Then she repeated the phrase in Spanish, just so nothing was lost in the translation. "I am . . . Apache."

"Apache!" Keegan looked shocked.

"Yes, Apache." She turned, snarling from either the pain in her hand or just her usual disposition. "You think I'd tell anyone that I am Apache? The men in Purgatory City would have cut my throat and cut off my hair. I am Apache."

"And the red savage that you killed?" the major asked.

"Yo-íí," she snapped. "Our holy man. Once a good Apache. But . . ."

Vasquez grinned. "Every man has his price."

"He paid for it."

The major rubbed his beard stubble. "How can you find Three Dogs's camp?"

"It is summer." She nodded at the mountains. "He will be there till winter comes, then he will move lower."

"How long has she been whoring in Texas?" the major asked Keegan.

428

Keegan tried to look shocked, but the fake Yaqui said, "Three Dogs is no fool. No one has found his camp. He will not move it. It is like the stronghold of our people in Arizona Territory. It is safe." Her head fell. "Had been safe. Until Yo-íí's treachery."

Vasquez grinned. "And now . . . your treachery?"

She glared at him. "For which I will be well paid."

"We need her, Major," one of the Rebs said. "But we ain't got no use for 'em boys."

"Sí," said a Mexican. "They kill enough men already."

Wildcat Walesja rose. "They go with me," she said. "Or we all die here."

Second Lieutenant Charles Tibbetts slapped at a mosquito. "Bugs," he said testily. "I wish we were back in that furnace."

"I don't," Three-Toed Charley said. The bloodsuckers did not have any interest in the surly, stinking scout, and Tibbetts could understand why.

The other scout, Tiny Olderman, then entered the wooded camp in the lower elevations of the Sierra Madres, pulling his horse behind him. Mosquitoes ignored him, too.

"Well!" Tibbetts snapped.

429

"No sign of 'em, boss," the scout said, leading his horse to the picket rope.

"Damn." Tibbetts found another mosquito. His left hand slapped on his right, and the lieutenant grinned with success at the bloody splotch on the back of his hand. But his impatience returned, and he glared at that lackadaisical, smart-talking scout. "I thought you said the Apaches were in these mountains."

"They are."

"Then why haven't you picked up the tracks left by Blood Moon and that Ranger?"

Three-Toed Charley stifled a yawn. "Because they ain't here, Lieutenant. Somehow, we beat 'em to these mountains."

"Maybe they aren't coming here."

The scout grinned underneath his beard. "Oh, they'll be here, Lieutenant, unless they's dead." He lazily pointed a finger east. "Nobody spends too much time in that hell." Yawning, the scout crossed his legs at the ankles and made himself comfortable for an afternoon nap. "We got us a good view of that desert from right here on this ledge. We just followed that dried riverbed right up to here. Got us lots of shade, too, and water just fifty yards away in that brook. We can see for miles and miles, and when somebody raises dust for these mountains, we'll see where they come in, then it's just all about getting to that spot and following them till you can get your scalp. So all we gots to do, Lieutenant, is sit and wait. Not move around too much because we want to find your Apache buck, but we sure as hell don't want no other Apaches to find us."

The haze never seemed to end. The journey went on forever. Matt McCulloch rode alongside Blood Moon now, the Apache still gripping the lead rope and pulling the mustang stallion behind him. Finally, the mountains rose before them. Higher than the Davis Mountains, Matt figured, and maybe a whole lot cooler. He found his canteen, lifted it from the saddle horn, and shook it, hearing the slosh of not even a quarter of a cup. McCulloch tried his best to wet his cracked, splitting lips.

He swallowed, and started to put the canteen, unopened, back where it belonged.

"Drink, White Eyes," the Apache beside him spoke without moving his head. "Water a few miles away."

"If it's like this damned riverbed we've been riding in . . ." McCulloch said, though his voice was so dry, he wasn't sure the Apache had heard.

But Blood Moon's face cracked as he grinned.

"Mexicans call it Río Muerto. Dead River. But it only dies in desert. Up there . . ." Blood Moon nodded at the Sierra Madres.

McCulloch decided not to look at the mountains. The mountains reminded him of just how long he had been in this steaming desert, and how close he might be to finding his daughter after all these years. He patted the pinto's neck, wet his lips again with his tongue, and stared at the ground below. Ground. Miserable stones and sand and cactus. And . . .

He reined in abruptly, startling the gray stallion behind the Apache's horse. Before the pinto had come to a complete stop, McCulloch's boots were planted on the earth, and he was kneeling, holding the reins in one hand, and fingering the dried horse manure in his left.

Blood Moon turned his horse and rode closer. The Apache looked down, but his expression did not change. McCulloch pitched the dried horse apple away, wiping his fingers on his chaps and moved a few feet away. This time his fingers dipped into a small dip, and traded the outline of a horse shoe. The depression of the dead bed, more stream than river, had protected it

432

from the blowing sand and never-ending wind.

"Shod horse." He looked up at Blood Moon, who showed no reaction.

"How old?" the Apache asked after a moment.

McCulloch jutted his jaw toward the horse dung. "My guess, two days."

"How many?"

The former Ranger rose, his knees popping. "Let's find out." He led his horse slowly south. Blood Moon dismounted, hobbled the stallion, and moved north. After twenty yards, McCulloch turned west, and so did the Apache. After ten minutes, the Apache had found something. Two minutes later, McCulloch knelt again and found more horse manure, dried. Tracks were hard to find, for the wind was like a washrag on a chalkboard at a one-room schoolhouse, but chalkboards, McCulloch recollected, weren't all that easy to clean. He found another print, which confirmed his theory that these tracks and dung were left two days ago, no more than three.

He glanced at the sun, sinking now just an hour above the tips of the mountains, when he returned to the hobbled stallion. Blood Moon rejoined him five minutes later in a deeper part of the Dead River. Now

McCulloch drank from his canteen, and so did the Apache. Both men also let their horses drink, even the stallion.

"Six men," McCulloch said, licking the moisture from the water off his lips, not letting one drop get away. "No fewer than that. Probably seven, eight. Two, three days ahead. All shod horses."

"Eight men," the Apache affirmed. "Two days."

"White men," McCulloch said. "They don't ride like Apaches."

Blood Moon nodded. "Pony soldiers."

"Yeah." McCulloch wrapped the canvas strap of his canteen around the saddle horn. "With a pair of civilian scouts."

"You make good Apache," Blood Moon said, and studied the mountains ahead of them.

This time, McCulloch let the insult pass without comment. He pointed east. "My guess is those troopers we set up for that set-to with the *Rurales* back . . ." He couldn't recall how long ago that had been, so he just shook his head, and drew his Colt, checking the loads. "They are one determined bunch."

Blood Moon pointed to the mountains. "If they reached that place, they soon be dead. They will search for Three Dogs, but be found by Three Dogs."

McCulloch shook his head. Blood Moon, for once, looked confused.

"Not if they want us. Well, not if they want . . ." He nodded at the Apache. ". . . you."

Now Blood Moon laughed. "You are Apache."

He wasn't going to let that pass twice. "I've told you —"

But Blood Moon held out his hand, palm facing McCulloch, and then pointed at the mountains.

"If they smart, if just one has wisdom, they wait and watch. Dust easy to see. So we wait." He sat down, Indian style, pulled out his sheathed knife, and began testing the blade. "We wait for dark. Then follow Dead River into mountains."

McCulloch moved to his horse to loosen the cinch. "You," he said without turning back to the Indian, "would make a good Texas Ranger."

Litsog sat upright in her lodge. She was shaking, sweating, and her chest heaved. Her wickiup was completely black in the stillness of night, and even the Apache fires outside had turned to nothing more than embers so that the women could build back

435

up for breakfast when dawn broke.

So how could she see so clearly inside?

"Yo-íí," she said, recognizing the squat figure of the old holy man of the Apache village.

His head tilted slowly in greeting.

"I thought you were gone," she said.

"I am gone," he told her.

She rubbed her eyes, felt a sudden chill that shook her to her very marrow, and when her balled fists dropped to her side, she thought the old man would be gone, a figment of her imagination, a dream.

But Yo-íí remained.

Litsog leaned slightly forward, staring at the old man's face. Blood had spilled from the tip of the bridge of his nose, with a ghastly hole between the eyes, and the blood, now dried and caked, closing his right eye and filling the canyons that time had carved in his ancient face.

"What happened to you?" she gasped.

"It is not important," he said. "Not now. It is the vision I saw. It is why I had to leave."

"I am glad you came back," she heard herself say.

"I have not come back."

The chill returned and she wanted to pull up a blanket over her shoulders.

"Before you were brought to us," the old

man said, "I told Three Dogs that no white woman should ever enter our camp. That it would cause trouble. That it would bring death to us all. Three Dogs did not listen to me." His voice dropped to a whisper. "Perhaps it was because of your yellow hair."

Her hand found the locks she had chopped off . . . how long ago? Days? Weeks? Eternity?

Her Adam's apple bobbed and she asked, "Will I still go home?"

"Yes." Yo-íi nodded.

"And you?"

"I am already home, Litsog," he said.

"I am glad you returned."

"I have not returned. I am with my ancestors."

Again she trembled.

"It is all right, child," he told her. "It is good to be with my ancestors. And soon, because of my transgressions, the Apaches of this village will be with their ancestors. Three Dogs is to blame. He is a great chief. But he is a fool. He never should have made camp here." He pointed. "The riverbed, long dried, that flows from here to the desert. The Mexicans have a name for it. Dead River. And that is what will become of the Apaches." His head dropped. "No. It

437

is I, Yo-íí, who has been the biggest of all fools."

The old man, she realized, was crying, and when he removed his buffalo headdress with his trembling hands, Litsog gasped. The wiry, silver hair had been ripped from his scalp. "My hair," he whispered, "no longer the black of the Apache youth . . . I thought they would not take it . . ."

"Who did this, Grandfather?" Litsog demanded.

"Why the scalphunters, of course. After they killed me."

She did not understand.

He brought the heavy headdress back to cover his head.

"What scalphunters?"

"The ones who are coming to this village. The ones I sent here."

A long moment passed as Litsog tried to comprehend what the old man had told her.

"Grandfather . . ." Litsog started.

"What is your name?" he said with a lovely voice, something like an angel might speak.

"I am . . . Litsog."

His head shook. "No. Your other name. I would like to know it."

Her lips trembled, and something wet ran down her cheeks.

"It is all right, child," he said in that soothing voice. "What is your name?"

This time, to Litsog's wonder, she had no trouble remembering, and the words flowed out as though she had never forgotten.

"My name," she said, "is Cynthia McCulloch." She had closed her eyes when she had spoken, and when she opened her eyes, Yo-íí was gone, an inky blackness had enveloped her wickiup and she heard nothing but the trees rustling in the wind.

"Yo-íí?" she called out.

The reply came from all around her.

"Farewell, Litsog," the holy man's voice said. "Now, you must do one final thing for me. Go to the wickiup of Three Dogs, my child. And tell Three Dogs that death comes to this camp at dawn. Go, Cynthia McCulloch. Go now."

Chapter Thirty-Three

Litsog was no longer. She had become Cynthia McCulloch, and Cynthia Jane McCulloch was scared. The blackness of night was ending, the skies turning gray, and she moved with intense purpose through the camp, frightening a sleeping dog, and came to the wickiup of Three Dogs. The flap was closed. She forgot her manners, and pushed her way inside.

The lodge smelled of smoke and deer meat. The Apache chief's oldest wife woke first, sat up, and barked at the intruder, demanding why she came into this lodge without invitation. The youngest wife rolled over and demanded that the old nag go back to sleep, that she was dreaming.

The voice of Three Dogs silenced both women. He pushed off the bearskin and stared into the darkness.

"Who is this and why are you here?"

She answered first in English, then shook

her head, and for the first time in years, she tried to remember how to speak in Apache.

"Litsog?" Three Dogs must have recognized her voice.

"Sí." Spanish came easier.

"What is the matter?"

The old wife muttered something obscene.

"Be quiet, woman!" Three Dogs rose.

"It is . . ." Cynthia had found the Apache words, but she stopped, not wanting to frighten the women in Three Dogs' lodge. She beckoned the chief, and slipped outside, moving to the nearest fire.

There, as the embers smoldered, she told Three Dogs everything she remembered from her dream. No, that was no dream. That was an Apache vision.

After Cynthia finished, Three Dogs squatted, found some kindling, and tossed them on the fire.

"Yo-íí is with his ancestors," the Apache chief said softly. "I cannot blame him for what he did. I kicked his son out of our village. A father loves his son more than he loves his own people." His head bobbed. "That is why he is not the chief. A chief loves his village more than his own life."

That's right, Cynthia remembered. Blood Moon was the only surviving son of Yo-íí. And then she remembered her own father, saw his face, until tears blinded the vision. "What does it mean?" Cynthia asked.

"It means . . ." Three Dogs found a larger piece of wood and pitched it into the coals, sending sparks flying. He threw another log on the fire. "It means that we will be ready for the White Eyes when they come to take our scalps. And they may kill us all. But what a price they will pay for our lives." He turned and barked loudly, telling the men to rise and paint their faces for war, to get their weapons ready.

The women came out, too. One barked out that she would fight with her man.

"Yes." Three Dogs nodded. He threw another log on the fire. "Let them come!" he shouted. "Let them come . . . and die! They will die in the Dead River."

In the gray light just before the break of dawn, Blood Moon nodded at the camp in the clearing below and signaled with his good hand five spread-out fingers, closed them into a fist, and then held up three fingers. Eight.

Matt McCulloch nodded. Eight men, most of them the Fort Spalding troopers McCulloch thought would have been limping back to Texas after the little fight McCulloch and Blood Moon had arranged for them back at La Aldea de las Siete Hermanas de la Fe — The Village of the Seven Sisters of Faith. They were steadfast. McCulloch had to give them that. Damned fools. But mighty persistent.

The Apache and the one-time Ranger had waited until darkness before leaving the flats of the desert and entering the Sierra Madre range, found a good spot for their horses, hobbling the stallion, and then rested and ate. Then Blood Moon had awakened McCulloch and they had begun moving through the woods and rocks, till discovering the camp of the American troopers.

Maybe, McCulloch thought, they had been granted permission to enter Mexico. But giving what all McCulloch had read in the Purgatory City and El Paso newspapers about the strained relations between Washington, D.C., and Mexico City, McCulloch figured that was unlikely. These boys must have been under the command of some arrogant martinet.

The men below snored, and the horses stamped their feet in the cool air. Only one man was awake, the sentry, a scout clad in buckskins, and he kept his eye out on the desert below. McCulloch tried to think of how he and the Apache should proceed. Kill them? Well, that would require some doing, even for men like Blood Moon and Matt McCulloch, who had killed many, many men. Rifle fire would carry far, alert the Apache camp that they had company. The best bet, McCulloch figured, was to just slip away. Let these damned fools just keep looking east, waiting for McCulloch and the Apache to signal their approach with dust clouds. McCulloch and Blood Moon could get to the camp of Three Dogs, McCulloch could trade the stallion for Cynthia, and get out — if everything went the way McCulloch prayed it might.

Fat chance in hell of that happening, though. Not with Blood Moon's hate-filled heart.

The scout made the decision for McCulloch.

He sprang out of his crouch, kicking a stone that tumbled over the side, and called out, "Lieutenant!"

Blood Moon was already looking at what the sentry had seen. He used his shriveled bad hand to point, and McCulloch could see the dust. Even in the dim light, he knew the men riding toward him numbered a hell of a lot more than just eight.

Blood Moon pointed south. McCulloch nodded, and they eased away from the camp of bluebellies, moving quietly until they heard the noise of men muttering, cursing, and making enough racket to raise the dead. That would cover their own footsteps, both men knew, and they hurried back to their horses.

How in the hell are we going to get out of this bloody pickle? That's what Sean Keegan was thinking as dawn began to break. Of course, Keegan had not come up with an answer that satisfied him.

Beside him, Jed Breen was thinking something else. *Who the hell is crazier, the Mexican Vasquez or that Johnny Reb from Alabama?* Breen shook his head. *No, no, that wasn't it. The Yaqui — no, Apache — whore's crazier. No, it's a toss-up between Keegan and me.*

That's when Wildcat Walesja spurred her horse into a gallop, Sean Keegan and Jed Breen glanced at each other, then kicked their horses and caught up to her.

Behind them, the scalphunters of the Mexican Santiago Vasquez and those riding under the colors of Major Block Frazer's Río Sangrieto Rurales charged after them.

"What the hell are you doing?" Breen roared at the Apache woman over the sound of thundering hooves.

Wildcat Walesja twisted in the saddle, holding the reins in her left hand and motioning at the scalphunters behind them to catch up, put the spurs to those horses.

"Are you crazy, woman?" Sean Keegan called out. He rode on the Apache's right. Breen was on her left.

She looked forward as the mountains drew nearer. "We tire out their horses," she said. "That way my people can catch them and kill them with ease."

"They might want to kill us, too, lassie darling," Keegan said.

"I will protect you," she said, leaning forward and giving her horse more rein. "Maybe."

"Watch them spyglasses, Lieutenant."

"Shut the hell up," Lieutenant Charles Tibbetts told Three-Toed Charley.

"Sun's coming up, sir," the scout said. "Them riders see that reflection off them lenses, and they'll know exactly where we are."

"I know what I'm doing, scout," the lieutenant said testily. But the binoculars quickly dropped, and Tibbetts pushed himself to his feet. He frowned, and his face paled. Turning toward Three-Toed Charley and Tiny Olderman, he said in a tight whisper, "That's not . . . ."

Three-Toed Charley cut him off. "You're

446

damned right, Lieutenant. That ain't Blood Moon and that white man ridin' with him. That's a gol-durned army."

"Not U.S. Army formation, sir," one of the bluecoats said.

"Nope." Three-Toed Charley spit out tobacco juice. "Scalphunters." Then he took off his hat and scratched through his thick, dirty hair at his scalp. "But what the hell is they ridin' so hard fer?"

The next thing Tibbetts heard was the deafening report of a Springfield carbine not twenty feet away from him.

He spun around and saw the white-faced trooper working the breech of his smoking .45-70, trying to find a fresh cartridge to load.

"What in God's name are you doing?" Tibbetts thundered. "They are out of range, you damned fool! And now they know exactly where we are?"

It took all the restraint Tibbetts could muster not to shoot the damned fool on the spot.

Matt McCulloch was working on the hobbles to the gray mustang when the gunshot echoed. He stopped, turned, looking north underneath the stallion's front legs. That was a rifle. From the camp of the U.S. Army boys.

He crawled from underneath the mustang, slipped around the back of the horse, keeping his hand on the animal's body so he wouldn't get kicked, and moved to the side of a boulder, crouching, staring at the desert floor below.

"Scalphunters," Blood Moon said.

"A hell of a lot of them." McCulloch frowned, but then a grin cracked his façade. "This might work to our advantage," he told the Apache, or maybe he was trying to convince himself. "Buy us some time."

He couldn't see the troopers from here, but figured the charging scalphunters would ride to the sound of the gunfire. While those scalphunters were tangling with the blue-bellies, McCulloch and Blood Moon could make their way to the Apache camp. They'd probably meet some Apaches on their way there, because Three Dogs' men would be coming to investigate, too.

He hurried back, crawled underneath the stallion, and started working on the hobbles.

He had just gotten the last strap loosened when Blood Moon spoke again. "Yes, White Eye," the Apache said as he swung onto his horse. "It will work just fine." The ruthless butcher kicked his horse's sides, and rode out of the clearing, finding the deer trail that they had followed up to get here.

"You yellow dog!" McCulloch hurried out from underneath the horse, started for his pinto to jerk the Winchester from the scabbard, but had to stop and grab the lead rope to the stallion, which fought briefly. He wrapped the rope tightly around a tree trunk, then made his way to his horse. Winchester in hand, he returned to the boulder, aimed.

Blood Moon galloped into his gunsights, and McCulloch looked above the rifle.

He let out a long sigh. Kill the Apache now, and what chance would McCulloch have of finding Cynthia. He was this damned close. If he went looking for the Apaches himself, they would find him. And his life wouldn't be worth a counterfeit penny.

Below, Blood Moon pulled his gelding to a sliding stop. The animal reared, and the Apache yelled and yipped.

McCulloch found the dust clouds. He could see the riders now. They were that close. Some pulled away from the leaders of the pack, and turned toward the Apache, who hurled insults in Apache, Spanish and English at the riders, before turning his horse and riding back into the mountains.

Swearing, McCulloch looked north. No doubt the bluecoats a quarter mile in the rocks had seen Blood Moon, too.

He rushed back to the horses, untied the lead rope, and swung into the saddle on his mount. Blood Moon thundered past him and rode southwest into the Sierra Madres. McCulloch put the reins in his teeth, ripped the Winchester from the scabbard with his right hand, and holding the lead rope in his left, he spurred the pinto and took off after that double-crossing Apache.

Second Lieutenant Charles Tibbetts told himself that he was no fool. He had the men mounted and riding out of the camp in fine time. The colonel would acknowledge that when he forwarded his report to department headquarters — after they had brought in the head of Blood Moon — and the newspaper reporters and the dime novelists and maybe even the President of the United States of America would do the same.

With scout Tiny Olderman leading the way and Three-Toed Charley bringing up the rear, they moved along what passed for a trail. Olderman reined in quickly in a clearing, and motioned Tibbetts ahead. He kicked his mount and hurried to the big, burly scout and followed his arm, hand and pointer finger down below.

It was an Apache, keeping his horse under control, beckoning the scalphunters, then turning his mount and galloping away, back into the mountains, not that far from where Tibbetts and his men were.

No. His mouth opened to draw in a quick breath. That wasn't just any Apache. That was Blood Moon himself.

"Hurry!" he told the fat scout.

"You bet," Tiny Olderman said, and Tibbetts turned in his saddle, smiling, and told his men. "We've got Blood Moon!"

But the woods here thickened, and they had to slow, moving in single file, between trees where the bark scratched both sides of Tibbetts's Army trousers. By the time they found a wider path, Tibbetts heard the hooves of horses. He had to lean to his right, to see past the fat tub of buckskins in front of him, but that was enough.

Blood Moon appeared on his horse, reining in briefly, barking, gesturing, then turning his horse and disappearing into the mountain forest before Tibbetts thought to draw his service revolver. A second later, a white man went galloping after the Apache killer. The white man had a Winchester rifle in one hand, and pulled a bareback horse the color of a Rebel frock coat behind him.

"After them!" Tibbetts bellowed.

But before he could put his Army spurs against his horse's flesh, three other riders appeared — two white men, one of them wearing a beat-up Army campaign hat, the other with the whitest hair Tibbetts had ever seen. They disappeared into the wood-lined trail following the third rider.

The third rider, the best Tibbetts could tell, was a damned Indian squaw.

Chapter Thirty-Four

Major Block Frazer had the fastest horse, and he pulled closer to those damned fools — the woman, the Yankee, and the white-haired hombre with the fancy Sharps rifle — but as his horse climbed up what passed for a trail, the others caught up with him.

Santiago Vasquez barked some Mexican insult, then used English to urge Frazer forward.

Instead, Frazer stopped his horse complete.

"No pares, maldito tonto," Vasquez said in a tight whisper.

"Shut the hell up, you damned greaser," Frazer growled back at him.

He had heard something, and then he saw them. A fat, bearded, ugly man in buckskins rode just above them, followed by . . .

"Yankees," he whispered, feeling his face flush.

They rode past, never glancing at the trail

below. The last man was another scout. Twisting in the saddle, he stared at Santiago Vasquez, who no longer seemed so angry.

"Eight," Frazer said.

The Mexican's head nodded.

Frazer grinned. "That Apache, the way I think, she's leading us into an ambush."

"Your wisdom almost matches mine, amigo," the Mexican said.

"That's how you had it figured, too, eh?" Frazer felt a mosquito buzz past his left ear. A damned mosquito. He almost laughed. It reminded him of home in Alabama.

"Sí."

"Pass the word," he told Vasquez. "We'll ride up to the trail, let the Yanks get ahead of us, and then we'll listen for the sound of battle. When the Apaches have butchered those bluebellies, we shall ride in and kill all them redskins."

"The woman," Vasquez said. "She will tell the Apaches that we will be coming, too, amigo. There will be no surprise."

He hated it when any man questioned his orders, and he shook his head.

"She won't have time to tell them," he said. "We'll be that close behind. As soon as the Apaches have finished their butchery, we'll be the ones doing the butchery."

Santiago Vasquez shrugged. What else

could he have done? While they had been talking, Frazer had pulled his Confederate-made pistol from his holster, and thumbed back the hammer. If the Mexican scalp-hunter had said anything but agreement, Frazer would have blown him right out of his saddle.

Of course, Santiago Vasquez wasn't that dumb. He was absolutely right. The Apaches would know fifty riders would be right behind those eight, and they'd be ready for them. But, what the hell. Block Frazer's Alabamans were already homesick, and they wanted to go crawling back and take the oath of allegiance after all these years, and go back to living under the oppressive blue-belly government's thumb. Major Frazer wasn't going to do that, and he'd be damned if he'd have his own men desert him like yellow dogs. So Block Frazer figured to have his last taste of revenge. He'd kill as many Apaches as he could, and then he'd join his wife and old friends.

He would die, sure. So would all of his boys. But, by Jehovah, they would die gloriously and take as many Apache fiends with him — and Vasquez's greasers, too.

He realized what they were following, not a deer trail, but a dried stream bed, the same one, just smaller, deeper, than the one in the flats. The Dead River. Río Muerto. The woods and mountains seemed to vanish, and McCulloch realized he had ridden right into the Apache camp. Flames glowed in the morning air in firepits. Wickiups surrounded the clearing, and Blood Moon raced his horse around the camp, screaming in rage, his face uglier than ever.

It was a large camp. More wickiups than McCulloch had ever seen.

But other than the gesticulating Blood Moon, Matt McCulloch couldn't see one damned Apache.

But he heard the riders, behind him, and still clutching Winchester and rope to the stallion, he kicked free of the stirrups and leaped off the pinto, which bolted in excited confusion between the two nearest Apache lodges.

He raised the rifle with one hand, but did not touch the trigger.

The first rider he saw was an Indian woman, and she jerked her horse to a stop, so hard the gelding almost fell onto its folded front legs. She had a small gun — a damned derringer — in her right fist, but she wasn't aiming at McCulloch. She snapped a shot that sent Blood Moon's horse bucking.

Then she was on her feet, hurling the empty hideaway gun into the dirt.

"You rat!" she yelled in English, then switched to Apache.

McCulloch didn't follow her. He found a wooden stump, and quickly wrapped the end of the lead rope around it as the mustang snorted and reared. Now he shouldered the stock of the Winchester and drew a bead on the next rider.

But his finger quickly moved off the trigger.

"Matt!" Sean Keegan shouted. And Jed Breen was right behind him.

Keegan couldn't figure out what the hell they had ridden into. He knew it was an Apache village, but the only Apaches he saw were fighting each other. Wildcat Walesja was running toward Blood Moon, who had been thrown off his bucking horse after the Apache woman sent a bullet at him.

But he saw Matt McCulloch. His old comrade had lowered the rifle, and was running back toward a stump, grabbing ahold of a rope to keep that gray stallion from running away.

Jed Breen leaped off his horse and shouted, "We got company, boys." Breen had drawn his Sharps before he dismounted, and now he turned, dropped to a shooter's stance, and let his fancy rifle sing.

The horse Tiny Olderman was riding just ahead somersaulted, sending the hefty scout flying straight into a campfire in the village. Only then did Lieutenant Charles Tibbetts hear the roar of a heavy rifle. Tibbetts had his revolver ready, though, and he made out the white-headed peckerwood who had shot a government-issued mount.

He recognized the assassin as Jed Breen, that jackal of a bounty hunter, stood and dived behind a felled tree that might have served as a bench.

Horses raced all around Tibbetts, but he swung his Colt. The squaw was fighting Blood Moon. Tibbetts thought he might get lucky. A .45 slug would probably go straight through that Indian witch's body and hit Blood Moon plumb center.

Just before he could squeeze the trigger, his hand practically disintegrated.

The Colt, unfired, fell to the ground, and Tibbetts dropped to his knees, clutching what remained of his right hand after a .45-70 round struck it.

Spitting out froth, he turned to find the Irish drunk, Sean Keegan, lowering his carbine and palming his Remington revolver.

By then the rest of his command were dismounting, drawing their weapons, trying to figure out who to shoot.

"Where the hell are all the Apaches?" Tiny Olderman yelled, standing in front of the fire pit, beating out his smoldering, greasy clothes.

An arrow answered the scout's question. It skewered the fat man's neck, the bloody arrowhead protruding from one side, and the feathered shaft quivering on the other side. Blood poured out of Olderman's mouth as he fell to his knees, his hands clutching both ends of the arrow, and then the man fell back into the fire.

"Oh, my God!" Tibbetts screamed for now Apaches, men and women, old and young, boys and girls, poured out of the woods, waving tomahawks. A trooper — Tibbetts didn't have enough time to see which one — was swarmed by women who raised their knives and tomahawks, then brought them down.

He spun around, looking for the reins of his horse, but that horse was long gone.

Seeing nothing but Apaches now, he raised his Colt, and shot a squaw in the back.

Two of his men — Wilson and Shultz —

stood arm's length apart as Apaches rushed toward them. They held their Colt barrels at each other's forehead. Smoke and flame belched from the weapons and both men dropped in a heap before the Indians were upon them.

That's when Tibbetts saw Three-Toed Charley, still mounted, and his horse raced past Tibbetts, knocking him to the ground. Quickly, the officer scrambled up and ran after the galloping scout.

"Charley!" he screamed. "Charley! Take me with you!"

The scout did not look back. His horse disappeared in the far end of camp, and Three-Toed Charley was out of his sight, following the ancient stream bed higher into the mountains.

An arrow hit Tibbetts in the leg, right where the knee bent, and he fell in pain. He tried to stand, but couldn't. He rolled over and saw women and men rushing toward him.

And just before they fell upon him, he remembered what Three-Toed Charley had told him.

You ain't gotta be faster than the bear. You just gotta be faster than your pard.

She was Litsog again. And Litsog was

proud. Other women cut down the attackers, but Litsog just stood and cheered. She sang songs for her people. She sang songs for the three white men who fought alongside the Apaches.

She marveled at the efficiency. Eight men had ridden into this camp to kill Apaches. Seven of those men were dead or dying, and the last man, a man dressed more like Indians than the soldiers he rode with, had disappeared on the trail that led higher into the Sierra Madres, then down back into the desert.

And suddenly . . . Litsog stopped singing. For now more men rode into the camp, and she knew what these men were. They were white, too, or Mexican, and scalps hung from many of their bridles and their uniforms.

Now she feared that Yo-íí's vision would come true. That the Apaches of Three Dogs' village would soon be dead. And maybe Litsog would die with them.

She stopped singing her song of victory and began her death song.

Until a word, a name, a voice — she recognized it all so clearly — rose above the sound of firearms and war cries reached her.

"Cynthia!"

■ ■ ■

McCulloch shouted her name again, then turned, saw Breen, tossed his Winchester to the bounty hunter, and ran toward the girl, the young woman dressed in Apache buckskins but with short — really short — blonde hair.

He ran for his daughter, seeing her first as the baby he had held with wonder in his arms, then the girl on a pony, and then the way he remembered her the last time he had seen her.

He still held the lead rope in his left hand and raced to the woman standing between two wickiups. The woman. By God, she was a woman now. He prayed that she would not run, and God, for some reason, answered the jackal's prayer.

Bullets sounded everywhere, echoed by war cries from Apaches, curses in Spanish, and the Johnny Reb yells that McCulloch had not heard since Virginia, better than a decade earlier.

He stopped in front of Cynthia Jane McCulloch, and said her name again.

Her lips opened, moved, and through the din of battle, McCulloch heard, not guttural Apache, but a Texas whisper.

"Papa?"

He wanted to hug her, to scoop her into his arms and never let her go. Instead, he found a hackamore on a post, and threw it over the stallion's nose.

"Sweetheart," he said, draping the lead rope over the stallion's neck. "Remember how you liked to ride bareback."

She just stared, not even blinking, oblivious to the savagery all around them.

He scooped her into his arms, and pointed with his chin as he swung her onto the stallion's back. "See where Charley rode out?" He pointed. "He ain't a bad guy, honey. He can get you back to Texas. You just gotta ride like the wind after him, and don't let this bad boy scare you. He ain't half as mean as he makes out to be. But he ain't full broke, either."

He lifted her onto the horse's back.

The words from his daughter's mouth brought tears to McCulloch's eyes.

"You always said no horse is full broke, Papa."

"That's right, darling." Cynthia leaned forward, and her knees tightened against the gray mustang.

"Ride like the wind!" he shouted, and slapped the horse's rump.

■ ■ ■ ■

The battle had carried Jed Breen to the western edge of the village. He drew a bead on one of those Alabama cutthroats and barely heard the report of the Winchester, but the Johnny Reb dropped to the dirt, twitching. The rifle felt like a toy in Breen's hand. Sounded like one, too. It didn't pack the punch of his Sharps, but his Sharps was on the dirt somewhere.

He backed up, levering another round into McCulloch's rifle, aimed, and put a bullet in a Mexican scalphunter's belly.

Then he saw Wildcat Walesja, sitting up, holding her head. Blood trickled through her fingers, and that cut, Breen knew, would take quite a few stitches.

If they lived.

He squeezed the trigger, and cursed, worked the lever, tried again, and pitched the rifle to the dirt. Empty.

Putting his hands on the Apache woman's shoulders, he waited until her eyes focused, then he asked, "Where the hell is Blood Moon?"

She didn't answer, probably too stunned, when something slammed into Breen's back and drove him into pine straw and dirt. He felt the weight on him, smelled the greasy, raw odor of an Indian, and managed to twist around and get his right hand up just enough to stop the knife the Apache held from finding a tender spot between a couple of Jed Breen's bruised ribs.

Breen wasn't sure how long he could keep the Apache off him, and it likely didn't matter, because through the sweat and gunsmoke he made out two other Indians, one a damned squaw, running toward him.

The blade inched closer to Breen's vitals.

Then Wildcat Walesja was on her knees, screaming into the knife-holding brave's ear. Breen couldn't understand what the woman was saying, but the warrior could, and he stopped forcing the knife down. Wildcat Walesja moved over on her knees and sang out orders at the two Apaches coming to help kill a gringo bounty hunter, even if Jed Breen wasn't one to take scalps.

The warrior stood, glared at Breen, then ran off to kill somebody else.

Wildcat Walesja helped Breen to his feet.

"Honey," he heard himself say, "I'm might glad you aren't a Yaqui."

As soon as the gray stallion entered the woods, Cynthia Jane McCulloch pulled hard on the hackamore. She had to pull harder than she was used to, but all those years of living with the Apaches, all those years of beatings by her husband and the other squaws, all the torment and abuse before acceptance . . . those had toughened her. The stallion stopped, fought the hackamore, and snorted in protest, but Cynthia spoke harshly in Apache, and turned and saw the carnage she was leaving.

She saw her father, brave Matthew McCulloch fighting alongside Three Dogs. She saw children she had fed, one she had helped bring into this world, and she saw her people, her Apache people, her real father. And she was not about to disgrace them by running away like many of the attacking White Eyes and Mexicans were now doing, only to be cut down by Apache men, women, and children, and less than a handful of white men.

Hates Everyone, that ancient old hag, stood over a crawling, bleeding scalphunter, pounding his back and arms and head with a busted rifle's stock, when suddenly another scalphunter came up behind her.

Cynthia screamed a warning, but the mean old Apache woman was too far away to hear. Blood erupted from her chest as the fiendish white man in a gray coat shot her in the back.

Hates Everyone pitched forward onto the scalphunter she had killed.

Pulling hard on the hackamore, Cynthia turned the mustang around, and kicked it hard in the ribs.

The mustang thundered back into her village, her summer home, and she sang out:

My husband was brave
But he was taken from our people
As I was taken from my people
When I was a child
But now I am a woman
And I love all my people
I will fight with my father
I will fight with Three Dogs
I will fight until I die
And maybe my name will remain
In the hearts of my people
Red and white
Forever
Forever
Forever

She sang the song in Apache. For she was Litsog again.

CHAPTER THIRTY-FIVE

"Major Frazer!"

Block Frazer turned around. He was on his knees over the body of an old Apache hag, whose scalp was not worth taking, but he found his knife with his right hand, made the slices, then ripped off the scalp with his left.

He used to enjoy the sound a scalp made when it was torn off, but he did not hear it because someone shouted his name.

"Major Frazer!"

He turned, saw Joseph William Henderson III, Oaxaca Joe these days, ducking. The boy came up, fired from the hip, and dropped a young Apache carrying a lance. That brave Alabama boy, hell, he held the reins to a horse in his left hand, the revolver in his right. It was Major Block Frazer's horse.

Frazer forgot about Henderson's past transgressions. That was just the wild mind of a young kid full of oats. Henderson wasn't a coward. And here he was, beckoning Frazer over. The boy had his commanding officer's horse. He was willing to let Frazer ride out of this maelstrom alive.

Then the boy spun, coming up, squeezing the trigger. Smoke shot out of the barrel, but Henderson spun around, releasing the reins to Frazer's horse. The horse bolted out of Frazer's vision. His eyes focused on that gallant Alabama boy, who pushed himself up to his feet, and tried to thumb back the hammer of his pistol, tripped over the rocks, and fell out of view.

It was the cliff's edge, Frazer remembered. He had seen it, glimpsed it really, early during the battle. Remembered the drop, maybe three hundred, four hundred feet.

A white man ran up, looked over the side, then turned aimed his revolver. The gun roared.

Major Block Frazer forgot all about the Apaches. He even dropped the scalp in his hand and ran. The white man fighting with these red devils did not see him until it was too late. Frazer pulled the trigger, but the damned Yankee gun he had picked up was empty!

The white man, Texan by his looks, pulled the trigger of his weapon, too, but it was also empty.

Both men heaved the weapons at each other, and both men ducked. Then Frazer charged, drove his shoulder into the man's ribs, just as the enemy's knees seemed to buckle.

That probably saved them both. If the man's bad leg hadn't given out, Frazer would have hit him squarely and driven both of them over the edge, to be crushed by the rocks below.

Instead, the man hit on the rocky edge, his head and shoulders in the air, Frazer on top of him, hands gripping the throat. Squeezing. Squeezing. Watching the eyes bulge.

Sean Keegan needed both hands to keep that Mexican killer, that Santiago Vasquez, from driving a dagger into Keegan's eyeball.

By the saints, Keegan swore, if he'd let some scalphunter kill him like this.

He twisted, and spit, and ground his teeth.

Then, he saw the horse racing past him, saw a sliver of a figure leap from the galloping animal, and saw this rail-thin, golden-haired warrior slam into the Mexican, driving him off Keegan.

Instantly, Keegan came to his knees. His eyes found the dagger the Mexican had dropped. The Apache with the short yellow hair rolled off, or was pushed off, of Santiago Vasquez.

The scalphunter came to his knees, reached for the dagger, and stopped. He looked up, finding his own dagger in Sean Keegan's right hand, and Santiago Vasquez spit and cursed as the blade plunged right below Vasquez's ribs, angling upward, into the black heart of the dirty dog. If the man ever had a heart.

If he did have one, it wasn't beating anymore.

The scalphunter fell onto his side, his eyes staring, but not seeing a damned thing.

Keegan walked on his knees and helped the Apache boy up.

"By the saints. . . ." Keegan stopped. "Jesus, Mary and Joseph!" the Irishman shouted. "Ye are no laddie. Ye's a lass!"

Blood Moon held the big Bowie in his right hand. Fifty paces ahead of him was Three Dogs, strangling some Mexican scalphunter with his bare hands. Now, Blood Moon would have his revenge. Now he would kill the Apache leader who had kicked him out of camp. Now . . .

Something on the eastern side of camp caught his eye. He turned. At the rocky edge, where children were warned never to play, where squaws dumped the trash and bones into the pit below, a White Eye in the soldier-coat of the Mexicans was strangling the Texan called McCulloch.

Blood Moon did not care. If McCulloch still lived after Blood Moon had exacted his revenge, Blood Moon would have killed the Texan himself. That was not what caused Blood Moon to stop walking.

It was what hung from the Mexican soldier-coat of the man killing the Texan.

Wiry, gray hair with streaks of white, silver and Apache black. Only one Apache in Three Dogs' camp had such hair. Even at this distance, through the smoke and dust, it was clear. There was no mistake.

That was the hair of Yo-íí — Blood Moon's father. *The scalp lock of his father!*

He raced forward, screaming, and the white man turned around, releasing his death grip on the Texan, and Blood Moon used his good hand to ram the blade of the knife into the man's chest — to the hilt. And then he fell with the white man into the abyss.

He heard two screams melding into one, one warrior's cry of battle, the other the gargling, dying scream of terror. Then the cries were stilled. Matt McCulloch rolled over, let his left fingers touch his bruised throat, and he looked down. Trying to catch his breath, he rolled back over.

"Papa!" Cynthia threw her arms around him. His arms enveloped hers.

"Careful." McCulloch managed to laugh. "I thought I was going over myself. Don't want you to come with me."

Keegan stood over them. He reached down, and pulled them both to their feet.

Swallowing hurt. McCulloch hurt all over. Even his leg was acting up again. But, hell, that was fine with him. His daughter put her right arm around his waist. She nodded at a dignified-looking Apache who stood in the center of camp. All around him Apaches sang out victory songs. All around them were the dead scalphunters, and more than a few Apaches.

But Cynthia was alive. So was Keegan. He saw Jed Breen walking toward them.

Life was good.

"Come on, Papa." He let his daughter escort him to the tall, noble-looking Apache. That had to be Three Dogs himself. "I want you to meet someone, Papa," Cynthia told him.

Jed Breen stared into the abyss.

"Ain't a rope long enough to reach down

there, me boy," Keegan said to him. "It's practically in the pit of hell."

Breen didn't speak.

Wildcat Walesja came up on the other side of Breen, looked, spit, spit again, and said something in Apache. She nodded at Breen, then at Keegan, and walked to the other Apaches, singing a victory song.

Victory? Breen thought. *With twenty thousand dollars lying in the pit below?*

"We could write out an affidavit," Keegan said. "Ye know. Swear on a stack of Bibles that ye killed ol' Blood Moon."

"Who'd take the word of jackals?" Breen said.

He felt Keegan's arm around his shoulder, felt the squeeze, then Keegan turned and wandered away. "No Irish whiskey within two hundred miles of here. Maybe there's some tiswin to be had."

Jed Breen stared below at the bodies of the dead men in the rocks and trash pile. Twenty thousand dollars. Gone.

The Apache voices sang out. Some joyful. Some mourning their losses.

Looking down at those mangled, crushed bodies wasn't doing Breen any good, so he turned and walked away from the abyss, staring at his feet.

Ten yards later, he stopped. He looked

up. At first he saw the gray stallion of Matt McCulloch's. A young Apache held the lead rope, while other warriors nodded in approval at the fine horse. Hell, even Apaches deep in Mexico respected a McCulloch horse. He turns slightly.

There was that brave Apache chief, Three Dogs, talking. He was talking, using sign language, of course, with Matt McCulloch.

Breen bent, picked up his Sharps from the dust, and butted it on the ground. Again, he looked at the gathering in the center of the camp, in the center of a bloody battlefield.

Matt McCulloch put his left arm around his daughter's shoulder, and the old Ranger stuck out his right hand toward the Apache. The Apache accepted the white man's hand, then put his left hand on the shoulder of Matt's daughter.

"Hell," Breen whispered. "I reckon that's reward enough."

ABOUT THE AUTHORS

William W. Johnstone has written nearly three hundred novels of western adventure, military action, chilling suspense, and survival. His bestselling books include *The Family Jensen; The Mountain Man; Flintlock; MacCallister; Savage Texas; Luke Jensen, Bounty Hunter;* and the thrillers *Black Friday, The Doomsday Bunker,* and *Trigger Warning.*

J. A. Johnstone learned to write from the master himself, Uncle William W. Johnstone, with whom J. A. has co-written numerous bestselling series including The Mountain Man; Those Jensen Boys; and Preacher, The First Mountain Man.

The employees of Thorndike Press hope you have enjoyed this Large Print book. All our Thorndike, Wheeler, and Kennebec Large Print titles are designed for easy reading, and all our books are made to last. Other Thorndike Press Large Print books are available at your library, through selected bookstores, or directly from us.

For information about titles, please call:
(800) 223-1244

or visit our website at:
gale.com/thorndike

To share your comments, please write:
Publisher
Thorndike Press
10 Water St., Suite 310
Waterville, ME 04901